PEN...

BLIN...

Paul Theroux has written over two dozen novels, including *The Mosquito Coast*, *Kowloon Tong* and most recently *Hotel Honolulu*. His acclaimed travel writing includes *The Old Patagonia Express*, *The Happy Isles of Oceania* and *Dark Star Safari*.

Fiction

WALDO
FONG AND THE INDIANS
GIRLS AT PLAY
MURDER IN MOUNT HOLLY
JUNGLE LOVERS
SINNING WITH ANNIE
SAINT JACK
THE BLACK HOUSE
THE FAMILY ARSENAL
THE CONSUL'S WIFE
A CHRISTMAS CARD
PICTURE PALACE
LONDON SNOW
WORLD'S END
THE MOSQUITO COAST
THE LONDON EMBASSY
HALF MOON STREET
O-ZONE
MY SECRET HISTORY
CHICAGO LOOP
MILLROY THE MAGICIAN
MY OTHER LIFE
KOWLOON TONG
HOTEL HONOLULU
THE STRANGER AT THE
 PALAZZO D'ORO
BLINDING LIGHT

Criticism

V. S. NAIPAUL

Nonfiction

THE GREAT RAILWAY BAZAAR
THE OLD PATAGONIAN EXPRESS
THE KINGDOM BY THE SEA
SAILING THROUGH CHINA
SUNRISE WITH SEAMONSTERS
THE IMPERIAL WAY
RIDING THE IRON ROOSTER
TO THE ENDS OF THE EARTH
THE HAPPY ISLES OF OCEANIA
THE PILLARS OF HERCULES
SIR VIDIA'S SHADOW
FRESH AIR FIEND
DARK STAR SAFARI

Blinding Light

Paul Theroux

PENGUIN BOOKS

PENGUIN BOOKS

Published by the Penguin Group
Penguin Books Ltd, 80 Strand, London WC2R ORL, England
Penguin Books Ltd (USA) Inc., 375 Hudson Street, New York, New York 10014, USA
Penguin Group (Canada), 90 Eglinton Avenue East, Suite 700, Toronto, Ontario, Canada M4P 3YZ
(a division of Pearson Penguin Canada Inc.)
Penguin Ireland, 25 St Stephen's Green, Dublin 2, Ireland (a division of Penguin Books Ltd)
Penguin Group (Australia), 250 Camberwell Road,
Camberwell, Victoria 3124, Australia (a division of Pearson Australia Group Pty Ltd)
Penguin Books India Pvt Ltd, 11 Community Centre,
Panchsheel Park, New Delhi – 110 017, India
Penguin Group (NZ), cnr Airborne and Rosedale Roads, Albany,
Auckland 1310, New Zealand (a division of Pearson New Zealand Ltd)
Penguin Books (South Africa) (Pty) Ltd, 24 Sturdee Avenue,
Rosebank 2196, South Africa

Penguin Books Ltd, Registered Offices: 80 Strand, London WC2R ORL, England

www.penguin.com

First published in the United States of America by Houghton Mifflin 2005
First published in Great Britain by Hamish Hamilton 2005
Published in Penguin Books 2006

2

Copyright © Paul Theroux, 2005
All rights reserved

The moral right of the author has been asserted

Printed in England by Clays Ltd, St Ives plc

Except in the United States of America, this book is sold subject
to the condition that it shall not, by way of trade or otherwise, be lent,
re-sold, hired out, or otherwise circulated without the publisher's
prior consent in any form of binding or cover other than that in
which it is published and without a similar condition including this
condition being imposed on the subsequent purchaser

ISBN-13: 978–0–141–01573–6
ISBN-10: 0–141–01573–X

A place where the unknown past and the emergent future meet in a vibrating soundless hum. Larval entities waiting for a live one.
—William Burroughs, *The Yage Letters*

CONTENTS

ONE

Drug Tour 1

TWO

Blinding Light 121

THREE

The Book of Revelation 205

FOUR

Book Tour 285

FIVE

The Blind Man's Wife 365

SIX

The River of Light 431

ONE

Drug Tour

1

"Wishing to go where you don't belong is the condition of most people in the world" was the opening sentence of *Trespassing*. The man with that sentence in his head had turned and lifted his sleep mask to glance back at the passengers who were masked and sleeping in their seats on the glary one-class night flight. The blindfolded people were strapped down, slumped sideways on their safety straps, with tilted faces and gaping mouths, enclosed by the howl of monologuing jet engines. The man excited his imagination by seeing them as helpless captives or hostages, yet he knew better. Like him, they were tired travelers going south — maybe some of them on the same drug tour, but he hoped not. This man slipping back into his seat and readjusting his mask was Slade Steadman, the author of *Trespassing*.

"Travel book" was the usual inadequate way of describing this work, his only published book, but one that had made him famous, and later, for unexpected reasons, very wealthy. He was so famous he would hide himself, so wealthy he would never have to write another word for money. This account of one of the riskiest and most imaginative journeys of the modern era was an obvious stunt remembered as an epic.

The idea could not have been simpler, but his seeing it through to a successful conclusion was another matter; that he had survived to tell the whole story was his achievement. Steadman had traveled through Europe, Asia, and Africa, twenty-eight countries and fifty-odd border crossings, defying authority, for all of it — arrests, escapes, illegal entries, dangerous flights, near disasters, river fordings, sneaking over frontiers — had been accomplished without a passport. No papers, no visas, no credit cards, no ID at all. *Covert Insertions* — the military term for his mission — had been a working title, but squirming at its ambiguity, the publisher had discouraged Steadman from using it.

Not only had he been undocumented during his entire yearlong trip, alone, an alien, struggling against officialdom to keep alive and moving; he had not carried a bag. "If it doesn't fit into my pocket I don't need it," he had written, and it was now as well known a line as the one about wishing to go where you don't belong. *Around the World Without a Passport* was the subtitle of the book: the plight of a fugitive. It was the way he felt right now, twenty years later, restless in his aisle seat on the flight to Quito with the blindfolded passengers who were trying to sleep. For all of those twenty years he had tried to write a second book.

He had not been surprised to see the young woman snoring in the seat behind him with a recent edition of his book on her lap. Readers of *Trespassing* — and over the years there had been millions — often took trips like this, involving distance and a hint of risk. The book had inspired imitations — the journey as a stunt — though no other writer had matched him in his travel. Even Steadman himself, who now saw *Trespassing* as something of a fluke, had failed to follow it up with an equally good book — or any book — in the decades since publication. And that was another reason he was on this plane.

They were two hours into the flight, after a long unscheduled layover in Miami, but the delay had been eased for Steadman by his spotting the woman at his gate reading a copy of *Trespassing*. It was the edition with the TV series tie-in cover showing the handsome actor who played the twenty-nine-year-old illegal border-crosser. And of course the actor wore a leather jacket. At the time of publication much was made of the fact that Steadman had traveled without luggage, wearing only a leather jacket. He had not realized how this simple expedient of not carrying a bag had made him more of a hero. The bruised and scuffed jacket with its many pockets was part of his identity, but when it became a standard prop in the television show, Steadman stopped wearing a leather jacket.

Watching the woman read his book with rapt attention — she did not see him or even glance up — and liking her trance-like way of turning the pages, helped pass the time for Steadman. He felt self-conscious at the sight of this old success, but gratified that so many people still read the book, even the ones who were following the reruns of the TV series. He had wondered if the woman reading it would be among the passengers on this Ecuador flight, looking helpless and passive. And of course she was.

In the seat next to Steadman, his girlfriend, Ava Katsina, stirred in her sleep. Seeing her, too, blindfolded like a hostage, he felt a throb of lust. The blood whipping through his gut and his fingers and his eyes made him jittery with desire.

That was welcome. The sexual desire he had once described in starved paragraphs of solitude in *Trespassing* as akin to cannibal hunger was something he had not tasted for a long time. Ava, a medical doctor, had said, "Are you past it? Do you want me to write you a prescription?"

At fifty Steadman was sure he was not past it, but his years of struggling to attempt another book had afflicted him and visited impotence on him too many times for him to believe it was a coincidence. Virility, he thought, was not just an important trait in an imaginative person but was a powerful determiner of creativity. Women writers were no different: the best of them could be lavish lovers, as ramping and reckless as men — at least the ones he had known when he had been the same. But those days were gone.

This slackness was another reason he and Ava had decided to split up, and the decision had been made months ago. The trip they had planned as a couple could not be canceled, and so, rather than lose their deposit and forgo the tour, they were traveling together. What looked like commitment, the quiet couple sharing the elbow rest, sitting side by side on this long flight, was their following through on the promise, a favor more than a duty, with no expectation of pleasure. When the trip was over, their relationship was over. The trip itself was a gesture of finality — this flight was part of their farewell, something civilized to share before they parted. And here he was, wanting to eat her.

For years Steadman had felt well enough established as a writer to shun rather than seek publicity. Now, he did not in the least resemble the author of *Trespassing*. That reckless soul was falsely fixed in people's minds as only a one-book author can be, a brooding one-dimensional pinup in a leather jacket. This man was his book, the narrator of that amazing journey. The book was all that was known. The mentions of him in the press — fewer as time passed, dwindling to a handful in recent years — described someone he no longer recognized.

Trespassing was still selling, its title a byword for adventure. He had paid his debts with his first profits and then began living well on the paperback rights. The big house up-island on Martha's Vineyard he had bought with the movie money. The TV series that came later made him wealthy beyond any of his earlier dreams of success. But the author who went under his name was a public fiction, elaborated and improved upon by the movie and the TV shows. The TV host and traveler was now pictured on the book jacket, and that well-known actor was fixed in the public mind and more recognizable than Steadman himself, but possessing the traits Steadman had established in the book. He was elusive, a risk taker, unapproachable, inventive, uncompromising, a free spirit, highly educated, physically strong, something of a Boy Scout, demanding, enigmatic, sexual, full of surprises.

The handsome actor who was identified with the TV dramatization of Steadman's book often made statements about travel, risk, and heroism — even about writing, with enormous confidence, even when Steadman could do almost no writing himself. As a stand-in for the reclusive Steadman, the actor was now and then employed as a motivational speaker, using the challenges of his television experiences making the show — most of it was filmed in Mexico — as his text. He did so portentously, in the tone of a seasoned traveler, as though he were responsible for the book. And *Trespassing* had spawned so many imitators it created a genre, inspiring a sort of travel of which this Ecuador trip was typical: a leap in the dark. Before *Trespassing* there had been travel of this kind but few persuasive books about it. Steadman had made it an accessible narrative, popularized it, given it drama. He had succeeded in making the world seem dangerous and difficult again, full of unpredictable people and narrow escapes, a debauch of experience, as in an earlier age of travel.

The merchandising that came later astonished him. Just the notion of it seemed weird, especially since he had not published any other book. A man he despised at the agency that had promoted it and sold it had said to him: "Don't write anything else, or if you do, make it another *Trespassing*. Don't you see what you've done? By not writing another book you've made yourself into a brand."

After Steadman licensed the name, it was more than a name; it was a logo, a lifestyle, a clothing line that was expressly technical, a range of travel gear, of sunglasses and accessories — knives, pens, lighters. The leather jacket had been the first piece of merchandise, and as a signature item it was still selling. The luggage came later. The clothing changed from year to year. The newest line was watches ("timepieces — 'watches' does not describe them"), some of them very expensive: chronometers for divers, certified for two hundred meters; a model with a built-in altimeter for pilots; many for hikers; one in gold and titanium. The licensed brand was Trespassing Overland Gear. The motto, a line from the book, was "Cross borders — don't ask permission."

How popular was all this? He knew a great deal from the revenue, which seemed to him vast and unspendable, but he often wondered what sort of people bought the stuff, because he so seldom went out and he avoided using any of it himself. Now he saw that the clothes on that woman behind him with his book on her lap were from the catalogue; and the man next to her, the others around her, all of them wore travel outfits bearing the TOG logo of a small striding figure in a signature leather jacket.

Merchandising and relicensing the name produced such a large and regular income that Steadman had long since stopped writing for money. He wanted only to produce another book worthy of his first one, but fiction — as brave an interior journey as *Trespassing* had been a global one. He had started writing the book, and spoke of it as work in progress, but for years he had regarded it privately as work in stoppage. What he published now, the occasional magazine articles and opinion pieces, were merely to remind the world that he was still alive, and this reminder was a way of promising another book.

Steadman liked to think he was in the middle of his career. But he knew that for an American writer there is no middle. You were a hot new author and then you were either an old hand or else forgotten. He was somewhere deep in the second half and wishing he were younger. Everything he had gladly done in the early part of his career he now avoided: the readings, the signings, the appearances, the visits to colleges and bookstores, the posed photographs and interviews, the favors to editors, the sideshows at book festivals — he refused them all and wanted the opposite, silence, obscurity, and remoteness. His refusals created the impression of snooty contempt; his brusque deflecting ironies were taken to be bad temper. Simply saying no, he was seen as grumpy, uncooperative, a snob. He did not want to convey to these strangers how desperate he was. Having all that merchandising money somehow made it worse.

Rather than agreeing to interviews and public appearances to correct the false impression that readers had of him, he withdrew even further; and in seclusion, without the envious mockery of journalists and profile writers, he began to suspect that he might have written better — that he could do better. He was hardly thirty when he wrote *Trespassing*. The book was full of hasty judgments, but why tidy it now? He was known as a travel writer, but he felt sure that fiction writing was his gift. Because so much of *Trespassing* had been fiction — embroidered incidents, improved-upon dialogue, outright invention — he knew he had a great novel in him. There was still time to finish the book that would prove this.

He had started writing it. Ava had praised it; they were lovers then, sharing their lives. In the course of their breakup she told him frankly that she hadn't liked what he had read to her after all. The novel in progress was a reflection of him: selfish, suffocating, manipulative, pretentious, incomplete, and sexless.

"Writing is your dolly. You just sit around playing with it."

This same woman, listening naked in their bed to him reading part of a chapter, had once said, "It's genius, Slade."

"You're probably one of the few writers in America who can afford to treat writing as your dolly."

He protested, ranting like a man in a cage. Instead of consoling him, Ava said, "You are such a fucking diva." He was demoralized for the moment. He told himself he would be better when she was completely out of his life. He took work for magazines — his factual story-chasing journalism had always been resourceful and vivid, even shocking. He said, "I write it with my left hand." The novel was what mattered to him. Yet what editor ever said, "Write us some fiction"? His struggle to continue his novel wrecked his relationship with Ava.

"You're just selfish," they both said.

When their love was gone, replaced by indifference and boredom, a new Ava was revealed — or, not a new Ava, but perhaps the essential woman: ambitious, sarcastic, resilient, demanding, predatory, sensual, much funnier and more resourceful than she had been as his lover. Her intelligence made these traits into weapons.

The delay in Miami proved her toughness. In the lounge, seated in the crossfire of intrusive questions and small talk, most of it from nearby passengers, expressing their impatience by gabbling, Steadman kept himself customarily stone-faced and silent, wearing the implacable mask he had fashioned for himself over the years of his withdrawal.

"On a tour?" one of the men said.

He was a big man, as bulky as his own *Trespassing* duffel bag, in his late thirties. His badly slouching posture made him seem slovenly and arrogant, and his anger gave him an overbearing and elbowing confidence. Steadman had noticed that he demanded more space than anyone else, an extra seat here in the lounge for his briefcase, his arms on both armrests, his bulgy duffel filling the overhead rack. Walking confidently on kicking feet toward the plane, he filled the jetway, pulling his valise on wheels that trapped people behind him, even his wife, who remained talking on a cell phone until the plane took off, and was on it again, urgently, saying, "I'll send you all the bumf with a packet of swatches."

Steadman took his time, and at last he said, "Are you?"

"For want of a better word," the man said, and looked up, hearing his wife say, "Hack?"

A dark scruffy man, bug-eyed and with spiky hair, was arguing with a clerk at the check-in desk, saying in an insistent German accent, "But that is falsch. I am on the list — Manfred Steiger. I am American."

Steadman thought: You went away to be alone — or, in his and Ava's case, on a deliberate self-assigned mission — and you discovered your traveling companions to be the very people you were hoping to flee, the ones you most disliked. In this case, young overequipped couples — rich, handsome, heedless, privileged, undeserving, and profoundly lazy in a special selfish way — from this generation of small-minded entrepreneurial emperors. And most of them were dressed in his clothes.

"God, how I loathe these people," Ava whispered to Steadman.

For one thing, they boasted of hating books and hardly read newspapers. *Trespassing* didn't count, because it wasn't new and was better known from movies and TV — Steadman was aware that some of the most obnoxious people seemed to love it for its lawlessness, its self-indulgent rule-breaking, and its tone of boisterous intrusion. *I've only read one real book in my life — yours,* such people wrote him. That alone was enough, but it was also an indication that you couldn't tell them anything. They didn't listen, they didn't have to — they ran the whole world now. *You turned me into a world traveler.*

The thing was to shut them down as quickly as possible.

Steadman had learned that, in an interview, if you fell silent and watched and waited instead of answering, people volunteered more detail. In this instance another man, a bystander, offered the detail.

"It's quote-unquote adventure travel," that man said.

"Eco-porn," Ava said. "Eco-chic. Voyeurism must be such a wet dream for you."

That man winced, but the man named Hack said, "We're traveling together. Didn't you see our T-shirts?"

He unbuttoned his khaki safari shirt, revealing the lettering on his T-shirt: *The Gang of Four.*

"Until they finish the renovation on our house," the second man was saying. "We're reconfiguring the interior of a lovely old Victorian. We've got twelve thousand square feet. It's on an acre in a lovely part of San Francisco. Sea Cliff? Robin Williams lives nearby, and so do Hack and Janey."

"Marshall Hackler — call me Hack," said the big slouching man, inviting a handshake with his carelessly thrust out arm.

And Janey was apparently the woman on the cell phone. She just flapped her fingers and turned away, but another woman who had been listening — she was pretty, bright-eyed, the one holding the paperback of *Trespassing*, in a bush vest and green trousers, dressed for a safari — smiled and said, "Ecuador. A year ago it was Rwanda. We were the last people in there before the Africans massacred the people on that tour. We had the same guide. He was almost killed. No one can go now. We were incredibly lucky."

The woman speaking on the cell phone broke off and said, "We're whole-hoggers. We want it all."

"Janey's doing the interior. But we're reconfiguring the outside, too. Swales. Berms. I've got the footprint and the plans with me — still working out siting of the lap pool. Downstream we'll be putting in a guesthouse and sort of meld it with the landscaping."

Hack put his arm around the man and said, "This guy actually wrote a book."

Dismissing this with a boastful smile, the man said, "For my sins," then took a breath and added, "Anyway, I sold my company and got into hedge funds. This was — oh, gosh — before the NASDAQ tanked in — what? Last April?"

Steadman leaned toward him, saying nothing, smiling his obscure smile at the self-conscious "oh, gosh."

"And I got in the high eight figures."

Hack said, "So he said to me, 'Let's get jiggy wid it.' 'Cause he's an A-player. He's a well-known author, too."

At the mention of "high eight figures" — what was that, tens of millions, right? — Ava barked loudly, as though at an outrage, and the woman in the Trespassing vest glanced over her cell phone and said, "Do keep it down. I'm talking."

"Wood worked for two solid years for that payday," the other woman said, looking up from Steadman's book.

His name was *Wood*?

Janey, Hack's wife, was saying in a wiffling English accent into her cell phone, "It seems frightful. But in point of fact, single people spend a disproportionate amount of time in the loo. The laboratory, as you might say."

Both couples were dressed alike, mostly in Trespassing clothes from the catalogue: trousers with zip-off legs that turned them into shorts, shirts with zip-off sleeves, reversible jackets, thick socks, hiking shoes, floppy hats, mesh-lined vests, and fanny packs at their waists.

Seeing them, Steadman wanted to say: I give away ten percent of my pretax profits from catalogue sales to environmental causes. How much do you contribute?

"This has something like seventeen pockets," the woman with the book said, patting her vest, seeing that Ava was staring at it — but Ava was staring at the TOG logo. She slapped it some more. "These gussets are really useful. And check out this placket."

And when Ava's gaze drifted to the woman's expensive watch — it was the Trespassing Mermaid — she said, "It's a chronometer. Titanium. Certified for like a billion meters. That's your vacuum-release valve," and twisted it. "We dive — Janey doesn't but she snorkels." The woman on the phone turned away at the mention of her name and kept chewing on the phone. "We're hoping to do some in the Galápagos."

Steadman was so delighted to hear that they were going in the opposite direction he did not tell them that snorkeling there was strictly regulated, but encouraged her instead. The man he took to be her husband was going through the sectioned-off pockets of his own padded vest. He brought out a folded map and his boarding pass and a wallet that looked like a small parcel, with slots for air tickets, dollar bills, and pesos. The wallet, too, was a Trespassing accessory.

"What I love about American money is its tensile strength. It's the high rag content. Leave a couple of bucks in a bathing suit and never mind. All you have to do is dry it out. It actually stands up to a washer-dryer."

"You mean you can launder it?" Ava said.

Janey, the young woman with the English accent, said "Ta very mooch for now" and "By-yee" and snapped her phone off, and collapsing it, she turned it into a small dark cookie. The other woman reached into another expensive catalogue item, the Trespassing Gourmet Lunch Tote, a padded food satchel with a cooler compartment. She handed her husband a wrapped sandwich.

"We always bring our own," Hack said, chewing between bites. "It's smoked turkey with provolone and tomato and an herbed vinaigrette dressing."

Noting that the man said "herbed," Ava frowned and turned away, and the woman looked up from her book and offered Ava half a sandwich, saying that she had plenty. Ava's tight smile meant "no thanks."

Tapping the cover of *Trespassing,* Hack put his arm around the woman and said, "That must be one hell of a read."

The woman said, "It's awesome."

"Like how?"

"Like in its, um, modalities. In its, um, tropes."

"You've been reading it for weeks and ignoring me."

"I read real slow when I'm liking something."

"So who wrote it?"

Steadman, who had been listening closely, braced himself, putting on his most implacable face.

The woman said, "This, like, you know, legendary has-been. The outdoor-gear freak. He's more a lifestyle than a writer." Then, "You guys married?"

Hearing "legendary has-been," Ava shut her eyes and smiled in anger. As for the question, everything about it, too, was wrong. The "you," the "guys," the very word "married."

"I'm Sabra Wilmutt," the woman said.

"I'm Jonquil J. Christ."

Sabra's face looked suddenly slapped and lopsided. She said, "I don't get it."

"The J is for Jesus."

As Ava spoke, the reboarding announcement was made.

What does it matter? Ava's expression said to Steadman, who had heard it all. But Steadman had been attentive to the woman named Sabra, immersed in *Trespassing*. It was just this awful flight to get through, and after that they would never see any of them again.

2

AIRBORNE ONCE MORE, isolated and blindfolded, with the slipstream crackling at the airplane's windows and fizzing along the fuselage, the passengers were at last silenced. Steadman reflected on what they had said. They were boasting, of course, but because most boasting was bluff and lies, really they had given very little away. He took them to be lawyers, even the one who had sold his company, because of their affectations. Lawyers never volunteered the truth, because the truth was debatable, and this was why they could hold two opposing views in their head, and seemed capable of believing both, as they tossed out challenges and suppositions, speaking in irrelevancies calculated to throw you off. The merchandising of *Trespassing* was a wilderness of lawyers waving contracts. Challenge them with a tough question and they handed you a sandwich.

But he said to Ava, "What was that all about?" for the way she had called attention to herself among those strangers. Steadman had described in *Trespassing* how it was always a fatal mistake in travel to be conspicuous. The greatest travelers made themselves invisible. An invisible man was a man of power.

Ava just shrugged, pretending he was worked up over nothing. Yet she knew she was motivated by their breakup. Underlying her sarcasm was the suspicion that if the people found out that she was with Steadman the famous writer, he would have to take the blame for her behavior: her insolence was his insolence. Breaking up had liberated Ava and made her reckless and indifferent to his worry, helped her see what a baby he was — "and writing is your dolly." She couldn't play with it, couldn't even touch it. He fussed with it in his room. And as time had passed the dolly had become more special, first a toy, then a fetish object, then a totem, and finally an idol that represented something approaching a deity. "Fucking writers," Ava had begun saying.

Steadman had carefully not asked the other people any questions for fear they would ask him the same things. He was on this trip for a reason, his own assignment, and he wanted it to be secret. He had covertly been taking notes, and he was still taking them. The meal trays had been cleared and he had just written the word *máscara*.

The lovely, dark-eyed, plump-lipped woman, looking like a prison guard in her black uniform, was the flight attendant. Brisk and busy, she murmured, "*Máscara, máscara,*" moving down the aisle, handing out blindfolds. Each passenger accepted one awkwardly (*as though they had been handed a condom,* he noted, *which in a sense they had*) and with varying reactions: bewilderment, suspicion, surprise, amusement, embarrassment. None had looked grateful, yet each had put the blindfold on.

Turning to size up the masked passengers, Steadman had taken a good look at the Trespassing Treads — the hiking shoes — and the Trespassing cargo pants and multipocket vests and the Trespassing daypack at Hack's feet. The woman named Sabra was reading *Trespassing* — or, rather, not reading it, since the thick thing lay spread open, turned over on her lap.

Just behind them was Manfred, the man who had announced in a heavy German accent that he was an American. He pulled the mask over his eyes and ratcheted his seat back and slept. He was wearing black Mephisto hiking shoes and a black hat and black leather vest. In their blindfolding they seemed to Steadman like participants in a solemn ceremony, some of them novices, some old hands. That did not make the blindfolds any less bizarre, yet it was somehow appropriate to this night flight to Ecuador, all of them gringos, more or less unprepared — willing and innocent and irrationally confident, flying blind.

Passing the blindfold to Ava, Steadman had noticed her trying to suppress a smile. She had not smiled for weeks, especially not that sort, a coquettish curl of the lips, with so much understood in it. When she put the blindfold on she was still smiling, looking helpless and eager, her mouth kissing air, like an amorous wink with her lips that suggested she knew she was being watched. Steadman touched her hand, and she snagged his fingers and squeezed. At that point Steadman put his own mask over his eyes.

He thought about the stopover, the delay, how the people who talk the most, using those clichés, pretending to be inarticulate, were often the reverse, and trying to hide something.

How much they had told him: the SUV, the house, the sale of the business, the shoes, the biking, the knife, the travel, the gear that he knew only too well — all of it could be summed up in one word, money. They meant it when they called themselves A-players, and were serious only in their jokes.

His desire as a writer, as a man, was to know them, to see into them, behind their masks. To translate what they said. To know them on the most fundamental level. But he knew enough now to dismiss them and go the other way, to use what he had found.

"You're a pornographer," Ava had said to him recently, to irritate him, another truthful piece of abuse from their breakup.

Yes, he thought, the truest expression of our being is our passionate engagement in the act of sex. To know that was to know almost everything, that we are most ourselves in sex, our most monkey-like, our most human, so why shouldn't he be fascinated? He realized this now because it was over with them, until last night no sex for months, only her hideous efficiency and angry humor and her long days and nights at the hospital.

Shifting in her seat, seeming to wake, Ava sighed. Steadman hated it when she talked to strangers. Once it had been he doing it, and he had thrived. But that ended, and now he listened to her. Her talk bored him, made him anxious; she never knew when to stop. Neither of them hid their annoyance. But what did it matter? This was their last trip. They had planned it for months, and the very planning of it, as the most ambitious holiday they had ever had, put such a strain on them, all the negotiation that collapsed into nagging and quarreling, that they realized how unsuited they were to each other.

They were certain now that they would split up, and this realization calmed them and released them from their struggle. Recognizing that they had reached a conclusion more final than a truce, they had the dull serenity and silent patience of a couple who know they have no future. It was better to see each other as a stranger than as an enemy, and in this slipping away they lost much of their history — the false, insincere part that had been their meaningless romance. They were tougher, not sentimental, hard to convince. No favors: with none of the frivolous generosity of lovers, they were, oddly, now equals. But more circumspect, less knowable, than when they had first met.

So this trip was practical. Though the planning had been full of conflict and taken so long, they went ahead with it. They had to take the trip or they would lose their deposit and forfeit the plane tickets. Ava said, "You actually care about the money?" The money was a pretext for the mission: he hoped the trip would lead him to his book.

Holding the blindfold, he said, "This thing cost two grand."

She said, "It's probably worth it."

To travel in separate rows, to pretend not to know each other, would have been ridiculous — they had discussed these strategies. They still needed each other, needed most of all to be let down gently, to part without drama. They still liked being together, even if they were no longer in love. The finality — the peculiarity of nothingness, no hope, no future — affected their sex life, gave it a vicious push. The night before they left they made love as though they were strangers, meeting by chance, emboldened by their anonymity to be selfish, even brutal, seeming to use each other. But the rough grappling in the dark room surprised and delighted them, afterward leaving them gasping, sprawling naked on the carpet, looking beaten and broken, as though they had fallen to the floor from a great height.

"I liked that," Ava had said. She knew that Steadman had too. It had reminded her of the first time, the blind recklessness of it, when they had just met and knew only each other's first name. "That was nice."

Ava had not been put off by the coldness of it, Steadman's apparent indifference to her, his concentrating on his pleasure. He probably had not noticed that she was using him, that only her pleasure mattered to her. And it proved that they were finished, it was over, she could say anything to him now, even tell him she didn't like what he was writing. They were strangers again in the dark room. She slipped her hand between his thighs and touched him and told him she wanted him again. She shocked him, she aroused him with her demand, her saying, "And if you can't get it up, what good are you?"

Afterward she had said in a teasing, greedy way, "Maybe we'll meet other people on the trip."

Blindfolded, he remembered everything.

Two hours into the second leg of the flight, and even taking into account the delay in Miami, the only people they had met were the talkative travelers who called themselves the Gang of Four, the Hacklers and the Wilmutts: big, loud Marshall Hackler — Hack — his English wife, Janey, the overly tidy reader, Sabra, and her husband, the competitor named Wood. The dark, bug-eyed German, Manfred Steiger, had hovered, wanting to enter the conversation, squinting, grinning, showing his teeth in a what's-going-on? face.

Here was the odd thing. Steadman felt he had met another person, too, and what fascinated him was that it was Ava, someone he thought he knew well, the woman he had once believed he would marry. She was someone else, someone new, a woman he both feared and desired. It was not just her lovemaking, her selfish sensualism that turned him into a voyeur, like a man watching a woman masturbate — that was how it seemed, and he had liked it. There was her frankness, too, her telling him his work was pretentious, her air of independence, and a toughness that made her seem strong. Most of all, her dealing with the other travelers, snapping "eco-porn" and "Jonquil J. Christ" and any other insulting thing that came into her head. He wondered if the fact that she was a doctor, used to giving reassurance and help, made it all the more thrilling for her to abuse these people.

Under his blindfold Steadman fell asleep, and the vibration of the plane, the engine howl, his damp palms on the armrests, and the smell of the dinner trays and dusty carpet and reheated food — it all entered his dream. He toppled and, still toppling, realized that he had lost his balance in an anatomical landscape. The valleys were the creases in a woman's body, and that discovery woke him. The plane was bright and stank of warm plastic and it was dawn, the just-risen sun blazing on the left side of the plane. Coffee was being served.

"Ever been to Ecuador?" he heard. It was the man named Wood, blowing on his coffee, speaking across the aisle.

Ava said, "Hey, that sounds like an invitation."

That was another aspect of the new Ava — her teasing, her mockery, the way she deflected questions like a child, like a coquette, being impossible and domineering, as though these people were trying to woo her.

"It's where this aircraft is going," the man said, maintaining his composure.

"Right. We're getting off at the next stop."

"How long are you guys going to be there?"

That "guys" again, and it seemed to Steadman that the man was preparing to ask what they were planning to do there, and Steadman hoped that Ava would resist answering the question.

She pleased him by saying, "That's kind of up in the air. How about you guys?"

"Three weeks. We've got a full program." He was boasting again. He said, "I bet everyone on this plane has to be back at work next Monday."

That was worth a note — that all these young well-off Americans were heading to Ecuador as though it were a holiday in Maine. They were probably on a tour of some kind, one of those expensive ones where someone else did all the arranging. Except for the Ecuadorians and a few missionaries and some obvious businessmen in wilted suits, most of the passengers looked like weary and apprehensive tourists. Steadman was glad that he was headed for Lago Agrio and Río Aguarico and the darkest, most distant downriver village in the Oriente. As Ava had said, they would never run into these people again.

"Wood Wilmutt," the man said, introducing himself. "You here on business?"

Ava said, "No."

"Pleasure then?"

"Probably not."

"What else is there?"

"A wet dream," Ava said.

The man's eyes went sharp and serious as his mouth became small.

"A leap in the dark," she went on, and Steadman wanted to hug her for quoting him. It was something he had thought, but he had studiously said nothing. He did not want to disclose that he was a writer on assignment. That kind of revelation always provoked questions and cast a shadow over a conversation, made some people inquisitive and bumptious, and others wary. At the very least it turned most people, including the writer on assignment, into bores.

"So you're on vacation," Ava said.

"If you will," Wood said, and Steadman made a note.

"And you're retired."

"For want of a better word," Wood said, and Steadman made another note.

"Meaning?"

"I said I sold my company, I didn't say I'd retired," Wood said. "I've been pretty lucky. Anyway, Sabra's still got her dental practice."

Steadman wondered whether Ava would divulge the fact that she was a doctor, and he thought she might, less for information than as a doctor upstaging a dentist; but she said nothing.

"*Was tun Sie, Fritz?*" Sabra said.

"*Ich bin Schriftsteller,*" Manfred said. His eyes were dancing in anger. "*Aber mein Name ist Manfred, nicht Fritz, danke. Sprechen Sie Deutsch?*"

"Kind of. I mean, I speak Yiddish."

"You are wrong if you think Yiddish is German. Yiddish is meaning Jewish," Manfred said. Then he spoke to the others. "*Schriftsteller* — writer."

"My husband wrote a book," Sabra said.

But Manfred was still talking. "My family is dealing in medical supplies, but I said no to the business. You are knowing Steiger Medical Fabrik?"

"Drugs?" Wood asked.

"Some. But rare varieties. Also uniforms. Glassware. Sterilizing appliances. Disinfecting agents. Rubber goods. Tubing. Syringes." He leaned forward. "Government contracts. We make good business."

"U.S. government?"

"German government."

That killed the conversation — and *sigh-ringes* had the others exchanging glances — until Manfred remembered something. He knelt down and pulled a thick book from his carry-on bag. He showed it to the passengers in nearby seats. It was *A Guide to the Medicinal Plants of Upper Amazonia*.

"I am writing some things," he said, and the others smiled at *sum sings*. His face tightened, as though he knew he was being silently mocked. He said, "Yah, I do journalism, but I am looking into psychotropic substances, too." He put his face near Sabra's and said, "*Ich bin Forscher und Wissenschaftler. Verstehen Sie?*"

Ava had been playing with her blindfold. She put it back on and smiled, as if reentering a familiar and hospitable room.

Steadman watched her for a while, enjoying the animation on her face, the shape of her lips, her shallow breathing. But he was thinking that he had not told anyone his name or where he was from or that he was a writer. And he was happy in his own anonymity. What people knew of you diminished you, robbed you of your strength. You were never stronger than when they were in the dark. Because of his reticence, Ava had taken charge. As a writer, nothing pleased Steadman more than holding a conversation in which the other person told him everything and he responded giving nothing away.

The seat belt light came on. The plane skimmed across the tufts of a pillowy layer of clouds. The pilot announced that they would be landing in Quito soon and gave a weather report and the temperature.

Still wearing her blindfold, Ava leaned over and whispered, "I'm glad I'm not your girlfriend anymore."

3

ON THE WAY into the cloud-dampened and sloping city, with its chilly, hard-to-breathe air, sitting next to Ava in the taxi, under overcast skies and the slope of the rubbly volcano Pichincha which was strewn with precariously sited huts, Steadman was thinking how this would be the last trip he'd ever take with her. The particular thought was not a sentence or phrase in his mind, not words at all, but rather a specific image, the sight of her nearest knee, pale from always being covered by her surgical smock, looking pinched and plaintive, as dimpled as a new potato, and representing a mute farewell.

That ambiguous little knee made Ava seem again like a stranger, enigmatic and yet unpromising. She had withdrawn from him, she was less helpful, a bit too brisk, and at times she seemed bored — not hostile but indifferent — casting her gaze beyond him when she looked in his direction. She was like the people on the plane, who had brushed past him at the baggage claim area and were now dispersing — Hack and

Janey, Wood and Sabra, the hurrying Manfred, who scuttled, bent over, spider-like, as though on extra legs, reaching as he moved. And all the others whom he imagined to be bird watchers, trekkers, and ecotourists in their Trespassing gear, colorful fuzzy jackets and hats and thick socks, wearing the most expensive sunglasses and wristwatches in the catalogue. Manfred had carried his thick *Medicinal Plants* book and studied it, making notes in the margins. He wore a black jacket and at his waist a soiled misshapen fanny pack. Sabra wore a small and neatly zipped TOG pouch. He'd had a glimpse of their luggage — slightly bruised Trespassing duffels and chubby leather satchels chafed at the edges and the best bags from the Trespassing line. Ava was now like one of these people, and Steadman was just a man who happened to be sleeping in her room.

This distant failing country and the strangers and the thin gritty air made their separation more emphatic. They looked lost here, they were alien to each other, and the foreign place represented their estrangement. He had heard of couples taking a long joyless trip, sometimes as a formality, in order to end a love affair or signify and seal an ending. Steadman understood that effort now. Some brutal landscapes, some lovely jungles, threw relationships into stark relief. You might go away with someone in order to make an announcement, and it might be a farewell. The far-off place was neutral ground. Steadman and Ava managed to be civil to each other, but they were through, it was over, and the other people probably sensed it. Then the others were gone, as though dissolved in the Ecuadorian air. "Good riddance," she said, and he knew she was talking about the others.

From the taxi window, filmed with dust and finger smears, Quito was both more orderly and more ramshackle than Steadman had expected. It depended where you looked. Off the fairly new main drag were side streets lined with hovels. Yet in the distance the hovels seemed substantial, and in the foreground the newer buildings were rundown and the gutters littered.

Steadman inclined his head and thought, In the Third World you smile at the strangeness, then you look closely and see ruin and misery, or that something is badly broken, or that woman is ill, that child is an old man. From the lovely veranda you saw mangy dogs and a man pissing against a wall — a wall on which someone had scribbled an angry slogan in Spanish, bracketed by exclamation marks, ¡FUERA

GRINGOS INVASORES! From the loveliest window you saw filthy-faced children huddled in doorways. The bottom of the heap was not far from the top, and all of it was home, turned upside down and stinking.

"*Mi casa, por acá.* My 'ouse down there," the taxi driver said, smiling as a street flashed past, and in that brief glimpse Steadman could see it was shallow and ruinous.

"Where is Nestor?" Steadman asked, since the driver had voluntarily spoken in English.

"Veesy. He see you later." His breath was moist with chocolate and tobacco. The man's pungent breath had a greater reality than his words.

"He didn't leave a message?"

"Yes. That is the message."

Though he was simple, even crude, the driver's succinct directness in basic English made him seem intelligent.

Steadman turned to Ava. He had felt slightly nauseated and lightheaded since the customs delay at the airport. A headache made of raw nerves tightened beneath his skull. He said, "The air's so thin."

"What did you expect at ten thousand feet?"

He expected something else. The high-altitude air was chilly, dusty with grit, and a dampness caught in his throat and scratched his eyes, like the furry air in a house of cats.

Searching the side streets for the grimmer sights, for it seemed that truth lay at the very margins of this ride, he saw a procession, girls and women in white smocks and black veils, boys and men carrying a tottering holy figure on a litter, shoulder-high.

"Is a fiesta," the driver said, sucking candy, his tongue gummy. He was small, in a tight sweater of pilled dusty wool. Though the sky was overcast he wore sunglasses. "Is coming Todos los Santos. And Día de Difuntos. How you say fiesta in English?"

"Fiesta." Steadman was staring at some masked children ahead.

"Halloween," Ava said. "They celebrate it here."

At the stoplight, the children approached wearing Halloween masks — cat masks, witches' hats. Their clothes were clean, they had good teeth. Steadman had expected urchins. He rolled down the taxi window and offered a dollar to one of the masked children.

"*Por su máscara,*" Steadman said, lifting the mask with one hand and handing over the dollar with the other. The black satin cat mask was trimmed with black lace and seemed like an obscure intimate garment, like a cache-sexe.

Hearing the driver's empty squawk of mirth, Steadman reflected that in places like this, demoralized and humiliated countries, someone's laughter seldom meant that something was funny. The driver had been disturbed, perhaps insulted, by Steadman's boldness — the dollar, the swap, the snatch. He winced and squawked again when Steadman put on the cat mask.

"That sort of scares me," Ava said, sounding stern. He knew that severe tone: she meant what she said. He took the mask off.

The hotel was the Colón. Ava said she had imagined it to be smaller and simpler, but checking in, Steadman reminded her that it was supposed to be only one night.

"Still no message from Nestor."

"Why do they all have names like that?" Ava said.

"He was recommended. Supposed to be an ethnobotanist."

"A nice name for 'drug man.'"

"You found him."

Their corner room faced a large park out one window, and out the other was the long steep side of the volcano. A cloud was flattened and raveling on the volcano's peak, and its slopes were dotted with houses. Steadman felt that up close they were hovels, but at this distance, in dim early morning, their lights still twinkling, they represented to his ignorant eyes the magic of a new place.

Ava had pulled off her T-shirt and was searching her bag for something. Her skin was luminous and blue in the gray daylight. Across the room, Steadman saw her as a strange woman who had materialized here, silent, careless, half naked, paying no attention to him. He was fascinated by her indifference, her naked breasts, the impersonal room, the sight of the huts out the window. It was as if he did not know her, that he just happened to find himself in this room with an attractive preoccupied woman. He watched her take off the rest of her clothes: her slacks first, which she folded; her panties, which she slid down with two thumbs and stepped out of, tossing them with one toe. She was headed for the bathroom, preparing for a shower.

Moving quickly toward her, Steadman touched her waist, just grazing her skin with his fingertips, as though stroking and steadying a cat, and then slipped the cat mask over her face, all the while staying behind her. She hardly reacted, except to straighten the fastening cord. He liked that; he could tell she was cooperating. And the mask and her willingness and this strange room in Ecuador aroused him more than love had ever done. Love had made him gentle, and love's querulous concern killed his desire.

This way she seemed his equal, a match for him, a black mask on her white body. He held her. He could not kiss her lips while she was masked, and that tantalized him the more — she seemed to like his frustration. Her mask dared him. She went to the bed and knelt, holding her hand between her legs while he watched, and then she opened her legs and, splaying her fingers, parted the dewy gills of her pinkness, and all the while her mask was impassive.

Watching her, Steadman roughly pushed off his clothes and was on her, slipping inside her, frantic. She murmured softly from beneath her mask, but when he leaned over and attempted to kiss the satin lips of the mask she moved her head away and arched her back, lifting her chin to expose her throat and the tightened cords of her neck. She seemed to exist in some blind private rapture of her own reckless anonymity.

Even when he was finished and on his back, blind himself and gasping, she did not take the mask off. She lay there beside him, so distant she could have been in another country, drawing the droplets through the hair between her legs, making this slickness seem like another mask, her parted legs showing at her vulva the image of a tarantula. And when she turned toward him, still masked and enigmatic, he thought that not she but he was the whore.

Over breakfast afterward — and it was Ava who remarked that it was still unbelievably only nine-thirty that same morning — they said nothing about what had just happened. The sudden wordless episode, the snatched sex in the room, seemed as remote as the long disruptive flight, the annoying passengers, the unhelpful taxi driver, the fiesta and its masks and costumes.

All that Ava said was "It's a real city. I was expecting something desperate. These places that people are always leaving to become maids and janitors in the States, I imagine them to be awful. But no, the places look fine. It's the people's lives that are awful."

All that Steadman said was "That bastard Nestor told us he'd leave a message."

But he said it casually and without rancor, for the sex had calmed him, had eased his mind and pleasantly wearied him and made him accepting.

They went for a walk to Old Town, down the main street that led from the hotel. On the way, seeing a hat shop, Steadman impulsively went in and tried some on.

"All from Montecristi. The best ones. Is the Optimo estyle," the saleswoman said, offering others. "We call these thee Natural. Look, thee weebing. So many months it takes to weeb one. You like?"

Steadman bought himself a Panama with a wide brim, and left the shop wearing it, walking self-consciously because of the hat. They saw more Todos los Santos processions, looking like Halloween kids, one small girl wearing the same mask — black satin trimmed with black lace — that Ava had worn when naked, making love. Steadman could not help attaching sexuality to the masked people, even the skinny-legged girls, whom he saw as teasing, even provocative.

As they approached the narrower roads of Old Town, the sky lowered and contracted with dark clouds. A rumble of thunder brought a torrent of rain. They ducked under a flat-roofed shelter at a bus stop and watched as hailstones, bright white and as round as mothballs, clattered onto the soaked cobbles of the road.

Then the rain eased. They resumed walking and were obstructed on the sidewalk by a small pretty Indian child, red-cheeked in the cold. No more than three or four years old, she sat in the middle of the wet sidewalk holding a plastic cup — and could not possibly have known what she was doing, though this was likely to be her life's work. An old woman across the road, probably Granny, eyed the little girl while begging herself, with two other children. There were ragged children all over Old Town, selling candy and bunches of flowers and combs and matches, assisting at stalls selling fruit, sweeping with clumsy-looking bunches of twigs that served as brooms. Medieval in its crude simplicity and desperation, this scene was repeated on other narrow streets, and some children carrying heavy loads in their tiny hands seemed like dwarf laborers in a cruel folktale.

At the edge of a large plaza, Steadman saw an elderly priest walking just ahead of an Indian man. The Indian, in a blue smock and bowl haircut, with a round face and bandy legs, looked like a big simple-minded child, except that he was doggedly carrying a bag on his shoulder, and the lovely leather bag could only have belonged to the priest. The Indian belonged to the priest, too. He had been domesticated and made to submit. Steadman looked at the clean hem of the priest's white cassock and his shiny shoes, at the Indian's stained smock and cracked sandals. The upright priest, the bent-over Indian: in their progress across the old paving stones of the plaza they seemed to represent the history of South America, if not the history of the world.

To Steadman all religious people looked like savages. Some of them were timid and innocent, most of them were arrogant, menacing in being so credulous and assured — the apes of an imaginary god, tyrannical simpletons who had invented that god and used the god's denunciations as weapons in their tyranny.

Among all these churches, Steadman reflected that he had no religious belief. The sight of believers aroused his pity but could also make him angry or sad, depending on the circumstances. Often he felt resentment that his skepticism could still shock people. His undogmatic sense of the spiritual was limited to preserving forests, nesting places for birds, shade for animals, roots keeping water pure. The symbol of his belief was a tree, and he had spoken in *Trespassing* of how many times he had been hidden and saved by the forests at frontiers and border crossings.

He could not bear the glibness of religious people. God spoke to them; they talked back. "God's testing me." God arranged everything. It was so easy for them to love life or have hope; they were taking directions from God. Yet how did a person like himself, with no faith, learn to love life? Perhaps by fearing its loss. Going away, as he was doing now — it was another message of *Trespassing* — was one way of seizing control of your life.

In a meaningless world he had devised ways to give his life meaning. Sensuality was meaningful; desire and the act of creation gave him purpose. The trip he had embarked on now in Ecuador was an expression of hope and, though he hated the word, his quest.

At the church entrances were Indian women, some with bags, others carrying babies — impossible to say whether they were selling something or just begging, but they were rooted there, looking immovable in their importuning. A blind woman whined at him, "*No sea malito!*" and superstitiously he pressed some money into her hand, making her smile. Black men hollered in Spanish, selling lottery tickets and newspapers. Stylish warmly dressed women slipped out of chauffeur-driven cars and hurried into shops. None of these people looked as though they were affected by the altitude. Steadman and Ava, exchanging an exhausted glance, were breathless and suffocated.

Pausing to rest, for even their plodding pace wore them out, they saw two people from the plane, Wood and Sabra. Wood nodded brusquely and seemed to mutter something to his wife, as if finding this chance meeting just as awkward as they did, for hadn't Ava promised "We'll never see them again"? Husband and wife were wearing new Panama hats.

"Janey's been robbed — her bag ripped right off her arm," Wood said. That was his greeting, as though he planned to deflect any pleasantries by introducing a note of drama — the theft. "All her credit cards. Her passport. Quite a lot of money. And she's been in the country — what? Three hours?"

"Maybe that's some kind of record," Ava said.

"It was a beggar, a blind woman!"

"Robbed by a *ciega*. That's a neat trick."

"Where was her husband?" Steadman could not remember the husband's name, and he did not want to say the wrong one because he recalled that the name was ridiculous.

"Hack was actually looking for her," Sabra said.

As though reproaching Ava for her callousness, Wood said, "Anyway, all her medicine was in the bag, as well as her valuables."

"I'll write her *una nueva prescripción*," Ava said.

Sabra said, "You speak Spanish."

"Obstetrical Spanish. *Abra sus piernas, por favor*," and she smiled at the woman's confusion.

She knew she was being offensive — she intended it. She did not like bumping into these people. She had not come all this way to chitchat with tourists. She seemed to enjoy the fact that the big bossy interior decorator with the English accent and the cell phone had been mugged. Not harmed, just taught a useful lesson. Meeting these other travelers from the flight was a shock, though. They had never thought they would see them again, and here they were, two of them on their first excursion from their hotel room.

"You got a hat, too," Wood said, tugging the brim of his own. "This is at least a grand back in the States. Maybe two grand."

They parted as clumsily as they had met and, heading for a church shown on the small map in their guidebook, Steadman and Ava took a wrong turn and entered a plaza, which was set up as a market area. Three more passengers from the plane, nameless gringos in newly bought Ecuadorian garb, Indian-made sweaters, one wearing a crisp-brimmed Panama hat like the one he had just bought, were haggling over trinkets at a stall. The sight of these people drove them from the market, and yet they saw others from the plane in the museum and in the Indian market and in the narrow streets of Old Town.

What was the point in coming this distance if all you achieved was that disgusting flight and the company of these timid adventurers? Steadman felt he had so far accomplished nothing. They were stepping over beggars, entering the church of La Merced, their original destination — lots of Todos los Santos activity here, in the shape of reverential women carrying lighted candles or slender flaming tapers.

The large soot-darkened paintings in La Merced depicted soldiers in armor and settlers in flowerpot hats, the history of the country from the Spanish point of view, unintentionally showing plunder and bamboozling priests and grateful baffled Indians. In one painting a blind priest was being led by a young boy acolyte, Jesus smiling down from the heavens. The text under it read:

*A los ciegos tú siempre iluminaste,
Testigo el sacerdote que curaste.*

"'You always illuminate the blind — witness the priest who's cured,'" Ava said, translating. "But it rhymes in the original."

The tall gold altar was as high as the church ceiling, with tiers of twisted columns, all thick pasty gilt and dazzling gems. A gigantic fatuity, this jewel box, looming among ragged people, some of them prostrate, others on their knees.

"But I had a strange encounter this morning at the hotel," Ava said. She kept walking, did not look back, slipped into a pew at the side of the church.

Steadman followed her. He sat and listened to her describe how she had taken her clothes off and a man had come from behind and slipped a mask over her face; how he had made love to her; how it had happened in silence — she told Steadman in an even voice, as though confiding to a stranger.

"You liked it," he said.

"I've never done anything like that before," she said.

He wanted her again, and seeing a masked woman pass up the aisle and drop to her knees, a supplicant at a side chapel, only aroused him more.

The masked woman was praying, her words remorseful and audible: "*Perdona nuestras ofensas como también perdonamos a los que nos ofenden — no nos dejes caer en la tentación . . .*"

"Tell me," he said, his tongue thick with desire.

"All this way." She spoke in a whispering mystified voice that trailed off. They were near enough to the chapel to feel the heat from the rack of small candles, a hundred flames lighting the jewel-crusted crucifix on the gilded altarpiece. "And all that expense," she said. "We're in these mountains, among all this gold and these cross-eyed Indians, and at best we are blindfolded."

"So what?"

"Did we have to come to Ecuador to find that out?"

"Obviously," he said.

"That's not why we came."

"I forget why we came."

They left the church and walked some more in the noisy clammy city. They came to a market and hoped to find handicrafts but saw only old-fashioned women's underwear, piles of men's shoes, stacks of brown trousers, folded blankets, and Chinese-made cooking pots. All this ordinariness in front of an ancient scribbled-on wall: ¡FUERA GRINGOS! Near the sign was a café, where they were greeted by a cheery woman who welcomed them, Ava saying "*Huevos*." Steadman felt sick before he had eaten much of his omelet. Ava said the beer she had drunk to quench her thirst made her feel dizzy. Was it the thin air? Steadman asked the waiter to take the beer away.

Throughout the morning walk in Quito he had felt they were getting on well, like an old married couple, but here — at rest, at the café table, dazed by the altitude and the indigestion it seemed to cause — Steadman realized that perhaps this apparent congeniality and easy company was the result of their decision to separate. Once they had said it was over, they had nothing to argue about — they had no future. They could be friends again.

Still, they sat at the café not speaking, not touching. The conversation in the church hung over them, the nagging echoey weight of unanswered phrases.

Rain came again, first like blown grit, then like pebbles tapping and softening in the gusting wind until the sound was more like a lash. Darkened by the weather, they were isolated and lost any desire to see more of the city. Steadman paid the bill and they caught a taxi that was parked near the bus terminal.

When they got in, the taxi driver was effusive, wearing a colorful scarf and a dangly earring. He spoke a sentence that Steadman could not comprehend.

"He says the rain is good luck," Ava said. "He's so pleased we are here. He has a friend in New York. Male friend, of course."

Steadman thought how rainstorms made strange cities familiar, exaggerated and simplified their contours. Yet here the rain did not drain away but puddled and flooded and held up traffic. This sudden downpour enclosed them, blurred the city, gave it a look of homely exoticism, made them need each other again. Now it was just the two of them. The sun might have separated them, but the bad weather brought them close.

Steadman said, "I'm starting to worry about this trip. If I don't hook up with this guy Nestor I'm screwed. I'm depending on him to get me into the jungle. He's supposed to be an ethnobotanist. If he doesn't show, there's no story."

Ava sat back in the taxi, drawing away from him, and said, "Oh, so you're a writer."

At first Steadman almost laughed and said, What are you saying? Of course I am! But he hesitated, because she was blank-faced, waiting for an answer while the taxi splashed through the flooded gutters, sending up gouts of water. That was the other thing about rain in such a country. It came down mud-colored.

Steadman said, "Yes, I am. And what do you do?"

"I'm a doctor." She smiled as only a stranger smiles at another stranger, holding the expression in check and yet hopeful.

The taxi driver took an interest. He said, "*Quisiera mostrarles cosas fantásticas.*"

"He wants to show us some amazing things."

Steadman whispered, "He's a sodomite."

Ava smiled again. She said, "Like me."

"What's your name?"

She said, "I'll tell you upstairs."

The taxi's seats were covered in torn leather. Hanks of straw showed through, and the pungency of the straw and the leather stirred him as much as her teasing words.

In the hotel lobby, Ava said, "I'm in three-one-oh-two. Give me a few minutes." She did not touch him. She turned and was gone.

Steadman liked this change of mood and the way she had given him this information, telling him what he already knew — so brisk and businesslike, as though she were an accomplished sneak, having rehearsed it many times. But he thought, That's what fantasies are — fantasies are rehearsals.

Liking the taste of the delay, he gave her more time than she had asked for and then went upstairs. She answered the door wearing a hotel robe, but slipped it off when he entered. She was naked. Steadman locked and bolted the door, and when he turned to Ava again she was blindfolded — the sleep mask from the plane — and held another blindfold in her hand.

"Wait." Steadman was kicking his shoes off, stripping off his shirt.

She knew what he was doing. She said, "I don't care what you wear, as long as you wear this," and handed him the other blindfold.

In the stumbling game that followed, Ava slipped away from him and then called to him from across the room. Fearful of hurting himself, Steadman got down on all fours and crept toward the sound of her voice, though she went on teasing him. Over here, she said. No, over here. Until he cornered her and took hold of her and kissed her and pressed his face against her softness, sensing her vividly as an odor and a warmth in the darkness of his blindfold. As they kissed, this darkness lifted and became smoldering light. But the act itself came much later, for they struggled, choking in a hallucination of desire, teasing, delaying, relenting, beginning again, two strangers becoming acquaintances, uttering the desperate half-laugh of lust.

The act was not about possessing her but about letting go, each of them doing so in the most private way, as though practicing this release. And they took turns, each one both a suggestion and a dare, as if in using only their lips and their tongues they were saying with mute eloquence, This is what I want.

Later, Steadman was the first to wake, but taking off his blindfold made little difference, for night had fallen. He saw a slash of meager brightness, the dim lights of the city through the curtain. Ava lay asleep, still blindfolded, sprawled between two chairs, embracing herself for warmth. She looked tossed there, her lips parted, her tongue showing, like a cat that has been hit by a car.

He too was lying naked on the floor. There was also a crack of corridor light showing in the threshold, enough light so that Steadman saw that a folded paper, probably a note, had been thrust under the door.

4

BEING WOKEN before dawn was like an intimation of sickness, a set of symptoms: the tremulous fragility of early morning in the high distant city, sniffing the thin, sharpened air in the dim fluorescence of the uncertain light, the rank dust, the muffled voices and humming stillness, his clamped head and crusted eyes. He was reminded that he had said something like this in *Trespassing* about this very place.

Steadman hated early starts, and downstairs he was jarred by Nestor's heartiness.

"Ready to rumble?"

When people like this knew American catch phrases, Steadman suspected them of trying to hustle him. Why else would a stranger take such trouble to ingratiate himself? Besides, their knowing such inanities proved that they had habitually associated with shallow boisterous Americans and knew no better.

Ava, used to a doctor's emergencies, was already up and dressed and lucid.

Nestor was a big confident man, no more than forty, with a beaky face and a mustache and deep-set dark eyes. He wore a heavy leather jacket, which Steadman remarked on. Nestor instantly seemed to know what Steadman was intimating and said, "You won't need it where we are going."

Instead of being reassured by Nestor's excellent English, Steadman was suspicious of his presumption. The man was clearly experienced, but he was impulsive in his movements, even in the way he walked — lunging — and so confident as to be carelessly clumsy.

Five other shadow-shrouded people sat in the back of the van, faceless in the darkness, hunched over in the chill of the early morning. A cassette of Andean flute and panpipe music was whistling in the van's tape player. They said nothing when Steadman and Ava got into the forward seat. They remained silent — Steadman guessed that they resented having to pick up him and Ava last, giving them more time to sleep. Waiting for them in the porte-cochère of the luxury hotel perhaps annoyed them, too.

"Six hours to Papallacta," Nestor said. "And then Lago Agrio. We stay in Lago tonight. We will be on the river in the morning. Tomorrow afternoon in the jungle. Anyone mind if I smoke a cigarette?"

"We mind," came a voice from a back seat, a woman's voice, like bolt cutters snapping through iron.

Nestor shrugged and unwrapped some chewing gum. He sat next to the driver, whom he announced as Hernán. Hernán was a capable driver, but Steadman disliked being driven except by Ava, who was efficient at the wheel, using her bossy doctor's manner in traffic, but she drove with caution, never speeded. The other passengers in the van were seated in silence, their heads down. Steadman had assumed, based on the high price they had paid up front, that he and Ava would be alone. But this was like a group trip for budget travelers.

Steadman reminded himself that he would not have been able to accomplish this drug tour single-handedly. They needed Nestor, and Hernán too, probably, for though he had been in Ecuador before, this was different. Even if Steadman had managed to find the village in the jungle, he would not have been able to negotiate the drug ceremony with the Secoya. He needed Nestor as a guide and go-between, but he also resented needing him.

Outside the city, the road widened into what seemed a highway, and after a short distance — though it was impossible to be precise in this darkness — it dropped down to a narrower, winding road. The van swayed on the curves; Hernán drove with his forearms on the wheel. In the deeper valleys it seemed that dawn was receding and night falling all over again. All that was visible was a short stretch of road ahead, rising and falling in the lights of the van, and at the margin of the road deep green sides of a forested valley.

"Like that road in Uganda," came the bolt-cutter voice from the back, faintly English. "On the way to that gorilla place."

"Bhutan," a man said with more certainty. "Bhutan's got roads like this. To the monastery. That burned down after we saw it."

"This could be Yucatán," a woman said.

"You been to Uganda?" Nestor called out. "Supposed to be awesome."

There were murmurs from the back, though Steadman was thinking that "awesome" was just the sort of word such an Ecuadorian hustler would know. A woman, not the harsh-voiced one, said, "Africa's finished. We're never going back. Some people feel sorry for the Africans and their AIDS epidemic, but I despise them for it. I hate them for being so irresponsible."

Beside him, Ava took a deep breath and released it as a sigh, a slow, barely audible whinny of exasperation.

"Billions of stars," a man said.

And ghostly moon-glow patches on the dark earth where there were thick, squat huts, with stones weighting the corrugated squares of their rusted roofs. To the south, the eerie brightness of a snowcapped peak, like a bed sheet crumpled on a black rock, just a glimpse that came and went. Strands of clouds, like torn spider webs, fluttered up from the snowfield and then were crushed by the darkness that poured from the depth of the valley.

"Dark matter," the softer-voiced woman said.

"I don't get that," the other woman said.

"Particles," a man said. "It's dark energy. What do you think is holding the universe together? Not the stars, that's for sure. They are, like, this tiny proportion of what's out there."

"What else is out there?"

"Dark energy. Quintessence. Gravity mass. It's a kind of invisible cosmic broth that keeps galaxies in place," the woman said. She was eating trail mix, stirring it in a bag with her fingers and chewing loudly as she spoke. "Or maybe not particles but overfolded space-time, like a new dimension. A whole different plane of being."

"You guys must be teachers," Nestor said.

"No teachers here," a man said in a weary voice.

"How many kilometers to Papallacta?" a new voice piped up in the darkness. Because the man was agitated, his German accent was more distinct than if he'd been calm, and he chewed it and turned it into a gargling speech impediment.

Nestor laughed and muttered something to Hernán, and at that moment a cell phone sounded two notes in the back of the van. A woman fumbled with it and tried to answer, the call failed, and the woman muttered, "Oh, knickers."

But for some time Steadman had known who these other passengers were.

Manfred was panting with impatience and now and then sighing with deliberate harshness as he fussed with the tangled wires of a pair of headphones. The others talked without letup, because of the darkness, because of their apprehension, because they were naturally assertive. Steadman did not blame them for being wealthy or for collecting destinations like trophies, but he minded their talking so much and so intrusively this early in the morning — dawn still distant, their voices contending in the van — and not conversing with each other so much as boasting to be heard by the eavesdroppers they hoped to impress. They were saying what all of them already knew, and everything they said had a gloating sound.

Wealth had made trespassing simple. With money it was now possible to go anywhere in the world. No courage was necessary, nor any planning. Steadman was fascinated by the choices: gorillas in Africa, temples in Bhutan, back roads in Yucatán. In Antarctica — so Wood was recalling right now in the van — they had wandered the rookeries of the emperor penguin. Though Steadman had imagined just himself and Ava on this trip, it was not surprising that they were with these others on the van ride to the jungle. Steadman hated the thought that he was like them, for his wealth had made this possible for him, too. But this was only the beginning. The real test would come later, down the river, in the jungle, at the village.

Still in this darkness the man who had been introduced as Hack said, "I still can't see a fucking thing," his face against the van window.

"Sabra and I heard about one of these quote-unquote raves outside London," Wood said. "I gave a taxi driver a hundred bucks and said, 'Just get us there.' It was some kind of industrial facility on the outskirts, a couple of thousand whacked-out kids jumping up and down. They all had taken this drug Ecstasy."

Sabra said, "One kid told me that he took a huge hit. Wandering around. Kids were just stepping on his face."

"The Secoya are much more civilized than that," Nestor said.

"One hit of Ecstasy and he's blind for six hours."

"A drug that blinded you might bliss you out."

"In your dreams."

"Yah, but some few plants give you fissions."

Dawn broke slowly, the buoyant light leaking into the air around them and seeming to hoist the sky as the darkness dissolved, leaving shadows like a residue by the roadside, on dense bushes and leaning trees. The soft brief light turned harsh and overbright within minutes and showed the littered road. Up ahead, near some frantic chickens and a tethered goat, was a low plank-built house at a bend in the road, its chimney smoking.

"Pit stop," Hack said as Hernán slowed the van.

"Anyone hungry?" Nestor said. "Also there is a restroom."

Beyond the house was a valley brimming with morning cloud, more spider web, some of it tangled, some of it close-knit and welcoming. Steadman walked over to the edge of the road and yawned and stretched. He turned, thinking that Ava had followed him, and saw Wood beside him in a blue jacket with full sleeves and a pair of warm-up pants.

"This cloth is actually a kind of ceramic," Wood said, stroking his sleeve. "While these Trespassing sweats are made from recycled plastic bottles. That's why they're so expensive."

"Ten percent of the pretax profits go to environmental causes," Steadman said, looking away.

"Tell me that's not deductible."

Steadman smiled and listened to a birdcall that was a tumbling whistle, like a showoff sound of beautiful wooing.

Hack crept to Steadman's other side and he too looked into the valley.

"Hold your nose if you're using the crapper here, it's like the one in

Cambodia," Hack said. He was still sizing up the valley. He said, "Good friend of mine from Wharton got jacked here on the local juice."

"Hack, check it out. Whole bunch of water over there."

Nestor called out, saying that breakfast was ready. Behind Steadman on the path, Hack said, "But Cambodia was great. On that same trip we went surfing in the Andaman Islands."

"Thailand's ruined," Wood said. "Bali's a toilet."

The women were seated at a table with Manfred, who was wearing headphones and had started eating before anyone else. He had a huge plateful of food — hunks of bread, deep-fried buns, gritty eggs, and wet boiled greens. Instead of sitting elbow to elbow with the others, Steadman stood, holding his plate with one hand and eating with the other. He marveled again at how Manfred seemed to have more than two arms, for the man was reaching and eating at the same time.

"Keebler. Like the biscuits," Janey was saying into her phone. A self-conscious singsong whine entered her voice, especially when she was attempting a joke. It came again. "No. Pfister. The P is silent. Like the pee in bath."

Janey began tapping her phone — she had lost the signal, she said. "You're eating that frightful tuck?" When Steadman did not reply she said, "It looks like something the cat sicked up."

He listened to Hack telling Ava, "We work hard, we play hard," and he wondered whether he should interrupt, to rescue her.

More coffee was brought and poured, and it was only now that Steadman noticed the people who were serving: small hurrying Indians, looking anxious as they moved among the visitors, smiling fearfully, in toothy terror-struck appreciation, whenever they made eye contact. Nestor gave one of the Indian men some money for the meal and said, "Now, let's boogie."

They reboarded the van with the brittle politeness of people who dislike one another, the sort of brusque formality that verges on rudeness. "Excuse me." "You are excused." And, "May I trouble you for a tissue?" "You may indeed trouble me for a tissue." And, "Thank you very much." "You're welcome very much."

"I am going to be terribly rude and put my cheesy feet up on the back of your seat," Janey said to Manfred.

Misunderstanding her, Manfred tapped his headphones and widened his eyes and shouted, "Weber! *Die Freischutz!*"

Janey peered out the van window as they drew away from the building of rough planks where they had just eaten. She said, "Everything here is so retro."

Planning the Ecuador trip with Ava, Steadman had imagined just the two of them with Nestor, negotiating the descent to the jungle from the plateau, Nestor confiding the secrets of the Oriente. Back then, this van and its occupants had been unthinkable. He had not counted on any intrusion, especially from tourists. And he had looked forward to being with Ava. He had wanted the journey to be singular, even risky. But it was over with Ava, they were not alone, and he felt disgusted and nauseated, resenting the other passengers, hating Hernán's driving, and with the sickly premonition that this was all a waste of time. He had wanted his Ecuadorian adventure to be the first stage in reclaiming his reputation as a writer, which he believed would be the making of him as a man. The drug tour that he had hoped would be unique, his own, was apparently a widely known trip down a well-traveled path, in the sort of full-color brochure that also described gorilla encounters in Africa and white-water rafting on the Ganges and treks to the Everest base camp and birding in Mongolia.

For a while, for too long, he dishonestly complained about his celebrity and his book sales — secretly, he had been delighted. But after that his complaints were sincere. He wanted to move on; he took any work that came his way. He was hired by magazines because he had established his name first with *Trespassing*, and the assignments he chose always involved travel. Ava loved to travel. For several years there was hardly any difference between his work and their vacations.

As the author of *Trespassing*, Steadman, a traveler, a writer, became known irrationally as a travel writer. He had been prevailed upon to take magazine assignments to write about cities and hotels and restaurants. In the beginning he could not believe his luck. "To travel writing," he would toast, clinking glasses with Ava over a sumptuous meal — and the meal might be lobster agnolotti followed by osso buco on polenta with baby carciofi, in the restaurant at the Hotel Cipriani — the crenelated, ecclesiastical skyline of Venice across the Giudecca Canal, San Giorgio Maggiore just out the window.

His assignments had been so pleasurable that he did not need to be told by editors that the underlying assumption in all such magazine writing was that the pieces would be friendly and positive. Most of the time there were no expense forms to fill out. Magazines sent him on press trips. The hotel or tourist bureau provided the airfare and treated him to meals and drinks. He was given helicopter rides and expensive presents and sent home with a press kit from which he was expected to write his story.

At first he did well. He had enjoyed himself; he expressed his gratitude in lush description, repaid the hospitality with praise. But the novelty was dulled by repetition, the travel became more laborious — more like work, even the luxury seemed humdrum and superfluous — and instead of the places seeming interchangeable, they became distinct, joyless, hardly human, and often odious to him. There was something peculiarly rigid and unspontaneous in the glamour. All this he described in travel pieces that he believed were fluent and truthful and sometimes humorous.

The pieces were not received well. One editor said, "You don't seem to have had a very good time. All you talk about is the bad driving and the dangerous roads."

Steadman was not discouraged. He quoted his line in *Trespassing* — *Travel at its most enlightening is not about having a good time* — and continued to go on press trips. But when they received his pieces the editors said, "This needs a little work," or "This wasn't exactly what we wanted," and would explain in vague, insulting terms how he ought to rewrite the piece — "Tweak it," they said — to make it publishable.

Steadman endured a terrible time on a press trip to Trinidad. The place was crime-ridden and dirty. It was noisy. Steadman hated the music. The Trinidadians he met were rapacious. He used the words "risible" and "jungly" and "sweaty" and "cacophonous," and all of them were crossed out by a subeditor. So was the word "stink." He had looked into the island's racial politics. The piece was rejected. "It was supposed to be for our 'Island in the Sun' slot. You didn't even mention the raw bar at the Intercontinental."

Steadman sent the editor a signed copy of *Trespassing*.

Sour or carping pieces were instantly rejected, irony was discouraged for its ambiguity, humor was unwelcome for its belittling, satire for its subversion, and any mention of ugliness or ruin was forbidden. In all such writing a note of fawning gratitude was mingled with submissive bonhomie. The theme of each excursion was pleasure: How lucky I am to be in this lovely place, eating this delicious meal, and you will love it too!

"It isn't travel. It isn't even writing," Steadman said. "This is advertising copy. I am expected to be an adjunct to the public relations industry." The magazines demanded pretty pictures and gusto and undiluted praise, in order to encourage advertisers and build income. It was how they prospered.

Real travel was risky, uncertain, difficult, and not very comfortable. What these magazines called travel were in fact beach holidays. For the upscale magazines it was the fake sophistication of gourmandising or the indolence of a luxury cruise — self-indulgent, undemanding, pleasurable, lots of sunshine, swimming, moonlight. Steadman had been hired because he was a real writer with a reputation, the author of a travel classic; but he realized that as an open-minded and wealthy traveler he was feared by the hosts, whose pretensions he would ridicule, and disliked by the magazines, which felt he would drive away advertisers. It took almost two years for Steadman to understand that he had no future in this business. He returned to struggling with his novel: work in stoppage.

And later, with the reading of Burroughs's *Yage Letters,* he yearned to take a trip to Ecuador — to visit a shaman; to experiment with *yajé,* which was also known as ayahuasca, "vine of the soul"; to revisit the drug that Burroughs had praised in his obscure book; to rediscover a true story and perhaps find the inspiration to go on with his novel. He needed fuel. He read the other recommended books — the ethno-botanical work of Richard Schultes and the more mystical Reichel-Dolmatoff. The drug literature was respectful, more about spirit and ritual and cultural roots than about thrills. But all the botanists mentioned the risks.

He had not guessed that this, too, had become part of the tourist industry, but now he knew that the people in the van, on this trip — Sabra, Wood, Hack, Janey, and Manfred — were like the people who were looking for the perfect mai tai on Maui, or the best snorkeling spot on the Great Barrier Reef, or the greatest nude beach on St. Barts. He knew now that they had trekked to see gorillas and gone bird watching in Botswana, been to Cambodia and Bhutan and Thailand, across the Patagonian pampas, down the Zambezi, up the Sepik. "I've got a Bontoc head ax. There's drops of blood on it." Scuba diving off Palau, they had been surrounded by sharks. Easter Island. The Andamans. Gauchos. Mudmen. Ifugao. Pygmies. Sea Dayaks. "Headhunters."

"India sucked except for the Ayurvedic massage in Kerala."

Trophies, all of them. And this — the trip to Oriente, the visit to a shaman in a jungle village, the search for a true *ayahuasquero* and the trance-drink itself — was another trophy for these romantic voyeurists.

"What are you planning to do here?" Ava had asked the others at breakfast.

"Same thing as you guys."

What Steadman believed he had elaborately devised as an original trip, using obscure anthropological texts and the works of ethnobotanists — a trip he hoped would help make his reputation as a traveler in search of enlightenment — had become nothing more than the highest-priced package vacation, a drug tour. Without her having said a word, he knew that Ava was also dismayed by the presence of the others on the tour. What he had hoped would be an adventure seemed no more than a school outing.

Yet he was determined to see it through. The trip had just begun; the others might panic and bail out. It happened — luxury cruise ship passengers got seasick, a woman on a press trip in Mexico was raped in her hotel room, and on the Trinidad junket a male travel writer from New York handed a woman travel writer from Seattle an envelope full of clumsy Polaroids he had shot of himself, nude, in a full-length mirror. And then the man had threatened her when she said she would turn them over to the police. Drama was still possible on this trip, but Steadman doubted that it would serve him. At times, being with Ava in this state of detachment was like being alone, for she had insisted on being a stranger, and that was an unexpected help to him, even a thrill, for her pretense and her manner of seduction.

He hoped the trip might result in a book, and perhaps he could make it one, part of the novel he had planned, an in-search-of book, exaggerating the dangers, profiling the people, attributing the sexual experiences he had already unexpectedly enjoyed, masked and blindfolded in the Quito hotel, to someone else, who perhaps he could say had bared his soul to him — or, coming completely clean, using his relationship with Ava. This travel-book-as-fiction would include food, drugs, sex, exotic landscapes, remoteness — snowcapped peaks rising above the green heat; the jungle in the shadow of Cotopaxi; romantic failure, disillusionment, disappointment; a breakup book, more about trespassing than *Trespassing* had been.

All this he reflected on during the long silent trip to Papallacta. The only words that had been spoken since breakfast were Manfred's "Weber! *Die Freischutz!*" Everyone but Steadman and Manfred had fallen asleep.

Just before Papallacta the van wobbled and swerved: a flat tire. They had no jack and had to flag down a car for help. The hour it took to fix it, and then get the spare repatched, put them behind. Lunch was late — just peeled fruit and warm beer in a parking lot near the hot springs at Papallacta.

"*Aguas calientes*," Nestor said.

Steadman watched Hernán approach a tall bush in bloom at the edge of the parking lot, just outside a low wall. He smiled and stroked the large white flowers.

"You know this tree?" Nestor asked.

Ava said, "It's pretty."

"Maybe you call it angel's trumpet?" Nestor said.

"I don't call it anything."

"We call it *toé*. There are many kinds. Brugmansia. Some we have down the river," he said, and tapped his head. "They are nice."

"And you know that because you're an ethnobotanist?"

"I am a *vegetalista*," Nestor said. "I am not a *toéro*, but I know this *toé*."

Steadman said, "It opens your eyes, is that it?"

"*Luz*," Nestor said with slushy sibilance, and goggled at him with a comic stare, then winced in exaggeration. "Is a light. Open eyes, close them, give you eyes like a *yana puma* — a *tigre*," he added, and spoke rapidly to Hernán, who laughed.

Ava hated it when people like this shared a secret in another language while laughing in her face. She believed they intended her to feel insecure and out of her depth, and she was insulted.

Insistently, she said, "What did you just say to him?"

"I speak in Quechua. You don't speak Quechua? I say, '*Toé — nino amaru*.' It is the fire boa."

Manfred fingered the leaves of the bush and said, "This is Datura Brugmansia. Is a separate genus now. A strong hallucinogen. Maybe containing the entheogen *maikua*. You call this *borrachero?*"

"Some people do."

"Is a solanaceous genus," Manfred said, bobbling his plant book, clawing at the tissuey pages with his sticky fingers.

Steadman was listening closely, fascinated by Manfred's dirty fingernails and his erudition; but Ava had turned away. "Why did we stop here?" she asked.

"Lunch. Then *baños*. Use the hot springs, then we go," Nestor said.

The hot springs' enclosure lay on a hillside, where there were terraces and stone steps, a shed that served as a changing room, and a shelter where an old leathery-faced woman in braids dispensed clean towels. The succession of pools set into the slope were linked by troughs and sluices down which steaming water ran. The pools at the top, near the source of the hot springs, were very hot — bubbling, perhaps boiling — and all of them were empty. Steadman put his hand into one and scalded his fingers. The larger, lukewarm pools were just below, surrounded by reeds, the water tumbling into them over a moss-covered spillway.

By the time Steadman and Ava had changed, the Hacklers and the Wilmutts were already sitting in the largest pool, up to their chins in the water, their heads wreathed in vapor.

"Plenty of room for you guys," Wood said.

"Ain't half hot!" Janey called out.

Steadman and Ava stepped into the steaming water and slipped down, seating themselves on the stone shelf, until only their heads were visible in the vapor. Four other heads watched them from the far side of the pool. A sulfurous odor hung in the mist over the bubbly gray water.

"Where's our German friend and his big book?" Hack said.

Janey cursed her phone and tapped the keypad irritably.

"I was promised roaming here."

Steadman noticed that a copy of *Trespassing* — it had to have been Sabra's, she carried it everywhere — lay on the wall next to the pool.

"How sweet it is," Wood said, thrashing like a child.

"The man of leisure," Hack said.

"I wish," Wood said. "I want to do another book."

"You're really a writer?" Ava said. She hadn't meant to say anything, but she was so surprised by "I want to do another book," it slipped out. She became self-conscious. "You mentioned your company?"

"One of my companies."

"He buys companies," Hack said.

"Writer, book packager, pretty much the same thing."

Steadman just stared at the man who was stirring the tip of his stubbly chin in the steaming water.

"*The Heights of Fame* — that's mine," Wood said. "One of mine."

"Full disclosure, the only one," Hack said.

"One of those is all you need," Wood said.

Ava smiled in surprise, for she had actually heard of the book — was it a book? Ava remembered it as a chart. She wondered if perhaps someone had given them a copy as a present — for a long time it was a gift item. It was regarded as a publishing phenomenon, widely publicized, reprinted many times, and unexpectedly and hugely profitable.

Wood said, "It was a great idea, but the worst part for me was its simplicity. So everyone copied it."

The idea had occurred to him, he said, while he had been reading a biography of Joseph Conrad. Conrad's height was given as just five feet.

"I had thought of Conrad as a giant — bearded, broad-shouldered, a big Polack sea captain. He was tiny!"

Wood read more biographies, he said, looking for the one fact. Diminutive writers seemed to be the rule. Alexander Pope had been four six; Lawrence Durrell gave his height as five four, but in fact he was just a little over five feet tall. Wood searched further. Keats had been five feet tall, Balzac five one, T. E. Lawrence five five — the same height as Marilyn Monroe. Dylan Thomas was five six, Thoreau five seven, and Robert Louis Stevenson five ten.

Wood said, "Melville was a munchkin! Henry James was a dwarf! Faulkner was a peewee! Melville was just over five feet. You think of him as a powerful whaler, wielding a harpoon, but no, he was a borderline midget, like most other writers."

Ava said, "Thomas Wolfe wasn't a midget."

"He's on the chart. He was six four."

Now she remembered: a foldout chart was included in the book. It was in the form of an enhanced tape measure, giving the name and height of each writer mentioned. This was to be tacked to a wall, and there was room on the elongated chart for you to write your own names on it. So your mother might be as tall as Conrad, your child the size of Alexander Pope, your basketball-playing nephew the physical equal of Thomas Wolfe.

"Graham Greene and George Orwell were both way over six feet," Wood said.

"Listen, want to hear something totally awesome?" Hack said to the others. Then he spoke to Wood in the tone of a quizmaster: "Edgar Allan Poe?"

"Five eight," Wood said.

"Marquis de Sade?"

"Five three."

Ava said, "William Burroughs."

"Five foot eleven and a half."

"Just your size," Ava said to Steadman, and Steadman smiled, for she knew that it was Burroughs's book that had started him thinking about this journey.

"Ever read *The Yage Letters*?" Ava asked Wood.

"Never heard of it. Who wrote it?"

"A man who came here once," Ava said.

As she spoke, Nestor appeared. He said, "He didn't come here. He was in Colombia, on the Putumayo. But it was still Amazonia and the quest was the same. Not a tour, though. Now we go."

Emerging from the steaming pool, they were chilled by the late-afternoon air and felt tired and stewed from sitting in the hot water. Drying themselves, they saw Manfred at the top of the slope. He always seemed to appear out of nowhere, as though dropping from an invisible line, like a pendulous insect. He was entirely naked and unembarrassed, thrashing himself with a loose towel, pink-fleshed from the scalding water, the hair on his head spiky and damp, his penis slack and swinging as he descended from stone to stone. He was wearing earphones and carrying a Walkman in one hand and had a small spray of flowers pinched in the fingers of his free hand, and he was smiling.

"Is a bromeliad!" — shouting because of the earphones.

Nestor said, "Next stop, Lago Agrio."

"How many kilometers until Lago Agrio?"

"I will tell you later," Nestor said.

"How many kilometers until 'later'?" Hack demanded.

5

THE FIRST INDICATION that they were nearing the town of Lago Agrio was a succession of signs, most of them lettered *Prohibido el Paso*, some of them showing a grinning stenciled skull, like a Halloween mask, and the single forbidding word *Peligro*.

"What's that supposed to be?" Wood asked in the darkness of the van.

"*Calavera*," Hernán said. "Eskell."

It was after midnight when they entered the empty streets, lurid in the glare of small orangy light bulbs, traveling first on a bumpy road and then the uneven pavement of the main street, flanked by the same ocherous shadows. All the shops were shuttered and dark. Only a handful of shadow-faced people lurked by pillars in the arcades, where some open fires were glowing, cut off oil drums serving as braziers. Ava and Steadman were first off the bus, and even in the semidarkness, smelling dampness, ant-chewed wood, moistened dirt, dog shit, rusty pipes, and the smutty smoke from the braziers, they sensed the town was ugly — not old but hastily built, a kind of blight in the jungle, a sudden wasteland of dead trees, a slum smelling of blackened pots and stale bread and frying and decay. Another stink in the air was subtly toxic, the sour-creamy tang of fuel oil.

"It's sensationally scruffy," Janey said in a tone of gloating satisfaction. Then she yawned. "Promise you will tuck me in, darling? I am so knackered."

Off the main road, down an alley, within a narrow courtyard that looked fortified by its high walls, the Hotel Colombiana lay in darkness. Hernán backed the van into the courtyard, stopping and starting.

"Wouldn't it be simpler just to park the van on the street?" Sabra said.

"Then the van would not be here tomorrow," Nestor said. "We are less than twenty miles from the Colombia border. You know the FARC? Fuerzas Armadas Revolucionarias de Colombia? They will take the van. They will take you."

As he spoke, he worked, catching the bags that Hernán passed to him and stacking them beside the van.

"You mean kidnap?" Sabra said.

"They are too busy for that. They outsource the kidnapping," Nestor said, and looked smug using the word "outsource" as he labored with the bags.

"So who does it?"

"Children kidnap you and then sell you to the FARC or anyone who will continue the ransom procedure."

"Charming," Janey said.

"What kind of kids would do that?" Hack asked.

"Hungry kids, with guns," Nestor said, and headed for the hotel office. "I will give you room keys."

The others complained about the hotel and were so aggrieved by Nestor's warnings that Steadman and Ava made a point of praising the place. They drank gin-and-lime in their hotel room, hearing distant voices, screeching women, roaring men.

While Ava sat facing the window and the wall of the hotel garden, which was fragrant with night-blooming jasmine, Steadman walked behind her and put a blindfold over her eyes.

They went on drinking, Steadman carefully filling Ava's glass, but she said, "It's not working."

Steadman said nothing. Perhaps she was tired. Was the whole blindfold business a self-deceiving gimmick, or was it a step too far? He resisted giving it a name. Surely such intensity could not be blunted after one day. Steadman put tonight's failure down to the fact that they had spent all that time together in the van. Being so close for so long, elbow to elbow, had tired him and killed his desire. Hers too, it seemed.

They felt awkward climbing into the same bed, clinging briefly though not kissing. And then they were asleep.

They were woken at seven — the jangling phone, Nestor summoning them to the café at the front of the hotel, where coffee, fruit, and bread were being set out on a table by Hernán. The others yawned and muttered, sounding irritated and weary. The morning was already hot enough to melt the butter in its sticky dish, and the humidity glowed on the faces of the travelers. The low hideous town was loud with traffic and scurrying people and hawkers, with new and sharper stinks and monotonous music.

"Anyone get kidnapped last night?" Hack said, peeling a banana.

"Hack, you are awful," Janey said, smiling in encouragement.

Nestor said, "Something stranger than that, my friends. Near here is the San Miguel Bridge to Colombia, at La Punta, the frontier. They call it Farafan. Early this morning, some people going across the bridge in their cars were stopped by the FARC soldiers at gunpoint. The soldiers gave them a choice. 'Set your car on fire or we will shoot you.' Twenty-two cars were burned on the bridge. Just here."

"That was this morning?" Sabra said, sounding terrified.

"It's okay, Beetle," Wood said, and hugged his wife. With angry emphasis, he said to Nestor, "What is the point of that?"

Nestor said, "Maybe they don't want people using the bridge, or maybe it's a protest against the hit squads here. Or maybe you should ask Tiro Fijo."

"Who's that?"

Hernán said, "'Sure Shot,' the big man of the FARC."

"Let's get out of here," Sabra said. She was squeezing her copy of *Trespassing* in anxious fingers.

"I think he's just winding us up," Janey said. "All I see in this grotty little town are nig-nogs in market stalls trying to sell us wickerwork."

Wood said, "Are we going to be leaving here in a timely fashion?"

"After we go shopping. We need food for the jungle," Nestor said. "There's not much gringo food down the river. Ah, here is the *estranjero*."

Manfred appeared, walking into the café from the direction of the Hotel Colombiana passageway.

The others, expecting someone new, looked up with disappointment. Manfred was in jungle gear, which made him seem darker and more predatory, his shirt tucked in and sweat-stained, his thick thighs tight in his trousers. He looked hot and uncomfortable, bug-eyed and blinking, his mouth open, breathing hard as he smiled and muttered at the rest of the people. He then seemed to take possession of the table, snatching at fruit, twisting bread in his fingers.

"You hear about the kidnappings?" Wood asked.

Manfred said, "Of course. Everybody knows. They enjoy kidnapping the oil people. This was all rain forest until the oil companies came. Texaco and Occidental cleared it. Now it's drugs, *putas*, gun sellers, and oil pipelines. High toxicity. Criminals. You blame the people here for hating gringos?"

"So what are you doing here then?"

Manfred became serious and said, "I am on a quest, like you."

"We're not on a fucking quest," Hack said.

"No need for effing and blinding," Janey said.

As a way of indicating that she was not interested in this abrasive back-and-forth, and loud enough for everyone to hear, in the manner of an announcement, Ava said to Steadman, "Let's look around town, shall we?" She glanced at Janey and added, "I want to see those nig-nogs and the wickerwork."

"Meet back here at noon," Nestor said. "Hernán will go with you. If you get lost, ask for the Colombiana."

"I'm staying right here," Sabra said. She opened *Trespassing* and lifted it to her face, as though to keep the world away.

Hernán led Ava and Steadman down a side street, explaining the stalls, some selling tapes and CDs — the music blaring — and others selling sneakers and sports jerseys and cheap clothes. Beyond the stalls were small shops, bars, and garages. The curio shops were stocked with blowguns of various lengths and darts, bows and iron-tipped arrows, crude knives, beaded belts, and woven baskets. Lining the walls were medicinal herbs in fat dusty burlap sacks.

"You want something special?" Hernán asked Steadman, and winked at a man in a curio shop.

The man took a long soot-blackened blowgun and inserted a dart into its tube and with bulging cheeks ostentatiously blew the dart into the ceiling of the shop. Then he led them past the sacks and more blowguns, behind a partition, saying "*Tigre, tigre*," and showed them a jaguar pelt and a jaguar skull with sharp gleaming teeth. The man spoke eagerly to Hernán.

"He will give you a good price."

"*Tigre!*"

Steadman looked at the empty eye sockets of the jaguar skull. The thing had long fangs among its sharp teeth, but the hollows where its eyes had been made it the pathetic parched shell of a small blind monster. On the table were dishes of animal teeth, feathers, quills, and patches of fur. He picked up an even smaller skull, the size of a baseball.

"Look, a little baby," Steadman said.

"Baby monkey," Ava said.

Seeing Steadman's interest, the man pressed the small skull into Steadman's hand and said, "*Mono.* Ees mankee. *En peligro de extinción!*" He flashed his fingers at him, saying "*Cinco.*"

"Who kills these animals?" Steadman asked.

"Hungry people," Hernán said. "Them too. *En peligro de extinción también.*"

In a glossy box, propped on hatpins, was a large, hairy-legged, pop-eyed spider.

"*Tarántula!*" the man said. He handed the box to Steadman.

Holding it up, Steadman looked hard at it. The creature that had seemed a horror in its box was, up close, a figure of sorrow. He marveled at its symmetry, its long jointed legs, its shiny bristles. But for all its complexity it was just another empty shell, like the animal skulls, a black thing crucified on the pins.

"Take. *Cómprala!*"

"I want a live one," Steadman said.

"A live one will kill you," Hernán said.

Now the shop owner was holding a dead bat, and he shook it in Steadman's face, calling out prices as Steadman backed away toward the door.

Outside, at the sidewalk table of a café, a teenage girl in a tight skirt and frilly blouse sipped a drink. When Steadman glanced at her, she stared at him and smiled, following him with her eyes. Steadman smiled back and greeted her.

"I think you've just made a friend," Ava said. "*Chingada.*"

"So funny to hear a woman say this word," Hernán said.

"What word do you say?"

"We say *chingada*. We say *puta*. We say" — he giggled — "*tiradora. Culeadora*. We say *araña*. We say many things."

"Lots of words for them."

"Because lots of them in Lago Agrio," Hernán said. "*Personas aprovechadas.*"

"I heard some clicking up and down the street last night," Ava said.

"Day and night," Hernán said. "The ones on the street are old and — how you say — *muy fea?* Agli. Most are at the *burdeles.*"

"What time do the *burdeles* open?" Steadman asked.

"*Los prostíbulos están siempre abiertos.*"

Steadman glanced at his watch. "It's nine in the morning. The whorehouses are open now?"

Hernán shrugged, and casually reaching toward the busy street and making a gesture with his fingers, he stepped back as a taxi drew to the curb. He said nothing more to them. Taking charge, he opened the rear door, and after Ava and Steadman got inside, he slid into the front seat. He muttered a word to the driver, "Pantera," and they were off.

Within minutes they were going slowly on a bumpy back road, the tires thumping large loose rocks. It was more like a dry creekbed than a road, and as it narrowed it steepened. They climbed a low hill, where at its brow they were struck by the hard glare of the morning sun, and passed a neighborhood of shacks and dogs and snotty-faced children. Descending the hill, their taxi had to stop to let a large foul-smelling truck go by.

"Cargo of meat," Hernán said, and looking back they saw carcasses and sides of beef swinging from hooks in the ceiling of the blood-splashed interior, and clouds of flies following.

More shacks, more children, and a short distance beyond this little slum the car stopped before a yellow-walled building. It was solid, made of cement, one story, with a big black cat crudely drawn on the wall and a painted sign: *La Pantera*.

Hernán led them through the door, toward the music, which was loud and Latin with a pulsing beat of drums. The sound of syncopation filled the large room but competed with other sounds, low animal wails of complaint, an agonizing mooing. The strange, seemingly empty room was the size and shape of a dance hall, with a high ceiling, which was the tin roof of the building. The wide floor was like that in a dance hall, but no one was dancing. Only the music and that horrible mooing filled it. The middle, which could have been the dance floor, was littered with tipped-over chairs and some empty tables and made of cement — a boy was slapping at it with a dirty mop and dragging a bucket.

At first glance the place made no sense — a big hollow noisy space, the music, the animal howl, the clutter, the boy with the mop. Looking harder, Steadman saw activity at the margins, groups of men seated in chairs drinking beer from bottles, scraps of bright color that were the costumes of women, some standing, some seated, at the doorways — a door every six feet or so, around the entire perimeter of the dance floor.

Of the fifty or so doors, there were women at most of the thresholds. The women wore bathing suits, most of them were smoking cigarettes, and they seemed demure, patient, passive, and vaguely attentive, as though waiting for a bus that was overdue.

Most of the women sat alone, but near two or three of them were clusters of men. The men sat talking together, their elbows on the tables. Steadman saw that the men were old and tough-looking, and in each case the woman nearby was hardly a woman but rather a girl, sixteen at most, looking watchful.

"*Hola,*" Ava said to one of the young girls, walking past the men. The men pretended not to be interested in or shocked by the tall light-haired woman and the man in the Panama hat behind her approaching the slender prostitute, who stood up like a schoolgirl, showing politeness.

"*Cuál es su nombre?*"

"*Soy Carmen. Mi apodo es Mosca.*"

She seemed shy and was so soft-voiced Ava could not understand her.

"*Vive usted aquí?*"

"*No. Vivo en Lago Agrio.*"

"*De dónde es usted?*" Ava asked.

"Guayaquil," the girl whispered, and entered the cubicle.

Ava followed her inside, and Steadman joined them, and there was so little room in the cubicle that the girl sat on the edge of the bed, which was just a mattress covered with a stained sheet, the two visitors towering over her, their elbows against the walls.

"*Cuánto vale esto?*" Steadman said.

The girl clasped her hands. She looked so awkward in her bathing suit and thick-soled shoes. She said softly, "*Dos personas juntas?*"

"You're scaring her," Ava said, and as she spoke she heard the men outside hoarsely conjecturing.

"I'm just wondering," he said.

The girl said, "*Por mí, normal — solamente normal aquí. Cinco dólares. Pero, número trece, número catorce*" — and she gestured to the wall, meaning the cubicles that way — "*por allí*" — and she became vague, and hesitated. She shrugged. "*Otras cosas.*"

But Ava had been right: Steadman saw a look of fear on the girl's face, something in the way her mouth was drawn sideways, a brightness in her eyes that was terror. He wanted to leave and he wanted to calm her. He gave her a twenty-dollar bill and motioned to Ava to leave.

The men gaped as Ava and Steadman left, and one of them — the oldest, the drunkest, grizzled and wearing a baseball hat — swaggered to the door, and before the young girl could step out he squeezed her face in his dirty hand and pushed her inside. She sat down on the bed and wrung her hands as the man kicked the door shut.

Hernán had hung back as Ava and Steadman went forward, passing the other groups of men, the single seated women, and toward the far end of the row of cubicles, all of which were numbered — a cot and a mirror and a small cluttered table were visible through each door. The women here were older, potbellied, with slack breasts, pathetic, even ridiculous in bathing suits. They did not look depraved, they looked sullen and badly fed. The music rang against the tin roof and this end of the brothel had a bad smell.

The old black woman in the last cubicle wore a tutu and high-heeled shoes and a pink turban and sunglasses. As they approached, her phlegmatic expression became alert and attentive. She frowned when Steadman met her gaze, but realizing that her head did not follow him, he motioned silently, an onward gesture with his hand. Just then, the racket of harsh wailing beyond the window became shrill, like an animal fighting confinement.

"Number fourteen," Ava said. "Other things."

The staring woman in the pink turban heard her and said, "*Soy Araña.*"

They kept walking past her, past the partition to the window, where that agonized wailing was louder. Steadman looked down and saw a gutter running crimson, bubbling where it was slowed, frothing over the sides, into the dust — a stream of blood outside thickening the soil, losing its redness, making the mud blacker.

Through one of the grimy and blood-smeared windows of the large building just behind the brothel, Steadman saw a blindfolded cow being electrocuted, howling and collapsing on twisted legs as the electrodes of a black clamp were fixed to its head, the cow shitting in fear, expelling great dark muffins of dung. Another window showed a scene of butchery, two men hacking at a bloody animal carcass on a stone slab, and other windows gave onto sides of meat on hooks, men skinning cows, tearing carpets of hairy hide from fatty flesh, knives and cleavers flashing.

"Is the abattoir," Hernán said, laughing at the absurdity of a slaughterhouse next to the whorehouse, the smells and noises mingled. "You want to see Las Flores. Is another *burdel,* but not so nice."

Some people began to dance on the floor that was still wet from the boy's mopping. But Ava and Steadman could not hear the music anymore, only the sounds of cows being slaughtered and the hacking of cleavers on slabs, the chucking sound of steel blades against thick bone and raw meat. Ava and Steadman backed away.

In the distance they saw Manfred in a stained T-shirt and sweat-plastered hair, watching them. He was carrying his beat-up bag, the weight of the big book showing in it. He turned and walked quickly past one of the girls, into her cubicle. She placed her cigarette in an ashtray beside her chair and followed him.

The black woman who called herself Araña was still sitting outside her cubicle. She cocked her head; her sullen look left her. She stood up and mocked them and, doing a little dance, spun slowly, wagging her bum at them, plucking at her buttocks.

"*Buenos días. Que desean?*" she said. And then, spittle forming on her lips, she said, "*Sodomita,*" making the word like the name of a delicacy. She leaned toward them, but they had taken a few steps, so her head was canted wrong: her sunglasses faced in the direction of the slaughterhouse, where they had lingered and talked.

Ava said softly, "She's blind."

Araña beckoned. She opened her toothless mouth and stuck out her tongue and wagged the long pink thing at them. Then she laughed hard, louder than the dying animals. And she clutched herself and repeated the word: "*Sodomita.*"

"*Lo siento,*" Steadman said to her, and Ava murmured to Hernán, "*No comprendo lo que dice.*"

Araña laughed and Hernán translated her shout: "'But why? Because you're not interested in this *culeadora?*'"

She went on shouting, and when Steadman nodded, Hernán continued to translate, but slowly, softly, with reluctance, as Steadman stared at the woman. She removed her dark glasses. Her eyes were pitted and scarred, with welts like burn tissue, a pair of wounds.

"What is *reflejo*?" Ava asked.

But Hernán was trying to catch up with the woman's shouts. "'You are not looking at me, you're looking at yourself,'" he said. "'Don't be so proud. I am you! Your reflection!'" She plucked at her flesh, her breasts, did a little dance, and she laughed again, sticking out her pink tongue. "'Take a good look. I am your mirror. You are me — the same. You are Araña.'"

Sensing that Steadman and Ava had turned, that Hernán was following them, still talking as they walked away, the woman pursed her lips and spat at them.

"Fak yo!"

"I got that," Ava said.

On the way out they heard metal chairs clatter to the cement floor and saw some men fighting, two big men hauling the arms of the grizzled man who had swaggered into the young girl's cubicle earlier. The old man shouted and kicked at the bouncers as they dragged him outside. When that noise died down they heard another shouting match: Manfred arguing with a man and one of the prostitutes, as though haggling over the price.

Hernán went over to Manfred and spoke to him. The German shrugged and, seeing Ava and Steadman, spoke to them.

"They try to cheat me. I want to leave. I want to go into the chungle."

Hernán tapped his watch. "*Vámonos*."

Over lunch at the café, Nestor said, "We eat, then we go."

"Any pork in this?" Sabra asked, using her fork to indicate the sausage in her soup bowl, but not touching the meat with the tines.

Wood said, "Porco?"

"*Puerco. Cerdo. Sí*, all pork," Nestor said. With a wink he added, "And a little bit *perro*."

Sabra peeled a hard-boiled egg, prying pieces of the shell with her long nails.

The rest of them ate impatiently, hardly speaking, but self-conscious in the silence, Janey said, "Oh, super. Elevenses."

Manfred reached for the dish of hard-boiled eggs and slipped three into his jacket pocket.

"I wonder if we get afters," Janey said. "Any pud? What about biscuits?"

Reaching again, Manfred began to tug at a covered dish, and when he got it nearer he lifted the lid with one dirty finger and exposed a bright crust.

"Crikey. There is pudding!"

"*Llapingachos*," Nestor said. "Pancakes."

"And a cuppa char would go down an absolute treat."

"Special Ecuador coffee," Nestor said.

"Look, Hack," Janey said as the coffee was served. "Just a manky little packet of instant."

Then they were all in the van again, with the boxes of food and stacks of luggage blocking the view out the back window. They were driven very fast down a narrow road fringed by tall grass and yellowish trees. At a settlement of shacks and shops — "Chiritza," Nestor said — they were shepherded to a riverbank and down a wooden walkway to a waiting canoe. Steadman sketched it quickly in his notebook, for it was less a canoe than an enormous tree trunk that had been hollowed out, its ends blunted, an outboard motor clamped to the stern. The travelers sat on the benches that had been lashed to it, and they watched as mud-splashed boys labored back and forth on the walkway with the luggage and food boxes.

While the lines were being unclipped from the mooring posts and coiled, Nestor knelt and reached into a bag. He took out some hanks of cloth and said, "Where we are going must remain secret. Please put these over your eyes."

6

THESE NEW BLINDFOLDS on the river made them fearful and garrulous, seeking reassurance, their yakking a frantic signal, like bat-squeal. In places, the river made odd swallowing sounds. Birds jeered at them from high branches, insects strummed and chattered, the heat and moist air left a film of damp scum on their skin and thickened their hair. Ill at ease, trying to imagine the scenes they were passing on the jungle stream, they went on talking, interrupting the birds and insects, interrupting one another. After a while they ceased to sound like bats, but instead squawked like anxious children, praising what they could not see, as though infantilized by the blindfolds, attempting to propitiate the river's menace.

"This is awesome," Wood said.

"Sweet," Hack said.

In a timid voice tinged with nausea Sabra said, "Like I'm traveling into some enchanted cave."

"As the bishop said to the actress," Janey said.

"Hernán is so shredding this river," Hack said.

Keeping his head down, Steadman lifted his mask with one thumb and was briefly blinded. He saw a rusted sign on the muddy riverbank, *Prohibido el Paso*, and let the mask drop over his eyes once more.

Hack said uncertainly, "This isn't that bad. Remember that smelly cave system in Mexico where we went diving? Santo something?"

"And the most awesome thing about it is the, like, smell of the darkness. Like you're in a tunnel."

"That is a veever bird," Manfred said.

As though Manfred's utterance were a cue, Janey said, "Jolly super."

The air on this part of the upper river was clammy, intimidating, and felt full of looming shapes. Some of these shapes seemed soaked in the fetid stink of fear, the musty forest-hum of an old corpse softening to the sludge of vegetable mulch. The bad smell silenced them like an overwhelming noise. And then Sabra spoke in an earnest voice.

"I think you're wrong — we are on a quest," she said. When no one replied, she added, "I want a healing."

Her seriousness seemed to silence the others. There was only the gurgly drone of the outboard motor, farting when it idled, and the mingled sounds of birds and insects, seeming to compete, their calls skimming across the river's surface.

"For me, yah, is a kvest."

"The longest distance on earth is from the heart to the head," Sabra said, as if she were remembering and quoting. She started to say more when there was a snort of derision from the bow of the boat, which in a bizarre echo was repeated by a birdcall, just as derisive.

"How long we must to wear this thing?" Manfred pleaded, in a different mood.

"What do you care?"

"I want to see things. Long ago, in 1817, came here von Spix and von

Martius. They found the unique species on the River Caqueta, on one place, name of Cerro de la Pedrera. I will go there for my book. And Nachtigall as well. For the *Schamanismus*. You know the *Schamanismus?*"

The motor chugged and coughed, sounding unreliable, and the water slapped the bow of the boat.

"Also, in 1905 up to 1922, Koch-Grünberg was here."

"That's funny. My mother's name was Greenberg."

"And Otto Zerries," Manfred said, remembering. "Also Schultes, of course."

"Oh, do put a sock in it," Janey said.

But no one else was listening. As the river widened and warmed in the sunshine, the air was less dense and the afternoon gave softer colors to the forest they imagined — greener trees and clearer water, a blue sky showing through the canopy of high boughs, and the louder birds they assumed were larger than others, with great beaks and spiky crests, toucans and hornbills with colorful drooping tails.

The light quieted them. They listened to the slurp of their wake against the bank.

"*Confluencia*," Nestor said as the boat tipped and seemed to slip sideways along a swifter current. "Río Arana. You say 'confluence'?"

After a while the brightness reminded them that they were exposed, and they became talkative again. One swirl of river sloshing in an eddy beside the bow Steadman took to be a fleeing snake, uncoiling in the stream. The air was humid against his face. In the shadows of trees at the level of the knobby roots were jaguars and ocelots. Sunlight glinted on the water like slivers of scrap metal, Hernán at the stern, Nestor at the bow, impassive, saying nothing except for their murmured directions: "To the bank" and "Stump ahead" and "Shallow here" and the repeated "*Siga, no más.*"

Janey Hackler seemed on the verge of speaking, asking a sudden question beginning "Europe!" But it was not a word. She was retching strenuously, her whole bulgy gut audibly convulsed, and a moment later she vomited over the side. She sobbed disgustedly, and when she got her breath she said in a pleading voice, "I've got bits of sick all over my fingers."

"I guess this is what you'd call dark matter," Hack said.

"Marshall, do be serious. I'm all sticky," Janey said, her gorge rising again. "Yoo-roop! Oh, crikey!"

"Wait," someone said. "Listen."

A canoe was passing. It had to have been a canoe: there was no engine, only the slurp and suck and drip of working paddle blades. People in the canoe called out a greeting, not Spanish but a chain of seesawing monosyllables, and Nestor replied in the same language, but flatter, seeming to repeat something he had once heard.

"What's that you're saying?" Hack demanded, but unsurely, in a nagging way.

"Secoya language."

They hate to be blindfolded, thought Steadman, who not only liked it, but unexpectedly took pleasure in being in the presence of blindfolded people, for all their revelations in the darkness.

"Lots of bird life," Wood said.

"This sucks," Hack said.

"But at least you're not covered with vomit, are you," Janey said, sobbing. "What are you grumbling about?"

"I can't see shit!" Hack screamed.

"I left my Leicas in Quito," Wood said. "They said travel light."

"The little Leicas, they weigh nothing."

And everyone sighed, because *Za little Leicas, zey veigh nossing* was so much more irritating spoken in the darkness. Yet the darkness was a soup of colors, and the colors were smells, not images, a swirl of odors, marbled like endpapers in an old book, the heat of the day making the color green almost black, and the crimson black, and the tree bark black. The green had the sharpness of cut leaf, the air was like sour dust, and the bark had the moldering odor of tobacco moistened by rain. The odors came in irregular layers, like the layers of a whole plant — leaves and roots and shimmering blotches of flowers they could actually taste.

Sabra said, "Rivers are borders. If you haven't crossed a border without permission, you haven't traveled."

Steadman held his breath, waiting for someone to comment on this oversimplified quotation from *Trespassing*. He heard the glugging of the outboard, some seconds passed, and then Manfred spoke.

"How much farza?"

Nestor did not answer.

"I thought this was supposed to be a doddle," Janey said.

They were now deep into the afternoon, and the day was thick with a heat and humidity that clutched them, and the highly colored smells all around them became stronger and mingled with the sound of the river.

"And it's a fag," Janey said. "And I have to spend a penny."

The colors reversed, blue river, green sky, shimmering trees, the decay in the air giving off patches of luminescence that showed through the hanging vines and stringy tails of lianas, and when they cut the engine and lifted it to paddle in the shallows between sandbanks, the shriek of insects was deafening — bright beetles and big-winged dragonflies and birds like paper kites and clouds of midges glowing in the slanting sunshine, a dream of deep Ecuadorian jungle.

"Okay, take your masks off."

They did so and were silent. Now they saw how wrong they were. Nothing was green here. The daylight was almost gone. The river was muddy and narrow and there was a whirlpool just beyond the landing place; the trees were so dark as to be almost black, the air heavy and hot, almost no sky. The riverbank was covered with smashed and bruised tree roots. Yes, there was decay, and where the soil was not crumbly it was mushy.

"Where are we?" Hack asked.

"*Remolinos*," Nestor said, "wheelpools," and pointed at the whirlpools. In the failing light the coursing water was scattered with floating blobs and divots, like hacked-off scalps and bubbly blisters and clotted soap scum.

But after they had taken their masks off they smelled nothing. Even the loudest nagging birds were invisible, but some insects looked as big as sparrows.

Someone called out up ahead, a small coughing sound, and then an echo in the person's sinuses, like a startled animal cooing in recognition, not a person but the incomplete ghost of a person, suggesting faulty magic. Some people stood on the bank, ragged and hopeful, like castaways amid the scabby bark of the tree trunks. Small people, some half naked, some in knee-length red smocks, whom they took to be Secoya, with damp hair in their eyes — the smaller they were, the nakeder they were — crouched in greeting, gaping at them with a passive curiosity that suggested imbecility. They were brown, elfin, laughing.

With a yelp, one boy in torn shorts seized the bow line and secured the boat. Still laughing, others hurried down the riverbank and, placing their feet apart, straddling the gunwale and the dock, began hoisting the bags and passing them to the boys on the bank. Standing at the side of a plank, a man helped the passengers ashore.

"Those bowl-shaped haircuts make them look like retards," Hack said.

Janey said, "Their hair looks frightfully nagged at."

Their mouths hung open, their teeth were small and worn flat, they were listening as much as watching. A naked child-mother clutched a naked baby to her breasts, and the baby, with dangling legs, looked limp and lifeless.

"*Como está?* How are you doing?" Sabra asked, and when she got no reply, she said, "Why are they looking at us like we're monkeys?"

Seeing that the boat was tipping in the wash of the river's eddy, one of the Secoya men, wearing tattered shorts with a Polo Sport label, scuttled down the mud bank and seized the noose of the stern line.

I have never seen a human being move like that, Steadman thought. The man had a skipping bandy-legged stoop-shouldered roll that made him almost invisible for the seconds that he was in motion. He snatched the rope and in the same gesture looped it round a protruding tree root.

"This man is Don Pablo," Nestor said.

Hearing his name, the man hesitated and looked at the passengers in the boat. He gabbled a little over his shoulder to the others crouching and staring on the bank. Some Secoya men murmured softly, their hands out. Hernán handed one of them a blue plastic cooler with a padlocked lid. The women and children said nothing.

"They sort of hate us, I can tell by their squiffy eyes," Janey said, fingering her cell phone. "And why do they look so stroppy?"

"Which one?" Wood asked.

"All of them. Him — he looks like a wet weekend." Janey called out to the man, "Oh, do cheer up. It may never happen!"

"But we're giving them business, right, Nestor?" Hack called, and turned to help Sabra out of the boat while Wood zipped his duffel.

On shore, the Secoya women gathered around Sabra, touching the stamp-sized butterfly tattoo on her shoulder, but Sabra hardly noticed.

"There's flies all over that kid," Sabra said.

"He's got a discharge, some eye thing, maybe conjunctivitis," Ava said. "I've got some cream for that." She took a tube from her waist pouch and said, "*Medicina. Crema para los ojos de su niño.*"

"Let's go!" Hack said.

But the word *medicina* had excited the watching people and they clamored around Ava, plucking at her clothes, until Nestor shouted. At his shouts they stepped back and made room for the visitors.

Without a word, Don Pablo turned and moved in his peculiar skittering way down the path. The others followed — Manfred up front, kicking leaves and striding to be first, but keeping one finger to hold his place in his big plant guide. Then Wood and Sabra, Hack and Janey, Steadman and Ava, and behind them on the forest path the Secoya boys carrying their bags.

Hack said to Ava, "I saw that medicine stuff back there. Are you in the virtue business? I hate people in the virtue business. Know what I think?"

"Who gives a flying fuck what you think?" Ava said with a smile.

From behind it seemed that Hack's ears were reddening. Janey turned, her thumb pressed into her cell phone, searching for a signal, and said, "You can't save everybody!"

"Know what, sister? You got vomit on your lips," Ava said.

Steadman enjoyed seeing Ava sticking up for herself. She was above all else a doctor, and in a place like this he knew her reasoning, the doctor's conceit: *In the end you will need me. I have the medicine.* Following them in single file, he wondered whether it was impatience or courage that was driving the others onward. In spite of the chattering in the boat when they had been blindfolded, they did not seem seriously daunted here. Or was it just the confidence, the indifference, of people who knew they were protected: tourists with a guide.

He was annoyed by the way the others made him self-conscious, by their irritating mannerisms, their very presence. Alone, he could reach his own conclusions, but with them everything had to be shared and either overdramatized or ignored. He had counted on this being an important trip but knew he would find it hard to write about, because seeing it with their eyes, it was diminished for him. Just as bad, as much as he resented the others, he was grudgingly impressed. They were determined to have their experience, and so far, even with their complaints they had not mentioned turning back. They were stronger and more single-minded than he had expected them to be.

"This thing's useless," Janey said, shaking her phone. "It's a pup."

"We had a doctor along in Bhutan," Hack said, tossing the words over his shoulder. He was speaking to Ava. "He got sick as a dog. He was asking *me* for advice!"

There were no animals or birds near the path. Steadman was on the lookout for snakes. He heard the sounds of prowling and looked back and saw children following. Some were naked, all were barefoot. But the people on the tour wore boots and leggings and long-sleeved shirts, and the two women wide-brimmed hats with mosquito veils.

Up ahead was the village, just a cluster of huts with thatched roofs in a clearing filled with long rags of white smoke from cooking fires.

Janey said, "Isn't that fun, the way they gather and finish those good strong reeds in the roofs? I could use that in my arbors and garden thatch. What would you call it? Something like 'distressed vernacular'?"

Nestor said, "We would call it poor people who don't have money for metal roof."

A small boy approached, running through the smoke, his hands out, gesturing, seeming to beg. Nestor muttered and waved him away while an old man came forward, also through the smoke.

"This is Don Pablo's brother. His name is Himaro."

The man nodded and glanced at the newcomers, their faces, their clothes. He wore shorts and a torn shirt, and on his head was a tiara of woven straw and upright feathers, and at his waist a belt of braided vines on which various totems dangled: a broken tooth, a yellow animal claw, a bunch of fluff, a hank of fur, a clutch of sharpened bones, which clicked as he stepped forward to greet the visitors. When he got closer, Steadman saw that the old man's eyes were weepy from infection as well as clouded and vague, searching helplessly.

"*Himaro* means *tigre*, the one we call *yana puma*," Nestor said. "That is a powerful animal here."

There was some palaver with Nestor in the Secoya language. The visitors stayed together, squinting at the incomprehensible quack of the words.

"We don't have a lot of time," Wood said, interrupting the flow. "Can you tell him that?"

Nestor said, "Yes, I could tell him that. But he would not understand."

What they could see of the village were straw roofs and glowing interiors and a smoky hut that might have been a communal kitchen. The brightest structure was a large platform beside an enormous tree, open-sided with a thatched roof, chickens pecking beneath it in the cracks of light from lanterns. Clotheslines were strung from tree to tree, and like dark cutouts, backlit by the bright lanterns, were Secoya, just flat shadows staring at the newcomers.

Janey singled out a low lashed-together hut and said, "That one's fun. It's a sort of Wendy house. Isn't it a pity that banana fronds always look so tattered?"

Hack looked around the clearing and said, "Fucking Discovery Channel bullshit," and motioned as though with an invisible remote switch and said, "Hey, guys, I can't shut this program off!"

When Steadman turned to speak to Ava, he saw that she had walked a little distance to where the women and children had gathered. He joined her there, noticing how the women were touching her, appealing to her for — what? Medicine, perhaps, some sort of handout. The old man wandered over, scraping his feet in the dust, feeling his way from shoulder to shoulder.

"They all have drizzling colds," she said, and touched the nearest ones. "This one has a low-grade infection. Look at this kid's shin. The sore is so deep it has eaten into the muscle. This old man could lose his eyes — he needs an antibiotic. He's rubbing them, for Christ's sake. *No toca, no toca.*"

"The *pajé*," Nestor said. "Himaro. The brother."

"He's also a shaman," Steadman said.

Don Pablo now appeared again. He wore a smock and a crown woven of slender vines and a row of stiff feathers. His eyes were wounded too, one weepier than the other, which was bloodshot and turned inward. The ailment made him seem more of a brother. Yet the shaman had a clumsy agility, and while he was anything but deft, his gestures were the more effective for being approximate, commanding attention and asserting control through his show of clumsiness. The Secoya near him were watchful in a shy, respectful way, giving him room as the old man worked his fingers like antennae, positioning them as though he had eyes on his fingertips.

Nestor signaled for them to follow when the old man turned and shuffle-kicked toward the stamped and smooth center of the village, where there were pots and baskets. Before the smoky fire were logs arranged like benches.

"Sit down. Have a cold drink."

Hearing this, Hernán dragged the blue plastic cooler toward the log, opened it, and passed out cans of soda. The white visitors drank, looking exhausted in their crumpled clothes, while the Secoya stared, naked, saying nothing, the children's noses dripping. Some men lying in hammocks humped and rolled over and, still horizontal, stared sideways at the strangers.

The pile of pots, the baskets of cut vine stems, the enamel bowls, on a shelved frame of lashed bamboo, suggested cooking, but nothing was on the boil. Near this paraphernalia some women knelt, grating manioc.

"This would make a super credenza," Janey said, gripping the bamboo frame. Then with a pitying smile she said, "But I peeked inside one of those huts. You know, they don't accessorize at all."

Irritably, Sabra said to Nestor, "Are we supposed to sleep here?"

"We're putting up hammocks, or you can find a space on that platform back there under the ceiba tree."

"What about washing? What about eating?" Wood said.

"I was going to give you some of the background," Nestor said. "This is a spiritual thing, like religion and medical combined. There is so many aspects. Maybe you like to know?"

"Yes, all," Manfred said.

"Skip the background," Hack said, lifting his elbows, creating space around him. "I'm going for a swim."

"We have manta rays in the river," Nestor said. "Hernán got stung by a ray and he was in his hammock for three months."

Janey said, "What about din-dins? I'm peckish."

Nestor leaned over and worked his mustache at her, smiling in toothy incomprehension.

"Hungry," she said.

Nestor spoke in Secoya, and one of the woman grating manioc replied to him without looking up. Still pushing the stick of manioc against the grater, she called out. A child's voice sounded from the direction of the big tree and the smoky hut, and within a minute two young boys hurried into the clearing with a pole through the handle of a large blackened stewpot. A girl followed, carrying tin bowls and spoons.

"What is it?" Janey asked.

"*Caldo* of yuca and *pavo*."

"Any pork in it? Porco?" Sabra said.

"No *puerco*," Nestor said.

Manfred said, "*Pavo* means a wild turkey. A kind of stew."

As the soup was ladled, Janey lifted her bowl and said, "I'll have a wee scrap more. There's masses going spare."

Hack said, "When do we get to drink the ayahuasca?"

"Don Pablo wants to speak to you," Nestor said.

The old man adjusted his coronet of plaited vines and feathers, and he stood behind Nestor, shuffling his feet, muttering. He put on a pair of cracked and twisted glasses.

"Look, he's got super gig-lamps," Janey said.

But the man removed his glasses and began rubbing his seeping eye with the knuckles of one hand.

"He says tonight is not good. You have just arrived. Some of you are angry. You must dissolve anger from your life. The women" — Nestor paused for Don Pablo to speak, and then he resumed — "he believes that one gringo woman here is having her moon."

"And that gringo woman would be me," Sabra said, and sat primly, her eyes glistening with annoyance that she had been singled out. She stared at a small dirty boy crouching in the dust near her and addressed him. "I'm unclean. I'm tainted. I've got the curse. They're worse than Hasidim!"

"Beetle, please," Wood said, cautioning her.

"In Secoya culture, sharing in a ceremony while having your moon is taboo. It is too much purification. Too much light, Don Pablo says. It can make the shaman very ill. He will see the huts dripping blood. So" — Nestor spoke directly to Sabra — "please keep away from the kitchen area. The food. Other people's dishes."

"Don't worry. I'll read my book instead. It's more exciting than this garbage."

Wood put his tin bowl of stew on the ground and crept beside her and awkwardly put his arm around her. She began softly to cry. "It's okay, Beetle. Let it out."

Manfred said, "They have rules. They must be obeyed."

"You Germans know all about obeying rules," Sabra said.

His face gleaming with sweat, his big teeth working, Manfred said, "That's right, I am a wicked German who started the World War and made all the camps, and you are a good person who does nossing bad."

"Woody, tell him to stop," Sabra said through her tears.

But Manfred was on his knees hissing at her, "I have been to Ramallah! You have seen Ramallah?"

"Oh, do belt up," Janey said.

Then Nestor rose and gestured with his hands to quiet the squabblers. He said, "Don Pablo wants to welcome you."

The old man was muttering behind him, shaking his head, and when he nodded some wisps swayed in his feathered coronet.

"Don Pablo has been a shaman for many years. In Secoya, the word *pajé* is shaman. It means 'the man who embodies all experience.' He says that some of the people he was treating were witches. A shaman always has enemies, because he is accused of being responsible for people's deaths."

"Where's he from?" Hack asked.

Nestor translated the question, listened to Don Pablo, then said to the group, "He didn't understand, but his answer is interesting anyway. He believes the Secoya were descended from a certain group of monkeys in Santa María — downriver from here, where two rivers meet."

The fire had died down, and as the crackling had diminished the jungle sounds had increased. Though they could only have been insects, they sounded to Steadman like a chorus of crazed birds — the honks and squawks issuing from the darkness around them.

"His father was also a shaman. He taught Don Pablo and Himaro how to use ayahuasca. Don Pablo became a *pajé* because he was very sick. He healed himself and became a healer. The best way to become a *pajé* — maybe the only way — is to be very ill and follow that path." Nestor listened to Don Pablo and spoke again. "Ayahuasca is like death. When you drink it you die. The soul leaves the body. But this soul is an eye to show you the future. You will see your grandchildren. When the trance is over the soul is returned." Don Pablo was still talking. Nestor said, as though summarizing, "He talks about 'the eye of understanding.'"

Manfred said, "Please ask Don Pablo to explain the meaning of this."

The question was relayed to Don Pablo, who turned away and answered the question while facing the trees and the darkness and the insect chatter.

"This eye can see things that can't be seen physically. Some people have this third eye already developed. And for others the eye of understanding can be acquired through ayahuasca or some other certain jungle plants."

Steadman sat feeling hopeful, and as he was listening another old man appeared, wearing a yellow smock, a feather coronet, and a necklace of red beads and animal teeth. He spoke to Nestor.

Nestor said, "This is Don Esteban. He is a Kofan. He wants to tell you that he learned to speak Secoya in one night from a parrot after drinking a huge amount of *yajé*."

"Is *yajé* the same tipple as ayahuasca?" Janey asked Hack, who said, "I guess."

"Don Pablo can turn into a tiger. He can visit other planets. He has been to many planets — he makes beautiful pictures of them. He can see into a diseased body."

"Who would have known — he's a fucking astronaut," Hack said under his breath.

In a seemingly cautionary way, Don Pablo spoke, and Nestor translated: "A flower may not talk, but there is a spirit in it that sees everything. That is the soul of the plant, which makes it alive."

Don Esteban added a thought, then shrugged.

Nestor smiled. "And, yes, a flower may talk."

Without another word, Don Pablo and Don Esteban signaled to Himaro and slipped away into the darkness. Nestor lit a torch from the embers of the fire and led the visitors down the path.

"Since I'm unclean, I'm going to my room," Sabra said.

Wood hugged her. "You don't have a room, Beetle."

Hurrying ahead, Nestor had planted his torch at the entrance to the high sleeping platform, the light whirling with small white moths. Fuzzy knuckle-sized insects buzzed and bumped the lighted posts. Watching the others approach it slowly, Steadman could see their reluctance in the way their dusty shorts were pinched between their bobbing buttocks.

7

From his rope hammock strung between two trees, Steadman lay as if trussed in the rope mesh, seeing the others thrashing on the sleeping platform, the Wilmutts and the Hacklers, backlit by the lanterns and surrounded by clouds of fluttering moths; all night their muttered complaints.

Steadman said in a drawling voice, "Sure you think it's romantic at first but wait till you sit there five days on a sore ass sleeping in Indian shacks and eating hoka and some hunka nameless meat, and all night you hear them fiddle-fucking with the motor." He paused and listened to the insect howl. "Burroughs was right. Tomorrow the river will be higher."

Manfred had slipped away. Perhaps he knew how persistently he talked in his sleep, asking questions, making declarations, usually in German, sometimes in English. Steadman had heard the gabble, and though he could not understand any of it, there seemed a coherence in its slurring narrative, like a story that Manfred had mumbled in his sleep many times before. But Steadman also guessed that Manfred had found a more comfortable hut or a better sleeping mat, or perhaps a companion.

Just as likely he had found a candle stump somewhere so that he could study his book of medicinal plants. The man was irritating, but in his reading and his note taking and his pedantry, the tenacity of his tactless honesty with the others, he was a reproach to Steadman, who swung in his hammock, regretting that his own notebook was so neglected. He told himself that he had refrained from writing so as not to appear conspicuous to the others, who might recognize him as the author and pester him with questions.

In her own hammock next to Steadman, Ava said, "That annoying woman is still reading your book."

Dawn came early but dimly, the tentative sun not penetrating the trees but lighting portions of sky, which were visible as tiny blue patches through the canopy of leaves. Beneath those boughs the air was pale green, gassy-looking, and filled with flitting insects and lazy filaments that swayed like the torn veils of spider webs, yet they were high up, draping the green air, where Steadman had never imagined spiders to live.

The birds had begun shrieking long before dawn, and one had a monotonous voice of objection that nagged through the jungle. Nimble, darting, unswattable flies kept returning to settle on and sting Steadman's face. Ants were everywhere, large and small, trails of them, clusters of them, black glossy ones, tiny flitting ones, some no bigger than sand grains. They gathered on Steadman's sandals, delved into his bag. The heat woke them; the heat seemed to make all the insects active: biting flies, white moths, big furry beetles, foraging wasps, and glossy cockroaches with tortoiseshell wings.

Walking toward the covered platform with Ava, Steadman picked up a fist-sized snail that was leaving a track of slime across the beaten-down earth.

"*Desayuno*," he said to a small Secoya girl who was watching him, and seeing her look of wonderment, he realized she did not speak Spanish.

The others were seated cross-legged on the platform, looking fatigued and miserable in rumpled clothes.

"My hair's a rat's nest," Janey said. She appealed to Ava. "We didn't get a wink of sleep. This whole bally place is a tip. We're so fed up we're about ready to leave."

Ava said, "I slept like a log."

Nestor was mounting the ramp to the platform. In great contrast to the visitors, he looked rested and bright-eyed, his thick hair combed straight back, and wore a clean T-shirt and jeans.

"I want to give you some instructions from Don Pablo," Nestor said.

Hack said, "Enough with the lectures."

Nestor stared at him, saying nothing, but with ironic jeering lips. Though he was a big man, his face was narrow, his black eyes set deep in his face, and he was the more intimidating for being calm and saying nothing until Hack looked away.

"I want to suggest to you," Nestor said, "that you are not home now. You are in Succumbios province." With his tongue between his teeth, he added, "Oriente."

Now Manfred appeared on the ramp, looking like a commando in his jungle gear. He swung himself onto the platform. He too looked rested, another reproach to the others who had suffered in the night. He was carrying a tin cup. He sat and sipped from it and swallowed with a hearty sigh.

"Ecuador *café*. Very delicious!"

Steadman smiled to see how Manfred aroused the hatred of the others, and how Manfred enjoyed it.

"Herr Mephistos," Hack said, gesturing at Manfred's shoes.

"I take from a pee-sant," he said, sipping the coffee.

Nestor said, "Please eat some fruit for breakfast, then nothing more. No food all day. But stay busy. If you drink — just water. The ceremony will begin after sunset in the pavilion over there. Later I will tell you what things to bring. The main thing to bring is a clear mind and a pure heart. And an empty stomach."

It was seven in the morning, sunset almost twelve hours away, and already the heat and the biting flies and the stink that rose from the sodden earth seemed unbearable.

"Why can't we have the ceremony right now?" Wood asked.

"Night is for ceremonies. We need darkness," Nestor said. "So you can relax."

"I didn't come all this way and pay serious money to relax!"

"You can maybe weed Joaquina's garden, then. She needs help."

"Hard cheese on Joaquina," Janey said. "She can weed her own garden. What a cheek. Imagine, faffing around on some scrubber's allotment."

"Or the Secoya women will show you weaving if you like. Or you can make pictures. Or Don Pablo will teach you the names of the plants."

Wood turned aside to Hack with an incredulous glance, mouthing the sentence "Do you fucking believe this?"

"We'll just hang out," Hack said, as though to calm his friend.

"I'm unclean anyway," Sabra said and, still sitting cross-legged, picked up her copy of *Trespassing*. "Look what this climate did to it!" The pages were thickened by the humidity, the binding curled, the whole book fattened and misshapen.

"At least you have something to read, to take the curse off this grottsville," Janey said.

"Are you hot?"

"Not half," Janey said.

"I wouldn't put that drug in my body anyway," Sabra said. "It's like a pact with the devil, drinking the magic potion so you can get visions.

I'm glad I brought this." She tapped the book. "None of that tricky stuff in here. I mean, the whole point of this book is that you can test your limits without putting crap like that in your system."

Steadman stared, his lips pressed together, and felt Ava's eyes on him.

Nestor said, "Anyone who wants to go on a jungle walk, Hernán will take you."

"That's us," Ava said.

They left after breakfast, just Ava and Steadman. Seeing them approaching the path with Nestor and Hernán, Manfred smiled at Steadman and said, "I would like to come with you." He sounded sincere, but more than that he sounded familiar, using a tone with Steadman that he never used with the others.

Ava said, "I'm sure you have something more interesting to do here."

"Yah. I want to see the cooking, for my notes. How the ayahuasca is prepared. How it is stewed. You say 'to stew'? The *yajé*."

Nestor said, "We say *hervir*. We also say *reducir*. They mix in some other plants."

"Of course, I know. I have read. They add other species of special plants. This I would like to see. You would like to see this?"

He was speaking to Steadman, but Steadman was so puzzled by the man's unexpected friendliness he just shrugged.

"They call the mixture *changru-panga*."

"You don't need me," Nestor said to Manfred. "You are a *perito*. Hexpert!"

Hernán nodded that he was ready to go, and he turned abruptly and set off, leading with a raised machete. A barefoot Secoya boy wearing a small canvas knapsack followed with a stick. They cut through Joaquina's maize patch and jumped a wide ditch. They were almost immediately slipping on a narrow muddy path under the tall trees, Hernán slashing at hanging head-high fronds and low thorny branches, the boy poking his stick at the dripping ferns at the track's side.

The land was level and the path fairly straight, but deeper in the forest the air was inert, hot, sodden, dense with humidity, whirring with insects. Some sunshine, in cones of light, penetrated from torn patches of the tree canopy, yet deep green shadow predominated. The shadow was wet, and the moss on the trees was like green foam.

After half an hour — they had not gone very far on the path — Steadman's shirt was soaked from sweat and his brushing the big, low-growing, dripping leaves. His shoes were heavy with mud. The bare skin of his forearms was scratched and dirty. Ava smiled at him but she was soaked, too.

"Where are we going?" Steadman called ahead to Hernán.

"*Paseo*," he said. "Walking only."

Perhaps feeling that he should be more informative, he pinched some leaves from a bush and showed them to Ava.

"The Secoya use this one for tea, if you have pain problem in you estomach."

"*Tortuga*," the Secoya boy called out sharply, and darted past Steadman and knelt in the mud. Steadman saw nothing, but within seconds the boy was holding up a small muddy turtle, its legs twitching and dripping.

"How did he see that?" Ava said.

"He is hungry, so he see everything," Hernán said.

Farther on, Steadman paused and said, "I always wondered where those flowers came from."

"We have many like this," Hernán said.

"I think that's Heliconia," Ava said.

The bunches of buds, red and yellow, hung on a long stalk like small brilliant bananas, little nips of color that were vivid among the gray ferns and shadowed leaves.

"You have this one?" Hernán said, and he indicated a tall bush with a profusion of white bell-like blossoms, thick and drooping from every slender branch.

Recognizing it as the mouthy blossom that Nestor had pointed out at Papallacta, Steadman said, "I saw one of those at the hot springs."

"Is good for this," Hernán said. He tapped his head and smiled at the Secoya boy, who was nodding eagerly, grinning and showing a broken front tooth. "See? Even he knows. He helps to gather this one."

"Angel's trumpet," Ava said, remembering what Nestor had told them. "What do you call it?"

"It is *toé. La venda de yana puma*. The tiger's blindfold." He smiled and widened his eyes as he said it. "We scrape. We boil the pieces. We drink."

They walked on for another hour, but slowly, because of the mud and the heat. Toward noon they came to an area where some trees had fallen and littered the earth around them with heaps of dead leaves and the withered trash of dead branches. Some of the trunks looked rotted and infested but one firm trunk remained, the right height for a seat. Ava approached it to sit down.

"*Mira. Espera un momentito*," Hernán said, and slashed the trunk with his knife, and it came alive with large frantic ants and clumps of tumbling ant eggs like furious grains of rice.

"I think I'll stand," Ava said.

Hernán took the knapsack off the Secoya boy and distributed bottles of water.

"*Paseo* is better," Hernán said, wiping his mouth. "If you sit in the village, you see food and you want to eat. Then, when you take the *yajé* tonight, you feel sick."

But Steadman had forgotten the ceremony. He was looking around at the great vaporous hollow of the fly-specked and thick tainted air, everything greenish, soaked and slick under the rain forest roof.

Flourishing in this remote seclusion, unaided by any human hand, was an obscure and eternal thickness of garden beneath the patchy heights of the forest ceiling. In the lowest shadows of the muddy floor were soft dirt-humps marked by the grubbings of tree rats and turtles. Flowering plants grew at every level, banking to the highest tree trunks.

More angel's trumpet, sallow and succulent, like white downcast funnels, and torch ginger with crimson flower pods, and the Heliconia that Ava had identified, its smooth curved fruit red and yellow and striped black; the labial petals of a rosy blossoming vulva on a bluish stalk; the orange beaks of Strelitzia; and the scalloped and splayed fragility of purplish orchids. Fingers of boiled pinkness pointed from a pendant vine, and on another tiny yellow bells on wing-like leaves. All of it glowed in the feeble light, and from the heights of the boughs immensely long, narrow roots, some of them hairy, trailed past gnats and flies.

He saw struggling butterflies and dangling worms, the crooked symmetry of the blue veins on big leaves, the frail luminous tissue like wadded silk of droopier flowers, the stiffer stems of wet black plants, the pale noodles of wandering tendrils, and the fuzzier knobs, like monster paws of nameless growths — all of this in a place where there was the narrowest path and no other footprints and only the dimmest daylight reached to the bottom of the forest. Here it was possible to believe that, though humans had passed nearby, none had interfered with the place, nor had ever bent a stem, nor plucked a flower. The whole world was blind to its beauty.

"*Mira — cuidado,*" the Secoya boy said sharply, and stepped in front of Steadman. Then the boy pointed with his stick, and Steadman saw the threads of a spider web glistening with dew. The whole thing was the size of a wagon wheel but suspended high, the center of it level with his eyes and trembling with the damp breath of the hot forest. If the boy had not spoken, he would have walked into it and wrapped the web across his face and all over his head. Just thinking of that made Steadman take a step back.

"Where's the spider?"

"*Araña,*" the boy said, indicating the creature at the edge of the circle of milky filaments.

Steadman saw the spider, and even though he took another step back in fear, he could see it clearly: a big purple fruit with the dusty shine of a plum, highlights of pinky yellow, looking ripe and heavy. It was hunkered on skinny legs, each one ending with a tiny toothy foot. It stayed at the edge of the web, its jaws apart like a pair of pincers. What unnerved Steadman was not its large size or its lurid fruit-like color; he was alarmed by its gaze, its glowing eyes like drops of poison turned on him and fixed upon his own eyes.

"*Escucha,*" Hernán said, tilting his head to listen and look up.

Only then did Steadman awaken from the trance state induced by the spider's gaze. All that Steadman heard was the racket of insects. The boy and Hernán were straining to hear.

Then Ava said, "What's that?"

There came a far-off chugging, like a motorboat plowing invisibly through the sky, and when it drew closer it became a more distinct yak-yak-yak.

"*Mira! Helicóptero,*" the boy said, his hair in his eyes, the complex word issuing from his smile and the space of his broken tooth.

Hernán said, "Is a chopper."

A shadow like a big brown cloud passed overhead, a mammoth belching airship, the largest helicopter Steadman had ever seen.

He started down the path after it, but Hernán shouldered past him and then the boy skipped ahead, his skinny brown legs working as he leaped like a fawn. The sound of the helicopter was still loud, not far off, perhaps circling or going lower.

The enclosed interior of the forest with its dome of branches and leaves prevented them from seeing the progress of the helicopter, yet they still heard it and were able to follow its percussive sound, the drumbeat of its engine burps in the distance.

They were off the path now and chest-high in ferns and big leaves as they saw ahead a brightness, an opening in the forest, perhaps a clearing, and then the descending darkness of the helicopter settling to earth.

Hernán and the boy were hunched in stalking postures, signaling for Steadman and Ava to stay behind and keep low. The brightness led them on and dazzled them, too, for the whole morning they had been walking in the dappled shadow of the rain forest, and now sunshine poured through the trees.

They were stopped by a head-high chainlink fence that ran through the forest, razor wire coiled along the top edge and skull-and-bones signs lettered in red, *Prohibido el Paso,* every twenty feet or so. Sunlight scorched the clearing within the fence — sunlight and steel towers and boxy prefab structures and oil drums and the huge sputtering helicopter, its twin rotors slowing as men in yellow hard hats rushed back and forth from its open cargo bay, unloading and carrying cardboard cartons.

The encampment was entirely encircled by the fence and the forest. No road penetrated here. And there was no break in the fence — no opening, not even a gate. Thus, the helicopter. When the sound of it died down, they could hear the softer but regular pulsing of an engine and could see a steel cylinder moving up and down in the center of the clearing, pounding the earth, pumping with gasping and swallowing noises and the lurch of unmistakable grunts that sounded like squirts of satisfaction.

"*Mira.* Gringo," Hernán said, seeing a tall man in a checked shirt and boots waving the workmen along.

But to Steadman that American was not the oddest aspect of the clearing, for near the entrance to one of the new bright boxy buildings was an Ecuadorian all in white — white shirt, white apron, tall white chef's hat — and he was conferring with another swarthy man in a short black jacket and striped trousers and bow tie. This second man, obviously a waiter or a wine steward, held a tray on his fingertips, and on the tray were a pair of thin-stemmed wineglasses and a wine bottle in an ice bucket.

Another man was climbing out of the cockpit of the helicopter. Steadman could tell from the casual way he walked, almost sloppy as he staggered on the gravel, and from the flapping of his big hand, his easy wave of greeting to the other man, that he too was an American. He had the carelessness of confident ownership.

"*Es él quien tiene la culpa*," the boy said.

Hernán translated: "That one's fault."

The two men shook hands and conferred, and the waiter approached with a flunky's obedient walk, upright and smiling and presenting his tray, and was rebuffed. The Americans walked toward a shelter — an awning propped up like a marquee — and the waiter followed them, the chef behind in his spotless whites.

"*Petroleros*," Hernán said.

The boy appealed to Steadman, saying, "*Nos gustan los Estados Unidos.*" Then he made a face and gestured to the oilmen: "*Pero!*"

"I wish I weren't seeing this," Steadman said to Ava. He regretted being there and for a moment forgot why he had come to Ecuador.

Then Hernán said, "We go now. We get ready."

Only then did Steadman remember the ceremony. As he walked the narrow path back to the village and the riverbank, the rain forest seemed much more fragile and less wild, not as shadowy, but part of a captive and violated world that he had always known.

8

THEY WERE GATHERED at the thatched pavilion in the failing light of day, looking pale and uncertain. Each person carried a hammock and a change of clothes and the items they had been instructed to bring: a sleeping pad, a poncho, socks and a jacket, and a bottle of drinking water. The shelter had looked simple enough from the outside, but now that they were inside and choosing places to sit, they could see how carefully the shelter had been made, the peeled logs lashed together, the slanted split-bamboo roof covered with tight bundles of thatch, the upright poles like columns that had been rubbed smooth. The whole structure now seemed less like a pavilion than a chapel in the forest, lit by sooty lanterns and flickering candle stubs.

Don Pablo and Don Esteban sat on stools at the far end, at what would have been the altar, had it been a chapel. They were monkish in their solemnity and their simple red smocks, with necklaces of orange beads and crowns of plaited feathers on their heads. Each man held on his knee a gallon-sized plastic jug sealed with a carved wooden stopper, dark liquid sloshing inside.

Other Secoya men, in T-shirts and shorts but just as serious as the two ornamented and costumed old men, were stamping on the earthen floor. There was no music, no sound at all except for the bird squawks and the piercing insect wail of the forest.

Some more Secoya men walked out of the darkness from the direction of the village, holding torches. Their entering the shelter, and lighting its interior, seemed to animate Don Pablo and Don Esteban, who began chanting, first in a murmur and then in a low growl that sounded to Steadman like the groaning syncopation of Tibetan monks at prayer.

Steadman and Ava had unrolled their sleeping mats to one side, near a lantern. They set out their clothes, their pillows, their water bottles. Steadman kept his notebook and pen by his side.

Manfred was at the front, nearest to Don Pablo, and the other four were gathered behind him, Janey leaning on Hack's shoulder, the Wilmutts squatting, coaxing their air mattress.

"They're supposed to be self-inflating," Wood said.

"Who's first?" Hack asked, and Steadman heard a note of apprehension, a quaver in the man's voice.

Sabra said, "It's like, 'Take a number.'"

Hearing her, Don Pablo stopped chanting and waved her away, and when she hesitated, he rose and stepped forward and poked her shoulder with his staff. Sabra backed away, glaring at the shaman.

Manfred was kneeling, leaning forward, holding an empty cup, so that when the moment came he would be ready, he would be first. He was watching Nestor for a sign.

But Nestor ignored him. He had been glaring with disapproval at Sabra all this time, hoping to catch her eye. He had told her before that because she was having her period she was not permitted near the shelter. Don Pablo had poked her so hard with his stick she was rubbing her shoulder, as though in pain. She backed out of the shelter, looking wronged, and became a shadow, slowly retreating.

Nestor said, "Okay, we can start, but it is not a good idea to be in a big hurry. *Calma*. There's lots of different energy here."

Manfred hesitated, the others murmured, Janey stepped back as if she had been asked a question to which she did not have the answer, and now Steadman was glad that he had not come alone. He could see that Ava was relieved that Manfred was going first.

"Don Pablo wants to show you the vines that went into the mixture," Nestor said, following the old man.

Manfred said, "Tell me the names of the others you mix with it. I mean, to the *caapi* maybe they add *rusbyana*."

"I don't know the names." He spoke to the shaman, then said, "Tobacco. And sometimes *toé*. What you call the datura."

"I want to know more about this."

"Do me a favor!" Hack said. "Like you want to do lunch at the Four Seasons and they show you the fucking kitchen. Hello! Can we start now?"

"What about *cosas cristalinos*?" Manfred said, ignoring Hack and speaking to the old man, who looked more and more like a goblin as he got nearer the fire. When the old man tilted his head, a vagueness that seemed to indicate "sometimes," Manfred began talking excitedly to Steadman. "Fischer Cárdenas was the first to isolate the alkaloid crystals from *yajé*. He called it telepathine. The crystals are very beautiful, like jewels. They are harmala alkaloids."

Don Pablo brought them to the edge of the open-sided pavilion. A pot was simmering near the fire, a brown liquid inside, twigs and broken leaves floating on the surface. Using a long fork, he fished up some cut segments of a thick vine. The liquid itself was muddy and clotted in the firelight.

"That's the Kool-Aid," Hack said.

"Psychotropic substance," Manfred said.

"Ayahuasca," the old man said.

The others became animated on hearing it, as though congratulating themselves, for it was the first word he had spoken that anyone could recognize.

Without another word or any ceremony, ladling some of the liquid into a large enamel bowl, he showed it, an opaque brew like overboiled tea that had stewed too long without being strained. He shook it a little, as if verifying its viscosity, then poured it back into the pot and returned to his seat at the back of the pavilion, where Don Esteban sat, still chanting, his lips rounded like a chorister's.

Steadman and Ava were sitting cross-legged. Manfred was kneeling, intending to be first. Wood sat with the Hacklers, behind Manfred. The Secoya men watched from the sides of the pavilion with eager, firelit faces.

"You go," Janey said to Wood. "You're the one who was so cock-a-hoop about doing it."

"Probably a big mistake," Wood said with an anxious giggle. He took the bowl, tilted it, and sipped at the rim.

"Drink it all," Nestor said. "Then lie down."

Wood did so — the others watching in alarm — and coughed and retched. Then he lay down, waiting for the drug to settle within him.

"Nothing yet. But it's real bitter," he said, and on the last word he retched again, tried to contain himself, doubled up, and instead of vomiting he heaved and clutched his face, clawing his throat and his eyes. Janey stared for a moment, then turned to Hack, who looked blank and helpless and who smiled in empty terror. Janey got to her feet and walked lamely, stumbling in fear and uncertainty, toward Wood, who was gagging.

Using his stick, Don Pablo stepped between them, not looking at either of them — and anyway, the shaman's eyes made Steadman think of burned-out bulbs. The shaman grasped a smoking bucket and from it he took an ember, and this he held over Wood's head, wreathing it in smoke and repeating a litany of quacks.

"Has the old man had any ayahuasca?" Ava whispered to Nestor.

"Maybe a little. He drinks to understand."

Wood was now lying on his side, batting at the smoke, still heaving and gasping, kicking his feet as though struggling for breath. Everyone stared, seeming shocked by this sudden casualty, who had been overcome and was sniveling with suffocation.

"Did he get it down him too fast?" Janey said. "He looks ghastly. Are you ghastly, Woody?"

"He's baked," Hack said. "He's fucking jacked."

"Choking," Ava said. She looked down at him as if in triage, examining a patient on a stretcher, staring hard, scrutinizing his vital signs, trying to size him up. "Some kind of convulsion."

Spasms shook Wood, then he retched some more, heaved without spewing, and kicked again, the veins standing out on his forehead and neck.

Steadman noticed that Wood was wearing new hiking boots, a style from the catalogue that Trespassing intended as an improvement on Timberlands. He found something sad in their newness, the bright toe caps, the unscuffed soles, the yellow laces. Wood's knees were filthy, his hands were dirty too, and they streaked his face as he dragged his fingers against his cheeks.

"Looks like he's swimming," Hack said, seeming detached now, almost relieved to be standing at a distance from the flailing man.

"Drowning," Ava said.

Wood began seriously to gag, inhaling and unable to exhale, filling with wind, and when he gasped, in an effort to breathe, he began to cry — to whimper, anyway, tears smearing his cheeks, dirtied by his hands. The effort quieted him, as if he were dying from lack of air. Then he slumped, drugged, a trickle of thin yellow vomit running from the side of his mouth and sticking his face to the mat, his eyes still open, seeing nothing.

All this while, Nestor had stood apart, his arms folded, frowning in satisfaction. "He will sleep a little. Maybe a lot." He turned to the others. "Who is next?"

"Not me," Janey said. She was looking down at Wood as she spoke. Wood lay awkwardly on the mat like a sick child, his fingers crooked, the mat rucked up from his having convulsed and twisted it.

Biting her lower lip, Janey looked horrified. Her wrinkled clothes made her seem childlike and pitiable, a fat girl out of her element, unconsoled by Hack, who was smiling in confusion.

"I'm not touching it," Janey said with an empty laugh.

Manfred struggled forward impatiently on his knees and said, "Yah, I go now."

Don Pablo raised his plastic jug and poured some of the ayahuasca mixture into a small bowl. This he held before the German, and when he lowered the bowl and nodded, Manfred got the point and rocked backward, sitting cross-legged again, unsteady in his attempt to look decorous. He accepted the bowl with two hands — they were very dirty — and he raised it and drank it slowly, glugging it like a stein of beer. Afterward, he wiped his mouth with the back of one hand and shook his head, seeming annoyed and impatient again.

"No anything. Just my fingers only." He flexed them and held them to his face. The splashed liquid had left blotches on his dirty hands, and he stared in dumb puzzlement at these dark stains on his skin.

The others stepped away, as though expecting him to explode. But he grunted, demanded more to drink. Don Esteban seemed to refuse, and he conferred with Don Pablo. Manfred was made to wait, and then he was given another full bowl. He drank it the same way, pouring it slowly down his throat.

Still he waited, and he looked at his hands, but in a different way, for his hands lay limp on his knees. He lowered his head to look at them, as if they belonged to someone else. He asked for more, a third cup, but before he could drink it he tottered. And with a dog-like motion of his head, he had just begun to complain when he toppled forward onto his face and vomited, his hands at his sides, and he lay there, his lips dribbling. He shuddered once and then was still, lying beside Wood, who was also motionless, his mouth open, the pair of them like poison victims sprawled on a puke-splashed mat.

"Okay, I'll do it," Hack said with reluctance, accepting the bowl, and bobbling it, splashing the potion a little. "I mean, this is why we came, right? I'm chugging it."

"Don't, lovey," Janey said, seeing the uncertainty in her husband's hands, the unwillingness in his fingers, his anxiety converted into clumsiness. "Marshall. Please don't do it."

Janey seized Hack's moment of hesitation and took the bowl from him. He let go easily, looking relieved, and then watched helplessly as she drank.

Janey caught his eye and gave him an insolent smile and licked at the brown liquid, teasing him until Hack glanced away, as though shamed by the woman. She said, "This is going down a treat," and did not gulp but rather sipped it slowly, creating more silence in her slowness, then set it down, sloshing the dregs and the residue. She hugged herself and concentrated, and when she lay down she began to moan softly and moved onto her side, away from Hack, and made swallowing sounds. She looked serene, breathing lightly, like a woman dreaming.

"Does this remind you of fucking Jonestown?" Hack said. He said to Nestor, "I'm not drinking anything until they wake up."

"Is your choice."

"I'm like the designated driver," he said in Steadman's direction, and Steadman could see in the man's nervous bravado that he was frightened. "These people are my friends."

Steadman said to Ava, "You want to try it?"

"I think there could be something toxic in it. All this retching. I'll watch. I might have to stick my finger down your throat if you have an adverse reaction."

So Steadman stepped forward and took his place on the mat and was served a bowl of the liquid. His tongue was dulled with a taste that was muddy and flat and twiggy, and he found it hard to imagine the cloudy concoction having any effect at all: it tasted sourly of the earth and the soupy bug-flecked air of the gray forest.

"Tastes like medicine."

As he reminded himself that he must drink it all, he looked at what was left, sloshing, and could not see the bottom of the bowl, it was so thick and dark. He tried to think of words for the taste. This is like drinking poison, he thought, trying to make a whole sentence. But before he could finish it he felt a separation take place in his body. Euphoria lightened his brain even as his body became nauseated and weak.

The bowl was taken from him. He propped himself on one elbow and shifted his whole body to the mat. Though his head and neck were at an awkward angle he did not have the strength or the willpower to change into a more comfortable position. But it hardly mattered, because a moment later he left his body and now hovered over it, looking down at the nauseated sack of flesh that was wearing his clothes. He was in the air. He was all bloodshot eyes in a hot realm of light.

The growling chant helped him steady himself in an aura of bright colors and scratchy sounds and an irregular echo of voices and birdsong. He heard the swish of a paper fan that he realized were a dragonfly's wings. Below him was nausea and the dense meat of his body, and where he hovered was light and air, streaked with primary colors, a prism of heat, and his mother, Mildred Mayhew Steadman, just passing by, airborne and soaring toward a distant planet.

Not ecstasy, not rapture, he was buried in a deep dream of tranquillity and solemn contemplation that saturated his body and warmed his nerves. There passed before his eyes a complex and highly colored panorama. A sequence, too, like zones of light breaking over him. Heavy rain came first, or it could have been a waterfall. Then, with muscle spasms, the pricking of bright stars, each a different color. Then darkness, then a translucence. Then snakes twined on trees, or they could have been vines, but vines with eyes and mouths. And families of spiders clustered like primates, the biggest spider like a silverback, moving its mandibles and speaking — not words but sounds that Steadman could understand as reasonable, even wise. The spider raised itself and came so near it resolved itself into a shrewd black light.

The vagrant light formed itself into a face, and the brightest parts of it were eyes; the mouth was whiskered like a cat and partly hidden. Not a nose but a snout, and furry ears. It was the head of a lioness in an Egyptian head scarf with blank staring sightless eyes and narrow feline cheeks and a woman's breasts, a real lioness, real breasts, with nipples like rosy spindles sucked smooth, on pale skin. The beautiful beast had wings — that was the first sound he had heard, the papery wings. The mouth could speak, it spoke to him, it did not move, yet it was insistent, calling him forward in a language he could translate.

He slipped forward, just his eyes, his mind, leaving his body below him in a piled-up shadow. The voice of the lioness beckoned him toward a light. The striped headdress of the lioness was friendly, the voice was soft, the nostrils were damp, the heavy breasts were a comfort, the distant light was a friend.

Even with a severe headache, Steadman was joyous with power and importance, translating the welcome in the vision of light, instantly knowing this language coming out of the cat face, its clucks and labials.

The growly voice said: *Find the heart of the flower.*

The solemn message was specific to him, spoken in a tone that implied that it knew everything about him — his few successes, all his failures, his anxieties, his weaknesses, his whole secret history. He was exposed. He was naked before this intelligence; and naked, humbled, known, he felt very small, less than childlike. He was a wisp of spirit — all his substance, the meat of his being, the coat of flesh that had always slowed him, had long since slipped away. He knew he was in two places.

In a green shadow, big pale bells tolled soundlessly, swinging softly on the limit of a low branch. One huge horn grew larger and began to emit white fuzzy notes of sloshing water, which Steadman recognized as the sound of the sea, breaking waves and surf growing louder, and the round bell-like mouth beckoning, a dark welcome that drew him on, for the bell resolved itself into a dainty flower, one he knew but could not name. The flower lifted to toll again, and he saw that the dark was pierced by a pinprick of light.

The risk in entering was that he would be swallowed and suffocated. Yet he never stopped staring at the tiny eyelet of brightness, like a single star of hope in the middle of all the murk, staring back at him from across a swamp of live rippling slime.

Find the heart. He knew he needed to enter the throat of the flower. He gave himself to the risk, remembering an odd phrase from somewhere in Borges, *the unanimous night,* and put his head forward and instantly knew he had penetrated a passage through the blossom of the angel's trumpet.

He was first blinded and then bathed and reborn in light, rejoicing in a vision of glory that was all the more powerful for being enacted over a dark pit, surrounded by a head-high fence, of wet snorting pigs and knotted snakes. The pit was striped in a slickness of oil that oozed through smooth punctures, and when he looked back it was impossible for Steadman to tell the snakes from the oil trails.

But by thrusting his tormented head into a familiar flower blossom he had saved himself.

The triumphant revelation of the light and the color and the warning and the wings was that they could be trusted; they were all true. And now he could discern great smoking oil pits where the swamp had been, and he could smell scorched flesh, charred bone, burned hair — the smoldering stink of burned human hair was unmistakable. But this was the whole smoking world, where he was known and small and ruled over by a blind heavy-breasted lioness. This truth entered his consciousness and, remembering the specific injunction to go forward, that time was short, he felt pity for that pile of frail flesh beneath him that looked like a corpse, and he began to cry, sorrowing for himself, for the little time left to him.

His sobbing was indistinguishable from his nausea. He gagged and wept and woke with drool on his cheek, hearing Ava say, "You're all right. Slade, can you hear me?"

Yes, he could hear, but he could not say so. He imagined speaking, he dreamed an articulate reply in which he described what he had seen.

But obviously Ava could not understand, because she was still asking him whether he could hear her. All this happened in his vision, but when he managed to open his eyes to the dim light of the jungle day under all the discolored trees, and when he saw Ava's face, her fear, he knew he had touched down and reentered his body again. After that, his body felt leaden and half alive, a corpse rising from the dead, more zombie than human.

"The others are over there," Ava was saying. "That woman Janey freaked out, Wood is detoxing, Hack didn't take any but he's acting weird. Manfred wants to do it again."

Steadman could not say anything. The vision was still within him, slowly slipping away, the light leaking.

"I decided not to take any," Ava said. "I thought I might come in handy if anyone seriously choked. This is pretty heavy stuff."

The old man and Nestor crept over to Steadman. And Steadman saw from the mottled sky behind the pavilion that it was now early morning.

"Good?" Nestor said. "You okay? You see some things?"

Steadman smiled and said, "A lion, a big cat. Beautiful, powerful, with" — and he made a plumping gesture with his hands to indicate a pair of breasts.

Nestor spoke to the old man, who all this time was staring into the middle distance with his damaged eyes.

"So, let's boogie," Hack said.

"Maybe better we stay here another day," Nestor said. "The people who took the *yajé* are tired. This is a good village — good people, and safe. We go back tomorrow to Lago Agrio."

"That's going to muck up our schedule," Janey said. But she spoke wearily, for the effects of the drug and the nausea were still evident in the slurring way she spoke.

"Shed-jewel," Nestor said, imitating the woman's way of saying the word.

"We're supposed to be flying to the Galápagos the day after tomorrow," Wood said.

"Oh, Jesus, it's Kenya all over again," Hack said. "Look, let them rest now and we can leave later — tonight."

Hernán said, "Even the Secoya, they no go about in the night."

Nestor said, "In the night here in Oriente, snakes sometimes drop down from the branches of the trees into the boat, and they don't say 'Excuse me.'"

There was no dispute after that, though there was more complaining, especially from Hack, who had not taken any ayahuasca and seemed stronger, and also from Sabra, who had been excluded and was angry. Wood and Janey looked weak; they were pale, they were quieter, as if convalescing.

Hernán said, "The Secoya say it is better not to take a bath today. If you do, you wash away the nice things you see and the *pinta*."

On the way back to the center of the village Nestor fell in with Steadman. He said, "The old man, Don Pablo, I told him what you said. He wants me to tell you that you did not see a lion. It was a *puma*, a tiger. Your dream was true. He knows — he had the same dream."

9

THEY WERE NOT used to failure. They took it badly, as though it suggested the weakness and defeat of character flaws, so they denied it. They were not ashamed but angry and blaming. "It's all Nestor's fault," Hack said. "What a loser." And Janey chimed in, "It's a bloody shambles" — she the one Steadman remembered looking at the village huts and saying, "Isn't that fun, the way they gather and finish those good strong reeds in the roofs? I could use that in my arbors and garden thatch." She was now saying, "We should never have come. The whole rotten thing's a dog's breakfast."

The others agreed: Nestor, hired to provide the ayahuasca experience, had let them down. The trip had been uncomfortable, the blindfolds had been unnecessary and disorienting, the village hideous, the people objectionable and unfriendly, the shaman an impostor in a ragged feather crown and elf's smock, never mind all his trinkets. Wood had almost been poisoned. Janey was still nauseated: "I'm feeling ever so precious." Sabra was frightened by everything she heard, and Hack, who had been appalled at the memory of his having been terrified, kept saying how shocked he was. "You could have suffered liver damage! Kidney failure!" he shouted to Wood. "And this food is crap."

"What's in this stew?" Sabra asked.

"Probably the same as before. Turkey. Yuca."

"Why not fish? There must be lots of fish in the river."

"Mudfish. Eels. Manta rays. Snakes. You want snakes?"

Nestor was impassive, smoking with one hand, picking at his food with the other. He said, "Not *pavo* today. It is *cuy*. Guinea pig."

The four Americans stopped eating. They dropped their spoons onto the food-splashed mat. They seemed beaten, their expensive jungle adventure clothes the more deranged and dirty-looking because they were so stylish, making the wearers like parodies of travel gone wrong. And the labels mocked them: Hack's crumpled North Face cap bore the legend *Never Stop Exploring*, the back patches on Sabra's jeans and Janey's fanny pack and Wood's windbreaker said, *Trespassing Overland Gear.*

"This isn't what we were expecting," Hack said. "My wife might be ill, and we've still got the Galápagos to do."

"You expect us to sleep another night in this village?" Wood said.

"There is such an incredible pong here," Janey said. "Even some of these flowers smell like stinky feet."

"Maybe you could try holding your nose," Nestor said. "You'll be in a hotel room in Quito tomorrow."

"I'm not talking tomorrow!" Wood howled. "I am talking now!"

Instead of being alarmed by the shout, the villagers smiled and crept closer to look at the big red-faced man in short pants waving his arms and stamping, his knees dirty, his chin dripping, sweat patches darkening his shirt.

With the morning sunshine slanting through the trees the clearing was full of luminous silvery smoke from the cooking fires and seemed haunted rather than miserable, the people more spectral than destitute. Stepping off the canoe two days before, the visitors had seen the place as filthy yet picturesque. But that was when they had believed they were just passing through. Now they were mocked by their first impressions: picturesque meant grubby. The prospect of spending another night there made the village seem dangerous, without privacy, and as Janey Hackler pointed out, there was nowhere to sit.

"I just want to wash my face," Sabra said. Then she walked a little way off, as though she might find a washbasin, towel, and soap dish, and after a few steps she screamed. "It's a spider! Get it away!"

Wood hurried to help her — "Get back, Beetle!" — but when he raised his stick to beat the spider out of its hanging web, Steadman stepped behind him and deftly snatched the stick, whipping it out of his hand.

"Don't kill it," he said.

"What's your fucking problem, man!"

"Just keep walking," Steadman said, staring him down.

With a low chuckle of approval, Manfred said, "Yah. Is not necessary to kill."

But the outburst soured the atmosphere further. The others were so humiliated they did not talk about their fear or their nausea from the ayahuasca. They blamed the village for being dirty and Nestor for not caring and said that they would be faxing the agency. That they wanted a refund. That they would ask for a meeting with the tourist board in Quito.

"I will make sure you get to Quito," Nestor said, and they hated his insolence the more for its being enigmatic.

In all this Manfred Steiger, who might have been expected to complain, had only seemed more enthusiastic. Steadman admired the man's animation and his pounce, the way he could fasten his attention on the minutest pedantic details of the plants and the ceremony. He was inexhaustibly nosy, as cheap people often are, and his parsimony made him impatient and a nagger; but when he did complain, his complaints were unconventional, and he never whined. He was boring, but in Manfred this was like a virtue, his dullness and his ponderous industry making him seem indestructible. He made notes, he consulted his plant book, he interrogated the Secoya boys — and was not deterred even when they smiled at him, not understanding a word he said.

He boasted that he never tipped anyone — didn't believe in it, did not pay his way if he could avoid it. He always took second helpings of food, and sometimes thirds. Steadman had noticed that he had asked for a third helping of ayahuasca. Manfred often stuffed food in his pockets — an extra orange, the hard-boiled eggs, sugar cubes, bananas. After wolfing down noodles at Papallacta, he had snatched fritters and wrapped them and sneaked them into his pockets. When something was offered, Manfred's empty hand was the first extended, and he always took more than his share, as though counting on the fact that everyone else would be too genteel to object. He was a successful predator, whose success depended on everyone else's being unwary or hesitant or polite.

His eyes were always working; his fingers, too — always flexing. He had a scavenger's restlessness. And now, while Steadman and Ava were listening to the objections of the others, who were shocked at the prospect of spending another night in the Secoya village, Manfred was making a circuit of the settlement, looking hungry and moving swiftly, his greedy eyes twitching busily in his jerking head.

On his return he nodded to Steadman. He gestured to him, indicating that he wanted to speak to him alone.

"You want to try something else?"

Ava said, "What did you find?"

But Manfred, who had shown no interest in Ava, did not turn to her. He kept his attention on Steadman, in the confiding and familiar way that unsettled him, as though Manfred assumed that Steadman was a friend, or if not an ally, then at least pliable. He walked a little distance, where a torn web dangled like a rag, and beckoned to Steadman.

"This is not yimsonweed," he said when Steadman wandered over to him. Manfred was pinching a twig still bearing leaves and thin ragged flowers. He sniffed it and held it close to Steadman's face. "Is a clone of Brugmansia. You see the leaves so shredded? The flowers — just strings? Its name is Methysticodendron. This is so rare, no one sees this but just a few lucky botanists. And maybe it did not exist before."

"What does that mean?"

"It means datura — highly atrophied."

"What happens with it?"

"I know a man, one German from Koblenz, who came through here. He was a chemist. He wanted to synthesize the alkaloids in this clone. They said, 'Try it first.' It was a scopolamine crystal. It blitzed him."

"Ayahuasca blitzed me," Steadman. "I've had all the visions I can handle."

"No visions," Manfred said. "I know a little about this one. They make tea from the leaves and stems. I read it in my book. Take the scrapings in an aqueous maceration." Steadman suppressed the urge to smile at the way Manfred sucked at his saliva as he said this. "It is great.

It change your head, it give you experiences. Only the question of money, but you have money."

Steadman glanced at Nestor, who was implacable, picking his teeth.

"So what's the point?"

Manfred said to Nestor, "He wants to know," but Nestor just shrugged — knowing yet noncommittal.

Steadman said, "Why are you telling me this, Manfred?"

"Don't you see?" Ava said. She had walked over to listen with Nestor. "It's something that costs money. He doesn't want to pay."

Even then, Manfred did not look at her. Instead, he shortened his neck and clenched his jaw, making it as compact as a clutch of mandibles. All his teeth bunched in his mouth, bulging against his lips.

Nestor smiled at Steadman, but his smile meant nothing except a challenge or a contradiction. He said, "In the Oriente you find out about these drinks after you drink them."

"Experience," Manfred said. "He knows."

"Knowledge," Nestor said. "Some people call that *borrachero*. Or *toé*. Ask Señor Perito. Mr. Hexpert."

"What about the others?" Steadman asked.

He indicated the two couples, who, a little distance away, just out of earshot, were squatting on logs near the covered platform, looking disconsolate, wanting to leave, hating the smoke and the smells, dreading the night they would endure in the village.

"Rich tourists," Manfred said.

The same casual belittling thought was in Steadman's mind, and it so annoyed him to hear this irritating man put it in words, he told himself that the description might be wrong. One of them appeared to be enjoying his book. And, after all, these people were doing the same thing he was. Like them, hoping for an adventure, he had hooked up with Nestor for the ayahuasca. The truth was that they were all on the same drug tour.

"You are not like them. You are an intelligent man — a wise man. Also brave." He tapped the side of his nose. "I know this. If you want to try it, we must do it now."

Steadman said, "Nestor, who else has done this?"

"Not many people. No one lately. It doesn't work on everyone, and it costs more. Five hundred each."

Without saying yes, Steadman said, "Five is doable."

"The Secoya don't take credit cards," Nestor said.

"Maybe you can loan me some money," Manfred said.

Ava jarred him with a laugh. She said, "'Loan' never means loan."

"I researched the information," Manfred said, nagging again. "What about the time factor? I negotiated with the Indian. I am facilitating."

Nestor said, "I'll just let you guys argue it out."

"See? I told you," Ava said. "He doesn't want to pay."

As though to put an end to the argument, she walked away with Nestor, back to where the others were standing, looking futile.

"I know who you are," Manfred said, putting his face into Steadman's. "Ever since Lago Agrio."

"You saw a passport at the hotel."

"Yes, but even if I never see it, I know," Manfred said. "You are different from those people. In the van I think, There is something about this man. And I see you writing notes."

"What do you want?"

"I want your story for my book."

"I'm not who you think I am, and I don't have a story," Steadman said, defying him and at the same time impressed that all this time Manfred knew who he was. "But even if I was and I had a story, why should I give it to you?"

He was not amazed by Manfred's presumption — writers he regarded as headhunters. This was typical, the arrogant conceit of the writer who took everything and used what he wanted; the same presumption was often in his own mind. And Steadman was annoyed again, because the German was giving voice to one of his own ideas, an ambition that was still unfulfilled, and his saying it aloud — like "rich tourists" — made it seem oversimple but valid. Steadman did not know what he wanted to write, but whatever it was, he wanted it to be his own, original, unexpected story, not something a stranger could guess at. And that was precisely what Manfred had guessed.

"I want your story" was the sort of thing a dwarf with an evil insect's face might say, bargaining with the harassed hero of a folktale.

Manfred was still holding the unusual plant with the strange torn-looking leaves and the even stranger blossoms. He dangled it, his eyes blazing, and said, "I have made the arrangement. Without me you cannot do it." He breathed harshly through his mouth. "And this is something incredible."

Whenever it became obvious that someone was brazenly trying to fob something off on him, Steadman felt his attention slacken and he lost interest. The more forceful and creative the sales pitch, the more Steadman resisted, seeing the salesman as an obvious buffoon. A persuasive sales pitch was no pitch at all, but rather something like a tremor that caused a distinct throb of aversion. The odd thing was that, knowing all this, seeing Manfred's motive as transparent, and even sensing resistance rising in himself as Manfred grew shriller, he still wanted to know more. And he was fascinated by his own reaction — that he was allowing this grubby wheedling man to tempt him with the misshapen blossom on the twisted twig.

Ava seemed to understand that Steadman was listening. She walked from where Nestor was crouching and said, "If you give this German any money, you're nuts."

Manfred said, "Yah, I am just a German," but his accent so overwhelmed him, his protest was a Teutonic yawp, which almost gagged him on the word *Chermin*. "When you see me, you see a German. Do you see a Jew when you see the woman Sabra? Oh, we are bad people. We persecuted the Jews. So we made our fate. We are the Jews now. You can say anything about a German and no one will *schrei* at you."

Nestor was squatting on his haunches a little distance away, smoking a cigarette, listening to the rant and watching the negotiation. Several Secoya men with him were similarly squatting, hugging their knees, puffing pipes.

As though anticipating a probing question, Nestor called out, "It is not part of the tour package." They looked at him and Nestor seemed to see another question in their faces, which he addressed. "So I am not responsible."

This hint of risk attracted Steadman and, raising his eyes past Nestor, he saw the others, the ones who called themselves the Gang of Four, looking disconsolate on their log, like monkeys in the rain.

Steadman was indifferent to the bargain that Manfred was trying to strike. Instead, he saw a chance to rescue something from this trip — something to write about, something new, which would be part of his own story. And the fact that Ava was against it was another reason for him to go ahead with it. They were at an end. This decision to try the rarer drug was something final that would demonstrate this. It was more than a gesture; it was like a new aspect of separation, an act of defiance.

"Don't listen to this cheeseball," Ava said. "He comes down here with his big fat plant book and puts himself in charge, and you're buying it?"

"Yup," Steadman said, and gave Manfred two hundred and fifty dollars, counting the bills into his hand. Manfred objected with a movement of his mouth. Steadman added, "You get the rest when it's over. But you can't have my story."

Ava said, "He's the devil!"

But Steadman smiled. He was amused by Manfred's meanness and manipulation, the transparency of it, especially when compared to the self-satisfied spending of the Americans and all their high-end gear — the contrast of Manfred's beat-up Mephistos and rotting socks with the Americans' expensive Trespassing Treads. Manfred's shorts and all-purpose black sweater had tears and pills; Wood's Trespassing jacket had seventeen pockets — so he kept saying — and Manfred had a greasy sack into which he stuffed everything, including the hard-boiled eggs he routinely sneaked.

Manfred's sunglasses were misshapen; the Americans wore titanium TOGs and peaked caps with neck flaps, like Foreign Legionnaires. When there was a brief flutter of rain the Americans took out their Trespassing rain jackets and Trespassing ponchos and crouched in the drizzle and waited it out. Manfred was the picture of discomfort, with muddy legs, bruised fingers, dirty nails, clawed sweaty hair, and a mud-streaked cheek from his having rolled off his sleeping mat in a convulsion during his ayahuasca trance. And at his muddiest he was capable of insisting, "I have good connections in Washington and New York. I am working on a book. Many people know my name."

"This watch is good for two hundred meters," Hack had said.

"See this watch? I found it," Manfred said.

Steadman liked Manfred's recklessness and saw him as a natural ally, the improvisational traveler that he had once been. That, too, made Ava insecure.

"Do you know anything about this business?" she asked Nestor.

"Only that it is done outside the village," Nestor said. "It is a shaman's drink. Not like ayahuasca. This plant is new. It is rare. It is an accident. I saw a couple of people take it. Only one of them got a buzz."

"What was the buzz?"

"That is the funny part. The guy just got quiet. He could not see. It was like we say, *una ceguera*, a blinding. Ugly to think about. But he knew everything that was going on — more than we knew."

"What is it?"

"The one he showed you."

"Angel's trumpet?"

"The *toé. Borrachero*," he said. "*La venda de tigre*."

Manfred tapped his plant book and said, "Datura. Methysticodendron."

"The tiger's blindfold," Nestor said. "He called it a crazy name. 'A necessary poison.'"

"It is not very far," the Secoya man said, pressing through the low bushes. His Spanish was as basic and approximate as Ava's — "*No muy lejo*."

"'Not far' always means it's far," Ava said.

She followed Steadman, knowing she wouldn't take the drug — and certainly not on Manfred's terms — but she felt protective toward Steadman. Her sympathy and patience were an unexpected reaction to their breakup, as strange as the sudden irruption of sex. But the desire to make sure he would be out of danger had nothing to do with their future; there was no question of compensation or reward. She had at last realized that they were each of them alone, and after the infatuation, the romance, the attachment had ended, and they were indifferent to each other's power, underlying it all were frailty and friendship — mutual understanding.

But there was an awkwardness, too, the realization that they did not know each other completely. They had withheld something, they still had secrets. Those secrets exerted a subtle force, and their being blindfolded had made them unselfconscious enough to exploit the secrets, made them strangers again in the eyeless darkness of sensuality, less inhibited. For Ava eroticism was anonymous hunger — "I am stuffing myself," she had told him with a greedy smile; never mind his pleasure.

She was free, no one's wife, no one's fiancée, no one's girlfriend; just his friend — she could do as she wished. Being with Steadman was her choice. She wished for the time when she would be certain that he would be safe. Then she would be finished with him.

The Indian had been accurate; it wasn't far. Beyond the bushes and split-bamboo stockade fence of the compound, another lashed-together pavilion stood a bit back from the riverbank and out of sight of the village.

"I guess we're on our own now," Steadman said.

Nestor had wanted to join them, but the Hacklers and the Wilmutts had demanded that he stay close to them, with Hernán, in case there was a problem. Nestor had mumbled "*Niños*" and stalked toward them, as though wishing them ill. Then he stood and ignored them and smoked, because they hated smokers and had not allowed it in the van.

Welcoming them to this different pavilion was the small smooth-faced shaman, Don Esteban, who had assisted Don Pablo in administering the ayahuasca. He had been the cook; he had stoked the fire, chopped and peeled the vine stems, stirred the pot; he had brewed the mixture.

Ava said, "He looks like he has a stocking over his face."

Hearing her speak, Don Pablo clapped Don Esteban on the shoulder and said, "*Vegetalista. Toéro.*"

And there were others: three Secoya men watching blank-eyed, or perhaps not expressionless but with faces so expressive, so peculiar, they could not be read — riddle-faced Indians squatting on their haunches and being obscurely busy, like scullions in a primitive kitchen. A frown might be a smile; their sniffing was like inquisitiveness; when they pressed their lips together it might have meant anything — pique, frustration, impatience.

Nor was language any good. In German-accented Spanish, Manfred said, "We start. I am first."

They ignored him and went on stirring the pot, stewing the peelings of the dry slender stems, crushing them into it and reducing the liquid until it was darker and thicker. Steadman saw that it was the simplest boiling and simmering. He thought, I could do that. They were making tea, but strong stewed tea. Don Esteban, the shaman they called the *toéro*, was working over another fire, ladling liquid into another pot and reducing it, mixing it with more plant fragments, stirring it until it grew soupy.

Manfred announced himself again with a question, but the Secoya were so preoccupied in their cookery they did not notice his standing over them, nor did they acknowledge him until, in frustration, he squatted, rocking on his haunches, and then called out to Steadman.

"This one is *Datura candida*," he said. "It contains alkaloids, such as tropane and scopolamine. Not like *maikua*, but strong still."

Using nannying gestures, the Secoya men directed him to sit. When he was seated, leaning forward, the shaman brought him a cup — a cracked porcelain cup — of the dark liquid. In drabness and consistency the liquid was no different from ayahuasca, a cup of muddy tea with a leaf of wrinkled scum on its surface. Manfred sipped, drank a little, then tilted the cup, emptied it, and blinked hard.

"Nossing," he said, and beckoned with his fingers. "*Más. Más.*"

The *toéro*, Don Esteban, considered this, let some moments pass, and refilled the cup. Manfred drank the second cup more slowly while the Secoya watched him.

Don Pablo, the calmest of the squatting Secoya, simply gazed and growled tunelessly, chanting through his sinuses, as if he knew what was coming next. Seeing Don Esteban, Steadman was reminded of that moment when a dentist administers a jab of Novocain and then turns his back and squints again at the x-rays hanging from clips over his tools, knowing that in a moment or so the jaw will be numb enough for the tooth to be drilled or yanked. Don Esteban had that dentist's confidence, which is also a look of indifference, part of the routine.

"Why it is not working?" Manfred said, his teeth against his lips. "*Esta medizina no fale nada.*"

But he was looking away from them, interrogating the carved wooden protrusion on the worm-eaten finial of a corner post of the pavilion.

"*Más, más,*" he said.

Don Esteban did not react. He was hunkered down, looking directly at Manfred, who was still preoccupied with the carvings on the corner post, grunting at them, perhaps finding a meaning.

Ava said, "He's toasted."

Manfred got up and stumbled a little, looked away, and then walked straight into the side of the pavilion, cracking his head on a beam. He staggered and sank to his knees, holding his ears, then slowly fell onto his side, his hands clutching his head, his elbows up. He was out cold.

Don Esteban shrugged and said, "*El resultado no depende de mí.*"

Before Steadman had been able to help him, as he struggled to his feet and reached, the shaman waved him away in a negligent gesture that seemed to mean, Leave him — he will be all right.

"I think they've seen this sort of thing before," Ava said. She gave Manfred's head wound a swift appraisal, as she would any drunken stranger lying comatose in the gutter. The Secoya were fascinated by the way she lifted his eyelid and looked at his dilated pupil. They seemed to gather from this procedure that she was peering through this opening, through his body, into his soul.

"You're next, darling."

Now Steadman was glad she was there with him. He needed her experience, her skepticism, her strength. Only since their breakup had he realized how tough she was. Perhaps that was why their sex was better, even if so much else they did together was worse.

"Please, stay right here until I come down," Steadman said.

He sat with his back flat against a corner post and accepted the cup from the *toéro*, then drank, sipping, and waited, and swallowed, then sipped again. He heard a mutter: "*Está bebiéndolo.*"

He knew that he had drunk the entire cupful of dark liquid when he lowered the cup and looked in and saw a large spider, flexing its legs against spots of rust-stained enamel on the bottom. The thing was not just alive but visibly growing larger, hairier, its eye bulbs swelling with sympathy as Steadman's own eyesight dimmed. From the spider's posture and gaze Steadman saw a friend, in an attitude of patient welcome.

Turning the cup toward Ava so that she too could see the spider, he smiled, and she smiled back. But he did not see her. He was looking through her, and from far off came the small dull clatter of a metal cup striking the ground.

Too much was happening within him for Steadman to speak. He was plunged into an episode in progress, twilit, people busy in the foreground. The dusty liquid in his throat was like warm stale tea, but the taste had nothing to do with the effect, for it had the smack of ayahuasca, the mud-puddle tang of dust, rain, smashed stalks, pounded roots, dead leaves — any weed would taste like this. It was a swallow of the earth. So with this muddy ordinary taste of a dull drink he was unprepared for what followed.

What he took to be twilight, a summer dusk, the looming shadow of night falling, was in fact dawn, a slant of light rising like the first sword blade of sunrise and lifting upward, slashing open the darkness so the whole sky was pierced with day. The difference was that the moon was still sharply visible, and so were the stars, as he remembered them on some of the clearest mornings of his life. This morning was full of bright stars in a pale sky, with the same important patterns of constellations — readable to him now, the complex skein of stars making perfect sense.

He had no eyes, yet his whole bedazzled body was an organ of vision, receptive to all images. He seemed to understand and receive these sights with the surface of his vibrant skin. He felt a transparency of being, a prickling awareness — not observing in a simple goggling way, but knowing, being connected, a part of everything that was visible.

No visions played in front of him. Instead, they glowed inside him — his body was the engine of the vision, the light was within him. He was hyperalert as though feverish, and the crystal world was composed not of surfaces but of inner states, what lay beneath the look of things, sometimes hilariously, for he had a glimpse beneath a mass of expensive adventure gear of a big pale body he recognized as Hack's — so odd to see this irrelevant American here and Sabra beneath him, making a cradle of her open legs. Not so hilarious was his understanding of his immediate surroundings, for there were snakes in the trees and spiders in the thatch and a clutch of nibbling rat-sized rodents in the undergrowth. Listening closely, he remembered and could understand everything that Manfred had said in his sleep.

No one knew him, no one saw his condition: the Secoya were indifferent to the state he was in. They were on the point of leaving the gringo to writhe, and he knew he was the gringo.

Turned inside out, he could think very clearly. He saw the blossom — he was inside the angel's trumpet. *This is what the ayahuasca told me.* He was blind in a powerful way, in the thrall of a luminosity he had never known before, so that blindness was not the shadowy obstacle of something dark but rather a hot light of revelation, like a lava flow within him, a river of fire, and he was euphoric.

He could fly in a dazzling arc over the people who were near him. There were many of them, some from the distant past, women and girls he had known. But he was the only one who could see. They could not see him, or even themselves, in their flattened shadowy state.

"Slade."

Ava was calling to him, whispering, imploring. He knew she was worried — more than worried, she was terrified. And he understood: This is her own terror of herself and the world; it has nothing to do with me. She is lamenting something within her, crying out to herself.

Speaking with his whole body, Steadman said, "I am not that man."

He was outside time, outside his eyes, outside his body, in the opposite of a dream state. He was a hovering witness, seeing everything, all the guts and gizzards, the nakedness of familiar people, the sadness of their deceits. Of his own deceits, too, for he was like them — his keenest illumination was just that, a glimpse of his resemblance to these people.

Light was power, and in this experience of power he knew what he had to do with his life, his writing; he saw his story. He realized why he had come to this village on the riverbank, and he knew precisely why it was necessary for him to be here with all those other people who sat before him. He knew them entirely. The process was glorious, yet what he saw — the human shadows turned into plotters of flesh and blood — appalled him.

Slowly he surfaced, as though rising from the depths of the ocean, recovering as the dim light of day returned, real dusk, real shadows, clammy air, in which the world was once again its own human smell — frantic birds, ragged leaves, shabby village, smoky fire. He was back on earth, and even as his knowledge was slipping from him, he suspected that outside that trance state he would never have had a clue that anything coherent was discernible beneath the stagnant surface of the visible world. He had an instant memory that he had seen to its heart, where all was light and everything obvious. But now that he was awake he could not understand much of what seemed only a murky liquefaction of time. And the light was gone.

"I don't think it worked."

"You were out cold."

"How long?"

Ava raised her wrist and showed him her watch, the stopped chronometer. "Almost four hours."

"*Una ceguera*," Manfred said, and Nestor shaped his mouth in a half-smile, as if to indicate "Who knows?"

Manfred was staring, looking greedy again, and somehow Steadman knew the man was disappointed and envious. He had inspired and facilitated the whole thing, and all he had gotten, so he kept saying, were convulsions and cramps and bouts of projectile vomiting. He wanted to know what Steadman had seen. Steadman was so groggy, so confused by the experience, he realized that he would have to take the mixture again in order to remember.

"You were blind. I shined a light into your eyes and got nothing," Ava said. "Why are you smiling?"

How could he explain? Blindness was the opposite of what he had experienced, but that was how he must have seemed to her.

"I was seeing in the dark," he said. Late that night he woke in his hammock. He said, "You know that line in Lévi-Strauss? 'The scent that can be smelled at the heart of a lily and is more imbued with learning than all our books'? That."

10

THE OTHERS did not sleep that night. They knew nothing about waiting, they hated to listen, they almost suffocated with impatience. All night they muttered, reassuring themselves, timidly plotting, too afraid to be truly angry. The village children — also awake, but frisky — played in the clearing by moonlight, while the Americans, hungry and uncomfortable, whispered like hostages, simply wishing to leave.

Before dawn, before the sounds of the assertive birds and the mutters of the Secoya women starting their cooking fires, when the Americans heard Nestor's call, which was just a murmured "Okay, we go," they were fully awake, and then noisy and eager. Hack threatened to report Nestor in Quito; Janey was tearful, still hung over from the drug; Wood and Sabra were subdued, Wood also queasy from his dose of ayahuasca. Manfred, talking loudly in his sleep, even with his hat over his face, had to be shaken awake. Steadman and Ava woke from their fitful sleep. Steadman thought, Each of us is different now.

In the hot dark morning of dripping trees and big-eared plants and powerful smells of foliage as rank as old clothes, there was no farewell. Blank-faced Secoya adults watched the visitors hurry down the plank to the big canoe while the children turned their backs on them. The Secoya women were the most curious, staring at the American women as though studying a troop of pale excitable apes unsuited to living on this riverbank.

Nestor handed out the blindfolds again in the boat, and Hack said, "You're actually afraid that we're going to reveal the existence of this place?"

"Do I look afraid?" Nestor asked, and waited for an answer.

The visitors put on the blindfolds and became silent, sulking like scolded children.

Steadman sat close to Ava, perspiring in the rising heat of morning, breathing the stink of the jungle, listening to the ambiguous birdcalls that sometimes sounded like teasing human squawks. He was sorry to be leaving and still felt the intensity of the village, which was for him a physical sensation, something he could taste, a tightness in his throat, a weariness, the subdued joy of having suffered through an initiation. He had no words for it and yet he felt changed. His sadness was the intimation that he would probably never see the place again, that he would have to keep going, no turning back.

The chugging of the outboard, the gurgle of the bow wave, the low voices of Hernán and Nestor, seemed to relax the others and embolden them to complain.

"I think my sponge bag was pinched," Janey said. "Couldn't find it anywhere."

"My daypack's all jumbled up," Wood said.

"Anyone see my knife?" Hack asked.

Sabra said, "Do your blindfolds smell as bad as mine?"

"I don't give a ruddy fuck anymore," Janey said.

But they complained in better spirits, dismissively, knowing they were leaving. The van was waiting at Chiritza, where Nestor gathered the blindfolds. They arrived before noon at Lago Agrio and had lunch. After the simplicity of the Secoya village, the town looked especially vicious to Steadman now, for he saw — somehow knew — that the town of drug dealers and gunrunners and whorehouses had once, before the oil boom, been a sleepy village on a riverbank. They boarded the van and took the long road to Baeza, ate there in twilight, passed by

Papallacta, and made the long climb to Quito in darkness. The village was not very far after all, yet it now seemed inaccessible.

Steadman wondered if he and the German had become allies in their sharing the datura.

"What did you see?" Steadman whispered as the van labored on the turns up the steep road.

Manfred shrugged and grunted and remained inert, frowning, saying nothing. Steadman smiled in a friendly way but was puzzled by the German's lack of enthusiasm, and disappointed, too, because he wanted to talk about the drug, verify details and doubts.

The others, united in their failure and humiliation, had taken a disliking to Manfred — "Herr Mephistos," because Manfred called attention to his sturdy shoes. Now Steadman knew the German did not share the bond of blindness — seeing with tiger's eyes. On the journey back, Steadman replayed the experience, and his episode of blindness unspooled, returning him to the dazzle that overwhelmed the ayahuasca nausea. The drug was the route to a cave, but a lighted cave with many echoey chambers, and not darkness at all but a vision, another self, another life, another world. He had been alone there. It was like love — a consuming happiness and a careless wishing for more.

Steadman gathered that Manfred had seen nothing or very little, though Manfred was animated by the experience. Finding the drug and persuading Steadman to try it had given him status, set him apart, made him talkative. And Ava occupied a special place for Steadman, having cooperated and watched over him.

Already the Hacklers and the Wilmutts, timid and exposed, were detached from this trip and mentally on the next leg of their journey, the Galápagos. They had come for the ayahuasca and they had a story to take home, even if it was not the story they had planned. The Galápagos would be another story.

As they were climbing out of Tumbaco, ascending the pass that led them to a clouded ridgeline and the thin air of Quito, there was an incident.

Nestor had said, "*Baños.* Anyone need?"

"Pit stop!" Wood called out.

Hernán slowed the van and parked it by the side of the road, near a café, but before he opened the door a commotion began at the back of the vehicle.

"Do me a favor!" Hack shouted, for Manfred had reached up to the luggage rack, bumping the Hacklers' backs. Janey said, "Do you mind!"

Manfred paid no attention to the protests. He dragged down his bulging duffel bag and unzipped it, taking out a large basket, not smooth like most of the ones at the curio stalls, but a bulky one of slender woven twigs still encased in their bark. From the wide opening of the basket he produced a human skull.

"My front."

The skull was dark and smooth, with the grain and shine of polished wood. The eye holes gaped at Ava, who stared back.

"Your friend has sustained serious trauma to the superciliary arch and the zygomatic bone. I think someone hit him in the eye with a blunt object," Ava said. "I hope it wasn't you."

"I buy him in the village."

Hack said, "And I got this," and unsheathed a crudely made knife with a woven raffia handle. He pointed the blade at Manfred and set his jaw and said, "A shank. To replace the one they stole."

Manfred said a German word and stuffed the skull back into the basket. Ava glanced at Steadman.

When they went outside to the café and the toilets, Steadman took Manfred aside and said, "That's amazing."

"Is old, the head. They call it *tsantsa*."

"But what I want to know," Steadman insisted, "is where you got the money for it."

"Was my last money," Manfred said, losing his fluency in his evasiveness. "Was why I require some loan from you."

Manfred swallowed and something stuck in his gullet and made his eyes go out of focus, as they had glazed over when he had seen Hack's knife blade pointing at him.

Ava said, "A loan is something you pay back."

Manfred had a bristly face and spiky hair. He had been sleeping in the van, his mouth gaping, his hands gripping his knees. Steadman admired him for the way he slept so easily, despised him for the way he took advantage, hogging a whole seat to sleep on. Steadman, who thought of himself as thin-skinned, easily offended by slights and criticism or even hearty encouragement — "When are you going to write another book?" — was fascinated by someone who did not care how much he was disliked. More than that, Manfred seemed to be energized at being singled out by other people's contempt.

Ava said, "He wants his money now."

Manfred did not turn to her, but he laughed, liking the aggression. "Ha! I don't have!"

This took place at a lookout point on the road, next to the café. A dog lay by the roadside in the dirt, probably sleeping but so skinny it was flat enough to be dead. The others who had used the *baño* — "It's just a hole in the ground, like Bhutan" — were now adjusting their clothes and squinting and sidling back to the van. They looked defeated. This return trip was a form of retreat, and their rumpled expedition gear made them seem greater failures, because the clothing was a symbol of their ambition and their conceit.

"You got Mister Bones," Steadman said.

"Is just a memory. A curio, so to say."

Steadman looked up to see Nestor smiling at their quarrel. He seemed impressed by Ava's presence, her tenacity, for she was smaller than Manfred but more aggressive than Steadman. With her as a bystander, the encounter seemed a more serious dispute.

Nestor said, "Who is winning, America or Germany?"

"I am American," Manfred said, so sharply the dog in the road jackknifed and raised its head to listen.

Nestor glared at him and said, "*Usted es una persona aprovechada.*"

Steadman said to Nestor, "What would an Ecuadorian customs inspector say if he saw a human skull in someone's luggage?"

"They like it," Nestor said. "They see them sometimes. They are very happy."

Manfred looked puzzled, and Steadman smiled, wondering what was to come.

"Because then they ask you for a *dádiva*, a fat *soborno*, a bribe." Nestor was big and confident and took his time, using his cigarette for drama and delay. "And you say yes. And you are happy, too, because they are so dishonest."

"You sink so."

"Yes. Because if they are honest, they do not ask for a bribe. They arrest you for breaking the law. If you ever see an Ecuador jail you know how lucky you are that they ask you for a bribe."

After that, they rode in silence up the escarpment to Quito. Steadman looked out the side window, seeing nothing, not even his reflected face, but only remembering his episode of blindness, the taste of the datura, and wishing he could remember more. He had his story, he had found peace, he was bringing something back. He knew he was selfish in wanting more, for his lingering feeling of the experience was like desire: the infatuation that had once made him obsessive with Ava, needing her constantly, his saying "I believe in pheromones — you have them," and her replying "You're cunt-struck. I like it."

Manfred, he could tell, kept wanting to start a conversation, so he turned away and held Ava's hand and imagined her blindfolded again.

In Quito, after the others had taken their bags and gone with Nestor into their hotel lobby, Manfred said, "I have no money."

"So I'll take something else."

The German frowned and pulled on his nose. He said, "You think I don't know you, but I read your book. When I read it I say to myself, 'If I can write a book like that I will be so happy.' That is why I want your story for my book. You are a great writer — better than me. You don't need money."

"This guy is just so incredibly smooth," Ava said, and Manfred scowled at her.

"He heard what Nestor said. When he goes through customs he's going to have a problem with his skull. I'll make sure."

Manfred smiled grimly, seeming to expect this as part of the negotiation. He wasn't flustered, he was nodding — calculating. He said, "Okay. I pay you. Tomorrow."

"You heard him, honey."

They were dropped at the Hotel Colón. They bathed, they drank beer from the minibar, and then, exhausted, they lay apart on the big bed.

Ava said, "What was it like?"

Steadman knew what she was asking, but he had no words for it. And he did not want to say that he was thinking how the trouble with the darkness here and everywhere was that it was not dark enough. The blindness he had known in the village just yesterday was so seamlessly black it was beyond eyesight, beyond vision, and really not the shadow he thought of as darkness, but a void of such profound blackness it was also its opposite, a brilliant light that endowed him with power.

In the morning he looked for Manfred. He was determined that Manfred would not get away without paying him back. He saw Nestor in the lobby with Hernán, and even before Steadman spoke, Nestor pointed with a knowing smirk toward the coffee shop.

Manfred was in a corner reading the *Miami Herald*. Steadman sat down opposite him at the same small table.

"Five hundred bucks," Steadman said.

"Is not even much money," Manfred said.

"But it's mine."

Manfred said, "The datura. You liked it?"

Steadman did not want to be drawn into replying; the experience had been private. He was annoyed by Manfred's bringing it up, especially since Manfred had not responded to the drug, and had only watched while Steadman came awake, his face glowing. He had not even wanted to talk about the experience.

"I give you some datura. You can use it, make it like tea. Better than money."

Steadman tried to disguise his interest in the proposition, yet he saw Manfred smile, for Manfred knew he had succeeded in his pitch. More of the drug was exactly what Steadman wanted.

"You brought some back?"

Manfred tugged at the cloth bag at his feet. He opened it for Steadman, who saw the skull resting in the big basket, empty eye sockets, splintered nose bone, toothy jaw.

"All I see is a skull."

"You don't see the basket?"

The basket, so big and so obvious as to be scarcely visible, lay on its side, like a badly made and fat-bellied clothes hamper.

"The basket is datura — best kind. Five kilos of it. They make it from the flower stems. Just a small amount boiled into tea is what you took in the village. This basket is all Methysticodendron, pure drug, but not a drug that anyone knows — not described in any official book. Is what I tell you. Is a clone of Brugmansia." He put his fingers to the lip of it and a small pinch of bark broke free. This crumbly fragment he showed Steadman. He said, "I know you want it. And maybe someday you will tell me what you see."

"Sure I will. How much for the basket?"

Manfred lowered his head and said, "Two sousand."

"Fifteen hundred. You already owe me five. I'll give you a grand." Steadman began counting the fifty-dollar bills.

They settled on seventeen hundred, and Steadman had to restrain himself. He would have paid much more. The agreement was that Nestor would hold the money. After Steadman had tested the datura tea and agreed, the money would be handed over. Nestor complained that he was being kept in the dark — "What's all this money for?" — but Steadman suspected that he knew exactly the nature of the transaction.

Then, narrowing his conspiratorial eyes, and with a movement of solemn intrigue — Steadman smiled at how truthful Manfred was in his tactlessness — Manfred eased him away from the others.

"You will like the datura, and sometime" — Manfred raised his arms to take in everything — "we will come back to Quito, and back here, yah? Just the both of us. Down the river, to the village. We will drink again. We will have fissions." Manfred fastened his gaze on Steadman's eyes. "You will give me your story."

Back to Quito? Down the river? To the village? Visions? He smiled at Manfred, and Manfred had never looked hairier or more spider-like.

"Sure," Steadman said.

Upstairs, Ava looked at him with the same who-are-you? expression Steadman had seen on her face in the village. Noticing the big bag in his hand that contained the basket, she knew that the matter had been settled with Manfred. She could tell that Steadman was satisfied — more than satisfied: he was so happy he hardly acknowledged her.

She said, "Nestor wants to give a farewell party for everyone tonight. His way of thanking us."

Steadman did not respond. He was examining the Indian basket, scraping at it with his fingernail. Loosely woven of thick, unpeeled, shaggy twigs, some of them splitting, it looked like a crude oversized version of many of the baskets he had seen in the curio markets in Quito.

Ava came back to her old question. "What is it? What did you see?"

If he told her that the drug had made him blind, she would have been misled, would never have understood, for "blind" was the wrong word.

"I have seen among the flowers, tigers in the skins of men."

"You're just being evasive," she said, which was true. "You've hardly said anything this whole trip."

That was true, too. No one had noticed how silent Steadman had been. That was not unusual. Talkers never noticed; only listeners tended to be aware of the back-and-forth of discussion. Steadman had passively encouraged the others to talk by not appearing to listen.

Ava turned away, went to the window, muttered something. He knew she was not looking at anything, just gazing at empty space, the way she had six days before when he had blindfolded her and made love to her. Maybe she felt that had been a charade and was now feeling futile, probably thinking: What a waste, all this time and trouble, what have we learned?

Apart from Manfred, who in his clumsiness appeared to be the shrewdest one of all, Steadman knew the others were dispirited, impatient to go elsewhere, needing more travel. They were talking about the creatures they would see in the Galápagos. "Big goofy turtles." They had not spoken about the ayahuasca. They were like children who had smoked their first cigar and gotten sick and said, "Never again." They had learned nothing.

Ava was still facing the window. She was at her prettiest with the light behind her. Possessing the Indian basket filled Steadman with confidence. He only needed a way to tell her. He saw that he had a future, not earnest hope but the certain knowledge of inspired work.

11

NESTOR LEFT A NOTE for them at the Colón saying that he had organized the farewell party in a private room in a hotel restaurant, and *el precio incluye todo* — as though emphasizing that the party was included as part of the tour price would tempt them to attend. Ava laughed and crumpled the note and tossed it aside, but Steadman picked it up and smoothed it. He studied the map printed on the back, then folded it and put it into his pocket.

Ava said, "You seriously want to go to this thing?"

"No choice."

The hotel was in the Mariscal Sucre district, within walking distance of the Colón, down the wide avenue called Amazonas, the narrow side streets leading off it full of strollers and youthful tourists on this chilly November night. No masks, no finery, no processions: the fiesta had ended. What costumed people they saw were Indians from the mountain villages, wearing shawls and beads and woolen leggings, selling woven mats and brightly colored rugs. Most of the shops on the avenue were shut, but Ava remarked that they catered to visitors who wanted jungle tours and Panama hats and leather jackets and raffia bags. The Ecuador experience.

"People like us," Steadman said.

Seeing them approach, Nestor waved from the foyer of the restaurant. Steadman could tell from the hostility that hung over them like the stink from cold ashes that it would not be a friendly party but an absolute farewell, something verging on the funereal, but a ritual of empty gestures, as though they were burying a stranger. From the outset no one made eye contact. Manfred had already gone inside the restaurant and taken his place at the table and started drinking.

"This kind of goodbye party, we call it a *despedida*," Nestor explained.

Janey's greeting to Steadman was "We didn't reckon you'd pitch up."

"The man of mystery," Hack said.

Steadman had watched Hack drinking from an elegant silver pocket flask, and Steadman's smile was his usual misleadingly mild one, his silence defiant and provocative.

"We have this feeling you think you're too good for us," Wood said.

"Is that the mystery?" Ava asked.

"The mystery is that he doesn't say anything," Hack said, and it really was like a chorus, this quartet of travelers. "The mystery is that we give a shit."

Ava said to Nestor, "We were looking forward to your *despedida*."

Steadman was still smiling. He knew that his smile was an irritant and that his silence and his gaze had worn them down.

"What is it about this guy?" Hack said, but it was less a question than an unfinished statement.

The hotel restaurant, Papagayo, had an Amazonian Indian theme — jungle foliage and macaws in cages and straw mats and even an assortment of oversized baskets that resembled the one that Manfred had sold Steadman. The floor show promised "folklore." Nestor obviously chose the place because it was attached to the hotel where the Hacklers and Wilmutts were staying, as some sort of barter arrangement.

The couples had changed their style of clothes, the women now in white shirts and loose slacks and sandals: they were the catalogue models again, and Steadman saw with dismay that they were loyal to the Trespassing logo. The men wore new Panama hats and safari jackets and freshly pressed cargo pants. They had conquered the jungle. They seemed fashionable, calmer, relieved; they had put their humiliation and disappointment behind them. Their adventure was over. It would never be repeated. They had their stories, their photographs, and on entering the restaurant each of them wore a weary look of triumph.

When Steadman sat down at the long table, they lost their confidence and became furtive again, uneasy and resentful, for this man was still a stranger to them. He had mentioned nothing of his experience, not a single word to them in all the days they had spent together. They had never learned his name. He was like a man who had vanished in a forest and reappeared after a long time without telling anyone what he had seen.

"Thanks for sharing," Wood had said in the van on the way back, in an attempt to provoke him.

Sarcasm was their way of showing frustration. Steadman's silences maddened them, especially as their own talking revealed them as querulous and ashamed, like naked people in the presence of a man in a tuxedo. In their attempt to tease him they were mocking themselves and feeling foolish.

"Aguardiente," Manfred said, sipping his glass of clear liquid.

"How about you?" Hack said to Ava. "Have a drink."

Ava felt that she too was being tested, for every apparent expression of politeness from them was like a challenge.

At the head of the table, Nestor ordered the dishes, saying, "This a specialty of Esmeraldas," and "The people in Riobamba make this chicken *seco* — like a stew but dry, *seco de gallina*," and "My mother, from Guayaquil, prepares the fish like this."

Even so, no one ate much. The altitude killed their appetite, they said. Only Manfred ate and drank with any gusto, and he had seconds. Steadman thought, He is silent only because his mouth is full of food.

While they picked at dessert ("I'd call this iced fancy a kind of macaroon," Janey said), Nestor made a short speech, thanking them for visiting his homeland of Ecuador and for being such great travelers.

"And maybe better not say much about where we went and what

things we did." He leaned forward to confide in them. "Is *secreto*. Is *escondido*."

And he put his finger to his lips. Conferring with the waiter, he quietly settled the bill, then scattered his business cards on the table. He backed away smiling, looking courtly, giving a little salute, leaving them to themselves and causing, by his departure, a conspicuous void that was like a reproach to the ones who remained there.

"He hates us," Wood said. "Maybe because we didn't tip him."

"Because the expedition sucked," Hack said. "Like, who would we tell?"

"Those natives in that scruffy village were cheeky monkeys," Janey said.

Hack went on, "Nestor was all attitude. That didn't sit well with me at all. Let's get out of here."

But he remained seated, drinking from a large glass, a green concoction, one of the local drinks the restaurant offered, *canelazo*.

"Rocket fuel," Hack said. He was drunk, though he had always seemed that way to Steadman because of his anger and loudness, his air of reckless violence; even his posture was like a drunken threat.

Wood said to Ava and Steadman, "Want to come upstairs for a drink?"

He didn't mean it — she knew that. His inverted politeness was not an invitation but a challenge. Out of a hostile reflex of false pleasantry, they were being asked to have a drink precisely because Wood and the others, who didn't really want to have a drink with them, disliked them.

"Just one," Ava said, accepting because she disliked them in turn. It was as though each were trying to expose the other. Had Ava and Steadman refused, their dislike would have been obvious.

Wood said to Manfred — more hostile ritual — "What about you?"

"*Fámonos*," Manfred said, wiping his mouth.

In the elevator, Hack turned to a stranger, a man in a track suit, obviously an American hotel guest returning from jogging, and said, "You American? Us too. Bay Area. Marshall Hackler," and stuck out his hand. "We just came from the Oriente. Lago Agrio? Aguarico River? We were staying in an Indian village. We took this psychedelic drug, no shit."

"Ayahuasca," Wood said. "I got ripped."

"It was all ghastly," Janey said.

"I'm not even supposed to be telling you this, but my friends will back me up. Anyway, the whole thing sucked."

"No way."

The man feigned interest, but seemed embarrassed to be at such close quarters with this loud man and this group of seemingly drunken people who filled the elevator. He pressed his lips together and said nothing more. He watched the lighted floor numbers change, and when the warning bell rang and the elevator stopped at his floor, he quickly squeezed past Hack, who was still talking.

"This isn't a country, it's a theme park. It should be turned over to a private company. Disney could run it."

"You said that in Kenya," Sabra said as the doors hissed shut again.

Conversation for them, Steadman saw, was returning again and again to a subject and harping in monotonous repetition on trivialities. He had heard this same banter several times already, in the van, at Lago Agrio, at Papallacta, at the village.

"Kenya's a fucking zoo," Hack said. "India's a total dump. China sucks big-time. Egypt's all ragheads. Japan's a parking lot. Want a sex tour? Go to Thailand. Want to get robbed by a Gypsy? Go to Italy. Want a truly shitty experience among dirtbags? Come here."

"Do shut up, darling, you're sounding bolshie and blimpish," Janey said.

"Make them viable. Put some American CEOs in charge. Run these Third World countries like corporations," Wood said.

"They got my hunting knife," Hack said. His eyes went small and turned more mean than rueful. He was making a fist with one hand, as though clutching the memory of the knife. "It was a real shank, cut from a solid block of steel."

"My posh Harrods binoculars were pinched," Janey said.

"I lost some cash and traveler's checks, but I'll get the checks replaced," Wood said. "This country is full of kleptos."

The floor bell rang again, the elevator doors hissed apart, Hack led the way to the room — adjoining rooms, as it turned out, a pair of deluxe ones linked by a large, shared sitting room. This one had a sofa and armchairs and a wide-screen television, and on the coffee table were magazines and newspapers and Sabra's copy of *Trespassing*. Manfred began asking aloud in a disapproving way what this arrangement had cost them and had they requested it beforehand? From the window they could see Pichincha, the twinkling lights from the mass of huts on its slope.

"You always travel together?" Ava asked, trying a harmless question because they seemed agitated.

Janey said, "Indeed, yes. We're the Gang of Four. Surely you saw the printing on our singlets?"

"I thought those T-shirts had something to do with China," Ava said.

"Have a drink," Hack said to Steadman.

"He doesn't drink anymore, really."

"You sound like his mother."

They had been cowed, uncomfortable, and defensive in the hot muddy village, but in the elevator and here in their tidy hotel room they were aggressive and rude, as though trying to erase the memory of that failure, or perhaps simply because they were leaving and had nothing to lose.

"I am ever so keen on our next trip," Janey said. "Tibet. We found a way of going there without going into grotty old China. You just charter a plane in Nepal."

Manfred said, "Maybe I come along. I was there. I wrote some things about the *Schamanismus* in Nepal. I know some important people, healers in Kathmandhu."

Steadman just listened. The lights dazzled him, his ears rang from the talk, he felt anxious, he hated seeing his book in the room. He noticed Hack leering at Sabra, he heard Wood explaining how you would go about running a country like a business. Janey sat, knees together, watching Manfred drink from a bottle of aguardiente he had swiped from the restaurant table. Steadman sensed a great emptiness in the room — after all, it was just a hotel room in which they were taking their turn as guests. But the vibrations of an unspoken drama among the people present animated his imagination, and he saw more than he had words for, like a nameless odor or the echoes of strange rituals.

He watched and waited for a silence, and then filled it as conspicuously as he could, saying, "Take me home, Mother."

"No one's going anywhere," Hack said. "You came here for a drink. You've got to drink something first."

Steadman said, "You don't want me here, really."

Instead of denying this or protesting, they stared.

"Just stay," Hack said. "And drink something."

"You don't mean that."

Hack turned his back on Steadman and said, "This guy is calling me a liar."

"You want the truth?"

Steadman was seated, facing them all, and the way he fixed his eyes on them, the tone he used in phrasing this question — his smile, his seriousness, his poise — silenced the room.

He asked for some water. Janey poured some from a hotel bottle of mineral water and handed him the glass. Steadman did not drink immediately. He took a small bottle of dark liquid from his pocket.

"Is the datura," Manfred said, as Steadman poured some into his glass and mixed it with a swizzle stick, muddying the water until it was the color of tea, with bits of broken and shredded stems floating on its surface.

This whole process was so pedestrian, so like someone taking a routine dose of medicine, the interest in the room shifted away from him and a buzz of voices resumed. Satisfied that they had persuaded Steadman and Ava to stay, the others felt they had won, so they ignored them, and it seemed they had forgotten Steadman's pointed question.

They expect you to be counterintuitive, Sabra was saying.

It's a good thing Big Oil is taking over crappy little countries like this, Hack was saying.

The redemptive thing about debt, Wood was saying.

I don't fancy being a whole-hogger anymore, Janey was saying. *I am done. Done and dusted.*

And only Ava and Manfred watched Steadman drink the tall glass of dark water — Ava with a puzzled smile, Manfred with recognition and a kind of envious joy that looked like hunger.

In the glow that was spreading through his body like warmth, Steadman became aware of an enlargement of his physical being — a bigness — of shadows slipping into him, separating his mind from his body, his nerves from his flesh. Something prismatic in his vision began this process of separation, too. It was what he had felt in the village: a sense of fragile surfaces. Everything he saw had an absurd transparency, but what lay beneath it was unexpected, like the spider he had seen in the village, rising from the bottom of his cup after he had emptied it of the liquid, and strangest of all, not a drowned spider, but a large one frisky with intelligence, on lively legs.

Steadman was so engrossed he had stopped pretending to smile at what he saw. The room was transformed; the people in it, too. The words they used were visible to him. They had weight and density and texture; understanding their substance, he knew their history. He could examine each one, and he was astonished at their deception, for he was able to study them and translate them, and each one seemed to contradict itself absolutely, as love meant hate, and black white, and joy sorrow. "I mean it" was its opposite, insincerity, the proof of a lie.

The room was much bigger now, and it held many things that had not been visible to him before. The ceiling was high, the sound from outside very loud, and even the smallest murmuring voice was audible to him.

He was able to reason that if a dream lacks logic and connectedness, is random and puzzling, it was the opposite of a dream, and was wonderful for its coherence. The version he saw of this room he took to be the truth. These people existed in their essence. It was no dream for him — they inhabited a dream from which he had woken.

Next to him, Manfred had been gabbling to Ava and had not noticed that Ava's attention was fixed on Steadman.

"My father teach me how to paddle a boat," Manfred was saying.

"Your father was a strange and violent man," Steadman said. He had no idea why he said this or what he was going to say next, but the words kept coming. "He was a soldier. You hated him. But it's a terrible story."

"Blimey," Janey said, for she had been on the periphery of this conversation and saw Manfred's face redden as though from a choking fit.

Steadman said, "Your father was a Nazi."

"That's not news, ducky. The Huns were all Nazis," Janey said, looking at Manfred eagerly — something horrible and gloating on her big plain face and the way her tongue was clamped between her teeth in her eagerness to know more. Sensing a secret about to be revealed, she wore an expression like lechery.

Manfred said, "My father was not healthy. He was wrong in the head."

"He was in the SS."

"Not the SS, but the SA, the Sturm Abteilung. But so what? Why blame me for my father?"

Protesting, saying *vaht* and *fazzer* and uttering the German words, attempting defiance, he sounded weak and emotional.

"He was captured," Steadman said. "He was in a prison camp."

"In Russia, working in a labor camp for the mines," Manfred said, "until the mid-fifties. Ten years after the war was over, the Russians released him. You know nothing of this. It was hard for us!"

"That wasn't the end," Steadman said. "After he got sent home he couldn't adjust."

Manfred said, "You don't know me! How can you know this?"

Now, with Manfred's clamor, the whole room was watching.

"And he killed himself," Steadman said.

"Why are you bringing this up? Can't you see he's upset?" Sabra said. "We were supposed to be having a drink for our *despedida*."

"You asked for the truth," Steadman said. "Manfred hates his father. He hates all fathers. He hates all authority."

"And that doesn't matter either."

"His hatred has made him contemptuous. He hates you all. He is positively subversive."

Manfred stared at Steadman with glistening eyes and sour insolence as the others waited for more.

"He's a thief."

"This is a lie," Manfred said. "I am important in my country. I know the biggest scientists. I am a writer on drugs and ethnobotany. I am a journalist in the States. Americans know my name."

Steadman ignored him and said calmly, "Those thefts you attributed to the Indians in the village and the people in the hotel. Your binoculars, your knife, your traveler's checks — that was Manfred. He stole something from each of us."

Janey said, "Is this true, Manfred?"

"Is a lie."

But just that denial and the way he swallowed and sulked seemed the clearest proof of his guilt.

"I'm not missing anything," Sabra said.

"He knows your Social Security number," Steadman said.

He surprised himself with his own fluency, for he said these things without being aware of knowing them. And time was irrelevant, for nothing was hidden and he seemed to have access to the past in perfect recall. He knew everything that he had seen, and beneath each surface, as though in a state of controlled ecstasy — Sabra fussing in her wallet and Manfred staring hard at her clump of cards, the Social Security card on top, giving her full name and number.

"He memorized your numbers. He has one of your American Express card numbers too, but there's a credit limit," Steadman said. "He has all your details. He can do a lot with them. Ever hear of identity theft? He can open an account in your name. He can access more of your information on the Internet. He can get a lot of money out of you long before you realize it. That's why he's leaving tomorrow. By the time you get back to the States, your cards will be maxed out."

The room was silent except for the coarse scraping sound of Manfred's breathing through his nose.

"I'm going to ask the hotel to go through his room," Hack said. "If they find my knife and Janey's binoculars, I'm calling the police."

"Go ahead, look," Manfred said, with energy the others took to be bluff. But he stood up and seemed to be edging toward the door, as if to prevent anyone from leaving.

"You look worried, Herr Mephistos," Wood said.

Hack said to Steadman in a slurry drunken way, matey, slightly cockeyed, "I don't know how you knew this, but if you can prove any of it, there's something in it for you."

Steadman said, "Maybe it's better not to look for the things that Manfred stole. I mean, what he said is true — he has quite a lot of influence."

"He's a thief. You said so."

"You're a thief, too," Steadman said.

Ava said, "Darling, please," as Hack bristled, stepping back, looking as though he were about to take a swing at Steadman, who was still seated impassively in an armchair. He stared straight ahead, looking through Hack's face.

"You've been sleeping with Sabra," Steadman said.

Sabra gasped and stood up and denied it. Wood went close to her and said, "Beetle?"

Janey started to cry, saying, "I knew it!"

Hack made a dive for Steadman, but was body-checked by Manfred, who simply stepped into his path and tipped the lunging man aside.

With this new revelation, Manfred was attentive to Steadman, who seemed to know everything.

"It's probably been going on for years," Steadman said. "For all the time you people have been taking trips together. Maybe it's the reason you've been taking the trips."

"Get this guy out of here before I fucking kill him," Hack said.

Wood said, "If there's any truth in this, Hack, I'll take you apart."

"What a muggins I've been," Janey said, sobbing.

Hack said, "Can't you see he's trying to start trouble?"

"But you're a cheat too," Steadman said to Wood. "You told me about your business, but your figures don't add up. That can only mean that when you paid off all your partners you were cooking the books so you could sell the company for an inflated price. That's just one instance. You are incapable of telling the truth. Every time you say a number, it's false. That book you claimed you wrote was written by some students you hired and ripped off."

"Bullshit," Wood said.

"All you've ever done is screw people and play with a stacked deck," Steadman said. "So it's kind of appropriate that your wife is a liar too."

Sabra said, "No, Wood, it's not true. Don't believe him."

But her protests were drowned out by Janey, who had slumped to a sitting position on the floor and was sobbing loudly like a big sorrowing child.

"This is the saddest one of all," Steadman said, still facing forward, speaking in a confident monotone. "Poor little Londoner, lost in America. She's having a nervous breakdown and doesn't even know it. Her husband is fucking her best friend. Both of them are lying to her. She thinks she's going crazy."

Janey was murmuring "No, no, no." Wood was glaring at Hack. Sabra's eyes were blazing. Manfred was smiling at the confusion, looking vindicated, and he loomed over Steadman like a protector.

Hack said to Ava, "If you don't get your boyfriend out of here I will fucking destroy him."

After all these revelations, spoken with assurance, Steadman rose to go and staggered slightly. Now grasping absently for something to help steady him, he seemed uncertain. He groped forward, seeing a different room, and then hearing Ava — "This way," she said — he stumbled and fell.

"What's with him?"

"He's blind," Manfred said, almost in triumph, as though Steadman belonged to him. "He can see nossing."

Sabra looked at Steadman with wonderment, searching his eyes. She moved her hand back and forth before his face. Steadman did not blink.

"I was right," she said in a hollow voice. "He doesn't know anything."

Ava went to him and helped him up. Steadman whispered with feeling, "I can't live without you."

He had never needed her more. He felt woeful, as though lost on a muddy star.

ID: 28
TWO

Blinding Light

1

STEADMAN ASKED, "What's that?" in a different tone, slipping into a small suspicious murmur and sucking air. He had interrupted himself in another voice, lost his fluency. His whole face went hot. He was reminded of his blindness only at times like this — the moment of intrusion by an unknown visitor, a dark noise, a sudden shadow he knew to be human.

You're in full flow, the most intimate description, your last word "lingerie," and now there's a distant glimmering, the gulp of a quickening pulse, the chew-grind of trodden gravel, pebbles masticated by advancing footsoles. Until then it had been an average afternoon in his many-gabled house, on his estate up-island on Martha's Vineyard. He was lying on the sofa with his back to Ava, dictating his novel — drugged, blinded. Then he heard the stranger's heartbeat.

His voice was sharp: "The back door. It sounds like someone. A woman."

"I don't hear anything."

"She hasn't knocked yet. Go look."

Narrating a sexually candid episode, he was unusually self-conscious; he had heard the sounds and felt like exposed prey. He lifted his head into the silence and moved like a listening animal, adjusting his body, tuned to danger, his alertness stiffening his neck, the whole room droning in his ears. He sensed that something was wrong. Anything unexpected here was like a threat to him.

"It's nothing," Ava said. She did not glance up — his back was still turned to her anyway. He preferred this paranoiac posture, especially in the more sensual episodes. Even so, he could feel the warmth of her body when she was near him, as she was now, waiting, glowing, radiating body heat.

Ava reversed the tape to play the last of Steadman's dictation, where he had broken off: *All he could think of was the woman waiting for him after the meal, the lingerie—*

Still poised upright, startled, animal-like, gone rigid in attention, listening as though in a green clearing, he seemed to see the shrouded head, the suggestion of a uniform, the reaching hands, the broken fingernails of a meddler. The staring eyes, the big heavy feet. Only such a heedless intruder would make those sounds. Someone who did not belong always announced the fact in clumsy noises, or in the glare of meaningless silences. Even without knowing who owned it, strangers were often attracted to the big Gothic island house set in a meadow behind high stone walls, its cupola taller than its oldest oaks; but all strangers were unwelcome here.

Then there came a loud knock, insistent knuckles on wood.

"I said, go look." His voice was breathless, his jaw set in aggression. He hardly paused before he added, "Doctor."

While Ava went to check the back door, Steadman touched the face of his watch, examined the hands, and turning he felt the warmth of a fierce sunset reddening the side of his face, the back of his hand. Great hot quilts of cloud spread across the sky, a broth of blue growing pinkish in a vast band of color, then quickening to fiery tatters, molten and purple — five seconds of that before sudden tumbled lambs appeared and gathered, were whipped into peaks to become a mountain range of gilded summits, subsiding slowly, pink again, just an orange stripe low in the distance. The whole stripe was simplified to a speckled egg, but a crimson one, and ultimately a blind eye.

He almost smiled to think that something might be wrong, that there might be an intruder. So much else had gone his way these past months that he was prepared to be thrown.

The glow was still in the sky, still on his cheek, and though the trees were cooling fast, the shade thickening in their boughs, some light and warmth remained in the western quadrant beyond the cove, like a lamp in the corner of a room, fading from pink to yellow-blue, the way embers go cold.

Ava entered the room holding something against her body — a package, a dense parcel, which she placed on the table. The way it settled told him the thing was heavy for its size.

"A woman," Steadman said.

"Right."

"Told you." He was the assertive man again, speaking in his own voice.

Instead of answering that, she said, "FedEx. The latest transcript of the book."

He saw it as Book. The manuscript was always capitalized in his mind, for he thought of it as *The Book of Revelation*.

That news pleased him — to think, after so many years, that he was embarked on a new book and was making progress. Even if he was just a name to some people, he had a large and appreciative public, eager for this book, and he was glad. For almost two decades he had struggled with this second book. And, writing steadily since his return from his trip downriver in Ecuador, he had finished perhaps a third of it. That trip had changed his view of almost everything in his life and in his writing, and had given him a sense of power.

"Shall we continue?"

Ava sat heavily in the chair. The way she dropped herself, making the cushion gasp, was emphatic, a whole blaming statement in the sound of her sitting down: *You are putting me in the wrong for hesitating to go to the door.*

Steadman felt her gaze as a shimmering light, as heat and reassurance, which said to him, *You have never been safer.*

"Yes, Doctor."

He did not mind that she was annoyed. He was glad that his instincts had guided him: the foot-crunch in his gravel driveway spoke to him more clearly than a watchman or a sentry. Delivery people were also intruders, and the more familiar they tried to be ("Nice place you got here"), the worse their intrusion. But seeing his suspicions confirmed made Steadman calm enough to resume the dictation — or, rather, not resume but find fluency in a digression.

All he could think of was the woman waiting for him after the meal, Ava wrote, at Steadman's talking speed, while watching the jumping columns of light indicating the stresses in his voice on the tape recorder. *Waiting in the candlelit conservatory, wearing the black lingerie he had bought for her. As he entered the room, saying softly —*

And he smiled, because this improvised collaboration was the best part of the day. He never wanted it to be spoiled by someone blundering in. When he came to the end of the day's work he changed his tone; it became intimate, and a full day of fictional inspiration became a halting description of how he wanted the evening to end.

Helping him, Ava said in a muted voice, "Over here."

Saying softly, "Over here."

"And he obeyed," Steadman said.

"Because he was in her power."

Because he found pleasure in submitting to her will, obeying her demands.

Steadman loved Ava for the intensity of her confident suggestions, for her knowing how to dictate to him. *I am yours. If you don't tell me explicitly what to do, I'll take charge,* she had said in the beginning. Her assertiveness had surprised him. Their sexuality was based on trust, on invention, on surprise; making it fictional excited him.

Because he was in her power, Steadman repeated, *and was helpless to do more than obey her. He faced her in the candlelight. The lingerie —*

"Loose panties of black silk that she had been saving for him," Ava said, speaking slowly, watching him closely for a reaction.

Dictating his novel to Ava, Steadman was always reminded of the consolations of storytelling, and how it had never been much different from this, the people in ornate halls, and little huts, and around the fires at cave entrances, relating stories of desire and its consequences, whole tales for a single occasion, bright eyes fixed on the narrator, the storytelling explicit and simple, tales of travel and discovery, of startling encounters, of adultery and deceit, the satisfactions of revenge, the reverses of fantasy.

He was afraid of them, the clothes, Steadman dictated, *for the way they transformed the body, like a mask or a blindfold or makeup. Afraid, too, because they excited him — the danger of that.*

She picked this up, continuing, *She realized that she had bought them for him, not herself, knowing that he wanted secretly to submit. Wearing them, she would tie his hands and slip off the black panties. She said firmly, "Put them on." But he was helpless and so she did it for him, slowly, complimenting him on his prettiness. Then the lipstick. He would protest but be so aroused, she knew —*

"That's enough," he said.

"Just as you were getting interested."

"Whose book is this?"

His face was serene, for she had thought of something new — she was expert, she was full of suggestions. He was reminded of how he would have failed in Ecuador without her: she had made all the difference then in her doctoring; she was making all the difference now as his listener and his lover. They had approached this fantasy before but had never ventured further into its details, the mention of lingerie and makeup. Thinking out loud was one of the pleasures of dictation: you could say anything, you could rewind it and erase it; it was just a story, it was vapor.

But Ava was much more than someone taking notes as he talked into the tape recorder. She was truly the doctor, watching over the man in a drug trance. Steadman, the writer, more confident than he had ever been, was reassured by her presumption. His success had begun with his dictation. He had used a typewriter and his travel notes to write *Trespassing*, but that was the distant past. Now he never wrote. He drugged himself and talked instead, and his novel, *The Book of Revelation*, was lengthening, engrossing him, a truer expression of the world he knew than *Trespassing* had ever been. Though the words were his, he never touched a pen or a keyboard, never made a note — that was Ava's work. He spoke his books in the dark, in his trance state. In the dark, words mattered so much more.

"How about a drink?" he asked.

There was no reply. Had Ava left the room? Their routine was such a fixed sequence he could not remember whether she had excused herself or announced the fact of her leaving. But it was the same most days, that break between the end of his writing day and the onset of night. The idea was that they would have something to think about before meeting again. Reflecting on the last of the dictation, he found it supremely pleasurable to sit in this twilit part of the day alone. Ava's elusiveness excited him and made him curious.

Deftly searching the coffee table where they kept the tape recorder, and using his hands like feelers, he discovered a cold bucket with a bottle of wine in it. Next to it was an empty glass on a tray.

He needed variation, for the day was so orderly. There was his work, and then the end of his work, this teasing incomplete fantasy, Ava taking notes and repeating them back to him. Ava's vanishing and the appearance of the wine signaled the end of dictation. The glass of wine meant the suspension of all work, the day at an end. At daybreak or earlier — for he could see in the dark — work would start again.

In this solitude he sipped his wine, liking the solidity of the house, the smell of books and carpets, the whiff of wood smoke from the fire, the aromas from the kitchen, always lamb or fish stews and chowders, and bags of fresh salads sent up every morning from a restaurant in Vineyard Haven, grateful for the off-season business.

The pale yellow Chablis in his glass was so rich that when he tipped his glass to sip, and righted it, he saw it was viscous, showing its legs sliding on the side of the glass. He tasted its sunshine on his tongue, in his throat, and its warmth relaxed him.

Some evenings Ava helped him off with his clothes, like a mother undressing a child, her clothes brushing his nakedness, her sleeves against his bare skin, nannying him with expert hands.

"I like that."

He could tell that she liked it, too, and though at these times there was no sexual pressure in her fingers, he could feel that she enjoyed touching him, her hands familiar and warm. This was especially so when she methodically shaved him, bringing a pinkness to his cheeks with the shaving brush and scented soap, lathering his stubble, sliding the razor and making a satisfying burr as the hairs were scraped away. And every two weeks she gave him a haircut, with clippers and a straight razor, standing quite close to him, leaning her slender thighs against him, her breasts brushing him. She was not just deft hands but a whole confident body, somewhat off balance.

Some nights she would wash his hair with a light touch, so gentle and yet with assured finger pressure. And then she would give Steadman a towel and help him into his robe. But tonight he bathed alone. The tub was full, the bathroom was fragrant with a scented candle. He could not eat until he had bathed and changed his clothes and had a drink or two. In clean clothes he was preparing himself for the next part of the day, and was a new man. It was all as deliberate as the ritual of dictating his book. He could not rush from his day of writing in his studio to Ava's suite. It was important that he pause and savor the interval. He needed to think deeply about what was to follow.

He groped his way to the dining room and praised it to himself in a murmur: the flowers, the candles, the chair pulled out from the table, the serving dishes steaming, everything arranged so that it was within his reach — the food, the wine, the single place setting at the head of the table.

While he sat there eating he knew that Ava was preparing herself in her room. He had tried every combination at mealtime. Earlier on in his experiments in blindness they had eaten together, but after the meal and all their familiar talk he felt sated and weary. They talked, they drank, they were friendly. But Steadman found that such congeniality killed his desire. Besides, Ava said, she needed to be away from him, too; to be on her own a bit after being with him all day alone, taking dictation.

The soup tonight had been freshly made in town, puréed tomato soup with herbs, the tomatoes simmered in wine and basil and this red pulp with a pink froth and a mass of golden seeds bubbling on top, and blended, then pushed through a sieve, becoming crimson. That was one of the pleasures of the Vineyard, fresh food from gardens and greenhouses, the soft ripe tomatoes, the tender eggplant, the crisp green peppers, whole baskets of deep green basil.

After the soup, he found another dish and lifted the lid. A braised lamb shank lay on a bed of risotto on the thick platter, the tender meat resting on the thick buttery rice, with florets of broccoli. Steadman served himself and ate slowly, chewing the tender sinews of lamb, licking his lips. The whole meal stimulated him, the bite of garlic, the citrus notes of the wine. He brushed flecks of food from his cheeks. He felt big and warm and pink, slightly tipsy and content. From this mood to sex seemed a simple transition.

He loved eating and drinking alone in a dining room of flower-scented air. It was like celebrating his own sort of mass in which a sexual surprise was the final part of the ritual: meeting a willing stranger. After a day of food and talk he needed solitude, the bath, being touched, the promise of sex, the seclusion of his own large house with the high perimeter wall.

In the beginning there had always been dessert, usually chocolate mousse or ice cream, something sweet to counter the heat of the meal. But an ingredient in it, perhaps something as simple as its fat or sugar content, reacted with the datura and nauseated him, producing cramps with violent vomiting. If the portions were small, the food did not alter the effects of the drug. He searched impatiently for the cup of datura. Usually he made it himself, brewing it before breakfast. Ava had become expert at making it too, stewing the scrapings of the twigs broken from the framework of the Indian basket, then straining the liquid and letting it cool. Not much of the drug was needed to make an effective drink. The strength of it lay in the reduction, the simmering that thickened it to an earthy darkness. A jug stewed on Monday lasted most of the week. Steadman could see that if he was careful in cutting the basket and cooking the datura he would have a year's supply of the drug, enough to finish the book.

He had been blind since morning, but in the evening his blindness seemed to lift, as though there were slashes in the fluttery veil before his eyes. Holding the cup in both hands, making a formal gesture of drinking the drug, he lifted the cup to his lips and swallowed it all. The taste was something he knew he would never get used to. It was the taste of the jungle — birds, vines, dark blossoms, the clammy scales of snakes, the sour tang of insects, the iridescence of beetles' wings — and it enclosed him in a tight and luminous bandage, as if he had been caught in a subtle web and wrapped in a spider's glowing spittle.

Tapping the finger pad of his cell phone, he sensed the heat of the number in its memory showing on the screen. He tapped again, and almost at once he heard a ring in the far end of the house, Ava's wing. No one else used that line; the number was like an endearment.

"I am waiting for you," she said in a summoning tone, authoritative, insistent, a doctor's order.

Getting to his feet, Steadman had to grip the table to steady himself, and he realized how impatient he was. He staggered slightly.

He shuffled through the corridors, growing warmer, sensing the flesh around his eyes getting puffy, his breathing becoming labored, his nose partly blocked, his scalp tightening as though a cap were shrinking on his head. Becoming sexually aroused affected his whole body with a kind of jitters, giving him hot spots, making him stumble, thickening his fingers and toes, filling him with blood and light, while a dark curtain twitched across his brain, leaving him pleasantly semiconscious. The druggy confusions of lust, the numbed muscles and quickened nerves, which were so pleasurable.

Going to see the doctor —

Nothing to him was more exciting than being in this heightened state and moving forward, through the shadows of these back corridors to

Ava's suite. That was the best of it, the foreknowledge — assured of the general plan and seeking out the doctor to learn the specifics.

The doctor was waiting for him, naked beneath her white doctor's coat —

He became excited, seeing the door ajar, the dim light, the glimpse of the woman's long naked leg. She was standing at the far side of the dim candlelit room, not lying on the bed as she sometimes did. She held a glass of wine, and she had posed herself before a mirror, so he could see the back of her head. Tonight her hair was short, like a boy's. She had a shapely head and slender neck.

She had transformed herself and become androgynous — another of her surprises. She looked so different he did not even try to make a connection between her and the woman who had been taking dictation all day. The white doctor's coat was only superficially clinical, for it was raw silk, a fluttery robe, and underneath, easily visible when she lifted her leg and placed her black high-heeled shoe on a chair seat, the black panties.

"Doctor," he said.

"Lock the door."

The mirror caught the light. He preferred seeing her in the mirror; he knew her better, desired her most, from her reflection.

Even from the few words she spoke he could tell that she had been drinking. That too made her less familiar. It was important that she be a stranger. Ava taking dictation had no body, no allure, no perfume; but the boyish doctor in this room, with red lips and bright eyes, was primarily sensual.

"I need you to lie down," she said.

Just before he obeyed, he pretended to resist, a second of delay that made Ava insistent, almost scolding, and he surrendered to her at once.

"Over here — none of that."

Seeing that she held some straps she called restraints, he lay on the bed and allowed her to tie his hands to the uprights of the bedstead. He smelled the wine and saw her glazed and greedy eyes. He was pleased knowing that she had been drinking, for when drunk, she was impulsive. Their encounters worked best when she was enigmatic and unpredictable.

Ava unclasped the heavy buckle of his belt and eased it out of the loops of his pants. With a chafing sound, stiff cloth against skin, she slipped his blue jeans off, giving his swelling penis a little slap, affection and severity in a single gesture.

"This is a swap," Ava said.

Knowing he was watching, his whole body alert, she used her thumbs to push down her panties, then let them slip to her ankles and stepped out of them, just a wisp of silk on the floor. Watching, he was overwhelmed, for what she had just done was an expression of power, not submission. She wrapped his leather belt around her waist and cinched it, jerking the end with one hand, against the buckle.

She climbed onto the bed and sat on him, facing away, and got the panties over his feet and up his legs.

"What are you doing?"

"You're my dolly," and she laughed, as if she were dressing a doll and did not have to answer back. And she gave him to understand that he was not any doll but an imposing one, a doll to cherish and play with, made to represent fantasies of her own. As soon as the panties were tightened on him he became aroused, and though she stroked him and he pleaded for more and tugged against his restraints, she would not touch him except through the silk, teasing him with her fingers.

"I'm going to give you a new face," Ava said. "A pretty one."

She placed a tray of bottles and jars on the bed and powdered his face, talking all the while, describing what she was doing. She rouged his cheeks, painted his lips with a small brush — lip gloss, she told him.

What had begun as play now seemed like a serious ritual, a sacrificial ceremony, for the body on the bed was like one on an operating table, and he was being worked on and transformed. He tried to imagine how he must look, terror in his eyes, a girl's face, a clown's mouth, a painted doll with bulging panties.

"You're in my power. I can do whatever I want with you," Ava said. "I am your doctor. Do exactly as I say."

It occurred to Steadman that this was what brutes dictated to their victims when they had murder in mind, yet she also sounded like a physician, reminding him of his weakness, making him submit to a medical procedure. Only as her victim did he realize how badly he needed her, for she was at that moment the only other person on earth.

The more feminized he became, the more he belonged to her; she took possession of him by making him her dolly, creating the image of someone she wanted. The more completely he was made submissive, the clearer he saw her desire, and the more powerful he felt.

"Why are you smiling?" she said, but lightly, as though she knew the answer.

She wheeled the full-length mirror on its stand nearer the bed, and in the long oval of cheval glass she studied him, moved his head a little and contemplated it, touched his lips with the brush again, dabbed at his cheeks, fluffed his hair.

"You've never done this before," she said, "but you've fantasized about it."

Steadman lay helpless, still like a doll, a bit awkward because of his tied hands, excited under her confident gaze. He had needed her to dominate him tonight, so he could see her charged with desire.

She kissed his lips slowly, licking his mouth, licking his face and neck, then painting him again — painted his nipples then kissed and sucked them, painted his belly and licked it, rubbed her face against him. She put her mouth on his ear and, breathing warmth into it, whispered that she was wet between her legs.

She lay beside him on the bed, tracing her fingers over his body, down from his face and chest to his stomach, moving them to where the panties were binding him, scratched the texture of the panties, and the stiffness beneath them, his engorged cock, like a snake thickening in a silken purse.

She toyed with him, saying nothing, so single-minded and meticulous that it was ritual, not play. He found the pressure, the tracings of her fingers, unbearable, he wanted more, he pleaded for it, but she did not reply. At one crucial moment she stood up, slid off the bed, walked across the room, and watched him, sipping from her wineglass. She had positioned herself so he could see only her reflection in the mirror. She peered back at him from the glass, lowering one hand, touching herself, and he strained to see better as he murmured and sighed.

"Look at you."

Her legs parted, she stroked herself with two fingers, watching his face. The room was hot, his face was damp, he could hardly breathe, now he was truly captive. After a while, teasing him from a little distance, she went nearer and put her damp fingers on his lips, ordered him to taste them, and then placed her hands on the panties, enclosing him, then clutching.

"Do you like it?"

"Please don't ask me that," he said.

He was fully aroused, his cock trapped in the tightened silk. And he had the sense that it was not his body she wanted. What she loved was touching her own panties on him, as though making love to herself again.

She lowered her face, nuzzled his thighs, pressed her lips and cheeks to the panties, groaning against him, speaking to his stiffness, murmuring into his crotch with a vibration that made him harder.

"Please," he said, half lost in delirium.

She knew what he wanted. She was still moaning, her face against him, telling him a long, incoherent story, like a fable of regret, her lips working, making him moan.

"Please." He could barely speak, his tongue was so heavy.

He longed for relief, he pleaded for her mouth. She delayed some more and then gave him what he wanted, and when she was on him she freed his cock from the panties and sucked it, holding it with her lips. Her mouth was hot, her fingers were stroking him through the silk.

But that was not the height of Steadman's pleasure. Just before he came in her mouth he felt her two hands throttle him, pumping hard, making him cry out. She was eager, sighing and swallowing with pleasure.

He sank into sleep just afterward. He dreamed, tumbling into dark depths, and just before he drowned he woke, gasping and helpless, but unbound, his hands untied, and he was canted sideways, like a man washed ashore, dumped on a beach, almost lost, regaining consciousness, remembering. He could see Ava seated next to him, seeming demure, her legs crossed.

"It's late. Work tomorrow."

She was being stern again, but distant and prim. Her primness aroused him as much as her sensuality.

"Time for bed," she said, and helped him to his feet.

As she propped him up, he muttered helplessly. All his vitality was gone, and drained of it he could hardly see anything at all — he never could in this state. Ava led him to his room. Again he slept. He hardly dreamed. He woke to a dimmer light, a different sunrise, another kind of wakefulness.

He had been blind. He had chosen to be blind. Now, on waking, he could see clearly, but was dissatisfied and impatient with the washed-out colors, the ugliness beyond the window, hideous midsummer with wind-tortured leaves, a sky like cat fur — the old world.

At breakfast, averting his eyes from the sickly light, he found the jug of datura tea. As he gagged — the concoction was clammy and cool, like a jungle in its darkest dripping hours — the day telescoped, all the sunlight flattened into shadow in just under a minute. He waited, knowing what was coming. Still at breakfast, his eyes dimmed, twilight fell, and he was ready for dictation, a blind man again.

2

FOR ALMOST EIGHT MONTHS he had prepared himself with the datura, the controlled blinding, a mask as exquisite as a falcon's hood, keeping to his secluded house. That had been a typical day: a whole day, including night. Darkness was a zone Steadman entered in order to know his mind and advance the narrative of his book. Daylight was unhelpful and ambiguous for seeming to be true, yet it was shabby and misleading. He spent his days dictating the revelation of his nights, which were bright and long and fictive. Engrossed in both sides of the day, dark and light, and both sides of his life, work and sex, he at last felt complete.

On this island he wanted no interruptions. He had never encouraged visitors to his house on the Vineyard. And few people came here in the bleak off-season months. For most mainlanders the island did not exist in the winter, nor even in the spring, which like the past one could be sleety and cold, the raw northwest wind scooping across Vineyard Sound and along the ponds and banks, flattening daffodils, tearing through his trees to claw at his windows. For Steadman it was writing weather.

In summer the island was full — more than full, spilling over, people clinging, harbors crammed with jostling boats, the roads dense with big slow cars. So in summer especially he had hid himself in his up-island house. And he had reflected that the Vineyard had not always been like this. He had fled to the island for solitude in the first years of his fame, when he had felt the need to hide, crouching like a hunter in a blind.

Time had passed and made the better places busier, and sometimes destroyed them. The Vineyard suffered, its beauties trampled for the very fact that they were beautiful — crowded and pawed by too many admirers. Even Steadman was sought out, like any other Vineyard curiosity. On his arrival he had announced that he was withdrawing, and the announcement had been like a challenge to the people who had pestered him. But the Vineyard was full of hiding places. He had found one in the green heart of the island, down a country road, behind a perimeter stone wall and high hedges.

Because he had bought the large estate with the merchandising and TV profits from *Trespassing*, the purchase was classified as celebrity news and reported in the newspaper columns listing hot properties. His scheme backfired. His very wish to be left alone made him a target. His taste for seclusion had singled him out, made him specific, a greater prize. It seemed the press was not interested in anyone who was accessible. A person who cooperated in publicity or agreed to be interviewed was regarded as a self-promoter and an easy mark. So reporters looking for a story tried to sniff him out because he was unwilling, a recluse.

To be first with the Steadman story would be a coup. No one succeeded, but that failure was a greater goad. Isolated, unwritten about, Steadman was more obvious, and was talked about more, speculated on, the subject of gossip. For some years his desire to remain out of the public eye became as much the basis of his fame as his book had, but the title *Trespassing* was like a dare to readers who wanted to know more about him. He was mentioned constantly, conspicuous by his absence, his name still attached to that one book.

Steadman did not in the least resemble the author of *Trespassing*. This was odd, for that person was falsely fixed in readers' minds as only a one-book author can be, a monochrome in one dimension. This man, the trespasser, was his book. The book was all that was known. The mentions of him in the press described someone Steadman scarcely recognized, which was another reason that for years he had stayed at home.

His fame disgusted him, not because it was hollow and cheaply won — he had earned it, he had craved it — but because as more time passed he felt unworthy. There was just that one book, the chronicle of a reckless stunt, and where was his second? His self-disgust made him cynical and envious, his inaction shamed him. He collected the names and studied the lives of one-book Americans — Salinger gone to seed in New Hampshire, Ralph Ellison teaching literature in New Jersey, Jim Powers drunk and frail in Minnesota. Steadman understood their anger and bitterness. They were not forgotten, but they had been abandoned.

People hardly talked about them anymore. If you didn't produce another book, you were as good as dead. That same sudden obscurity befell Steadman; he realized it when the phone stopped ringing and the talk ceased. Once he had pleaded to be left alone; then, years later, he had his wish and he was at sea. There was no need to hide, no one to hide from. Who cared? As the Vineyard had grown in popularity, his own fame had slipped, and it had gotten to the point where, though the title *Trespassing* was well known, his own name was not linked to it. The book was associated with the TV series, the bad film, the branding of the outdoor clothing line and the licensed accessories — waterproof watches, footwear, binoculars, sunglasses. His own name was forgotten, or perhaps — suggested by Sabra in Ecuador and her referring to him as a "legendary has-been" — Steadman was thought to be dead.

In old age most writers fell silent and existed without force, in a precious obscurity indistinguishable from death. Mute, aged, feeble, unremembered, they were little more than moth-eaten ornaments, wheeled out for prizes, for ceremonies, the indignities of being patronized for giving keynote speeches and getting honorary doctorates, the ridiculous robes and unwearable medals, the pompous tributes of philistines who served merely to remind an indifferent public that such forgotten fogies were still alive. You saw them looking like tramps or mad uncles, with wild hair, twitching fingers, baggy trousers. Old writers were uglier and crazier-looking and smellier than other civilians — shuffle-hurrying to the men's room after the ceremony, and the next thing you knew they were actually dead.

In his first years of seclusion Steadman had wanted to write a novel as original and strange as his travel book. But all he wrote were magazine pieces, travel stories that were the opposite of *Trespassing,* the opposite of what he wished his writing to be. And he told himself that he had another writing life, which was more real to him for being his secret. He was confident in his own ideas — the unwritten books, the stories that were just jotted notes, the sheaf of false starts. There was time for them — why spoil a good idea by being hasty? He didn't want to rush his book. He wrote nothing substantial.

So much of writing was pure silence, forethought, meditation, a kind of Zen, summoning the mood, achieving the mastery to begin; and writing poorly — the false start — was more damaging to an idea than not writing at all. So Steadman reasoned. He despised the vanity of writers who raced into print; he loathed looking at their clumsy sentences and upholstered paragraphs. He hated hearing them talk. "I'm doing a novel." This paltry bookmaking merely repeated the banalities of the past; and Steadman swore that if he could not write something new — a novel so original as to be disturbing, in language coined for the purpose and ringing with reality, a book as powerful as *Trespassing* but an inner journey — well, then he would not write fiction at all and only volunteer for pieces if they interested him.

Then he stopped writing the pieces, and in the years before traveling to Ecuador he did nothing but live in obscurity, doodling at his desk on the Vineyard. He remained on the seasonal party list, a sought-after guest because he so seldom showed up. Parties and tennis and the water preoccupied the summer people, for whom the Vineyard was the greatest summer camp on earth. These people were cliquey and gossipy like campers, too. "How's the book coming along?" he was sometimes asked, and he smiled and said, "Slowly. It's only been twenty years."

Publishing nothing because he refused to write badly conveyed the impression of virtue and made him self-important for a while. A writer's obliquest boast was that he or she, so tormented and blocked, was not writing. But eventually people stopped inquiring. Much worse than their gauche questions about his work was their tactless not-asking, like people made awkward by a bereavement, pretending to demonstrate their concern by not commenting on the deceased. He avoided the parties for embarrassments like these. And he hated himself for his delay in writing another book. Or was delay the word? Perhaps he had nothing to write. He had had one book in him. He had been young, like Salinger and Ellison, and now he was middle-aged and depleted, perhaps kidding himself that he had anything more to give.

Yet he could not be calm, did not have the stomach for this. Not writing now seemed to him the cruelest form of self-denial, a kind of mutilation.

He had changed, he was older, he was better read; he saw that *Tres-*

passing had been a marketable mythographic idea. It was a young man's book, but now — he had never thought this would happen — he was neglected and ignored. To succeed in society you had to stay the same. That was also true of the most vulgar success in publishing: you had to stay true to the brand and repeat yourself. What had made him timid about writing the confessional novel he had planned for so many years was that it bore no relation to *Trespassing;* it was against the rules.

For years all he had ever heard from editors and publishers, and especially from the agency that sold merchandising rights, was "Give us another *Trespassing*."

As time had passed he had become somewhat self-conscious about the success of his book — doubted its integrity precisely because it had been a success. What he had regarded as an achievement now seemed like a fluke. The only book they wanted was the very book he refused to write. So he did nothing, and he might as well have been dead.

The Vineyard was the perfect place to be dead. Except for the summer months it was an island of natives, exiles, and castaways. The off-season population was divided between millionaires and menials — the rich who were allowed to stay and the tenacious land-poor gentry who actually ran the island, through a network of obscure relationships, support systems, and productive rivalries. Being a wealthy summer resident on the Vineyard simply meant having a house on a piece of land; but the house was little more than a ticket to live there, and only a season ticket in most cases. On the Vineyard money was not a significant factor in acquiring power. Money didn't even buy influence, because only influence mattered, and it could not be bought. An almost Asiatic system of loyalty and dependence, trust and cooperation, got things done, and without it life was impossible in any season. Your name mattered most. Everyone was known, or at least knowable. The oldest families, the most deferred to, the ones with power and influence, were by no means wealthy, though some still owned land. In every respect, as the years had passed, the Vineyard had become more and more like an island in the South Seas — inbred, enigmatic, with complex alliances and unsolvable issues of land and power — like many of the destinations in *Trespassing*.

The descent of the summer people overwhelmed the island. They were suffered for their revenue and their obedience. The crowds gathered in early June and the numbers swelled until just after Labor Day.

Among the summer people were some of the island's stalwarts — the celebrities, the money people, the fundraisers, the patrons, the ones for whom the Vineyard was a worthy cause, an art colony as well as a refuge. Most of them came to see each other and to glory in another golden summer. The village of Edgartown was house-proud and self-important and snobbish, attached to its history, and until just the other day was adamant in its tacit understanding of Whites Only and No Jews. Vineyard Haven was a working port and commercial center; Oak Bluffs, geographically in between, was upscale black; Aquinnah was Indian; Chappaquiddick, the most recently colonized, was New Yorkers and lawyers and trophy houses; South Beach was new money; Lambert's Cove was old farmland and big houses. Scattered throughout, in the woodlots and among scrub oaks and bull briars and thickets of sumac, were the islanders, the old-timers, many of them living in hovels and bungalows, amid a clutter of pickup trucks and kids' toys strewn on the lawn and, here and there, untidy stacks of lobster traps.

Up-island was harder to define, because there were so few solid landscape features. The presence of old families was one aspect — Mayhews here, Nortons and Athearns there — and so was the crossroads at West Tisbury. Squibnocket was another. Alley's store and the old churches were landmarks. But most of up-island was hidden houses and steep meadows surrounded by high hedges and stone walls. One of those estates was Steadman's, at the end of a gravel track that was more a country road than a driveway. For him the Vineyard did not grow smaller with time, and he did not get the "rock fever" others talked about. The longer he lived on the island the larger it appeared, and sometimes it seemed as vast as Australia. Yet it remained a place with no secrets.

For years Steadman believed he was hiding, and that he was being pursued and pestered. But at last, so thoroughly had he insisted on his privacy, people stopped seeking him out. The press stopped caring; there was no scandal and no new book. Steadman had had a succession of live-in girlfriends, but none of them had taken to the island. The winters were too quiet, the summers too loud, and Steadman never mentioned marriage. He was silent when asked "Where's this thing going?" But the women knew that the very fact that they were asking the question meant the answer was "Nowhere." Then he had married, but disastrously, the marriage shorter than the courtship. That was Charlotte — Charlie. Ava, whom he had first met at the Vineyard hospital, was more a wife to him than Charlie had ever been.

As one of the few doctors on the island, Ava was in demand; electricians, plumbers, housecleaners, carpenters, and handymen were also courted, because there were so few of them. Some were enticed from the Cape and flew over in the commuter jet from Hyannis to perform mundane tasks — mend a roof, stop a leak, rewire a house. When Ava took a leave of absence from the hospital to help Steadman with his novel, the hospital management screamed in frustration and begged her to come back.

The Vineyard was the real estate phenomenon of Steadman's life. He had gone there from Boston as a child when it had been a hymn-singing island of fishermen and vegetable farmers, odd-jobbers and lobstermen. His mother had been a Mayhew; it was a return for her. Then the island became a version of America — a choice destination with an unflagging building boom, too many newcomers, mutual suspicion and class conflict, environmental battles, unsustainable development crowding areas of natural beauty, a dwindling labor pool, heavy traffic, drugs in the summer, race problems, angry Indians, and now and then a knifing in Oak Bluffs: Hometown USA.

Still, it was home for him, and for that reason, prettier than anywhere else. Old money built discreetly and dressed down and didn't show off and was famously frugal. Old money fraternized with the locals, formed alliances, got things done — or, more often, managed to be quietly obstructive, meddling for the good of the island. What new money there was remained intimidated by the locals, gently browbeaten, never understanding that the gentry prided themselves on and gained self-esteem by knowing the workers, for the boat builders and the fishermen and the ferrymen and the police and the raggedest Wamponoags were the island's true aristocrats.

"How long have you lived here?" Steadman was sometimes asked.

"I went to John Belushi's funeral," he said. "And my mother's people, the Mayhews, have lived here for three hundred and sixty-five years."

These days, as an addict — there was no other word — he often thought about Belushi's drug habit. He knew enough about it to understand that it was the opposite of his own. Poor Belushi shot himself full of speedballs and was incoherent and out of control, comatose and futile. Steadman's addiction was benign and enlightening, healthful and productive.

The blinding light bestowed by the datura inspired and strengthened him and gave him back the past; granted him something just short of omniscience; was revelation and remembrance. He had heard that blindness was sensory deprivation and had believed it to be something like a thick bag over the head of a doomed man in a noose. Never had he imagined that such blindness would grant him power, that he would be given such vision. Darkness was light, the world was turned inside out, he saw to the essence of things, and it was prophetic, for at the heart of it all was the future.

Blindness was his addiction and his obsession — his entire waking life was given to it; his whole world was transformed. No one knew what he knew. How deluded sighted people were, insects twitching in a stick-figure tango, animated by their feeble impulses, seeing so little.

Drinking the muddy mixture, Steadman was blinded and uplifted. In the glow of his sightlessness nothing was hidden; the world was vast and bright, and its vital odors filled his soul. The simplest touch roused him by the pressure of its tragic eloquence. He learned a whole narrative of smell, a grammar of sound, a syntax of touch.

At first, preoccupied with dabbling in the datura, he had done no writing at all. He had sat big and bright as though enthroned, overwhelmed by the luminous warmth that blindness had kindled in him and by the insights it provoked — he was truly seeing the world for the first time. Writing could wait. He had fantasized that as a blind man he needed round-the-clock nursing. Well, it was partly true.

He did not begin writing immediately, but when he did he realized how incomplete *Trespassing* had been, how thinly imagined, and not a fluke but a failure. Yet even failures had the power to delude the reader. Once, he had wondered whether he would ever write anything again. *Trespassing*, for those who remembered that he wrote it, might be his only literary legacy. Now, with the datura, he could not see any end of creation. He could barely keep pace with the tumult of his visions, the record of his nights and days, in the god-like realm of the erotic, the doctor by his side, his dark dreams fulfilled and revealed.

On some days of dictation he felt that he had poisoned himself and died; that in death he had entered the shimmering chambers that some people had glimpsed but none had described, because unlike Steadman they were unable to come back from the dead. He died once a day and woke, delivered from death, freighted with revelation.

He worked alone, with Ava. No one else knew how he had been transformed. Steadman remained secluded as the bleaker seasons passed into the cold Vineyard spring, with its spells of frigid sunshine. He had no need to go anywhere. His writing was the one constant in his life, and he was content with the conceit that, blinded this way, he contained the world.

But late May brought warmth and color. After the clammy winter and the cold northwest wind there were some uncertain days, and then at last the Vineyard was enlarged with more assertive sunlight, and the rain diminished, and the wind swung around and blew from the southwest. He knew the island would be sunny and pleasant for the next four months. The first flowers were the biggest and brightest, the daffodils and early Asian daylilies, the azaleas, the rhododendrons, the white viburnum the locals called mayflowers, the blossoms he preferred for their fragrance, for the more extravagant the flower, the more modest its aroma. He was no longer tricked by his eye. One of the lessons of blindness was that night-blooming flowers had the most powerful perfume.

After the long winter up-island he prepared himself for summer — the pleasures of spring lasted just a few weeks. Steadman wondered what the season might bring. The winter for him had been perfect: safe and sexual, turning him into an imaginative animal. After his day's work, he ate and rutted and then slept soundly. He woke and blinded himself first thing and resumed his dictation. He felt as confident as a prophet. He spoke his narrative as the book was revealed to him.

His writing was not work — it was his life, flesh made into words, the erotic novel rehearsed at night. He was like someone conducting an experiment on himself, then writing up the results. Blindness was his method and his memory; the drug created in his consciousness a miracle of remembering and invention.

He was most himself in his blindness, an eyeless worm on the move; most himself in his sexuality, and paired with Ava absolutely without inhibition. He was convinced that his sexual history was the essential truth that demanded to be written as fiction.

He was satisfied with his progress so far: enough had been transcribed and printed for him to begin calling it a book. The book contained his world; he inhabited the book. The act of creation became understandable to him: it was brilliant transformation, not making something from nothing, but giving order to his life, turning darkness into light. He knew now that the travel in *Trespassing* was a delusion. There was no travel on earth like the distances he was covering now, locked and blindfolded in his hidden house.

A satisfying solitude was returned to him, and he delighted in its stimulation. For years he had longed to write the fictional counterpart to *Trespassing,* a novel as an interior journey that would also be an erotic masterpiece, wandering across areas of human experience that had been regarded as forbidden — like the sort of fenced-off frontiers he had crossed in his travel book: sex as trespass in the realms of touch, taste, and smell; sex as memory, as fantasy, as prophecy. And fantasy, because it was ritualistic, became something like a sacrament that gave him access to the truth of his past.

He had been so hesitant to go to Ecuador; it had taken an effort of will to submit to the drugs; he had needed to be tempted; he knew it was his last bargain. But the datura had made all the difference, had revealed his book to him, and the months of productive seclusion he had spent since arriving back on the island were the happiest he had ever known.

And he had discovered through the drug's blinding light that the truth was sexual: the source of truth was pleasure itself, fundamental and sensual. Everything else was a dishonest aspect of an elaborate and misleading surface — all lies.

He intended his book as a confession and a consolation. In a world full of desperate and bloody imagery, how could such a thing as sex be shocking? Yet he was interested in describing only the nightmarish intimacies of his sexuality. For the traveler who had gone everywhere else on earth, this was the undiscovered world of his mind and heart, the basis of his being, his inner life revealed, not anyone else's. No one could say, "Not true!" when he knew it was his own truth, that he had risked blindness to understand.

One day in early summer he was with Ava in his library, working on the novel, when she handed a card to him. He framed the card in his hands, then smoothed it, touching the raised lettering with his fingertips, and said, "An invitation. I can just about read it. The Wallaces?"

Ava said, "The Wolfbeins. Party at their house."

The noise Steadman made in his throat, adenoidal, approving, sounding interested, put Ava on the defensive.

Ava said, "You could do without going."

She was the one who usually wanted to attend parties, and when they had stayed away she accused Steadman of being vain, of sniffing at his old friends, of being a prima donna. The Wolfbeins' summer place was in Lambert's Cove, which necessitated a long drive from Steadman's up-island house, and for the past few summers Steadman had avoided such parties. Yet he was interested.

"I think I should go."

"Are you serious?"

"My debut," he said.

"What a word."

"To show myself as I am."

She laughed loudly. "You sound like such a fairy, saying that."

"You don't get it." He was smiling, with his face in front of her, his blank gaze. "I mean go blind."

He could hear Ava's whole body react, seeming to stiffen in objection.

"That's just a stunt," she said.

"I am most myself when I'm blind."

"It's a drug!" Ava said. "You are seeing phosphenes — they exist outside a light source. It's a dazzling delusion, a kind of migraine. And what will you do when it wears off?"

Steadman turned away from her and said, "I have to go there."

He was thinking of the future — his desire to move on, because he needed to distance himself from *Trespassing* and its youthful half-truths. And since taking the drug he had thought a great deal about death. He might die at any time. And the man he was now bore no resemblance to the man people thought they knew. He imagined them praising him in a eulogy, putting themselves in charge of his history, writing his obituary, speculating, for no one was more presumptuous or untruthful than an obituarist.

"No one knows me," he said. "No one ever knew me."

Ava was silent. She did not need to insist or even mention that she knew him, that she was the only one. She said, "Finish the book, if you want to reveal yourself."

He shrugged, because that was obvious and it had always been his intention. He was obsessed with writing the one book that would say everything about him, disclose all his secrets. He would have to call it a novel, because the names would be changed, but the rest, the masquerade of fiction, would be true, for a man in a mask is most himself.

"I want people to see me like this," he said. "My friends, anyway."

"Going to the Wolfbeins' is going public," Ava said. "It's always the A-list."

He was silent again. He could see she wanted a fight. And anyway it was true — he wanted to go public.

"Your blindness is a lie," she said. "It's temporary. The phosphenes are in your brain and your optic nerve, caused by whatever shit is in the drug."

"No," he said.

"A game," she said.

"A choice," he said. "And I want to see these people."

"See?"

"Know them," he said.

3

STEADMAN WORE DARK GLASSES, he carried a narrow white cane. He did not need the cane, except as a prop and a boast. The insect eyes of his lenses and his thick pushed-back hair emphasized his sharp inquisitive face. Ava had chosen his clothes. He could have passed for a stroller at the West Chop Club — white slacks, yellow shirt, white espadrilles, a slender whisking cane.

"You putz," Harry Wolfbein said. And to Ava: "What's with him?"

Steadman said, "Relax, Harry. I'm blind."

A rush of air was audible at the word, and in a vacuum of embarrassment that followed it Wolfbein breathed hard in apology.

Steadman wished only to state his blindness, not discuss it, not be

146

clucked over and pitied. So, to cut him off, Steadman said, "There's some sort of engine noise over there I've never heard before." He gestured beyond the house, toward the big garage. "Transformer, generator — what is it?"

"Bug zapper," Wolfbein said.

Steadman knew he was lying. He said, "Then what's all the auxiliary power for?"

Before Wolfbein could recover and respond, a man entering behind him said, "Oh, God, another rat-fuck."

Recognizing Bill Styron's voice, Steadman greeted the writer and his wife, Rose. They said they were glad to see him. He did not announce his blindness; everyone would know soon enough. As for his dark glasses and cane, the Styrons just smiled in sympathy. In his nonwriting years, as a reaction to his obscurity, Steadman had affected odd habits of dress and behavior, as a defense, so that his raffish eccentricity would be noticed and not his silence.

"Rat-fuck" was the right expression for a party where a mob of people stood and drank and yelled in your face, looking past your head as you looked past theirs, for relief, for escape, for someone better known or wittier. At a certain point a party was just that: a loud room of coarse static, like a rookery of big frantic birds.

The moment he had arrived at the Wolfbeins' house in Lambert's Cove he knew the party was unlike any other summer thrash. He did not discern the contours of people; he understood their essence. He needed to be blind to feel the voltage, the pitch and whine of it, like the whir of a spinning ball of molecules. The furious hum beneath the chatter that drifted from the house kept Steadman listening and in that hum discerning the distinct character of people. If he had not been blind, would he have been aware of the woman — all eager atoms — who had begun to stare at him and stalk him from the moment he stepped onto the front porch?

He heard her heartbeat, he sensed the woman as a pulse in the air, as an odor, a hot eye, in the deepening shadow. And when he drew near her and was surrounded by other guests, she touched him, probably thinking that he would not be able to distinguish her from the others — stroked his arm, touched his mouth, left a taste on his lips. It was not her touch that lingered but an oily dampness, as if her salty sweat-warmed hair still clung to him and got into his nose and onto his tongue. He had caught the animal scent and kept sniffing it, the trail of it that curled from the woman's body like a distinct invitation in all that noise.

As a younger man, Steadman had liked such party loudness for its concealment. The noise was like darkness and made your plea inaudible to everyone except the woman you were imploring. A party was an occasion for a dog-like mating ritual, for bottom-sniffing and innuendo. In a large noisy crowd in which anyone could be touched, a party was a liberating prelude to sex. A crowd became a sort of dance, in a room in which you paired up with someone and got her to agree to see you later, meet you secretly; it was an opportunity, a beginning, an abrupt courtship.

But this event at the Wolfbeins' was not that at all. It was a gathering of older, milder, successful people, all of them friends, and well past the frenzied adulteries of their earlier lives. Steadman was a friend, too, but different in being a year-rounder on an island where summer people believed they mattered most.

The summer-camp atmosphere of the Vineyard in high season was so intense and infantilizing that Steadman hardly went to parties. Besides, when the summer people departed just before Labor Day, the year-rounders were on their own, and it was awkward for them to admit that in the off-season the islanders seldom met except at the supermarket, the post office, or the ferry landing.

"The guest of honor isn't here yet."

"Steadman thought he was the guest of honor."

"Maybe he is, now," Wolfbein said softly, with a new sort of reverence. "It was really nice of you to come, Slade."

The gratitude in Wolfbein's chastened voice Steadman heard as piety — that Steadman, crippled and handicapped, was doing them all a favor by showing up, being brave. Like a limper dragging himself into daylight, the proud damaged man was going public.

If only they had known. Steadman believed himself to be gifted through his blindness, superior to them all, with the power of special insight. He had come just to be visible, to declare his blindness. He was Ishmael, believing that no man can ever know his own identity until his eyes are closed. Steadman thought: No one can ever claim to know me now.

And, as he had suspected, the fact of his blindness at the party gave him a kind of celebrity. The only way to reveal his secret was to present himself here, where most of his friends happened to be, none of them his confidants, since he had none. He was greeted by Mike and Mary Wallace, Beverly Sills and her daughter, Alan Dershowitz, Mike Nichols and Diane Sawyer, Mary Steenburgen, Walter and Betsy Cronkite, Skip Gates, Evelyn de Rothschild and Lynn Forester, Olga Hirshhorn, Ann and Vernon Jordan. He would either keep his blindness a secret or allow these people to know. He could not be selective in telling people on this island, where people talked — did nothing but talk.

"I feel like Zelig," Dershowitz said, bumping into him, then profusely apologizing, before inquiring about the cause of his disability, as though appraising his condition in a bid for a possible personal-injury lawsuit.

"All my fault," Steadman said.

"Our own Tiresias," Styron said with his customary gallantry.

Steadman did not mind being seen as a tragic hero. The only alternative was to joke about his blindness, and he saw that as vulgar ingratiation — not beneath him, but a distortion of how he regarded his blindness. When his book appeared, his true responsibility would be known.

As though commiserating, Wolfbein was talking about someone he knew who had macular degeneration — how sad it was — and Steadman seemed to surprise him by saying, "That might be the best thing that ever happened to him. What's his profession?"

"That's the point," Wolfbein said. "He's a writer, like you. He needs his eyes."

"He doesn't. He'll be a better writer," Steadman said.

"I don't get it."

"Our eyes mislead us," Steadman said.

"I hope you're right."

"You're looking at me as though I'm a cripple," Steadman said. "Your eyes deceive you."

"What do I know?" Wolfbein said, insincerely, helplessly conceding it, as if deferring to a cripple, changing the subject.

Steadman said, "Harry, you're not convinced. You're thinking I am a poor bastard trying to make the best of it, putting a brave face on his handicap, saying, 'Cripples have a lot to teach us!' Because I'm a hopeless case, banging into walls, grinning into empty space, stumbling down stairs, with food on my chin."

"I don't think that," Wolfbein said, but still he sounded insincere.

"'The blind man shits on the roof and thinks that no one sees him,'" Steadman said. "Arab wisdom."

"Don't be a putz."

Steadman could sense the man's uneasiness. Wolfbein was trying to be a friend. He was so overwhelmed by the sight of Steadman, transformed with dark glasses and a white cane, he did not know how to conceal his pity. And so, more than ever, Steadman was sure he had done the right thing in showing up here. He would never have known this otherwise.

But between his up-island house and this party — between the seclusion of his Gothic villa, with its long blind nights and sexual revelations, and the glare of this public appearance — there was nothing. Anyway, wasn't that the point? He was glad to attend such a lavish party, because it allowed everyone he knew here to see at once what had happened to him.

When he had said that to Ava, she had replied, "They're seeing what *didn't* happen to you. Why are you misleading them? This is such crap. You can see perfectly well."

"No. I can see better this way. Only they don't know it."

Ava cringed whenever the partygoers expressed their sympathy for him. And it was worse for her when they commiserated with her, confiding their fears. They clucked and urged him to be brave, and all the while Steadman was laughing and protesting, "I'm fine. I'm working again. I'm doing a book."

Wolfbein said, "No reflection on Ava, but are you seeing a good doctor?"

"I am seeing what is not visible," he said. "And I am seeing more of Ava than you will ever know."

Wolfbein had been joined by his wife, Millie. She kissed him, her large soft breasts cushioning her embrace. She said, "I'm really glad you came."

"So am I," Steadman said. "I didn't realize until I got here that it was such a big deal. Whom are you expecting?"

In the silence that ensued he could tell that she exchanged looks with her husband, hers a meaningful frown that mimed, Who told him?

"It's someone important," Steadman said, sure of himself.

"Whose mind have you been reading?"

"There are so many people here who don't belong. I don't mean guests. I mean lurking heavies, muttering men. The tension, too. Some people suspect, some don't."

He knew Millie was smiling, and he could hear the flutter of her heart.

"All this apprehension," he said. "What are you waiting for?"

"POTUS."

"What's that?"

"Elvis."

"I knew it."

Millie squeezed his hand and left him, and a heavy breather he knew as Hanlon massaged his shoulder, said, "Great to see you" — the blind, Steadman now knew, were constantly being touched. Since arriving at the party he had been pinched, fingered, handled, steered, all by well-intentioned people.

Even Ava touched him when she reappeared. He said, "The president's coming."

"Cut it out," she said, but he sensed her looking around and recognizing the oddities — the generator, the buzzing phones, the extras, who must have been security men.

The president was on the island — everyone knew that — and there was always a possibility of his appearing, since Wolfbein was a friend and a fundraiser. But of all the guests, Steadman alone knew with certainty that it would happen. He understood the voltage that seemed to run through the party, heard the scattered cell phone crackle, the awkwardness of the advance team.

The party guests saw only the people they knew; he saw everyone. The deck and the garden were full of people, but near the big garage and among the trees were the president's support crew and the mute, watchful Secret Service people. Beyond this crowd was another crowd.

Before anyone else, before the Wolfbeins even, Steadman knew that the president's car had drawn up at the front of the house, and after the president was greeted in the driveway by his hosts, Steadman was the first to know when he came near and presented himself. It was a pulsing in the air and a heartbeat — distinctly the president's, distinctly quickening, an ugly flutter of embarrassment.

The moment the president entered the room, Steadman felt a change in the atmospheric pressure. Then some people turned; others were still talking. There was a rattle in the air, an anxiety, the president exposed, prowling yet seeming like prey. The hot concentrated gazes of the guests were all directed one way, making a crease in the room.

"I can't believe he's talking to Mike Nichols."

"Roth," Steadman said.

Philip Roth was chuckling. "Mike is saying, 'I should have put you in my movie. You're perfect. Why did I use John Travolta?' See his face?" Then he clasped Steadman's arm, a bit too tightly. "Oh, Jesus, Slade, I'm so sorry."

But Steadman said, "I can see his face. He looks more complicated than I expected."

The party became circular, electrified and orderly like a magnetic field, the whole house in motion, with the president at the center and the first lady at the periphery, another eddying motion, people wheeling around her.

Noticing that Steadman was carrying a white cane and wearing dark glasses, the unmistakable props of blindness, with his head alert, looking proud in his obvious posture of listening, the partygoers gave him a wide berth, which allowed him to slip nearer and nearer to the current of the force field, toward the president, whom he could make out as a warm pink smiling being, hyperattentive and talkative at the center of a large admiring group.

Likable, friendly, sexually obsessed, everyone knew his traits: charming, needy, subtly competitive, willing to woo, craving power and adulation in such a compulsive way, yet indifferent to personal wealth, not materialistic, funny, intelligent, eager to please. And because of all of this, especially his strange deflecting smile, he conveyed the strong impression of trying to live something down, that he was burdened by secrets.

To Steadman he was like a high school senior from an ambiguous background who fought desperately for influence, eager to charm everyone, to be the student-body president. He had the high school attitude toward money, too — the insight that money was not power, that only persuasiveness and approval were power, and the president craved approval.

The president was speaking in his easy unhesitating drawl to Mike Nichols, an enthusiastic assertion about a movie, but he was also speaking to his dazzled listeners. Steadman approached and at once the group parted for him, and the way the human heat was bulked in that opening conveyed to Steadman the physicality of the man, the confident way he was standing, gripping one man's shoulder, holding a woman's hand. He eased her against him for a photographer, all the while talking to Nichols about the movie, which was *The Barefoot Contessa*.

"I was fourteen, fifteen, just a kid, sitting there in the movie theater in Hot Springs and going like this!"

Steadman saw the self-mocking dumbfounded face and heard the grunt and the appreciative laughter. And then the president reached out and drew Steadman beside him, into the center of the circle of listeners.

"Slade Steadman, Mr. President," a wheezy man said, stepping forward, cutting Steadman off, trying to be helpful.

This meddling was Steadman's first experience of his blindness marking him out as a deaf lump of inert flesh, incapable of fending for himself.

"I know who this guy is," the president said. "How're you doing?"

"Changed a little but doing fine."

"Harry told me you might be coming. I am really glad you could make it."

Steadman replied to the president, but looked at the wheezy man as he said, "I see more than you might think."

"You are one brave guy," the president said.

"You mean these?" Steadman said, and tapped the black lenses of his glasses. "Like Ishmael says, darkness is indeed the proper element of our essences."

He was going to say more, but the president interrupted him. "I mean *Trespassing*. I can't tell you how much I admire it."

"I know you've got taste, Mr. President. Friend of mine, Redmond O'Hanlon, was at Oxford with you and said you had a whole shelf of Graham Greene."

The president touched Steadman again, and like the others at the party kept touching him, as if to reassure him. It was a gesture Steadman had begun to hate in bystanders, for the insult of its pity, for its patronage, its distrust, its intrusive fuss. And yet the president's touch was different — revealing — giving so much away, the man's anxiety and weakness and secrecy in the uneven pressure of his fingers, as though he were steadying himself, drawing off energy and finding his balance by holding on to Steadman.

"I had no idea your vision was impaired."

Another person who did not dare to use the word "blind."

"My vision is excellent," Steadman said. "It's my eyesight that's a little faulty."

"It's not getting you down. That's just great."

"No, because, bad as it might be, it's better than anyone else's."

The president, Steadman saw, needed to be looked at. He was the embodiment of self-consciousness. Every word he said had conviction in it and a suggestion of, Remember this. He had a wonderful please-love-me laugh. He had a way of exaggerating his facial expressions, as though to indicate, I am laughing, I am touched, I am intently listening, I share your feelings.

"I like that. You've got a real good attitude," the president said.

He was all calculation. But beneath the surface of his confident facial expression was a shaky heart and trembly attention, an insecurity, the fear that someone might see what he really felt, what he actually knew — his woe, his close-to-despairing feeling that he might be found out. Standing next to him, Steadman felt these vibrations — that the president needed to keep his secret even more than he needed to be loved for his candor. He was at the core a watchful anxious man who had spent his life being observed, who could not bear unsympathetic scrutiny, who hated to be alone. There was something explosive in him, too, that he was keeping in check. And not one secret but many.

"I will get you the finest doctors," the president said. "We can fix this thing."

How can I help you? was his mantra, because helping people was the key to earning their gratitude, their respect, their support. Steadman liked the man for understanding that power was something that you had to earn, that people gave you, not something you snatched and squeezed from the unwary. The president had been poor. The long climb from poverty, a history of favors asked for and repaid, had given him a sharp memory. He still had aspirations. Even in this easy group of rich well-wishers he was campaigning. Everything about his social posture — his smile, his banter, his kindness, his generous nature — said he wanted your vote.

Someone — a woman, the same woman as before — took Steadman's hand and placed a cold glass into it. Her perfume, the pressure of her fingers, the softness of her skin, the warmth of her hand, the way she brushed him, her soft skirt, her tight thigh — all this told Steadman she was slender and young and sure of herself. And she was aroused — so obvious to him now that he was blind — a hot humid tenderness to her skin, a sticky quality to her lips, and the close dampness of her breath that her perfume did not mask.

"I mean it," the president said, speaking of his offer to help.

"That's very gracious. Thank you, sir."

But the president, who missed nothing, had noticed the woman too, and he was attracted. Steadman realized how other people's reactions were helpful, and now, in these past few minutes, feeling the heated gaze of many people, he had become the center of attention.

Because Steadman had become the most conspicuous person in the room, the president hung on, began needing him — Steadman could sense that, for by being next to him, he was peculiarly visible. That vanity in the president was mingled in a paradox of conceit with sympathy and kindness.

The others' shock was apparent: no one had expected Steadman to show up blind. People who had found him arrogant or distant or offhand now pitied him, and faced him more squarely, emboldened by the strength, a swagger of wellbeing, that onlookers feel in the company of someone frail. For in their judgment Steadman was powerless and lame as a blind man, needing to be steered around by his elbow, no longer a threat or a source of sarcasm; he was impotent, he was pitiable, a cripple, and without help he would trip over chairs and bump into walls.

Steadman smiled at the thought of this, for the truth these people did not know was that he was perhaps a greater threat to their privacy now. He could gain access to and probe any of their secrets, was nimbler and more acute and virile than ever. Nothing was hidden from him.

Holding on to his arm, as much a new pal as a helper, restraining him a little, the president seemed to understand Steadman's insightfulness. He introduced him to a few people — men and women whom Steadman already knew — and in doing so, the president was claiming him as his own, possessing him for his aura, his power to command attention.

The blindness fascinated the president, like a peculiar gift, a unique asset, a signature trait. Which it is, Steadman thought, all of that and more.

Still holding on to him, more tightly now, the president moved him through the party. Steadman understood the president as blind in a simple and old-fashioned way, fearing exposure. The poor man could not see himself at all. He was desperate in clinging to his secrets — secrets that to Steadman were obvious in his whole demeanor. Never mind what the secrets were — they smoldered like half-smothered fires in the president's soul and shone in his fragile and easily readable face.

The president wanted everything, but most of all he wanted to be needed. And so he took charge of Steadman, possessed him and seemed proud, as though he'd captured a country or successfully wooed a woman — he had what he wanted.

He kept touching Steadman with deft slender fingers, and when Wolfbein appeared and introduced people to the president — "Mr. President, I want you to meet an old friend" — the president deflected him, and with Steadman on his arm said, "This is Slade Steadman. I'm sure you know his work."

Steadman had become his prop, his cause, and though the president had put himself in charge, and was big and busy on his behalf, Steadman could see how wounded he was. The man was next to him, holding him, kneading his shoulder. Steadman could feel the warmth, which was more than warmth — the scorching heat and life of his eagerness and something like shame. He was fully alive, but what had he done that had made him so hot with guilt?

His pulse, his touch, told Steadman how appearances mattered to him, how surfaces meant everything, though he was the most watchful human imaginable. Perhaps he recognized this trait he shared with Steadman. He seemed like someone who was forever stalking, with an insatiable appetite, his hunger beyond the hunger of anyone else.

Also, what looked like guilt or shame was neither of those — they did not cut deep enough; it was undiluted embarrassment. He was brave in his secrets, not sorry for them but only fearful of being found out. His need to be fully visible was at odds with his need to conceal, and made him an active and distracting presence for his furtive alertness, and had given his smiling and much too reliable face a profound pinkness.

So he latched on to Steadman, because it proved that he had sympathy and altruism and charity. He was here at a party, not carousing — he hardly seemed to drink anyway, had barely touched his glass — but propping up a blind man, though Steadman was aware that it was really the other way around.

Ava joined them, was embraced by the president — "You're a lucky gal" — and she took Steadman aside to say that she had been talking to the first lady.

"She's amazing — she's lovely," Ava said. "She looks straight at you and tells you exactly what she thinks."

"I saw her when they came in."

Whenever Steadman referred to his seeing something, Ava reacted, made a gesture, not quite doubting, but impatient.

"And what did you notice about her?"

"The snot in her nostril," Steadman said.

As though he had spoken the truth, Ava became defensive. "She's beautiful. She's strong. She really knows him. It's a real team."

But another glance in the direction of the first lady told Steadman that there was almost nothing there except a chill between the husband and wife. She was much poorer at pretending than he was.

"She's his prisoner," Steadman said.

He walked outside, down the stone steps to the lawn. Many of the guests had gone out to enjoy the fragrance of the evening. They were drinking, laughing gently, reminding each other of what a lovely summer it was. "We've been on the island since July Fourth," Wolfbein was saying. Through the slender scrub oaks the Sound was glowing in the last of the sunset.

In the luminous half-dark of dusk on the lawn, a little apart from the other guests, he felt euphoric, seeing everything clearly while unseen and unknown himself. He was reminded of how, in this euphoria, he resembled the celebrated novelist he wished to become, a narrator among his characters. He was convinced of the purposeful insight of his blindness, his apparent blindness, and that at last his novel would be the book he had longed to write.

Sensing someone behind him, Steadman tilted his head to listen. He was touched on the hand by soft, damp, imploring fingers, and his arm groped too, each touch an appeal, a plea, an invitation, the clutching of slender bones. The people who had touched him at the party believed they were unseen, unknown — and they were, except by Steadman, who saw each one, the big bold woman, the sidling blonde, the dark fox-faced woman with searching hands who had crept over and stroked him, announcing herself when he had arrived. She was small — smaller than Ava — and she had touched him without Ava's knowing. And she was back, on the lawn, grazing him again with her hand, her heart beating like mad as she moved quickly away.

Sunset had come fast, a deepening shadow in the sky, a dampness of light dew gathering on the grass. Being touched, in his memory, was like being brushed by the low boughs of leaning trees, by the leaves of bushes next to the path, tumbled thickets and groves growing at the edge of the bluff, its sea grass and sand still holding the dry hum of the day's heat.

And with the darkness, the smoke-stink of flares and torches was more apparent — orangy flames, flat and ragged, on head-high bamboo poles jammed into the ground.

"Down this way!" Wolfbein called out. Looking like a cop in traffic, one arm raised, he directed the guests toward the narrow stony path where, in the flapping light of the kerosene torches, handsome young men in white shirts, employees of the catering company, as orderly and solemn as soldiers, escorted people along the path to the lip of the bluff, where a flight of steps led down to the beach.

"I'm all right," Steadman said when one of the young men reached for him.

Steadman tapped his stick on the wooden treads and looked down, deliberately holding up the other guests, who paused and watched the blind man's slow descent, talking as he stepped slowly.

"Nobska lighthouse," he said, waving his stick at the flickering light across the Sound. Then he looked down. "Checkered tablecloths. Lots of tables. Lanterns. Crimson lobsters stacked on seaweed. A washtub of steamed clams. Buckets of corn. A tureen of chowder. A basin of chopped salad greens. More torches. And the water lapping the table legs."

"That's amazing," someone said, hearing him, and there were supporting murmurs.

"I was at this clambake a few years ago," Steadman said.

"It's still amazing. I hadn't recognized all that stuff until you started describing it."

"Memory is vision," Steadman said, still descending the stairs, and as he spoke he heard Ava groan.

At the bottom of the stairs, Ava said in a low scolding tone, "Why are you calling attention to yourself?"

"That's why I came."

"How can you be so fucking pompous? 'Memory is vision.' Jesus!"

But he was smiling, feeling his way forward. He brushed the piece of paper Ava held in her hand.

"What are you reading?"

"The seating plan."

"Where am I sitting?" he asked.

"You tell me," she said, challenging him. "You can see in the dark, right?"

All this in whispers.

He knew Wolfbein as a friend who would have assured him a good seat — and everyone was extra-nice to the blind. He said, "I'm sitting with the president."

Containing her fury, Ava's body convulsed: he had guessed right. And then he heard her shoes treading the stones on the foreshore as she stalked off to her own table.

And a woman's hand rested on his lower back, a woman unseen by Ava.

Steadman said, "Who are you?"

The woman touching him turned quickly and stumbled slightly on the shingly beach, leaving a wisp of fragrance at the level of his head.

He was the first to sit, and so when the others joined him they spoke to Steadman, positioning themselves in front of his face to address him. Although they were friends, and he knew them as soon as they spoke, they said their names, as though he were feeble — Walter and Betsy Cronkite, Olga Hirshhorn, Bill Styron, Millie Wolfbein, and finally the president, who was finishing a conversation with Vernon Jordan.

"You're going to be fine, man," Vernon said, looming over Steadman, bestowing his blessing before walking on.

"Hello, girl," the president said to Millie, and gave her a hug. Then he said, "Slade's doing good. I think he sees more than we do."

It was true, and he knew it. The president was uncomfortable, Steadman could tell, which was another reason he wanted to possess the blind man and disarm him. He feared the blank stare behind the dark glasses, he feared Steadman guessing his secret. Steadman did not know the details of the secret, only that it was a woman, and because it was sexual the president was both embarrassed and eager. He was happy, he was pink with confusion, rendered younger and more readable — all the grinning traits of being smitten.

So when the drinks were served and the talk turned to movies, the president reminisced about himself as a boy — the interrupted conversation he had begun earlier in the house, about *The Barefoot Contessa*.

Styron said, "I went to high school with Ava Gardner. She was a lovely simple girl, just a farm girl. Came over the state line to Newport News from North Carolina. We called her a Tar Heel."

Steadman said, "You could have taken her to the prom."

"Well, she was a year behind me. But, yes, I could have," Styron said, and he stroked his face as he did when he was self-conscious, and gave his deep appreciative laugh.

The president said, "In that scene where she drops her dress and it just falls. Oh, my."

Everyone at the table was watching the president with pleasure.

He said, "I couldn't breathe!"

The laughter exploded as soon as he spoke, but Steadman saw the truth of the revelation. It was distinctly confessional, and it was also a dream of yearning and power in a crowded movie theater in Hot Springs. Steadman saw a boy in a seat, wide-eyed and with his mouth open, wanting the world.

As the clambake progressed and the food was distributed, the waiters bringing plates piled with corn and lobster and steamers, a group of young men lined up, a dozen or more in identical red shirts. They paid their respects to the president and greeted the diners. One of them, announcing that they were the Tiger Tones from Princeton, took out a pitch pipe and blew a note, and they began to sing. They sang one song after another, old tunes, "Chattanooga Choo Choo" and "Hey, There" and "What'll I Do?"

The president watched attentively, smiling appreciatively, and sang along. He was an unspontaneous man who knew that people were constantly looking at him, and he was at pains to demonstrate that he was just what he seemed, an open and benevolent person who had nothing to hide.

The Tiger Tones' spokesman came to the table and asked the president for his requests — any song he liked.

"You go ahead. You're doing just fine," the president said, which was shrewd, because a request was also a giveaway.

Steadman said, "Do you know Chuck Berry songs? How about 'Maybelline'?"

"Sorry," the young man said, and repeated it more loudly when he noticed Steadman's dark glasses and the white cane propped against the table.

They sang "Up on the Roof."

The president said, "I had Chuck Berry at the White House."

"That's great."

"I could get him for you."

Steadman was touched — not by the offer but by the spirit of it, the sense he had noticed earlier, that the president was saying not "love me" but "please need me."

He was mouthing the words of the songs, appearing to know that everyone was looking at him and he was doing the right thing for them. He would never want to be seen doing the wrong thing, which was why his secret was engrossing to him, and it had to be a forbidden woman, for what else could have made him so pink?

The president was so much *there*, so willing to respond, so quick to read reactions, so present, that he had to be hiding something. Evasion and calculated secrecy were important to him, for he was both puppet and puppet master. But he searched with such close attention, charmed so completely, he took possession.

Only Steadman saw through him, and he was fascinated, as though watching a man balancing on a high wire, while the others at the table spoke to him in such a respectful way. The aged Cronkite, so courtly as he leaned forward, said, "Mr. President, forgive me for wondering, yet I can't help . . ." And the president nailed the question with an even more courteous reply.

The man had something on his mind. He was always a fraction late in his responses, as if the lapse were another voice in his head, distracting him and demanding to be heard. What was he thinking about? Perhaps a matter of national importance, yet Steadman felt deeply that it was something else — an embarrassment, a source of shame and strength.

"Is that the ferry out there?"

Aware that he was being observed by Steadman — uncomfortable under his blind gaze — he seemed to be struggling for relief.

"That's the big ferry," Olga said.

"Might be the *Uncatena*," Betsy Cronkite said.

"Crossing the Sound with a bone in its teeth," Walter said.

Steadman said, "To Woods Hole, just to the left of the flashing light. That's Nobska."

The people at the table stared at him, and the president hitched his chair back on the sand to have a view of Steadman and the things that Steadman described.

"The lights to the west are the Elizabeth Islands. The scoop of darkness is Tarpaulin Cove. To the east, past Nobska, the Falmouth shore, Falmouth Harbor, Falmouth Heights, East Falmouth, Green Pond Harbor entrance, Waquoit, and Cotuit around that flung-out arm of lights."

The president was relaxed and grateful, for scrutiny had been suspended, all eyes off him at the moment.

He said, "That's wonderful. That's amazing."

Steadman then named some of the stars in the northwest sky.

"I don't see a thing!" Olga said.

"Light pollution," Steadman said.

Walter said, "Slade knows these waters well. I like having him on board when we take the *Wyntje* out."

Steadman said to the president, "The white line just offshore is the standing wave in the chop on Middle Ground Shoal. Sort of foaming in the moonlight. Great fishing spot."

The president, seeming to be lost in this conversation, said, "We had a real nice sail yesterday in James Taylor's boat."

Just then a weak blade of light crossed the president's body, and a man looking official, perhaps someone on security detail, dressed in a dark uniform and swiping the ground with his flashlight, crept to the president's elbow and shone the light on a piece of paper that was crumbly and insubstantial. It had to be a fax, for the way it crinkled and did not lie flat.

Now Steadman was more aware than ever of the president's slender, almost feminine hands and long, delicate fingers, his small wrists, his tremulous touch. The fax paper rattled softly as the president read it, looking grave, all his attention on it.

"Keep me informed," he said to the man, who nodded and slipped away.

"There's been an accident," he said, his self-conscious solemnity commanding the attention of the table with its drama — and all around them, on the shore-side tables of the clambake, there was a gaiety that gave this single table the look of a séance. "Princess Diana was hurt in a car crash. Her friend has been killed."

As Steadman touched his watch face — it was a little past ten o'clock — the president was answering questions: "Paris . . . that very night . . . in the hospital . . . No other news."

The president seemed to relax, not in an idle way but with great solid confidence, like a man in an important chair, at the center of things, directing operations, like a captain taking command in uncertain weather and setting a course. And because he was in control of this serious business of leading, no one questioned him or scrutinized him. He was accepted, trusted, needed — he had what he wanted.

Steadman perceived the man's secret through the man's relief; yet the relief was temporary and the secret was a scar on the man's soul, an obsession that had become a wound.

"Do any of you have memories of Princess Diana?" he asked, as chairman of the table. "Some of you must have met her."

This was brilliant — easing the pain of worrying about her injury by remembering the good days, as a whole, healthy memory of something hopeful.

Walter Cronkite said, "There was a rumor going around that she was staying with us in Edgartown and was seen sailing with me on the *Wyntje*, sunbathing on the deck as I steered. My goodness, how I wish that had been true."

"She was supposed to visit the island this summer," Styron said. "Rose said something about it."

The president said, "She had been in touch with me. She wanted to come to the States. She was very concerned about land mines."

Millie said, "I met her in London at a movie premiere. She was really sweet. There was no sign that anything was wrong in her marriage. She might have had a lover. I certainly would have if I had been married to that twerp Charles."

The president smiled. "She came to the White House. She was so beautiful."

Betsy Cronkite said, "And did you dance with her?"

"I wouldn't have missed that for anything."

"Let's toast her health," Styron said.

Millie said, "It would be so horrible if she died."

"But if she did," Steadman said, "my advice is, don't die tonight."

"I had no plans to do that, thank you very much," Olga said.

"But if any of us did, no one would know. It wouldn't be news," Steadman said, realizing that his sightless eyes gave him an importance that transfixed the table. "The papers tomorrow will be full of this story."

"So what if we did die?" Millie said.

Steadman smiled at her and leaned over. "When did Aldous Huxley die?"

No one knew. Steadman could see that the president hated to be asked a question to which he did not have the answer — and by a blind man, who was now the center of attention.

"I have no idea," Olga said, and giggled a little.

The others murmured, but Steadman waited until they had gone silent again and were staring at him. He had begun to enjoy this reverence for his blindness, like the veneration of believers before a mute statue of a deity.

He said, "November 22, 1963."

"The day JFK was killed," the president said.

"And stole the headlines — the whole paper."

"Don't die tonight, dear," Betsy said to Walter.

The president was impressed and pleased, not because Steadman's challenge had given the table more drama and depth, but because the diversion was a relief, obscuring the president's secret.

While the others fretted, Steadman stared at the president and saw him stripped to his nerves. Did he suspect this? He was so sensitive, so quick to know, it was possible. It was clear to Steadman that he was upstaging the president, at the same time as the president closed in on him and held on to him for a photographer, who was passing the table. On the face of it he was making Steadman a poster boy for blindness — Give generously, so this man might see again! — but the reality was that he needed Steadman badly, his sudden celebrity, his inner light, as a cover for his secret passion.

The president became strangely possessive and familiar. All his life he had advanced himself with his knack of making important friends. He remembered everything, less like a politician than like the greatest friend, or a desperate and fearful animal.

Now he had risen from the table and was telling the Diana story to a larger group of party guests, and he had assumed an air of calm authority, in contrast with the misery and panic on the faces of the listeners. The story had already become polished as he spoke to them.

"Just a horrible crash, apparently. And we'll just have to wait and see."

While Steadman listened, the woman returned and touched him again. Steadman sensed that the president saw her. But she was not the only one. Women seemed to be fascinated by Steadman's blindness, for it licensed them to touch him, hold him, steer him, take him in their arms. His sightless face seemed to have a sexual attraction — the women felt freer, almost maternal, liberated from a man's scrutiny of their bodies and their clothes. They were reassuring voices and eager hands.

In what he had called his debut, being visible, his blindness known and gaped at, he began to understand how the women were eager to mother him. More than that, they wished to be seen as mothers in the drama of a pietà, holding his wounded body so they would be judged on their altruism and sympathy, not on how they were dressed.

But he could feel the heat in their desire. They were aroused. They wanted to possess him. He could smell the ripeness of their lust, like raw salty flesh, as they touched him, kissed him like an idol, something inanimate that might be given life through their hands.

The president's back was turned. He was still delivering the Diana news — not much news, but even this small amount had the weight and value of tragedy.

"Can I borrow Mr. Steadman for a minute?"

Steadman knew that touch, those fingers. He listened for Ava, but she was nowhere — the party had broken up in the wake of the Diana revelation. Many people had gone up the stairs from the beach to the house, to see what was on CNN.

The woman guided Steadman into the darkness along the shore, away from the glare of the kerosene torches, nearer the lap of the water and the low hooting of a foghorn. The damp breeze off the Sound was against his face.

"If it weren't for the light pollution, you'd be able to see Buzzards Bay," he said.

The woman was not listening. She took his hand in a commanding way and lifted her dress and touched herself between her legs with his fingers. Her wetness had the slippery feel of a sea creature, a small warm squid, like the fish salad he had poked his fingers into earlier, but warmer, wetter, softer.

Then she lifted his hand and helped him taste it and, still holding him, led him back to where the torches still blazed and the president was still speaking to the people, being reasonable and reassuring.

"She's a fine woman."

But as the president spoke — and he could only have been referring to the woman who had led him away — the woman vanished.

The president led Steadman up the stairs to the house, and the remaining guests followed. Clutching him like this, the president was still revealing himself. He was wounded, carrying this secret inside him, and the secret made him clumsy.

But he said, "Does Harry Wolfbein know how to get hold of you?"

"Oh, yes," Steadman said.

And then, seeing Ava approach, the president let go, and embraced her, and told her again how lucky she was.

The president was hoarse and still talking to a group of people as Steadman and Ava left. Waiting in the driveway for the valets to bring his car around, Steadman was approached by Wolfbein.

"I think you've made a new friend," Harry said.

4

AFTERWARD — as early as the next morning, when he woke to squirm in bed and squint in the dirty slanting daylight — the whispers began. So distinct and so insistent were they, he could hear them from his seclusion: the words, the tone, even the hot breath, the beat and glee of the gossips. Was it the timing — the awful event, the shocking news? Steadman believed he got greater sympathy for clinging to life, or seeming to, because the world was in mourning for Princess Diana, while he stood uncomplaining at the periphery of that tragedy.

Steadman's blindness seemed to make him another object of that outpouring of grief and pity. He was brave, wounded, still alive, a limping survivor, staring at the world with dead eyes. He seemed to represent hope, for there was defiant life in his damaged body, and people were kinder, clinging to him, because of the awful news of this sudden bereavement, the car crash in Paris, which was overwhelmingly the topic in all the newspapers. On the Vineyard everyone was talking about Steadman, too. He drank the datura and the shadow fell over him and he heard them clearly.

The whispers said, *Slade Steadman is blind,* and some went further, explaining, *Slade Steadman, the writer*—Trespassing—*just like that, lost his sight,* as though he had reappeared after many years' absence. Not just showed up but magically materialized, descended from the heavens, covered in glory, his blind eyes blazing like a luminous sky over Buzzards Bay late on a summer afternoon from a profusion of scudding smoke that was a ballooning jumble of gray-bellied clouds and pink plumes and feathers slipping from a great flock of molting flamingos with green-yellow highlights — appropriately lurid for a wounded artist to burst through and step forth from volumes of smoke backlit by fire, a whole sky of it, and pure gold slipping behind all of it, and in the crucible of rising darkness only the gold remaining to drain into the bedazzled sea.

Those were Steadman's images, fanciful, because that is what he imagined they saw, a heroic visitation: the ideal way to show up after all that time. People seemed so glad to see him. And Princess Diana's messy death helped give contrast, for her departure — the public sacrifice of a cheated wife, a slighted heroine, a sidelined royal, a celebrated risk taker — had made him seem a survivor against the odds.

Fearing his affliction, the whisperers wanted to care about his life, they wanted to help, they were manipulative and bossy, they knew eye doctors, they had heard of miracle cures, and they mentioned the possible causes — infected cataracts, macular degeneration, diabetes. Their caring was part of a ritual of warding off the evil of the misfortune. They were so relieved that the shocking ailment was his and not theirs.

The whispering was not all praise, not only amazement. Some of the whisperers were oddly gladdened — because they had been spared, gloating over their good fortune — others were appalled. Some whispers were dark, some blaming, mocking his foppishness, his hat, his cane, his arrogance — his spelling out what he saw in the Sound, like a deaf man whistling Mozart. Some envious guests exaggerated his conceits, for Steadman had been sitting with the president, and what they knew about him they had learned secondhand or had glimpsed in the twilight at the clambake.

The whispers made him a marvel, a freak, a figure of obscure power, somewhat remote even to his friends, known for his arrogance, who was both pitied and feared. He knew that on the Vineyard he was celebrated less for his book than for his being a multimillionaire as a result of the clothing catalogue. So it often happens with such tragedies: in their panic and ignorance people look more closely at each other and notice how frail they are, how damaged and failing, and give thanks for being alive in the shadow of death. Alert to his blindness, saddened by the death of Diana in the mangled car, people went on whispering.

In the succeeding days of gossip Steadman relived the fame he had known as a new resident of the Vineyard, when he had been in the headlines and had kept himself hidden. He was reminded of his notoriety, the fatness of it, his pleasure in the enigma of being satisfied, seeking nothing. Yet there was a great difference, for he was aware that the renewed interest in his work contained a deeper respect, and his writing was now a larger achievement because it was an aspect of his blindness. The handicap he had surmounted was now seen as a strange gift, and in his sad eyes a sort of holiness.

All this in less than a week. Steadman heard the whispers before anyone actually called. He knew that something amazing had occurred, his coincidental link to the death of Princess Diana by his having been sitting at a Wolfbein clambake with the president when the flunky appeared with the fax and the flashlight. The people at the president's table had been among the first in the entire world to learn the terrible news. These few people were the earliest whisperers, and they approximated the curious admonition of the blinded Steadman, saying to the president and others: *Don't die today. No one will remember.*

At last the phone rang, acquaintances called — he had no close friends. Most were the people from the Wolfbeins' party, the inner circle of celebrities, who lived at such a remove from the ordinary, and kept to themselves, that Steadman was sure the news of his blindness would not travel far, at least for the time being. But because of their celebrity these people would eventually carry the news to the wider world. Soon everyone would know.

In some of the commiserating calls there was a note of concern, less for Steadman than for the speaker, who nearly always sounded fearful and somewhat vulnerable. Steadman wondered if what they feared was the insight granted to him by the crisis of his serious condition — how losing his sight made him especially watchful and alert. He was no longer the aloof and arrogant money man. He was an extraordinary victim. And what could these helpless people say to console him? The truth of the world of mortals is that people fall ill and weaken and die. As a wounded man Steadman was nearer to death than to life, and was reminded of his fate, and so life meant more to him, and he knew more of it and was a hero.

In a few of the phone calls he heard something rueful, almost a lament, bordering on jealousy, for on this island of celebrities his sudden handicap contributed to his being a greater celebrity, as though blindness were not a sickness at all, not a defect, not a disability, but a sort of distinction conferred on him, something to be resented and envied.

He was indifferent. No one knew him well enough to understand the truth of his blindness or the prescience it allowed him. All that mattered was that when the fact of his blindness became common knowledge, as he knew it would, and his name as a writer became known again, he could honestly say that he was working on a book and that his blindness had helped him resume his work.

To be writing was to be alive, to wake up happy and to pick up where he left off. His thinly fictionalized narrative expressed the deepest part of himself, exploring the farthest recesses of his memory, his oldest and most enduring feelings, in the ultimate book of revelation. He knew many writers who had published whole shelves of half-truths and evasions, made-up tales, fables, and concoctions. Sometimes it seemed that was all that writers did — spin yarns. "I'm doing a novel." "I'm working on a story." "I'm trying to develop an idea." But if you used your own blood for ink, and what you wrote was the truth, and your life was the subject, one novel was enough; there was nothing else to know, no more to see, a heart laid bare. So he believed.

What disconcerted Ava was that in the days following the party the callers were mainly women. First were the wives of Steadman's male friends, inquiring in the kindest way, and then the women he had known for a while before Ava, more oblique than the others, summer women, the unattached, the available ones, the speculators, the still-pretty, the newly divorced. Finally, the urgent callers, women who were strangers to him, who kept to the fringes of the Wolfbeins' circle, and these were the most insistent on seeing him soon.

"I want to help you."

What one woman said one morning, demanding, offering everything — this mothering, rescuing, bossing — stood for all the long conversations. Steadman took the calls while Ava sat nearby, halted in her dictation, glaring into the middle distance where the tape recorder lay turned off, exasperated, in an accusing silence, resenting the calls, hating every second of his being on the phone. All this was the consequence of his showing up at the party.

"That's very kind of you."

"Anything." Was this the woman who had touched him, embraced him, offered herself to him at the party? "What can I do?"

"I'm busy at the moment."

"I know how tough it must be for you."

She was kind but persistent, like so many of them. There was something awful in the tone of the pitying people he knew, who possessed the clinging manner, hectoring voice, and unstoppable intrusiveness of telemarketers.

She said, "I could meet you today — this afternoon. Or later. Tonight I am completely free."

Not hearing the words but somehow knowing, Ava sighed, exhaling harshly, amplifying her breath through her wide-open mouth, almost loud enough to be heard over the phone, making Steadman self-conscious.

"I have to go," he said. "I'm working."

Yet before he could resume his dictation, before Ava could make an unanswerable remark in a tone of scolding pity, the phone rang again.

"Slade — I feel I know your work well enough to call you Slade." Another woman. "I've had an enormous amount of experience with visually impaired people."

She was young, sweet-voiced, solicitous. Steadman imagined beautiful skin, lips close to the receiver in her damp hand, her tense receptive body slightly canted to listen to him.

"My vision is not impaired," he said.

"I could read to you. I'd love that."

Ava wanted him to bang down the phone, he knew. But he could not move the phone away from his ear — he kept it clapped against his head. He was fascinated: the woman was offering herself, pleading *Take me*.

"Where did she get the number?" Ava said.

She knew the caller was a woman, knew what she was saying, knew everything, which was why she was angry at the intrusion.

"Tell your friend that I care about you" — the woman had heard Ava's question and was answering it. "All telephone numbers are available if you know how to access them."

"Tell her —" Ava began to interrupt, but was cut off.

"There are no secrets," the woman said. And just before she hung up: "I'm here for you."

Then Ava said, "I was afraid of this."

"Women chasing me?"

"Your calling attention to yourself. That charade at the Wolfbeins'."

"'There are no secrets.' That's what she said."

"That should worry you."

Pretending to sort his papers, aligning his pens and pencils, squaring up a set of notepads, moving the tape recorder, he said nothing and hoped she would stop.

But she spoke into his face: "Because there's nothing wrong with your eyes. You haven't even been to the eye doctor. Out of some weird look-at-me bravado, you went to a Vineyard party pretending you were a blind sage and got the president of the United States to believe you."

"It was worth it."

"Because you had the best seat in the house to get the lowdown on Diana's death trip?"

"No. The president. I saw into his soul."

"Oh, please."

Ava began to snort, jeering at his pomposity, the grand manner that seemed a posturing part of his blindness. The manner itself was another form of blindness.

But Steadman merely stared at her with his dead eyes and waited for her to stop, knowing that if he persisted in his scrutiny he could unnerve her by boring a hole into her skull with his blank patience. And he felt that maybe he had succeeded, that she was taken aback, because she stopped challenging him with mockery, and when she spoke again she did so in a more reasonable tone.

"When you say things like that I don't know whether to laugh or start worrying about your sanity."

"He's tormented," Steadman said. "I really pity him. A part of him is lost and he doesn't want anyone to know it. Imagine the dilemma: the man with the secret is the most conspicuous person in the world."

"What sort of secret?"

"Something forbidden, something that shames him, like being helpless, smitten." Steadman's blank gaze was still fixed on her. "Cuntstruck."

Ava said, "I'm sure the president would be reassured to know that you care."

"I agree, strangely enough. Everything matters to him. He's very thin-skinned. And very tenacious. He came from nowhere. And he wants to be a hero."

"Maybe that's what you have in common."

The phone rang before Steadman could reply, and he snatched the receiver as he had all the other times, before Ava could intervene.

It was a different woman. She said, "You touched me," and hung up.

"I hate this," Ava said, seeing the expression on Steadman's face. "You're pathetic and they're sad."

She told him angrily that he was deluding himself in enjoying the phone calls from these strange women. Instead of being strengthened by his blindness, as he had maintained, he had the egotism of an invalid, demanding attention and wanting to be cosseted and needing for his infirmity to be noticed.

"'Look at me — blind as a bat!'" Ava said, satirizing him. "You love it."

He wondered if this was true. Yes, he had liked being noticed at the party. It had reminded him of the great days when he had been a celebrated prodigy.

"So I'm as vulgar and susceptible as everyone else — so what? Hey, what about the president?"

"You liked upstaging him."

"Probably," Steadman said. "Then Diana died and upstaged us both. What a night."

He knew that Ava was still staring at him, still annoyed, from the way she breathed.

She said, "Not everyone wishes you well."

"What does that mean?"

"I'm sure there are people who are glad you've been taken down a peg, and others who suspect you're faking. Anyway, why haven't you asked me to find you an eye doctor? I could refer you to a specialist."

"You think I'm faking," he said. "You've been cold."

The party and all the gossip afterward, the fact of his having reappeared among all those people, this abrupt visibility, were jarring, and so their evenings were changed. The sexual masquerade at night, the delicious routine, was over for now. His being with Ava, blind, for the hours of that party, the president's arm around him, had had a powerful effect — had sobered them, made them self-conscious, kept them from their usual intimacy. More than that, all this had let blinding light fall on them and exaggerate the space between them.

"I guess so. You're someone different."

"I'm writing again," he said.

Until that night of visibility he had felt that this woman was also inhabiting his skin. He had loved the intensity of their seclusion, loved the shadows over them, the shadows within, the shadows they threw in the bedroom. But going public for the first time since arriving back from Ecuador, and being noticed, even praised for his handicap, had altered things. It was a change of air. Allowing other people into their lives, they had revealed Slade's secret, the spectacle of his blindness, shocking everyone with the obvious ailment and keeping the deeper truth hidden.

"It's a trick," she said.

Not blindness at all, she went on, but a state of luminous euphoria brought on by a jungle potion. You reached for a bottle, you took a drink, and you were in a brighter, blazing room, and the room opened onto the world.

That last telephone call ("You touched me") had exasperated Ava and left Steadman murmuring. They faced each other, seeing only the walls.

"Deny that it's a trick," Ava said.

But Steadman had no denial, nor anything else to say. Then, nagged by what he remembered, he said, "What do you mean, eye doctor? Why should I go to an eye doctor?"

"You have a condition without a name."

"It's called blindness."

"Blindness is a result, an induced condition, because you've been taking that drug," Ava said. "Or why else do you have it?"

Steadman turned away and stumbled slightly, hating his unsteadiness, resenting Ava's accusations and wishing that he was dictating his book to her instead of listening to her. She was still talking!

"Blindness always has a cause. It has an etiology, a pathology. Do you want a lecture on the visual cortex and the neurological basis of visual imagery? Blind people are always experts on their condition. They lecture doctors about retinitis and macular degeneration, they know all about PET scans and functional MRIs. About cataracts, the various ways of operating, the recovery time, the risks of infection."

"So what?"

"For you it's metaphysical. It's mystical. All you do is gloat over your blindness. You love the attention. You love people talking about you and calling you. Those sentimental women."

"They don't ask why I'm blind."

"But the president did. I saw you squirming and evading the question. He wanted to help you. He wants to find you a doctor. You looked ridiculous in your hemming and hawing."

"He understood that I'm blind. He also understood that I'm hypervisual, I'm prescient. I see more than anyone. I could smell his anxiety, I could hear it when he was talking about something completely unrelated — his mention of Chuck Berry. I could differentiate people at the party by their smell alone."

"Do you want people to know that you got your blindness out of a bottle?"

Now he saw what she was hinting at. She was right: going to the party had exposed him to the possibility of questions he couldn't answer truthfully. And there would be more questions. He needed a better explanation; he needed a story.

"They want to help you," Ava said, and she laughed at the thought of it, but it was a shallow, wounded laugh.

"What would be the point of seeing a doctor?"

"So that you can say you've seen a doctor."

"You're a doctor."

"I'm the blind man's lover."

5

HE WOKE much too early, seeing the whole day ahead in Boston and feeling cross, thinking of how he loathed medical doctors, their absurd authority, their bossy arrogance, their airs — you were familiar, they were formal; you were small, they were large: "Wait here, Slade, the doctor is busy at the moment." A doctor posed as a figure of power and wisdom, knowing how to ease pain and cure sickness and save lives. Those skills were like a higher form of plumbing, mastered by earnest drudges, yet they regarded themselves as shamans and did not want to be judged like ordinary mortals. They hated their learning to be called into question, and they never listened.

Ava was different from every doctor he had ever known. She read books for pleasure, she did not advertise herself as a doctor, and she did not disagree with him when he declared that doctors caused illnesses, that hospitals were disease factories, that most new drugs were poorly tested and overprescribed. Doctors made people sick with dirty drugs. The ideal doctor-patient relationship was his love affair with Ava, or the Secoya shaman's with his ayahuasca-taker. To be humbled by the chanting shaman and granted visions by his drug — that was the purest healing.

That week of revelation on the Aguarico River reminded Steadman that they had not left the Vineyard since arriving back from Ecuador last November — had been buried alive all winter and spring and into the summer, those dazzling months of work and sex. And then at nine, starting for the airport, Ava at the wheel, Steadman furious in the passenger seat, scowling at an impenetrable line of traffic they were trying to join, they came to a dead stop at the junction of his country lane and the main road.

Summer people in crawling cars, sunburned and squinting in impatience, children's bored bobbing faces at the windows — an unbroken line of cars going nowhere. Disgusted by all these intrusive strangers in their Jeeps and minivans and truck-like vehicles with big wheels and bumpers and bike racks, only ten minutes into the trip, Steadman regretted agreeing to the eye appointment in Boston.

"Take the shortcut." He was staring at her leg, praying for it to articulate her gas-pedal foot.

"I can't even get into the traffic."

Trying to force a space for herself, Ava eased the car forward, but when a Range Rover hesitated and a space opened, a man on a moped darted into it, as though sucked into a vacuum, and after him a procession of bikes — dad, mom, wobbling kids, and another adult in skin-tight spandex on two wheels towing a bike trailer. Then the urgent inching cars closed the gap. A red-faced woman in the passenger seat of a convertible peered at Steadman, and with her arms folded and her head forward she opened her mouth wide, her nose pinched white, and yawned irritably, with a coarse goose-hiss that he could hear.

"Go home!" he called out.

The woman smacked her lips and blinked and calmly mouthed the words "Fuck you."

Ava sighed at the slowly moving line of cars and headed into them, forcing open a space angled sideways, in the path of oncoming cars, but still only half inserted, for the traffic had stopped again in what was a two-mile backup into Vineyard Haven. The shortcut to the airport was still almost a mile away.

Mopeds veered in and out of the stopped cars, cyclists bumped along the side of the road, and two women jogged ostentatiously past, sweat-soaked in their scanty clothes — a dog barked at them, thrusting its loose spittle-flecked jaws out of a car window, sounding outraged. Someone's radio — the convertible in front? — was very loud, and among the unmoving cars in the still summer air someone's cigar smoke reached Steadman and Ava.

"The president was puffing a cigar at Wolfbein's, did you see?" Ava said, just to make conversation, because the delay was so serious and she wanted to calm Steadman's anxiety about the plane they had to catch.

"What the fuck is this traffic all about?"

Steadman's anger was a gumminess in his mouth and grit in his eyes and his guts churning with frustration. He felt like an innocent loosed upon a mobbed and noisy world. He was upset and angrier for the way that Ava, with that pointless cigar remark, was trying to distract him from the bikes, smoke, noise, strangers, New York license plates, joggers, the leafy road blocked with cars — and the most annoying thing about slow traffic was the visibility of bumper stickers on the SUVs. The more expensive the vehicle, the more frivolous the message.

"Look at the size of them. They're made for jungles and deserts."

Ava said, "That reminds me. The agency wants you to sign off on a proposal from Jeep for some kind of Trespassing Limited Edition. Like the Eddie Bauer Ford Explorer."

He imagined the vehicle in the Trespassing style, the safari look, the earth tones, the sturdy seats, the loops and brush guards and compartments, the compass, the altimeter, the gear bags, the khaki, the canvas patches, the leather details. All this because he had written a book. He went sad and silent.

Ava said, "Anyway, there's another flight at noon," and kept on, sounding hopeful, offering consolation, until she became aware of the silence from Steadman.

Gazing straight ahead, smiling slightly, licking his lips, Steadman held a small bottle in his hands that Ava could tell was empty.

"What did you just go and do?"

Instead of replying to that, he said, "The traffic's moving" — though it wasn't — so he added, "A mile down the road," for he was blind again, in another dimension of understanding, relaxed, seeing past the jammed-up cars and the bikes, and calculating that they would easily make the flight.

At the airport, Steadman was smiling behind his dark glasses as they checked in.

"Just carry-ons," Ava said to the woman behind the counter tapping the computer keyboard.

Steadman said softly, as though to himself, "That traffic was in my head."

Swishing his white cane, he loped confidently toward the small plane, ahead of Ava but following the other boarding passengers.

"Brother Steadman, how're you doing?" a man said from one of the forward seats.

"Bill," Steadman said, recognizing Styron's voice and, sensing him begin to rise from his seat, "Please don't get up."

"You're doing just fine," Styron said. "Wasn't that a great party at the Wolfbeins'?"

"A historic occasion."

"You made it so. You're a brave guy."

"Cut it out."

"No, you're a trouper. I was fetched by the sight of you talking to the president. He was mighty impressed, too."

Ava's embarrassment was visceral — Steadman sensed it powerfully, feeling what she felt, tightening like a cramp, reproaching him, and he said, "Please don't say that, Bill. I'm the same as always, maybe a little brighter."

"You're right here, sir," a woman said — the flight attendant, Steadman knew, directing him to a seat on the aisle. Ava took the window seat.

Steadman was aware of being close to Styron, just behind him, an odor, a mutter, the crunch of Styron's folding a thick newspaper, the sense of his fragile fingers, his knuckles on the crease.

"You going to Boston, Bill?"

"Just to change planes," Styron said. "Susanna's filming *Shadrach* in North Carolina. She invited me down."

"I'm seeing a doctor at the Mass. Eye and Ear Infirmary."

"I hope it's good news."

"Whatever. I'm happy."

"That's what I mean by brave."

And again the contraction, the cramp of shame from Ava beside him, though they were not even touching. But he resented her reaction now, like an intrusion into his serenity.

"I'm working on a book."

"That means everything," Styron said.

They taxied, the small plane's wheels bumping; they took off, as though suddenly caught and lifted by a sling of wind, and the aircraft twisted and vibrated, the engine noise filling the compartment until they were well aloft and cruising, bumped by hidden angles of clouds and gulps of air.

"I could fly this thing."

"Sure you could," Styron said, with magnanimous authority and a little chuckle.

Steadman threw off his seat belt. He hoisted himself from his seat and walked to the cockpit door, which was propped open.

"Hi, Captain."

The noise was loudest here, the pile-driver racket of pistons and propellers, but one of the pilots sensed him standing at the door. He smiled when he saw the white slender cane and the dark glasses, the Panama hat, the elbows out, head upright, face forward, ears cocked, in a blind man's alert posture, a listening animal.

"Why are you flying along the canal? That's not your usual flight path."

"Incoming traffic's stacked up to the west because of weather. We've been given a slot on the south-facing runway, so we'll make an easterly approach. Hey, how did you know our bearing?"

"Sunshine," Steadman said. "The canal entrance is down there. The Sandwich power plant. The harbor. The marsh. The dunes to the east. Scusset to the west — and now we're banking toward Plymouth. Duxbury coming up, and we're hitting the headwind, northwesterly today —"

"Better take your seat, sir."

"Let me spell you at the controls."

Shortening his neck in apprehension, one pilot hunched forward, gripping his wheel protectively, while the other pilot kept his gaze on Steadman, looking alarmed at this smiling talkative blind man offering to fly the plane.

"Move over," Steadman said, nudging the man with his cane.

"I'm going to have to insist that you return to your assigned seat and fasten your seat belt," the man said, seeing himself and the copilot reflected on the mirror lenses of Steadman's glasses.

"You think I can't fly blind? I can fly better blind."

"We'll be landing in just a few minutes, sir," the pilot said, as though to a madman.

"I knew that," Steadman said, and tapped his cane again. "Marshfield, North River —"

"Step away from the controls!"

At last, Ava touched his arm and said, "Please, Slade."

Returning to his seat, he brushed the terrified and anxious body of the flight attendant, who asked Ava in a murmur whether he was all right.

Ava was too embarrassed to mention any of this in front of Bill Styron, and was relieved when they had landed and said their goodbyes and were in a cab a few minutes later. She was about to raise the subject of his bizarre behavior in the cockpit when, going through the Sumner Tunnel, Steadman took charge, saying, "Take a hard right after the exit. We're going to Quincy Market. I'll tell you where."

"Nothing wrong with your eyes, sir," the cab driver said. His own dark eyes and big nose and part of his smile filled the smeared oblong of the rearview mirror.

"Right here," Steadman said, and then, as if reading the signs but without looking at them, "Martignetti Liquors. La Rosa Deli. Mama's Pizza. The Big Dig labyrinth."

Silenced by Steadman's talk, the cab driver began to frown, as though he were being mocked.

"Stop here. We'll walk."

"You said Quincy Market."

"But you're not moving. The Union Oyster House is on a one-way street. It's quicker to walk."

Then he was out of the car and Ava was paying the fare. The driver was nodding at the side mirror and saying, "Where's the fire?" Steadman had hurried ahead, and when Ava caught up with him he was striding, slashing his cane at the sidewalk.

"Why are you doing this?"

He didn't answer, he walked ahead of her, whipping his cane, scattering the other strollers, who, noticing that he was blind, seemed to regard him with a mixture of fear and awe. Farther on, he reached toward the bow window of the Union Oyster House and felt along the single panes, the thick cracked paint, and tapped his way into the entrance.

A man and woman leaving the restaurant stepped back at the sight of this tall blind man — dark glasses, one arm outstretched, the other swishing a white cane, digging its ferrule into the threshold. A young waiter swept by him and bowed, almost genuflected, and said, "Right this way, sir." Steadman followed the ingratiating voice to a side booth. A dangerous-looking man was always "sir."

Ava was sliding into the seat as Steadman said, "Too near the bar."

"The bar is empty, sir."

"I don't want all those stools and bottles in my face."

The waiter was probably thinking, But you're blind!

"What about there?" Steadman's white cane swung like a compass needle to indicate an empty table.

"Reserved, I'm afraid."

Steadman peered at him and said, "Has it escaped your notice that I'm blind?"

"I think we can accommodate you, sir," the young man said, clearing two of the four place settings from the table in a clatter of silverware. "I'm Kevin. I'll be your waiter today. May I offer you a cocktail?"

Ava was tense, silent, fearful of what Steadman might say next, for he had an unsettling habit of joshing waiters, being amiable and ironic and overfriendly, which was worse than being stern, for it threw them off and sometimes insulted them. But he tapped the menu without looking at it.

"No cocktails," he said. "I'll have a dozen oysters and a bowl of chowder."

"The lobster chowder is my personal favorite."

"Then why don't you order it, Kevin? I'm having the clam chowder."

Ava said, "Lobster salad and a glass of iced tea," and when the waiter had gone, "Slade, I wish you would calm down."

"I'm blind. I'm in another world from you. Maybe you shouldn't have come."

She considered this. It was true that he had noticed things she had missed, but he seemed not to notice much that was obvious. He was especially sensitive to textures, odors, and voices.

"I hate it when people talk on cell phones in restaurants."

After scanning the room, Ava finally located a man holding a cell phone to his ear at a far table; but she could not hear him.

"And those people in that booth are whispering about me."

As soon as the oysters on the half shell were served, Steadman ran his fingers around the plate, counting the shells, and without hesitating selected the bottle of Tabasco sauce from the cluster of condiments and sauces at the side of the table. He shook drops on each oyster and then, squeezing a lemon wedge, passed it over the plate in a circular motion. His hands, held high, fussing a little, exaggerated the act, calling attention — and it was true, those women in the nearby booth (how did he know they were in a booth?) were whispering and commenting on Steadman's precise gestures.

"You're showing off," Ava said.

"I'm in Boston."

"I like you better at home."

"Do you really?"

He could tell she was trying to humor him. She ate quickly and nervously, feeling observed, apprehensive because of Steadman's impulsive behavior. His blindness made him an extrovert, excited him, gave him a look of stealth and adroitness. He glided like an animal with night vision, even sniffed and held his head like a hypersensitive animal. Blindness sharpened his senses, but it also seemed to change his manner of walking and moving. He had a clear recollection of seeing a Secoya man emerge from the jungle on the banks of the Aguarico and thinking: I have never seen a man walk like that. Then, he had not been able to say what made the man's walk so unusual, but now he knew it was a gait of total alertness.

Hurrying from the cab to the restaurant, Steadman had had a similar skating walk, though his posture was straighter — his blind gestures were less tentative, more assertive and fluid, his gaze steadier and more intense, his head angled to hear better, for his eyes were empty. He seemed to see with his face, his lips, the surface of his skin, his fingertips, receiving pulses from the air.

"I've never been to Boston as a blind man."

He hated Ava's taunt — "showing off" — as though he needed to perform! He could see her so clearly now with his tongue, with his teeth, with his forehead, with his nose.

"The city's the same," she said.

"It's different for me. I see more, so I'm responding differently. Why are you making me say this? I hate to explain things. It smells of building in progress — the stink of destruction, diesel oil and pulverized cement. All that and the discontent of tourists, the way they prowl, so uncertain. Most of them are lost. This restaurant, filled with strangers. It's disconcerting. Because I'm not lost."

"We should have taken a later plane. Your appointment isn't until two."

"I like having the spare time. You're in a different city from me at the moment," he said. "You're sleepwalking."

"See what I mean? Bullshit."

"I am fully awake."

"You're wired."

"Because of all the talk. I hear too much. Blindness bothers bystanders. They want to help, they don't know how, they're worried I'll fall on my face. I heard someone say, 'Look at that blind man, how fast he's walking.'"

"I think you were doing it on purpose."

That was partly true, he knew, but he objected to the onlookers because they gaped without any comprehension; did not know enough, didn't see how clever he was. He wanted to be noticed, perhaps feared, or at least be seen as someone powerful. He felt deserving of praise, not pity: he saw more than any of them.

Ava said, "I think you're secretly enjoying yourself."

"I went to school in this city," he said. "Scollay Square and the Old Howard used to be right up the street. Burlesque, strip shows, Irish saloons. Two streets away from here at the market I remember horses and pushcarts and vegetable sellers. My father used to take me, not for local color but to buy fresh fish." He moved his plate away. "Fresher than this."

"You've got two oysters left."

"Bad ones."

"They look all right."

"That's the trouble. But they're poison." He turned aside, for the waiter had appeared with the dessert menu and he knew the man had heard his last words. He pointed to the plate and said, "They're dead. Give them a decent burial."

After lunch, with an hour more to kill and Steadman still restless, inquisitive, needing to move, they crossed City Hall Plaza to Cambridge Street — "It's heartless. It's a cheat. It's a stage set" — and walked all the way to Charles. They passed the turnoff to the Mass. Eye and Ear Infirmary, threading their way among the taxis and ambulances and waiting people — some of the people looking damaged and newly mended, with bright white bandages taped over their eyes. Steadman hurried ahead of her.

"Where are you going?"

Saying nothing, making a show of his blind man's ability to move quickly, he picked up his pace, crossed the main road, kept walking, found the Fiedler Footbridge ramp with his cane. He moved swiftly on the arch, over Storrow Drive, toward the sound of splashing and a racket of eager screamy voices. Without hesitating, he made a shortcut across the lawn to the chainlink fence at the perimeter of the public swimming pool. He stood there, his arms high, his fingers hooked to the fence.

"I used to come here as a little kid, before we moved back to the Vineyard," he said as Ava caught up and was next to him. He was gratified, feeling superior when he sensed Ava was out of breath.

The swimming pool was a confusion of caged-in shrieks and chattering laughter, the slap of bare feet running on the cement apron of the pool, the explosive plunges — the noise and water and youthful exuberance, high spirits amounting almost to frenzy — and amid the howling the occasional shrill tweet of the lifeguard's whistle, the smack and rap of the diving board stuttering on its chocks whenever anyone prepared to dive. In the heat and the sunshine and the full-throated screams, there was pushing and shoving — no serious swimmers, only jumpers and splashers, kids fooling.

"They excited me," Steadman said, seeing the past, "all those skinny flat-chested girls in tight, too small bathing suits, with pruny fingers and blue lips, running and shrieking. I could see that they weren't afraid to take risks."

A thin pale-legged girl exactly matching Steadman's description loudly dared a boy to push her off the edge of the pool.

"They were the nakedest girls I knew. I used to squeeze them and touch them underwater. When they laughed I knew they wanted me to fondle them. One of them reached into my bathing suit and touched me and I was in heaven. Her little fingers finding me in all that water."

Still hanging on the fence, he smiled at the splashing and the howls, boys shouting like monkeys, girls' meaningless shrieks and joyous objections, the free-for-all.

Then Steadman's tone hardened, and in a flat urgent voice he said, "There's a kid in trouble. Over there. He's going under. You see him?"

At first Ava saw nothing but the mass of heads, the wet hair and beating arms in the pool, but one boy was saying nothing in the churning water, was not even struggling, just sinking at the deep end and — his mouth was open — giving a barely audible groan of surrender that was like a helpless and sorrowful farewell.

"Help him!" Steadman called out, in a demand so loud he silenced the cluster of boys and girls on the other side of the chainlink fence.

In the brief silence, the groan came again as a watery solemnity, a softer whisper of goodbye, and now Ava yelled, and when she caught the lifeguard's eye, she pointed toward the struggling swimmer.

The lifeguard threw off his baseball cap, vaulted from his high chair, and leaped behind the drowning boy. In the same movement he seized him and boosted him to the edge. The boy, all loose arms and legs, looking indignant and in shock, resisting the help in his bewilderment, began to choke and weep, miserably spewing water.

"We're done here," Steadman said, and turned, hurrying ahead of Ava, tapping his stick toward the hospital.

6

PEOPLE PUSHING CANES and shuffling behind him, wearing eye patches and dark glasses, circulated in the hospital lobby, looking just like Steadman. But every one of them had a guide, moving slowly on the tucked-in arm of a spouse or nurse. "This way." "Over here." "Be careful." They seemed so feeble that Steadman was determined to keep walking alone among them, ahead of Ava. And now Ava let him lead.

She was appalled and impressed, seeing how he moved with conviction, commanding the space in front of him by sweeping it with his cane and taking long strides, shouldering through the crowd, half of it aimless casualties. The blind and near-blind kept close to the walls, out of the way, and Steadman's only collision was with a fully sighted man laughing into a cell phone. Steadman spoke the word "asshole" and raised his elbows and walked on, ignoring the man's apologies.

They reported to the reception desk, summoned by a woman at a computer terminal. Ava took the folder of forms and began filling them out.

"He's here for his physical."

"Are you family, ma'am?"

Ava kept writing, did not look up. She said, "You can call me Dr. Katsina."

"Just take a seat," the woman at the computer said when the completed papers were handed over.

The doctor kept them waiting. They sat in awkward, unwilling postures among magazines that were wrinkled and damp, having been picked through by so many anxious fingers. Hearing their names, people got slowly to their feet and entered small rooms to be examined. Steadman saw them as poor, weak, naked flesh, struggling to stay whole, flunking their tests, humiliated in their failure.

"I don't even know why I bothered to come here," Steadman said. "I know what the verdict will be."

"I wish I knew."

"That's what I'm saying. They won't have the slightest idea."

Saying this, he stood — he was being summoned by a stammering receptionist. He was aware of the voice a fraction of a second before Ava heard anything.

"Follow me, please," the receptionist said. And to Ava: "If you don't mind waiting."

Steadman was shown to a room where a woman wearing white was seated. She was the doctor. She was heavy, inert, her body as pale and dense as cheese, the swags of flesh on her slack arms squashed against her sides, her gaze fixed on a computer screen. Her smell of antiseptic and talc put Steadman in mind of plastic flowers, of disguise and decay. Her ankles were swollen, overflowing her shoes. A wall clock behind her was ticking, and the face of the clock resembled hers. He detected a sadness in her but, offended by her officious manner, rejected the thought.

She did not rise or look at Steadman when he entered. Instead, she leaned away from him and shifted her heaviness onto the hams of her thickened thighs. When she picked up a pencil and clipboard her body filled the tight white uniform, binding it. She seemed to him like a keeper in a madhouse, chosen for her bulk. She had a bully's body, and was probably a bit mad herself for her airless days in this sorry room, sitting in judgment on the sick. He disliked her for not greeting him — he a cripple, a blunderer, a blind man measuring his steps in the room with the tip of his cane.

Without engaging him in conversation, she watched his progress as he tapped with his stick and found a chair to sit in.

"When was your last complete physical?"

"Does it matter?"

"Lift your shirt for me," she said, and he heard the squeak of her chair's casters, the tug of her crepe soles, as she rolled toward him with more orders, abbreviated ones: "Sleeves up. Mouth open. Lift your tongue."

She took his blood pressure and temperature without commenting, but all the while she breathed through her nose with a rasp of the bristly hair inside her snout.

Scratching with her pencil, her plump hand chafing across the paper, she entered numbers as though carving them with the chisel of her pencil point.

"What sort of work do you do?"

He could hardly believe that the doctor, staring at his name, did not know this simple, well-known fact; that she was swollen and slow did not explain it. Everyone knew his name, which often annoyed him when someone recognized it and greeted him. In the past it had been like a mockery of him, for what he was not doing.

"I'm Slade Steadman."

The pencil lead trembled against the paper, then began paring at the page like a knife point. No other sound came from the doctor except the bump of her bare forearm on her desktop, like the skid of raw meat, a fat rind of cold pork slapped onto a butcher's block.

As she began to write, and it sounded like an indictment, her scraping the paper with her pencil point, Steadman inwardly objected again: another doctor dominating him, behaving as pompously as a priestess, hinting that she had power over life and death, knew the diagnosis for all mortal ills, if not the cure, protective of the special language of illness, the code words of doom, a superstitious idiolect, a lingo that was all about fear and flesh. He was supine; there was no sympathy here.

He had come to believe that many doctors caused disease. Ava was a notable exception, yet he sometimes looked at her and thought, But you never know. He could rant on the subject of physician-assisted illness. Gnawing in secret like the canniest rats, worrying your confidence and good feeling with their arrogance and secrecy, doctors were at the bottom of it all. Steadman was certain that doctors brought healthy people down by uttering dire warnings and attaching the most grotesque meaning to the commonest and least harmful symptoms. "Your headache might be a brain tumor," and "Your cough might be more serious than you think," and "That skin blotch might be melanoma," and

"What you think is just bad eyesight is macular degeneration — you are going blind." They were the bearers of fearsome news that made sick people sicker.

Or they told you nothing at all, treated you like a pickled specimen, a sample ailment, a case number. Then they squinted and scrutinized, frowned and scribbled, as this fat uncommunicative harridan was doing now. They were drug dealers with the dirtiest drugs, which cleared up some symptoms but gave you others: dizziness, nausea, insomnia, anxiety, impotence, skin rash, hair loss, depression, renal failure, the shakes, and you were incapacitated by these side effects, or died. A few doses of a vaguely named antipsychotic drug and you ended up palsied, with all the outward symptoms of Parkinson's disease. Check into a hospital to fix a painful rotator cuff and you picked up bacteria that triggered arthritis so crippling you couldn't get out of bed. Hospital air was soupy with germs. Shot-happy doctors made people ill, as this woman had already begun trying to do to Steadman, demoralizing him by ignoring him, by breathing hard, a kind of poisonous exhalation. But he knew better.

"What is your name?"

"Dr. Budberg," she said in a panting breath, surprised by the sudden question, but not so startled that she forgot to give him her title.

He wanted to remind her that all ignorance needs a name. She was really no better than a Vineyard lout doing yard work, who smiled resentfully at words like "threadbare" and "profusion" and "extricate," and was insulted when Steadman used them, saying with aggression, "I guess I'll have to write that down, Mr. Steadman."

He said to Dr. Budberg, "I do the same work as Herr Grass and Dr. Canetti and Mr. Wolcott." When she did not react, nor even raise her head, he added, "Señor García Márquez, Mr. White, Mr. Milosz, and Mrs. Gordimer."

Her hesitation showed him he had rung no bells — her head still down, her pencil motionless, poised over the blank line headed *Occupation*.

"They won the Nobel Prize for literature," Steadman said, and wondered what she would say. She said nothing. "I haven't so far, but may I say you have a strange scotoma?"

She looked at him and — given her specialty, this seemed odd — blinked in confusion.

"Writer," he said.

Just last week the president of the United States met me, he wanted to say. And: How is it that this exalted man knew my name and work, and you, arrogant lump that you are, did not?

Dr. Budberg was wearing what he took to be her game face. Doctors learned early how not to look fazed. She was proof of such scientific posturing, busying herself with an eye chart, shifting in her chair, rolling it on its casters as she skidded and stumped with her lisping crepe-soled infirmary shoes. She adjusted the viewing hood, and Steadman knew he was no more than a pair of goggling eyes attached to an insurance policy.

But in the studied scorn of her indifference, a bit too contrived, she lost her poise and knocked her pencil to the floor. Before she could retrieve it, Steadman stood and walked four steps and snatched it, played with it a little, fingered its lettering, made her wait for it, then handed it over and sat down again, all unhesitatingly and without using his cane.

"Put your head in here. Use the chin rest," she said, fitting the metal viewer bracket onto his face and staring at his eyes.

"Can you read anything?"

"What do you want?"

"How about the top line?"

Steadman read the top line.

"Can you read the next line?"

Steadman read the smaller letters, the whole line.

"Can you see anything else?"

Without pausing, Steadman read four more lines.

"The last line you read isn't on the chart," the doctor said, as though Steadman had uttered something fatuous.

"Move the chart up," he said.

She did so, making the yellow projection of the lighted rectangle jump, and the newly exposed bottom line was the line he had recited.

"How did you know that?"

"Because I'm not reading it," he said.

The heavy woman shunted her weight and became clumsy in her confusion, heavier-seeming, not liking what she heard, fussed by the illogic of it, snatching at the arms of her chair. She was still fussing, swinging the binocular mask of the viewer bracket away from his eyes.

"What do you see now?"

"Nothing," he said.

"So you can't read anything?"

"I can read everything." He kept his chin on the metal rest and stared straight ahead. "I've seen all those lines before. Why don't you people get new eye charts?"

She leaned and shone a light into his eyes and peered into his skull — the warmth of the light brushed his cornea like a feather. He could smell the doctor's sour body. She said nothing, but he could tell that she was disturbed. He was reminded of his first impression, how sadness penetrated her flesh and was eating at it from within.

"You're getting no response. My pupils are still dilated and you don't know why," he said. His chin hard on the chin rest restricted him from easily opening his mouth and made his voice sound mocking and robotic, a tone he instantly became fond of and exploited. "No sign of trauma. You're bewildered."

"I am not bewildered," she said too loudly. "It could be neurological."

"You say 'could be' — so you don't know."

"Are you presently taking any medication?"

He said no, but warily, using the chin rest to disguise the unease in his voice.

Fixing and clamping his head again, the doctor swung a new arm out of the apparatus and leveled it, like a small pistol aimed at his right eye, and she fired a bullet of air into his cornea. She repeated it with his left eye.

"My pressure's normal," Steadman said. "Why don't you tell me these things."

She was briefly abashed and then she recovered and became formal again. She said, "This is a little unusual."

"Are you suggesting I am a little blind?"

"I didn't say that."

He could tell he was annoying her, and he was at last happy. He lifted his head from the hollow of the viewing stand and smiled at her.

"I am totally blind," he said. "Now you know."

His teasing made her obstinate. She said, "You read the chart perfectly."

"No. I remembered it. I've had eye tests my whole life."

The doctor became insistent. "You didn't see the chart? You saw darkness?"

"There is no darkness. Have you heard of a man named Shakespeare? A writer. I now know that his most inaccurate line is 'Looking on darkness which the blind do see.' Black is the one color I can't see."

"You can see colors?"

"I am like Jorge Luis Borges, who made that observation. A writer. He was blind. 'I live in a world of colors,'" Steadman said, and still in his quoting tone, "'The world of the blind is not the night that you imagine.'"

"What sort of colors?" She was holding the pencil again in her stubby fingers.

He faced her and said, "Monkey-ass purple, clitoral pink, venous blue, nipple umber."

But Dr. Budberg had turned away, her jaw set hard, swelling her jowls. She interrupted him, saying, "So you were unable to read the eye chart."

"My reader's and writer's sight is gone," Steadman said. "When something ends, something else begins. There are all sorts of vision, not all of them measurable."

Working her legs and feet, the doctor rolled herself to her desk. She said, "You'll have to come back. We'll schedule a PET scan and an MRI. Make an appointment with the receptionist."

"You didn't even know I'm stone blind," Steadman said. He began to laugh, poking his face at her.

"This examination is over."

"Now you know I'm blind, but you don't know why," he said. "Why not admit it?"

She was insulted, he could tell. Doctors might be habitually hearty, but that was a distracting ruse to josh you; they refused to be teased themselves.

"I'm a medical miracle," Steadman said.

"Really," the doctor said in an uneasy murmur, hardly parting her lips.

"I see more than you do," Steadman said. "Who knows more than a blind man?"

"Then why did you bother to come here?" she said. Her voice, intending insult, went shrill.

"Maybe for verification," he said. "Maybe to give you some timely medical advice."

She drew back from him. It was what strangers had been doing all this day in Boston, reacting to him, stifling their feelings, looking fearful, because they saw he was blind — the pilot, the flight attendant, the cabbie, the waiter at the Union Oyster House, people on the sidewalk and in the elevator. He went closer to the doctor, putting on his dark glasses, lifting his cane, looking fierce, like a swordsman.

"If you can't do anything to control your weight," Steadman said, "how do you expect me to trust you with my precious eyes?"

That was too much for Dr. Budberg. She rose awkwardly, stumbling a little, snatching papers and folders from her desk. She hurried out of the examining room, leaving Steadman to find his own way to the door.

But now that she was gone he saw her clearly, as he had suspected at the outset, and was alarmed, for at the moment of the doctor's abrupt departure, when she was in motion, Steadman realized his error. Dr. Budberg was in mourning. He had been too severe with her. He had not understood. The way she walked, slightly lopsided, her head tucked into her shoulders, holding one arm crooked — her whole posture of grief — told him that she was miserable, bereaved, and he had hurt her a little more, made her sadder, kicked her. Feeling sorry for her didn't help. Someone close to her had died. Grieving had deprived her of sleep and made her inattentive and unintentionally remote and slow and officious.

"What did you say to piss her off?" Ava asked when Steadman entered the waiting room — and he knew that the doctor had preceded him.

Steadman wanted that twenty minutes back; with shame he recalled his rudeness. He went to the reception counter and handed in his file folder to a woman in a white smock sitting at a computer.

"Want to schedule an appointment?"

In a low voice, Steadman said, "Dr. Budberg — someone died in her family."

"Daughter," the woman said, narrowing her eyes, her face crumpling. "Terrible to lose a child."

He did not want to know more than that. Details would only make him feel worse.

"What's wrong? You act like you got some bad news," Ava said.

"I was a little hard on that doctor," he said, touching the face of his watch. "We've got two hours before our flight. Let's find a cab."

A taxi was waiting by the front entrance of the hospital. The driver got out to help but Steadman waved him away and snatched the door open.

The driver said, "Where to?"

"You know the Two O'Clock Lounge?"

"It's not called that anymore."

"Does it matter?" He could tell that Ava was staring at him. He said, "I need something life-affirming."

The place was called Pinky's, at the same address on Washington Street where the Two O'Clock Lounge had once been. Leaving the hot sidewalk, they entered the darkened doorway into a room of loud music that was cool and poorly lit and dirty, smelling of spilled beer. He sniffed again: naked flesh, two women dancing slowly on a mirrored floor, a pair of long-legged nudes, seeming to ignore the beckoning men.

"I hate places like this," Ava said. "I'm a doctor. I don't need it."

"You need it *because* you're a doctor."

"Please not down front."

But Steadman insisted, and she followed him through the darkness to the edge of the stage, where they sat holding hands among men in attitudes of intense concentration, almost worship. One woman, wholly naked, twirling in a slow dance in high heels, approached. She smiled at Ava, looking curious when she saw Steadman's dark glasses and white cane, so confident in his blindness, not seeing her and yet smiling.

"Now she's squatting," he said.

"I see some pretty tortured labia. Some warts."

"Please stop being a doctor."

When Ava fell silent and he felt her fingers, warm and moving in his hand, he was aroused, sensing her sudden awkward interest.

She said, "I've never been in one of these places before."

"Think of it as an examining room," Steadman said. "Slip a five-dollar bill into her garter and you can give her a physical."

She let go of his hand, groped in the shadow beneath her, and fished in her bag. He loved the furtiveness of her movement, tipping the naked dancer with a self-conscious gesture of concealment, woman to woman. He savored the silence as the other woman came near and squatted and opened her legs, and Ava said, "Such pretty girls, such beautiful bodies — what are they doing here? Is it that they have low self-esteem?"

"How is this different from a hospital?" Steadman said. "Look at the interns at work."

The solemnity of the men whose heads rested between the knees of the naked women, the attentive way they studied what they saw, a complex pinkness, like a live blossom — yes, they could have been the most serious medical students.

"Or like boys playing doctor."

"It's also like a temple," Steadman said, and he explained: a bit of magic, some mirrors, ritual glimpses of the forbidden. "They're not weak — these women are in charge. They're priestesses. The men are helpless worshipers."

That squatting woman, seeing Ava smile, had pursed her lips and made a kissing sound when Ava rewarded her with a folded and tucked-in five-dollar bill.

And then the kneeling woman leaned slightly and reached behind Ava and drew her head closer, placing it between her naked breasts. Ava laughed a little, then realizing she was caught, her mouth against the cleavage, she became flustered as the woman moved quickly from side to side, slapping Ava's face and cheeks with the weight of her loose breasts and laughing in triumph.

Steadman had heard it all, no single word but the beat of it, the smack of flesh on flesh, and he was aroused by the fact that his lover had been surprised that way by the naked woman.

Ava's eyes were shining, her mouth slightly agape, as though she had changed places with him, and she was stunned by the slap of the breasts on her face.

"If you like, we can stay," he said.

"I have a much better idea." She kissed him, her eyes still glittering, as the naked dancer looked on approvingly and winked.

They left Pinky's and flew back to the Vineyard in the dark — much simpler at night, and an easier landing, a lot less traffic on the nighttime road. They were home in twenty minutes, Ava driving.

He kissed her inside the house. He held her. He said, "Now let me see."

7

RISING FROM DARKNESS to light, abruptly dazzled, Steadman understood how religions caught fire, for what was revealed to him was not just the ardent power that blindness had granted him but the deception of sight. Where others saw opaque blobs, he saw symmetrical flames illuminating the passage of time, like a torchlit path, giving continuity and coherence to his memory. Not hallucinations and fantastic visions but the plainest, most persuasive reality, what he took to be truth: a lit-upness of his life.

He whispered to Ava, "Everyone I see is naked."

"You're boasting again," Ava said. She challenged him with denials and evasions, because of his extravagance.

"No, you don't understand. Nakedness is a kind of concealment, the most misleading kind. It subverts fantasy."

Yesterday in Boston, at Pinky's, he had been reflective, for nakedness was like defiance. The dancers had been girlish and coy, playful, teasing, protected by their nudity. Even the barest woman in the place looked peeled and raw, just feeble startled limbs, going through the motions, and others seemed more like pork to him now. Because he saw too much, something important was missing. The essential woman was hidden inside all that naked flesh.

Though the trip to Boston had been exhausting, it had been worth it for the sight of Ava in the bar, face forward, her cheeks slapped by the fat breasts of the dancer, her eyes alight.

"You liked it," he said.

Ava said, "Couldn't you tell — I wanted to go home with her. But I'm trying to keep you honest. The women who've been calling you up don't care about your writing. And if you think you're preternaturally prescient, then you're a freak."

His rattle of laughter disturbed her even more than his white sightless eyes.

To give herself confidence, she mocked him. "You're like the kid who always wins at Pin the Tail on the Donkey. After a while everyone suspects that he's peeking over his blindfold."

"They'll read my book and see that my power is real."

"What happens when you lose it?"

"Sight and blindness are the same to me. Blindness is special sight."

"You can't keep up this pretense forever. Someone will find out and expose you."

He laughed. Her challenges excited him by keeping him alert; he enjoyed repelling her attacks. He wanted her to fight him, or else later, embracing her, there would be nothing left to believe in. He smiled and said softly that he was not afraid, that the book would vindicate him and — as books seemed to do, as *Trespassing* had done — displace him.

"Ask Dr. Budberg. She was baffled. I told her I'm a medical miracle."

"Oh, please."

Ava seemed to think that her defiance might stimulate his humility. She kept at him, accusing him of being absurdly proud of going back and forth from blindness to sight. "You think you're better, not because you're blind but because you're both, that the ability to switch makes you superior. You're drinking flower juice from the jungle. That's all."

"Some people drink it and nothing happens. Remember Manfred?"

"That creep," she said. "He was the one who got you into this."

Because the drug was so effective on Steadman, he felt singled out, not lucky but chosen. He could see that Ava was weakening, but he relished her antagonism. Her doubt was necessary; he did not want a slave, he wanted an active partner; he needed her doctor's skepticism.

"By the way, you've got wine stains all over your shirt," she said sharply.

"And you're having your period."

"No," she said, and then lamely added, "It just started."

"Isn't that what I said?"

He was like a goblin, but he was writing; he was living for his new novel. Only he and Ava knew that its wildest parts were the facts of his life, the most outrageous of his conceits the plain truth.

The many-sided trip to Boston that humid summer day, his stumble-strutting like a proud cripple and slashing his bone-white cane, finding his way, raising the alarm for the drowning boy, reading the doctor's grief, understanding the implications of nakedness, had vitalized him and made him greedy for more. Being among strangers had always made him impatient and alert, and his blindness electrified him and endowed everyone he saw with a blue aura of revelation.

"Borges is right. Blindness is a gift."

Still resisting, Ava said, "My worst patients are always the ones trying to prove they're not sick."

"I'm not your fucking patient!"

She shrugged and switched on the tape recorder and took dictation. He blinded himself and continued his book, speaking fluently, the storyteller reclining on his sofa. He came to see that the trip to Boston had been an interruption — necessary to preserve the appearance of having seen a specialist for his condition, but a disturbance of a routine on the island that he had found satisfying and productive.

Strange women still called, offering themselves to him. *I know how you must feel. I'm sure I can help.* Ava laughed insincerely at these anonymous calls, which were more frequent after dark.

Steadman teased her into taking him to see *Titanic,* at the Island Theater in Oak Bluffs, and he blinded himself in the dark, gulping his tonic covertly like a habitual user. Ava mocked the movie, but gaping at the screen, Steadman found it both melodramatic and upsetting. As he was watching, he was aware that across the road from the theater the harbor brimmed with a high tide, and far-off children's voices, carrying across it with the sound of the sea, saddened him.

Afterward, in the night air, walking the streets of Oak Bluffs, blind among restless youths, many of them black, he felt even worse, and murmured, "They are prowling here. They have absolutely nothing to do. All these stalkers going in circles, looking for risks to take." Their lazy muscularity terrified him, and their watchfulness alarmed him. They had such hunger. He said, "You have no idea how they glow."

"Are you turning into a racist?"

"Some of these kids are angrier than you think."

"They seem to be having a good time."

"You have no idea."

He said that what Ava took to be their taunting humor was really rage and envy and rivalry. They were too oblique to be observed in the normal way, but he saw their essence with his third eye; their appetite and energy were a set of readable odors. Where she saw boys in baggy pants with their caps on backward and girls in tight shorts, he saw a scrum of people trying to claim a place for themselves.

Another day they went to South Beach, using the fading of his blindness — had the dose been too small? — as an excuse to take the afternoon off from dictation. But the harsh distorting daylight pained his eyes, and daring himself in the wind that was filled with pelting sand grains, he blinded himself again. He was so daunted by the greater brightness, he ran headlong through the dunes before he leaped into the surf. Much more buoyant in blindness, he let himself be borne by the waves for a long time and then tossed into the rim of wet sand at the tidemark.

"Are you all right, Mr. Steadman?"

Leaning over him was a young woman with hot skin and an aroma of slippery kelp on her soft thighs, like a dripping mermaid with damp twisted hair and fish lips.

"He's learning to hold his breath underwater," Ava said, and the young woman shimmered into the sea and danced across a wave.

"She was offering herself," Steadman said.

He shopped blind, he walked blind, he sailed his catboat blind, he drove blind to Squibnocket. He never lost his confidence, did not waver. But in spite of the authority of his gestures, he sometimes bobbled a line or dropped things; and though he did not falter himself, he made others falter — Ava especially was wrong-footed by him again and again.

The nighttime drive to Squibnocket was a cautious charade, a much shorter distance than Steadman realized or admitted. Ava meant it when she praised him, though she was overly sincere, a little too insistent, as if humoring a drunk or a madman.

In the street, dogs barked at him, and when children stared he screeched, "I'm a bat!"

On the day of the sail he handled the boat expertly, but did not know the tide had turned and was ebbing west, sweeping his small boat on its beam through the harbor to the lighthouse until, jerking on the main sheet, he found himself rocked in the troughs of West Chop. Ava took the tiller and guided them into the harbor entrance to Tashmoo Pond, because they couldn't buck the outgoing tide at Vineyard Haven.

"You sailed the hard part," Ava said.

Steadman knew he was being patronized by her, but didn't mind her tone because she was in the dark, not he. He was compulsive, he needed to be blind, it was liberation to him.

This was his year of blinding light. He hoped for many more of them, light-years ahead. He had turned his life around. He was writing again.

He hated to use the word "blind." Blind meant struck down and helpless, and he had been elevated and inspired. The decision was his, the secret too — datura was not blindness but a mask in a play of revelation. He loved putting it on, he was reluctant to take it off, and when he did, it was an act of will, like throwing his head back and stabbing his eyes with needles.

He did not miss the irony in the image of needles, for he had become like an addict, needing the visions granted him in the darkness he brought on himself. Datura was a paradox, blindfolding him, giving him sight. Until then, all he had ever seen was a one-dimensional world, shabby and insubstantial in its shallowness. He realized on leaving it, borne by the drug, that he had spent his whole life truly blind, seeing only one plane, one surface.

Datura gave him night vision, like the superior sight and heightened senses of a nocturnal animal, one of the big yellow-eyed cats that dozed by day and prowled at night. He saw himself as the feline prophet of a new religion and his writing as revelation. What Nestor had called *la venda de tigre,* the tiger's blindfold, had admitted him to a world of visions — the gauzy light, the luminous shapes, the peculiar phosphorescence all around him, the way black light was active, and most of all the smells, the touch, the taste of darkness. But the experience was also deeply physical. Nothing stirred him more sexually than this palpable darkness.

Dr. Budberg wrote him a brief blunt memo in which she confirmed his blindness. It was "of unknown origin." She encouraged him to seek a second opinion and to consider more tests.

Ava said, "It would have helped if she had suggested a cause. Then we would have some sort of description for your blindness."

Steadman said, "She's the blind one!" — still annoyed that she had never heard of him, or at least pretended not to know his name. But she had problems of her own, her grief like a disease, bloating her and making her slow and sour.

"She was highly recommended. She comes to the island sometimes."

In a list of scribbled notes on the "Additional Comments" page, she stated that he had no apparent vision, had failed all the tests, nothing registered, all the measuring instruments said so. He was a mystery, a problem, his sight was zero, and she had neither hope nor any remedy except a referral.

In the report it was as if Steadman's eyes had been gouged out and the sockets sewn shut. No one was blinder — that was the story. But his cheerfulness and wit, his emergence from his solitude, had given him fame on the island — an island that was connected to the greater world. People on the Vineyard who knew him admired him; he was envied rather than pitied. In the island talk, which was constant, he was becoming a hero of handicap.

No one but Ava knew the truth, that his blindness was his choice, and reversible; his own decision. The effects lasted six or seven hours and then wore off, leaving a residue of craving, a longing for what had just ended, a memory of light, of commanding power.

He no longer questioned the datura but was only grateful for its being part of his life. He could see more clearly than ever, could feel, too, with intense sensitivity; his skin, his muscles, his nerves were electric. Sex seldom satisfied him completely; it made him greedier. It was something tactile that convulsed him, but was more than ever a brilliant spectacle, something ruthless and sudden even when it was anticipated.

"Because sex is the truth."

The summer was passing. He dictated a portion of the book every day to Ava, and his dictation, which was taped and later transcribed, was often a dramatic episode, a set of instructions for a sexual encounter with her in her nighttime role as a seductress, Dr. Katsina. Summer days, summer nights, living and writing the erotic narrative that was his book. Blinding light, exquisite heat.

There were more parties, and — though Ava objected — Steadman was frequently the center of attention. When someone asked him what had happened to his sight, he explained that he had been blinded in such a simple way that he was amazed it had not happened more often. Why weren't more people blind? Eyes were just blobs of jelly, like a pair of trembling oysters, the softest, most vulnerable parts of the body. Nothing violent had befallen him, just a series of preventable errors, so he said.

He had been traveling — spending some of the fortune he had made from the merchandising and licensing of *Trespassing* — and had been in Hawaii. He had a residential address there, having leased a beach house for the winter. On a whim, he applied for a driver's license and, placing his chin on the metal rest for the eye exam, had looked into the chart and seen a blaze of light and faint, sketchy letters. He could not read a line, even with the glasses he sometimes used, and was failed by the apologetic clerk, who said, "Maybe you need new glasses."

After trying many combinations of lenses on him, an eye doctor shone a light into his eyes and said he had severe cataracts. He would need immediate surgery.

"I was amazed. I said it was impossible. I was hardly fifty."

But it was not unusual, he was told, especially given his extensive travel. Cataracts were sometimes hereditary, but there was also his exposure, in the years he spent outdoors, to ultraviolet rays. His father had worn thick glasses, the old inadequate remedy.

"It's an easy operation," the doctor said. "A slam dunk."

Everyone said that, though Steadman believed that the expression "slam dunk" had come to mean, for him, certain failure. And so it seemed, for Steadman had both eyes operated on, separately, six weeks apart. Not laser surgery, he explained, but a procedure under a blazing light, the scraping sound, the murmuring of the surgeon and her assistant, a knife in each eye, but such a small incision that no sutures were needed.

For a brief spell his vision was no longer yellow-hued but clear, bright as a Hawaiian lagoon, impressive in its depthless clarity. But he saw another blue, and for a brief period he enjoyed the piercing sight of crystalline imagery.

He followed all the post-op instructions. He used the drops, took the antibiotics, did not touch his eyes with his fingers, but still — was it the snorkeling? the sea water? the swimming? — the tiny incisions became infected. He was put on stronger antibiotics, to which he was allergic, and in the days he refrained from taking them, the infection got a grip. He went back to the doctor and was informed that he was losing his corneas.

He remained in Hawaii, he said, awaiting a cornea transplant, his eyes bandaged. Blindfolded in all that sunlight! The transplant was done and he flew back to Boston, only to be told that the operation was a failure.

"The doctor looks at me and says, 'Your corneas are decompensating.'"

They tried again, this time with a world-class medical team: the waiting, the suspense, the exhaustion of the surgery. And those corneas, too, were rejected.

"I accepted this condition. Maybe someday I will get a healthy transplant that will take, and you'll see me reading on the beach. But that's out of my hands. I don't want to live on false hope."

That was his story. Except for the mention of snorkeling in Hawaii, none of it was true. But it didn't matter, for with the datura he was truly blind. With his stick and his unhesitating gait he had emerged from seclusion to become a dramatic public figure on the Vineyard party circuit. There was renewed interest in his life and work. And somehow people knew that after years of silence he was working on a book.

It was easy for people to believe the fiction that he had been rendered blind from an infection and his cornea transplants had gone wrong. Medical mistakes were so common, everyone understood. Many people countered with a medical mishap of their own — misdiagnosis, wrong medication, unexpected side effects. "He went in for tonsillitis and they gave him a vasectomy."

People agreed with him when he said, "Doctors make you sick." And he was surprised that his explanation was so easily accepted, glad that he did not have to elaborate on his lies. It helped his story when Ava agreed that his doctors had been incompetent.

He knew that nothing would have been harder to explain than the drug he had happened upon in the Secoya village down the Aguarico River in the Oriente province of Ecuador, when he had been looking for ayahuasca and been introduced by Manfred to that rare datura, the ragged and attenuated clone of angel's trumpet; and how the blinding light had allowed him a downward transcendence into a new life, with a new vocabulary of sight.

"Phosphenes," Ava said.

The word that science offered was inadequate for the visions that were now his.

At one time he had taken pleasure in the act of writing, had enjoyed filling a page, crossing out half of it, beginning again, adding improvements and variations in the margin, preparing a fair copy, like a monk scratching away on vellum. But now, with the prevision of his blindness, setting down the words seemed much less important than contriving a sequence of images in his head. Why write when such visions were so intense? And the fact was that the very writing of them seemed to diminish them.

And when the moment came, using a pen was out of the question, and he had no use for a keyboard. He needed a tape recorder, needed a woman to stimulate him — not any woman but someone he desired, and now there was only one. He was so enraptured, so possessed by his vision, and given such fluency, that he needed to speak his book and for Ava to set it down as well as record it. His book was an exuberance, an intense erotic prayer; her writing it was not submissive but a form of interrogation. The act of his dictating and her murmuring and saying "Yes, yes" or "Wait" was sexual, too, because she was an essential and active partner in it, just as obsessed.

Ava was sometimes Ava and sometimes Dr. Katsina, depending on the time of day, and their nighttime relationship was the more passionate for their daytime detachment. Needing her so badly in order to get on with his book, he was grateful for her being there, but he was so dependent he was at times resentful — not toward her but toward the whole scheme of creation. He wanted to be a beacon, a prophet. And the fact was that without her he would have been nothing but a harmless paranoiac, a secret king, living in seclusion, impotently, frivolously fantasizing to a whirring machine.

THREE

The Book of Revelation

1

Once, not that long before, Ava had seemed just a face and figure, another woman, but loving, desirable, bright. Now she was the living embodiment of his ideal woman — a comforter, a partner, a protector, a helper, a healer, a friend; and she was hungrier than he was. He loved to think that she never said no, that she initiated sex. *I am waiting for you. Come here.*

She had become his life, his greatest friend, and his need was deeper than love. She was his companion, she was his mistress, she dominated him, she attended him, she was both his soothing submissive nurse and his bossy doctor. He depended on her for everything. She took orders, and in serving him she guided him, became part of his days and nights. Though she had said she would never do such a thing, she had vacated her Vineyard Haven house and moved in with him up-island. Now the whole estate was as much hers as his. She was his secretary, encouraging him in his dictation and operating the tape recorder. She was everything but his eyes — he had his own eyes. But she was in his work, helping him live it, helping him write it. She was half his book, as she put it: the blind man's lover.

She still fought him, accusing him of pomposity, but the proof that he had been profoundly changed was evident in his work. He admitted to her that the moment he had felt the most liberated by his blindness was the moment he needed her the most, realizing that he could not live without her. He did not question this paradox. He could not separate those two contradictions. In his darkness he held out his eager hand to grope forward, and she grasped it with her uncertain hand and led him onward.

"I feel responsible for your blindness."

"Now you're the one who's boasting."

"Wasn't it an awful shock?"

"No, I'm a new man."

A year ago, it had been her idea to go to Ecuador, on the jungle drug tour. The blindness that resulted, Steadman said, was his good fortune. He had gone looking for an idea, anything to write; he had never thought he would have a second chance, another book, a real life. In the face of Steadman's apparent irrationality Ava desired to take the blame. But there was no blame. He had seen into her heart, he needed her, he was only grateful.

"You've given me life," he said.

"My life, unfortunately — I'm not working, I haven't done any doctoring for months, and the hospital keeps calling to say they're shorthanded," she said. "But maybe that's what love is, a kind of selfish sacrifice. The illusion that you're giving someone your life."

"Don't call it love," he said, and became extravagant. "You're a shepherdess, a shaman, a priestess."

She said, "Just don't ask me to marry you."

He laughed with surprise and relief.

"Because I never want to give you that power over me. And I don't want any myself."

"What do you want?"

"What you want — pleasant surprises. Go into the library and wait for me."

He did as he was told, and saw that the stained-glass windows he had installed to protect his books from the sun were darkened by the gloomy afternoon, each color in each panel like a distinct aroma that was fading. He stood, not knowing what was in store, but savoring what he knew would be pleasurable. Facing the dim colors of the windows, he heard the library door open and shut.

She had changed her clothes: she wore a white blouse, a short skirt, high heels. She walked to the leather sofa in the corner of the room and sat on its far end, in the shadows.

"Touch me."

He approached, trying to suppress his eagerness, and he knelt before her, sliding his hand between her thighs, plucking at her panties.

"You're wet."

"Not enough." She guided his hand until it seemed to sink, and she sighed as he stroked her.

Then she leaned forward, unbuttoned the front of her blouse, and tugged his head forward as the dancer had done to her in Boston. She slapped his face with her breasts, holding them, one in each hand, manipulating her nipples.

"Touch me again."

He did so, with his face cradled in the warmth of her breasts, and found that she was wetter, sweetened with moisture, her panties clinging, heavier. He lifted her skirt, parted her legs and began to mount her.

"No," she said, and taking advantage of his getting to his feet, she gripped his cock and folded her breasts around it and chafed the hard thick thing between their softness, and when he began to pant she used her breasts to lift it to her mouth, and finished him off by sucking him slowly into her throat.

All this without removing her clothes. She passed her fingers over the slickness on her lips, swallowed again, and said, "That's what I mean."

She knew him so well, and she was able to say so in a mock-dramatic way, teasing him with her understanding. She could demonstrate, like that, the interlude in the library, that he needed her. Now he felt safe with her. He had never been so content, so stimulated, so greedy for more. He could depend on her, could share all his secrets.

Early on, the second time they had met, when she was just starting at the Vineyard hospital, delivering babies, setting bones, performing appendectomies, tying tubes, he had said, "Like everybody else, I've been married before."

Her smile, her reckless eyes, made her seem strong, and so his expression softened. She said, "Generalizations are great. They show you're impatient and not fussy."

"You mean about everyone being married? But it's true. It's like everyone gets a driver's license. And later you're amazed you passed and that you didn't have more accidents."

"Some people need to be single," she said, with a confidence that meant she was single. "And some people need to be smugly married."

He made a pretense of thinking a moment, so that the delay, the silence, would help her remember. Then, eyeing her, he said, "And some people learn by doing."

Steadman's marriage had been brief and, from the beginning, bewildering. The wedding — ridiculous, expensive, a mockery — was just confusion, like a pretentious ritual before a bloody battle; and later, when arguing exhausted and confounded them both, and there was no obvious purpose in fault-finding except pettiness, he took refuge in a despairing silence. The silence that lay between his wife and himself he remembered as a true darkness.

Marriage seemed to him a sudden loneliness with someone familiar — maybe this happened all the time? — someone who by degrees turned into a stranger. They had met at a party, soon after he had arrived back from his two years of trespassing. Her name was Charlotte, "but please call me Charlie. Everyone does." He said, "Then I'll call you Charlotte." She said she was in marketing, an account executive. He had no idea. She seemed intensely animated in the first weeks of their friendship. Sex made her desirable for her teasing elusiveness, and his infatuation blurred her even more. He had to have her no matter what. He told her he loved her, he promised her everything. Yes, I want to marry you! Her excitement made her beautiful, she said she would do anything to make him happy, and he promised her the same. But marriage made them first strangers and then quarrelers and finally enemies.

The confusing part for him was that her strangeness stimulated their sex life. The stumbling sense that he hardly knew her, that they did not share a common language, made her desirable. He did not know where to begin, so when she made a suggestion — and it was nearly always crude: "I am so horny," yes, he understood that — he was immediately aroused, as though the foreign woman he had been staring at from across the room at a party approached him and, reading his mind, said, "Now," and led him into a nearby bedroom and kicked the door shut.

Charlotte's haste, her need, and her mood of anonymity were a pleasure to him — perhaps the only one — for she was more a stranger in bed than anywhere else. "Bed" was a euphemism for the various places they made love: the back seat of the car, the bathroom, the hidden pocket beach below West Chop lighthouse. He did not want sex as a gift; he wanted it as a command — and to take turns giving orders. Charlotte taught him that, or at least helped him realize what he wanted. As a stranger she had no inhibitions; she could demand anything of him, he could say anything to her, they could be irresponsible and reckless. She used him, he used her — those were their happiest days. He loved the fact that sexually she was hard to satisfy, always behaving badly, like a selfish person taking advantage of someone unsuspecting.

Early on, she had dropped hints. "Look at that," she said of a lacy low-cut dress, "it's real slutty." And of a pair of stiletto-heeled shoes, "I want a pair of those hump-me pumps."

Ordinarily she had little conversation, but when she was in the mood for sex she was like a cat, demanding, rubbing against him — or not like a cat at all, but like a predatory woman, a coke whore on a back street pleading for sex. Steadman liked her snatching him and insisting, "Go down on me — yes — more," while she held his head with both her hands. "Use your finger, too. Yes, like that, harder, deeper, don't stop, make me come."

And after she came, convulsed, gagging and squealing, her body bucking, she could be even hungrier, more demanding, but in a pleading and submissive way, on his behalf. "Be rough with me. Call me a cocksucker. Go ahead, make me blow you." When Steadman was tentative — Where do I begin? — she said, "Rougher, spank me, force me," and then, as she kicked and he slapped her small hard buttocks, she growled against his cock and became noisily ecstatic, whinnying as she drank him.

Otherwise, most of the time, and always in public, she was a rather prim and passive woman.

She bought clothes, she had her nails done once a week, she read the *Wall Street Journal*. She was absorbed by her work. "I've got a marketing meeting in Cambridge with the salespeople, and I haven't edited the pitches or read the spreadsheets." *What?* Her work was a mystery to him.

But this strangeness, this unexpectedness, made her combative, too, and he often wondered, Who are you? At last Steadman was indifferent. He worked on his book and was so absorbed in it he ended up not knowing her. Fighting with her was meaningless. Their house seemed emptier when they were both inside. He wanted her to go, but he was so exhausted that when he suggested that she go, his voice sounded lazy and detached — so hopeless and speculative he hardly cared.

"I think it's over, Charlie."

A year before, during their courtship, when she had become flustered by his excessive questioning, she had said to him, "What you see is what you get," as though emphasizing her simplicity, almost boasting of her shallowness, primary colors in one dimension, a paper cutout, a little doll. Her facetious warning not to look deeper became her mantra: she had no subtleties, nor any inner meaning. "I'm in sales and marketing! Doesn't that say it all?"

When he said he doubted that — "You're not being fair to yourself. There's always more" — she complained in a rueful wronged tone that she was not hiding anything and that he was the most complicated man she had ever met in her life. He was impractical, he had no savings, no real income, no investments. He had spent his money on a two-year trip around the world. How could you be both a writer and a traveler? Writers stayed home and drove people crazy; travelers didn't sit long enough to write. But he did both, a profound mystery to her.

"I've got to read one of your books," she had said soon after they met.

He did not tell her that there was only one, that it was not done yet, that he had no money left of his advance.

All this in the last months of his finishing *Trespassing*, when the manuscript was sitting on his desk. He was so tired from the physical effort of typing the book and imagining it at the same time that he could not look further ahead to its publication. He had never imagined the overwhelming success, the transforming miracle of it: the fame, the wealth, and then the celebrated seclusion that made him notorious and sought after.

But that was afterward, after his tentativeness with Charlotte, his believing that she would understand him only if she had read what he had written.

"I really want to read it," she said.

The stack of paper, the *Trespassing* manuscript, was almost eight inches high. He had typed it himself on a manual machine, banging the keyboard with the claws of his hands, watching stiffened insect legs fly up from the oily basket and kick letters onto the page as the bruised ribbon fluttered. The book proceeded letter by jumping letter. He had sickened himself smoking cigarettes while doing it, his pores oozed with tar, his throat ached, he felt poisoned; and that was the end of his cigarette smoking.

She was not daunted by the size of the manuscript. She repeated that she was eager to read it. "Your book, look at it," she said, in an overly patient, uncritical way, with a slightly affected smile, as though she were describing a puppy.

"There's a lot of geography in it," he said. "But I've got a set of maps — you won't get lost."

How often he remembered his innocence and self-deception in those days, seeing two people quietly talking, the stack of manuscript between them in ream-sized boxes, hopeful and happy, in a kind of paradise, before the whole world knew and began to intrude.

She was the book's first reader. She buried herself in it. But she had a disconcerting habit of reading the manuscript with the TV on, glancing up from the pages to follow a sitcom, smiling at the show, frowning at his pages. At last she said, "I like it." He wanted more from her — more praise, more detail, an extended rave, alluding to all the passages she particularly liked. Even though he was starved for praise after all those years of indifference, he managed to say this in a tactful whisper, or at least not seeming to be pleading.

"I liked all of it," she said, protesting, surprised that he should want more than that.

"The typescript is almost seven hundred pages. Did you finish it?"

"I read practically all of it. What do you want me to say?"

He shrugged. He realized he was asking too much of her. After all, he was unable to evaluate the twenty or so pages of a marketing plan she sometimes showed him, though he was able to correct her spelling and grammar.

Following her simple verdict on the book, she had said, defending herself — and she never looked prettier, more bright-eyed, lovely lips, full breasts, delicate hands — "What you see is what you get."

Don't look for more or you'll be disappointed, she was saying. I am only surfaces.

That was a complete lie, it turned out. Perhaps deliberate, perhaps an honest misunderstanding, but a lie he could no longer accept. "Crap," Steadman raged. "Dog shit!" For later, as his wife, every day some new annoying aspect of Charlotte was revealed, always a shock to him because of her insistence in advance that there was nothing more to know. Wrong — there was everything!

She cried easily, she was hurt by the slightest word, she was insecure.

She reacted hysterically to a chance remark or the wrong question — she saw questioning as a form of assault. "I don't know the answer! I guess I'm just stupid!" She told defiant lies. Mention a book, any book, and she always said casually, "I read it so long ago I can't remember much about it." He stopped talking about books so as not to put her on the spot. She had not read anything except books about sales and marketing.

She, the businesswoman who said "As soon as you lose your temper you've lost the argument," who had never raised her voice to him, who had seemed the soul of calmness, turned out to be a screamer, the veins in her neck standing out like blue twisted cords as she howled at him. And then, after all this noise, she would sulk and say nothing — she could sulk for days with a stubbornness that would have actually impressed him with its resolve had it not been such a maddening provocation.

"Say something," he would plead at these times, trying to encourage her, and he would end up shouting at her, his frustration seeming to give her satisfaction in her spitefulness, for he had proved he was a brute.

"See, you're raising your voice," she said in a triumphant tone, having infuriated him. "You're shouting. You're swearing."

What he had seen was not what he had gotten: he had married a placid, mildly agreeable woman and he had gotten a shrill, unpredictable woman who was impossible to please. It was as though he had taken the simple complacent face of a new clock to be the clock itself. He had not guessed its guts and workings could be so complex and unpredictable, with all the cogs and springs and teeth and noise that made it run, and sometimes it was just a clock face, a pretty dial with unreliable hands that did not run at all.

"It's you," she said, and she blamed him for being difficult. A writer, a traveler, the two selfish professions combined into a single act of egomania.

What could he say to that? His book was done but not yet published.

Charlotte's objections to his behavior were precisely his objections to hers. And so they were equal adversaries. Still they made love, and sex took on a cruel unexpectedness with their underlying antagonism; while it lasted it was satisfying for being vicious. For a time, whenever they had an argument they were gripped by a passion that turned sexual, and they ended up on the floor or the sofa, her clothes torn and twisted aside, his pants at his ankles, while she clawed him and struggled, his body smacking hers in furious slaps. Afterward, lying motionless, with the fish-stink of sex on their skin, stuck together with sweat, all their anger burned away, the stalemate resumed.

At last he realized that he was an irritant to her and the whole relationship was unfixable, for she was unhappy, and she had been unhappy long before he'd met her. What she needed he could not offer her.

"It's you but it's not your fault."

"Don't patronize me."

"Okay, I won't. You've got a borderline personality disorder."

"What about you?"

"Of course I do. Isn't it the human condition?"

He had made her very unhappy. Her sadness was a great deal different from her anger. It was heavy and silent; it killed his desire. He did not think of making love to her now, not even in the drooling doggy way he had done just a week before. She was gloomy, and he left her to her unhappiness. It was either that or accommodate it.

Though she was still passive and low, she claimed she was angry, that she felt abandoned.

"You're the same person," he said. He meant: I don't know you — you're a stranger that emerged from the body of a friend whom I had found familiar and even beautiful. I was able to fuck the body but not the person inside it.

"You're a bastard."

Meaningless abuse; he was capable of the same. It was another stage in the disintegration.

But it seemed to him that she wanted to hold him responsible. It was almost as if she had been looking for a husband in order to find someone to take on the burden of misery within her, which had been part of her since childhood.

Dishonestly, he had wanted to sigh *Women!* as she had often shouted *Men!* But that was ridiculous. "We are not raccoons," he had said to her one day. It was unfair to see her only as a woman, for she was different from any other woman he had ever known. She was Charlotte and sometimes Charlie. They had tried. They had failed.

Trying to analyze her didn't help. The attempt made him insincerely sympathetic and seemed to obligate him. She talked about her parents, and it seemed like a weird parable of perverse and cruel people: hag of a mother, bully of a father, brute of a brother, who had done everything except love her. He hated listening, for whenever she talked of these people he saw damage. The worst of it was that since she really did not like herself very much, how could she love anyone else?

Yet she had friends, all of them women, none he knew well, for she kept them to herself and, he suspected, secretly complained about him to them. He could tell from the way they treated him — distantly, coolly, sometimes mocking, sometimes loudly contemptuous — that they were acting on her behalf.

Her closest friend was Vickie. In one of Charlotte's low periods Vickie came to stay for a week. He suspected a week would be too long, that it might undo him, but he made attempts to be conversational.

"Have you ever been to the Vineyard before?"

"Years ago."

"When was that?"

Vickie couldn't remember. It had to be a lie. He asked her what sort of work she did.

"Depends on the day."

She was being elusive. He knew Vickie was a marketing manager from Los Angeles. Charlotte had said so. They were both part of a business plan that was being written. Vickie had a long-term relationship with a man in New York. Steadman asked about him. "He's delightfully eccentric." Charlotte had told him the man was very wealthy and that Vickie was wealthy, too, but all Steadman saw was an aging sharp-faced woman who had a demented male friend and who had shown up empty-handed and contradicted nearly everything he said.

"Beautiful," she said of a small *santo* on a pedestal, its gilt chipped. "I was going to buy one in Mexico."

"This is from the Philippines."

"Mexicans make the exact same things," she said. "You're limping."

"Gout," he said.

"Gout's terrible. Sometimes you can't get out of bed. You get gout in every joint."

"That's not it. Have you ever had it?"

"No, but I know quite a bit about it."

Wondering why he was going to the trouble, Steadman explained that you never got gout in every joint. He had been severely dehydrated on his travels and had fainted one day in Assam, before trespassing into Bangladesh. The resulting kidney damage had produced the gout. Gout was nearly always limited to one joint, often the podagra of the large toe of one foot.

"It's like having a broken toe."

"Oh, is that all?" Vickie said, and turned to Charlotte. "I had a broken toe when I was a dancer. It didn't hurt at all."

"This hurts."

"If you'd drunk more water," Vickie said, "you wouldn't have gotten dehydrated."

Steadman smiled, raging within.

"This was in India."

"They're starving in India," Vickie said.

"Have you been to India?"

She averted her eyes. "Years ago."

She stayed in the guesthouse; she whispered with Charlotte, whom she called Charlie; they shopped in town. Steadman saw them only at mealtimes. Though she was a snob about food — "Avocados are really fattening," "Fruit juice is all sugar," "You don't have any soy milk?" — she didn't cook. Vickie wouldn't swim in his pool — she hated pools, all those chemicals. When he offered her blueberries in a bowl she said she hated blueberries, and so he followed up with raspberries and she shrieked, saying she hated them even more. "They're so hairy." She said she wanted to give up business and be a masseuse. She often massaged Charlotte's neck as she talked. "You're all tight here. Why are you so tense, Charlie? These knots. Feel them? Let me work on those." Steadman wondered why he had never massaged his wife's neck. Vickie said her ambition was to live in a deluxe hotel, preferably in Europe, maybe in Vienna. She had been there once, it was so clean, better than Italy, where they threw trash everywhere.

"The narcissism of minor differences," Steadman said.

He had become fascinated by her disagreeable opinions and ignorant evasions. She believed she was delightfully eccentric, like her New York boyfriend, while he knew she was simply annoying. He realized that it was a relief for Charlotte to see someone else battling him, but couldn't she tell how pathetic the woman was?

She looked up, though her fingers still clutched at Charlotte's neck.

"Freud," Steadman said. "He was from Vienna."

"Everyone knows that."

"And the quote's from *Civilization and Its Discontents*."

"I know."

"You read it?"

With a wave of her hand, "So long ago."

Harmless affectations, white lies; and if she always surrounded herself with people like Charlotte, she would never be found out. More serious was her continual gossip. She had gotten close to a mutual friend, a man Steadman had met a few times but who was closer to Charlotte, a business associate to whom she had introduced Vickie. And Vickie, the passenger, the floater, was now a friend of the man. He saw her regularly, he confided in her.

"I shouldn't be telling you this, Charlie," Vickie said, and giggled, and then told them both the secrets the man had divulged to her: of his wife's past, his children's problems, his financial worries, his weaknesses as a businessman — weaknesses, she suggested, that she and Charlotte might easily exploit.

She spoke in the tone a person might use when offering a special gift to a lucky, much-valued friend, giving them the secrets and letting them share the information, which made them powerful, too. The confidences were beyond gossip: they had the effect of reducing and emasculating the man, and created the illusion — as some betrayals did — of making the listener stronger.

Charlotte was delighted, rapt, as Vickie went on leaking.

"The key to his marriage? He married his mother. She makes all the decisions. You gotta wonder about their sex life."

Steadman found himself more interested than he should have been. But pondering what was being divulged, he became wary, for here was the indiscreet woman in his own household, a confidante of his secretive and dissatisfied wife. At some point in the future he would be talked about that way. *You gotta wonder...*

Seeing Charlotte with this woman friend, he perceived aspects of her personality that had been hidden from him before. She laughed hard at Vickie's small smutty asides. She was delighted by her confidences, her betrayals, her gossip; she asked for more. Vickie brought out a dismissive, philistine side of Charlotte, one that was also tinged with mendacity. She was untruthful because she was snobbish, aggressive, competitive, mean.

And Steadman noticed that half the time he was either ignored or belittled by the woman, whom he had begun to dislike as much as he disliked the weak aspects of Charlotte's personality that the woman patronized.

The days of Vickie's visit went by slowly, but it served to show Steadman a different, much more dismaying Charlotte: heartier, crueler, easily won over, more comfortable with this woman than she had ever been with him, a woman he could never love and yet one that seemed more self-sufficient than he had previously imagined. Now, having seen her together with her friend, he knew for certain that their marriage was over — was surer than if Vickie had been a man enjoying his wife in a week of adultery. Charlotte would be all right; for her, the break would be painless.

He was hurt, humiliated by the failure, felt deceived, yet he knew that the failure was as much his fault as hers. His pride was injured; he knew he looked conspicuous, a bit of a fool, someone people pitied or tried to ignore.

The marriage had been a straightforward declaration, a contract, the binding part of the ceremony lasting minutes, a simple affirmation. The divorce was a lengthy agony strung out over many months, a set of legal questions with no clear answers, a tedious and painful disentangling that was like major surgery after a car crash, a messy amputation.

In the first remorseful months of his divorce, a bitter time of private pain, *Trespassing* was published, with its dedication ("To my wife") withdrawn. No acknowledgments page was included, though there were many times just before publication when he had fantasized writing a dense paragraph of small print to be inserted at the end of the text, under the title "No Thanks":

> To my ex-wife, Charlotte, who was too busy to finish reading this book in draft, eat me! To the many foundations that turned down my requests for financial assistance, fuck you! To the MacArthur Foundation, which did not consider me a genius but saw genius in a thousand preening mediocrities and rewarded their tedious efforts with absurd sums of money, eat my dust! Up yours! to my editor, who seldom returned my phone calls, and Piss off! to my bank, when at a crucial

stage of the writing it refused me a loan. To all the people who told me not to go on my journey, or said they could not see the point of this book, or belittled the title, or said the text was too long, go fuck yourself! ...

He had had no help at all, had only obstacles and stupidities to contend with. "Be careful!" people said when he set off. Were any words more unhelpful or antagonistic? The difficulty of writing the book had reflected the difficulties he'd had in taking the long, dangerous trip. Sometimes the imagining of such a list of no-thanks late at night had soothed his mind and helped him get to sleep in his empty bed.

The reviews were good, approving, and numerous. "A new kind of travel book," and as something different in a market that craved novelty, the book's sales were brisk, the film and TV rights sought after and bid upon, as the book itself became more widely noticed. His idea of trespassing from country to country without a passport was the basis of a "major motion picture," a board game, a ghostwritten sequel, a licensed book by another author from the point of view of a woman, and a popular television series, which inspired the merchandising. The Trespassing line of outdoor clothing became a bigger brand than The North Face and Patagonia, because the catalogue also retailed the TOG line of luxury accessories. The high-end items were the moneymakers — titanium sunglasses, watches, and knives. The knives alone occupied one division in the company and seven pages of the catalogue — folding knives, camp knives, bowie knives, some with staghorn or abalone shell or mastodon ivory handles (one or two designs with the rubric "Limited to 50 Pieces"), and each, in the hollow of the guard, embossed with the Trespassing logo. People who did not know Steadman's name and who had never read his book coveted the sunglasses and watches and knives. And the unexpected profits, fabulous even to his wealthy Vineyard friends, allowed him to buy and expand the up-island house, giving it the size and look of a château, complete with perimeter walls and orchards and garden statuary.

Although he had been careful to exclude any mention of her, Charlotte was associated with the book, and many people believed she had been partly responsible for it. That she was given some credit for it angered Steadman more than anything else, for he had conceived and written the book alone. The fact was that she had hindered him; he had overcome that and ignored her dismissals. The success of the book was a relief and a pleasure. He told himself — and for a long time believed this was true — that if he never wrote anything else, he would be happy being a one-book wonder. It was a good book, big and solid, that inspired a new generation of risk-taking travelers.

After Charlotte left, after the divorce was final and the property apportioned, after the early part of his success was established and he had gone to ground on a remoter part of the Vineyard, she wrote him a letter. It was apologetic and humble: she was glad for him, she wished him happiness. She complimented him, said she was sorry she had helped him so little. She said she was living in New York, which was much more expensive than she had imagined, and "I guess you know what's coming next."

He agreed to give Charlotte the very amount of money that she had asked for. Steadman's only condition was that before he handed anything over, she sign a paper waiving any further claims, demands, or requests. She did this gladly, by return mail, notarized and witnessed. Then he was rid of her. She took the money, and was perhaps thrilled initially, before thinking (Vickie would have egged her on): I should have asked for more.

For his book kept rising, there was more money, enough to support him for the rest of his life. The amount she had asked for, which had seemed so much at the time, was a pittance compared with what later accrued to him. When his lawyer complimented him on his savvy, he was not pleased — it was petty to feel vindictive or triumphant. He knew the No Thanks page that he had imagined was mean-spirited and unfunny.

Reflecting on Charlotte later, as his ex-wife, his former lover, he was remorseful. He could barely believe that he had once vowed to love and protect her for life; he was astonished that he had desired her, ashamed that he had broken solemn promises made so publicly. He could no longer remember the color of her eyes or the shape of her face. But the beautiful swell of her buttocks as she lay on her stomach, crying out to be penetrated; the curve of her thigh; the brownish birthmark in the shape of Madagascar at the small of her back; the way she sniffed and blinked like a rodent when she was anxious — he could call up these images at will.

She probably hated him now, but why? Because the marriage had not worked? But she had made promises, too, not that the marriage would be easy, but the awful lie that she was simple, no more than she seemed. Now he knew that no one was. People might believe their own words, but it could be fatal for you to believe them. He did not distrust her, or the next women he met. He deeply distrusted himself for believing that Charlotte would be happy to be his partner, and hated himself for thinking that he wanted no more than that, when in reality he had expected her to do housework, and be witty, and help him with his book, and love him for being intelligent and hardworking and a hero.

Preposterous expectations — he was better off alone. He said, "Never again."

2

NO WOMAN WOULD EVER console him in his distrust, he felt. The one he wished for did not exist, for he wanted a woman to lay a healing hand on him, bind a blood-pressure cuff on his upper arm and cinch it, touch his forehead, take his temperature, use her fingertips to tap for clues on his back, peer into his throat, check his heart, perhaps only a tender physical examination, in a manner of speaking. But how could there be such a woman?

Years passed, girlfriends came and went. He shrank as his fame grew, that famous author of *Trespassing* resembling him less and less. Rather than leave his farm, he continued to enlarge it until it became an estate so vast, so productive, so valuable, that he would never need to leave.

The land was fertile. He grew much of the food he ate. The physical activity tired him and displaced his writing hours. He started stories, he sketched out ideas for novels, for plays, for an opera. The publishers wanted another *Trespassing*, but that book he knew was written and done, and he told them so: there would be no other. He took comfort in the fact that among his summer friends, the most secure and happiest were those who had done one thing well — a book, a movie, a play, a picture — the unique thing by which they were known.

Growing flowers, cultivating vegetables, gave him consolation and wearied him enough to ease the passage of time. Whatever he began to write on any given morning, doodling at his desk, he always ended up abandoning the effort and digging in his garden. And when he was not hoeing or watering, he would sit on the cast-iron love seat at the garden's edge and peer at the plants and exult in their size, imagine that he was watching them grow. He put in a heated greenhouse, an enormous tent-shaped conservatory of glass, so the whole year was his for cultivation.

The labor of gardening was a gift. He spent days lifting heavy sacks of manure for his potato field, bending and straightening, heaving and slinging them over the high fence that kept out the deer and the rabbits. When that chore was done he lay inert in his bath, stewing his aching bones and muscles. And one day when he looked in the mirror he saw that his left eye was crimson where there had been white: the eye was full of blood, opaque and frightful.

What surprised him was that there was no pain in the bloody eye. Still, it shocked him enough that he overcame his hatred of hospitals. He drove himself to the Vineyard hospital, squinting, shutting the right eye, apparently using the gory but functioning left one. He registered, was told to wait — a Thursday night in early May, hardly anyone around. He found a mirror and marveled at his hideous eye.

A woman in white appeared. "Mr. Steadman, please come this way."

He was friendly with the woman, wondering if she was the doctor. She was small, compact, efficient — those white silent shoes. She asked him if he was taking any medication, and was he allergic to antibiotics, and what exactly was the reason for his visit? After the woman recorded his answers, she smiled and asked him to wait. She was the nurse.

Another woman entered, older, bigger, dressed in white. She took his temperature, strapped his arm for his blood pressure, then jotted down the numbers. She led him to a small room and left. So it was a series of steps, a gaining admittance by degrees, wait here, now wait there, refining the questions, advancing toward the final room by passing through a set of subtle antechambers.

"Yes?"

Another nurse, probably, another stage of waiting, more questions. But she said, "I'm Dr. Katsina," and shook his hand.

He was at first anxious and then inexpressibly relieved, for she was attractive — long-legged, thin-faced, lanky light hair, full lips, her lovely blue-gray eyes staying on him with a curious and intelligent gaze. He guessed she was in her mid to late thirties, athletic, brisk, with a bike rider's calves, a good grip from handlebars and hand brakes.

As she washed her hands she said, "You've been doing some hard work."

Steadman looked at his hands and wondered what she had seen.

"What have you been lifting?"

He loved her coming straight to the point, the swift deduction, the summing up.

She smiled and put her scrubbed pretty face close to his. She was warm and clean and her nearness was like a remedy for the yearning in him. Placing her thumb near his left eye and the other fingers at the back of his scalp and tilting his head, she looked into his eye as if through a keyhole, and then she used an instrument to peer.

"Any pain?"

"No."

"Not too serious."

"What is it?"

"A subconjunctival hemorrhage. A burst capillary. That's real blood. You were bending, lifting something heavy."

He smiled at the accuracy of her diagnosis. "Do I take anything for it?"

Dr. Katsina shook her head and, washing her hands again, said, "It looks scary, but you're fine. It should subside in a week. If it doesn't, come back. Was there anything else?"

Steadman was so relieved he felt excited, grateful, restored to health. He wanted to hug her. He said, "What can I do for you?"

"I'm okay," she said, finding this funny.

Detecting a trace of unease, for he was staring at her with his bloody eye and looking eager, Steadman said, "How about a drink?"

"That's against hospital rules — and unprofessional. I'm a doctor. You're my patient. Anyway, I have a woman in labor. She's due any minute but I have a feeling it will be two A.M. It always is."

Dr. Katsina made a gesture of helplessness and departure that was also a signal of dismissal — time's up.

"How do you deal with someone in labor?"

"I wait until I'm paged."

"Maybe we could wait together."

She equivocated with her shoulders. It was like a yes, but she said, "Not today."

He didn't insist, because he felt she was cooperating, and now that he knew her name, he was certain he wanted to see her again. Instead of phoning her, he wrote her a note, wondering when she would be free. She did not reply. He told himself that doctors were busy. He tried again, giving her his telephone number.

She called him a few days later, saying, "This is Ava Katsina," and it took him a moment to recall who she was, for she hadn't said "Doctor."

He said, "I want to see you — please."

"Okay," she said, "but this means I can't be your doctor."

"I'll agree to anything."

Her laughter reassured him. She said she was free the following day. He waited by the emergency door of the hospital, gladly at ease, watching through the window, seeing her dress tighten against her body as she bent forward over the counter to sign out.

"I have to leave my pager on," she said, getting into the car. "I have another woman in labor. I can't go far."

He drove to Oak Bluffs, parked at the Dockside Inn, and they climbed to a second-story bar overlooking the inner harbor. He was struck at once by its roughness, the sourness of spilled beer, the loud music. The place was a bit too busy for May, perhaps because there were so few other bars open, the drinkers not vacationers but islanders, an after-work crowd of shouting friends. The porch was chilly, damp, uncomfortable, noisy, and when the sun went down there wasn't enough light to read a menu. The service was slow, and along with the discomfort and din was the chill in the air, one of those days in clammy procrastinating spring when people called out, "Not summer yet!" and the Vineyard felt more than ever like a remote island, detached and dark, the Cape hidden by low clouds, the north wind thrashing the water, making whitecaps on the ebbing tide and pushing corrugations of froth across the Sound.

Steadman had been so preoccupied with these distractions — he had hoped to find a quiet bar or café — he had turned away from Dr. Ava Katsina. He looked at her to apologize, to make a joke about the place being so awful, such a dive, and to smile at her.

She was crying. She saw his sudden concern, something like alarm, and she said, "I'm sorry. I can't help it."

He was always torn by tears, anyone's tears, and a woman's sobbing undid him. He had no reply, he was helpless. Please stop, he wanted to say.

"It's just that I don't believe it." And she went on softly sniffing and swallowing, dabbing at her eyes with a ragged ball of tissue. "I am so happy."

He smiled again, hoping to encourage a smile from her.

"You're the writer," she said. "*Trespassing*."

Steadman nodded, he clinked his glass against hers, he drank not knowing what to say.

"I was wondering if we'd meet. I knew you lived here."

"Everyone lives here."

"In the summer," she said. Her tears made her look young and inexperienced, as unlike a doctor as it was possible to be. She blew her nose and wiped it, reddening the rims of her nostrils, becoming plainer, innocent, almost boyish. She sniffed. "I'm so sorry."

Steadman took her hand and felt her gentle fingers; she let him comfort her. He could see she was shaken but happy, her tears like the glow of a rapture. He liked her emotion, the change in her face, the way she looked younger with tears on her cheeks. He was the doctor, she the ailing patient, needing reassurance, emotional, as though sobbing in relief.

"Take it easy."

"No, I'm happy. Really."

He could see she was, even with her wet eyes and dripping nose.

He was about to embrace her when her pager sounded — important, a dull repeated note, demanding to be noticed — and immediately she scooped the thing out of her leather bag and studied its message. In a clear efficient voice, scoured of tears, the tone of a timekeeper, she said, "I have to leave here right now to see to that delivery."

Like that, in a flash; and now it was he who was impressed and helpless.

The waitress appeared — young, fresh-faced, with a beautiful smile and thick tumbling blond hair that she arranged with tosses of her head. She held a pen and a pad and said, "Some more drinks for you guys?"

"Just the check," Dr. Katsina said.

Steadman watched the waitress leave, shimmying through the crowded bar, and then said, "I can tell you're a really good doctor."

"I know what I'm doing most of the time. And I can go on being your doctor — but that's all," she said.

"What's the alternative?"

"Find another doctor. I'll be your friend. I'm a good friend. You won't need to make appointments."

She spoke with an intensity that had to have come from her being so solitary, so hardworking. A sociable person would never have said it that way. He tried to take her hand, but she was already rooting in her bag for her car keys.

He hardly recognized her the next night. They had agreed to meet at a restaurant on the harbor in Edgartown, but when he was led to the table, reserved in his name, he did not see her. In Dr. Katsina's place was a blonde in a red blouse, applying lipstick. Seeming to see Steadman behind her in the small mirror of her compact, she clapped it shut and looked up at him, fingering the ringlets of her hair, not smiling, looking intruded-upon.

"It *is* you," he said, and sat down.

Then she smiled. "I saw you staring at that waitress in the bar last night and I thought, Why not? Anyway, I'm a doctor and we don't do things like this, which is why I did it. It's a wig. Want me to take it off?"

Amused and fascinated, he said, "Not now."

It was another cold evening but a quieter place, and she told him how she had delivered the baby, a normal delivery, a little girl — happy mother, nervous father — just like that, eased a whole child into the world, dripping and squalling, and wiped its wet head. Her lipstick, her blond wig, made the clinical details of the childbirth story wonderful and slightly improbable.

"I can drink tonight," she said. "My pager's off."

She was strong, she was confident, she alluded without apology to old boyfriends. ("This guy I used to date turned me on to your book.") She told him stories of the operating room, and Steadman was fascinated by her conceit, for while there was something incomprehensible and mystical in it, there was also a mastery of anatomy, the ultimate in physical transformation — a cesarean section, cutting out an appendix, ridding a person of a diseased organ, setting a bone, snatching a sick person from the brink of an abyss. A patient staring horror-struck at death she was able to restore to health. She knew the chemistry of drugs, she had the authority to order them, she knifed open flesh, she sewed it together with stitches, made a healing seam in the skin. All of it a vigorous challenge of his belief that doctors caused illness.

He was so conscious of his skepticism that he said, "You're like a shaman."

She laughed at his hyperbole and denied it with a hint of insincerity — the medical doctor's confidence, the surgeon's arrogance: she knew her power. She was the only truly fulfilled person he had ever met.

"I'm glad you think so."

But as though to deny it she told him how at medical school they had fooled with cadavers to take the curse off them — she and a boyfriend with a corpse. Or saying nothing during a long operation she performed jointly with that man, while dropping sexual hints, knowing that after the thing was done and the patient wheeled away they would hurry to his house — this was in Boston.

"The rush you get from a successful operation — I mean, working together, the tension, the efficiency, the body lying there on the table between us," she said. "When it was all over we'd go and fuck."

"The private life of a shaman," he said, but he had been taken aback by her frankness. "Too bad you can't be my doctor."

"I can be other things."

"My friend."

What she said next was so memorable to him, he kept it to himself as a wicked secret, and never recalled it afterward without seeing the redness of her lips and tongue, the unsuspicious smiling Yankee with his tankard in the white blouse and the silly improbable hair on the Sam Adams beer sign, the slant of light and wooden threads on the screw bung of an ornamental wine cask, the saltshaker shape of the fat, squat Edgartown Harbor lighthouse, the outgoing tide swelling and chafing at the edge of the On Time Ferry plowing a dark furrow through the current near the Chappaquiddick side, a woman walking nearby on the beach with a cigarette in her mouth and a scarf twisted on her head — all of it fixed in his mind with her blunt statement.

"Statistically, only six percent of the women who give blowjobs get any real pleasure from it," she said.

Steadman's mouth was already dry; the words he had attempted had shriveled and blistered on it and were gone. He was looking helplessly at her lipsticked mouth, her damp swollen lips.

He anticipated what she was going to say next, and his ears were already ringing, all the louder because he could see she wasn't smiling, only relating an established fact. Yet he was shocked. It was one of the boldest sentences he had ever heard from a woman — a taunt, a tease, a promise, the ultimate pickup line delivered as a statistic. She seemed to understand the effect it had on him and to desire him for being shockable, as he desired her for being able to shock him, Slade Steadman, reclusive author of the well-known book of surprises, *Trespassing*.

"I'm in that six percent."

Except for his facetious response, which he delivered hoarsely and hopelessly — "So what's in it for me?" — he did not remember the rest of the meal, only his urgency that they finish and hurry home, and she seemed as eager as he was.

That began the summer of hot nights in the walled compound of his up-island house — nights when she was not on duty, nights so dedicated to their desire that often they met in the dark and drank and touched and groped and uttered nothing but sighs, twitching and tearing at each other's clothes and bodies. She held him off, she said, "Let me, let me, I like it" — holding him down, mothering him, sucking him — until he could not stand it anymore, and as the night grew darker, their bodies glowed. He loved it because it turned them into blameless animals, monkeys rutting for the play of it and the pleasure she took in arousing him. And when she was aware of the closeness of his panting, that he was seconds from exploding, she squirmed free and got down on him and held him in her mouth and pumped with her hand until he came with a roar while she squealed and licked it from her lips, her eyes rolling up as she became sightless, white-eyed in ecstasy.

"Do you love it?"

"I love it," he said.

"Now do as I say."

Then, after she had cared for him, searching his body in the most intimate way, she insisted that he please her — and he was unexpectedly gladdened as the moans crept from her throat, as she directed his hand or, opening her legs, seized his head with all her fingers and thrust it against her, smearing his face with her desire.

He loved his nights with her for her demands, and her fairness, for she encouraged him in his demands. Whole greedy nights of saying nothing, or muttering disconnected words in a darkness in which their hands spoke and everything was allowed, everything insisted upon. Or the opposite: talking all night, pressed together, kissing, telling each other their most elaborate fantasies. And the intensity of their single-minded desire kept them strangers to each other, communicating on the lowest frequencies, dwelling on their satisfactions, loving what they shared, and needing each other for their secrets.

Their secrets were safe — trust was what bound them together in the beginning, as they became ever more candid about their needs. At the same time, all this while, Ava remained a woman in white, the most skillful doctor at the hospital; and he began to work with greater confidence and with renewed imagination, the inaccessible writer in his up-island seclusion, smiling again. Yet still they remained strangers. Their lives were separate, only the act of sex joined them, they knew each other in the dark but nowhere else. They did not believe they had any future, and felt certain that all desire, fierce as it seemed, hot as it might burn, had an end in ashes that cooled and dispersed like the dust they were.

Steadman loved having her because he had so little else in his life. Charlotte was gone. He did not resent the divorce, but he questioned his own judgment: how could he have been so wrong about her? The girlfriends were gone, too. After his first struggles to be alone on the Vineyard, with his curt answers, his evasiveness, his lack of cooperation, he had actually succeeded in keeping people out of his life — and, at last, after the first years of his reclusiveness, keeping the press and interviewers away, they ceased to care. He had no new book. He slipped beneath the surface of events and seemed to sink. Except for the summer people who invited him to parties and were polite about his work, keeping their inquiries vague, there was no one. The summer people were his friends, though, and more than that: for a season they were his world. When they left around Labor Day he had remained on the Vineyard, wondering what to do with himself. Now he knew. He had Ava.

Of course everyone talked, for on the island, summer people and locals alike were passively nosy in the Vineyard manner, watchful while pretending not to care, and always alert for gossip. They were noted for their attention to detail and for their long and remorseless memories. They knew he was having an affair; they knew with whom. His car, her car, the groceries, his movements, even his moods, his happiness — it was all monitored and noted and whispered about. People were glad for him, for her too, for though she was a recent arrival and was hardly known, she was respected for her efficient doctoring. The islanders took an ignorant pleasure in commenting on how different the two people were, the wealthy risk-taking writer with local roots and the modest physician from off-island. Steadman was aware of those rumors and thought: If only they knew how reckless and greedy she was, how depraved and demanding, how lavish in bed, how she made a happy slave of him.

"Desire me," she said. She was content, she almost crooned the words. "You don't have to love me. Love is a burden. It's a pain. It causes unhappiness. Just be my friend."

He knew the deceptions of love and its meaningless language. He told her that it was also a delusion. It came, it went, and made you crazy. It was mainly about wanting to possess someone. Sex was something else: it promised nothing, it had no future, it was magic enacted entirely in the present. They did not expect the affair to last. They hardly met in the daytime, they made few plans, and Steadman assumed that the ashes of their desire, the useless fragments and residue of its end, were not far off.

She knew that without his saying so; she always seemed to know what he was thinking, and when he was sunk in silence, she knew what was in his mind.

"If I ever write anything more," he said, "it will be about this — us — the feeling in the flesh, the two of us at our most monkey. How the truth can be drawn from sexual pleasure. Knowing that we are going to die. Everything that lies beyond love."

The way he dismissed the delusions of hope and the self-deception of future plans and the farce of romance moved her. She said, "I'm glad we found each other. I want to be your friend. It's purer. It's much better. Friendship asks nothing, it gives everything, and friendship with desire is paradise."

"I agree. Love doesn't make you better. It excludes the whole world. For a brief period you have an adoring partner, and later an enemy. Love is like some horrible twisted religion the way it changes you. And afterward, when love ends, you're lost."

"Please don't marry me," she said one day outside the hospital, still smelling of disinfectant. She laughed with conviction: the words were like an aphrodisiac to them both.

"I promise. I will never marry you," he said, and embraced her, kissed her, feeling beneath her loose clothes and her doctor's smock, the girlishness of her eager body.

"Let's be friends."

"Yes, yes."

"We have no future," she said.

"None at all."

From his marriage to Charlotte he had learned love, and you could not know love without knowing its opposite. He remembered now how his marriage had ended and the love soured and he had been cut loose — like one of those mute and damaged men released after a long spell in prison who find they cannot function in the crowded world of decent people, and turn to crime again, and get sent back to a cell to sulk. That was how dangerous he regarded loving. It was waywardness and weakness and failure.

"Friendship is so much better," Ava was saying. "You have to love your lover, but you can be truthful to your friend. Love isn't blind — it's sickness, it's surrender."

The extravagant talk was the self-conscious reassurance of two people passionately attached and at pains to be kind to each other, aching for each workday to end, for night to fall so they could be together.

She, the stronger, more confident one, strengthened him. The manner in which she bucked him up made him long for her.

"This is what I want you to do to me tonight," she would say, usually in public, a bar, a restaurant, the supermarket, a neutral place where they would hold hands, nothing more. And she would describe in the minutest detail where she wanted to be touched, and how, and what she would be wearing, and the way she wanted him to be dressed. It was her script for the evening, but it was not complete until she said, "And this is what I want to do to you."

In these fevered dialogues, in her insistence on order and ritual, the stages of their lovemaking, she could be almost clinical, as if running through the phases of what would be a brilliant but tricky operation, the object of arousing her, bringing her to orgasm. But when the time came, what ensued was anything but tidy, and it was less like an operation than the rehearsal of a black mass.

"You have more germs in your mouth than in your ass, didn't you know that?" she said, turning him over and tonguing him. And when she was done, she said, "Now it's my turn for a black kiss."

She challenged him to go further. "Deeper, deeper, deeper," she would say. He had never known a woman to be so explicit in daring him. Theirs was nothing like the sort of courtship or love affair in which by degrees trust was gained and plans were made for a future together. Next month, next year, a vacation, children, a mortgage — none of that. They had no future; tonight was enough. They wrecked themselves on each other, and yet the following day they met again, like insatiable conspirators, for more.

She was able to surprise him as no other woman had ever done. One night she said, "I've got something for you," and he expected exotic lingerie or Polaroids, as in the past. But if she promised something new, it was original, all hers, and certainly new to him. She did not disappoint.

That night she met him at the Dockside bar wearing a dark tailored suit and slacks, a wide tie, a felt fedora. He smiled — he had never seen this suit on her before. She looked like a decadent schoolboy. On the way home she told him to pull into a side road and park. "I want to make out with you," she said, and kissed him, let him grope her, fondle her breasts, and she opened her knees and held his hand against her. He felt something hard, like a rubber truncheon, between her legs.

"A strap-on," she said. "That's for both of us."

And when they set off again, Steadman became sweaty, anxious, eager, and fearful, as she described how she was going to use it on him. But in the house she would not go into the bedroom. She lazed on his sofa and pulled the thing out and played with it and refused to take any clothes off. "On your knees," she said, "get me in the mood," and forced his head down. Seeing how he was making her happy — she screeched with pleasure as she gagged him — he became aroused by the madness of her voluptuous laughter.

Again and again he had to remind himself that she was a physician, respected in the hospital and on the island. Yet how was it possible, knowing the most delicate surgery and all the anatomy — the name of every tissue, every muscle, every organ — that she could lose herself in the darkness of the body in which nothing had a name? A doctor was trained to see the body as something coherent, namable, dissectible, like a symmetrical cabinet of flesh and blood. But that was her daytime preoccupation; at night she stripped him naked and operated on him with her mouth and her fingers, devouring him, nameless part by nameless part, as though they were hardly human.

"You are my meat," she said.

That summer passed. People saw them together, the writer and the doctor, but as Steadman and Ava always looked semidetached and distracted, like friends, never a couple, the people observing did not speculate unduly. They were glad to see Steadman at last out of his self-imposed captivity. His good mood seemed to indicate that he who had published nothing in years might have freed himself from his seclusion by finishing a book and would be publishing it soon.

There was no book, and now his silence was a virtue, for he was spending time with Ava and glorying in her paradoxes — the medical doctor who was a debauched sensualist. Summer faded into fall, and fall declined into winter, and the cold weather made them more companionable, allowing them to possess the darker, emptier island. Winter was perfect, their solitude complete. The Vineyard seemed to belong to them. The hospital was less busy, there were no parties, hardly any social events, no "Taking another trip?" no "How's the book coming along?"

And there was nothing more exciting to him than Ava's phoning him in midafternoon: "Tonight — a house call," then *click,* and his anticipating her arrival in the early dark of winter, frost gleaming on the grass, and the approach of her car, the fat tires announcing her on the gravel driveway, and her kiss, her warm breath, her open mouth, "I want you," and her taking off her laboratory smock or her ER scrubs and revealing herself in a pretty dress or lingerie. The great room of his house was so warm they were comfortable lying half naked on the sofa; the candle flames, the mirrors, her sighs, which became low howls of pleasure. Out here, in the winter, she could scream — and sometimes did, foul-mouthed in uncontrollable desire, shocking him with men's words — and no one would hear, for they were in the middle of a dark ice-bound island.

When they were done, drenched in sweat, panting for breath, they lay in each other's arms.

"I hadn't expected you to call."

"I had to see you," she might say. "We lost someone today, a nice old man. I needed to do something life-affirming."

He smiled, he held her.

"Something human. Something perverted."

But he would sometimes stare, seeing only the elderly blood-drained face of a patient yellowing on a pillow, open-mouthed, as though having died screaming.

"Now I'm better. You cured me. Gotta go." Abrupt, all business, like a man on a mission, she was out the door and in her car, and at last two receding red lights.

Spring came, full of equivocating winds and low temperatures, dawdling promises, daffodils in April, drizzle and mud in May, reminders of the previous spring and their first meeting, and somehow giving a sense of repetition to their days and weeks. They had been together for a full year. In the second summer Ava was busier at the hospital, in greater demand, and he was the one who was made to wait. Waiting was hard for him, because he had no work. He wondered if there was someone else; he couldn't ask — that was their agreement, proposed by her. "When we're together we should possess each other. When we're alone we have no claims." Steadman had thought that was a good, enlightened idea, but as the summer passed and he saw less of her, he became insecure, suspicious, jealous.

"I think I have a rival," he said one day, hating himself for even raising the subject.

"Two rivals," she said. "A man with emphysema, on a ventilator, with pneumonia, whose family wants to pull the plug. And a man in constant pain, in a head and neck brace, who fell from a roof he was fixing and cracked three cervical vertebrae, whose heart is too weak to let us operate. Who just wants to die."

She was the strong one, and understanding this he was ashamed of himself. He felt more like one of her patients than her lover, but a fatuous and fussing patient, whining for her attention. He sometimes wished that there really had been something wrong with him, so he could justify seeing her more often. She had a busy life that was determined by the urgencies of medical procedures. She was sometimes so reflective that she fell silent when she was with him, and he knew she was thinking of a critical case, someone at the hospital.

Her work was full of life and death — rescue and cure, real flesh, real blood. What had he to offer in return? Blank pages and complaints, the insubstantial fictions of someone who had forgotten how to write, who might have nothing to write. By the end of the summer she was polite but preoccupied, and though they remained sex partners — the blunt, unsentimental expression was hers; she often described previous lovers that way — the passion was gone, and with it the sexual innovation. She was a good doctor; he did not feel let down, but he knew she was caring for him.

"I'm still very fond of you," she said, and he laughed, because the expression was empty of desire. It was like a way of saying goodbye.

He knew it was over. "Fond" said it all. "Fond" was the opposite of her teeth and lips, her torn panties, her stabbing finger, his flogging her smeared face with his cock as she teased him with her tongue.

They made a ritual one night of burning their Polaroids. In their solemnity they were so reproached by what they saw, they hardly recognized their own bodies. They spoke of needing to find a way to end the affair, to formally seal it somehow.

As lovers they had talked of going to South America. Maybe following through with that was the answer. Ava had found the Ecuador tour on the Internet while searching the ethnobotany Web sites, especially the ones that were obvious drug tours dressed up as culture quests. It was all her idea — the river trip, the *yajé*, the Secoya village — a possible journey for Steadman to find a subject to write about. It had everything: Indians, rain forest, drugs, difficulty, exoticism. She had contacted Nestor and bought the tickets, because she felt certain that it was their last trip, an innovative goodbye, "a ceremony of farewell" was how she put it, like the *despedida*, a word she was to learn later. He agreed. Months before, they had stopped making love. That coincided with his abandoning his writing, as though writer's block was another expression of impotence. Neither of them imagined that the trip would keep their relationship together — blind him, inspire him as Burroughs had been inspired, arouse him, fire him with the idea for a book.

How were they to know that the farewell would become its opposite — the way home, truth-seeking, a renewal that was a kind of betrothal? They now saw that the trip to Ecuador had been a revelation, for from the moment he was overwhelmed, fearing he was lost, Ava took charge.

At the onset of his darkness she gave him light and propped him up, so he hardly knew the terror of blindness — or, more precisely (for he wanted to be precise), what he knew of it, the descent of blackness had so terrified him that he was not even aware how long it lasted. In that seemingly endless loop in the hazy time-scheme of a dream, just before he woke from his datura trance and she was holding his hand, he understood that it was not blackness at all but rather a bedazzlement, a blinding light of revelation, more than he could bear by himself.

Ava promised not to leave him. She left the hospital instead. She asked for a leave of absence. "I need a break. I'm tyrannized by my pager."

She moved onto the estate with him, and he began his book. Writing occupied his whole day now. He talked, she recorded it, she took notes; she played his words back to him. She was full of suggestions; he needed her encouragement and approval. And his prose always sounded better to him, with a ghostwritten concision, when she repeated it.

He was living at the margin, trespassing again, and delighting in being on the frontier. The shadows had always given him a clear view of the world. He had Ava's word on this. The man in the book was him. The women, all of them, were Ava.

She repeated that his taking the blinding datura was an indulgence — his conceit, his arrogance — but in the same breath would admit how fluent and observant he became in his blindness.

Saying "Now let's finish it," she praised him for noticing particularities, for remembering so much.

All the rooms he had known as a sensualist, their odors like reeking ghosts, and every disfigurement of their ceilings; the peripheral sounds of birdsong, wisps of music, muttered remarks, far-off voices — these and more. One entire chapter was background, no foreground, although all that was implied — a love scene, in fact. The man on the floor, the woman kneeling astride him, facing his feet — this was suggested by the movement in the mirror, the tugging of the carpet, the frantic cheeping of the caged bird, the shapes they cast on the wall, like Javanese shadow puppets — more subtle for being elongated — and the way it all sounded to a thirteen-year-old girl named Flora passing in the street outside, walking her dog. It was the dog that first noticed, frisky at the almost inaudible sounds. Then the young girl looked up at the jumping shadows and the fluttering candlelight, and she stopped to watch and remember a scene that might not make complete sense to her for years.

"And what did Flora say?"

"Flora just watched."

Flora just watched, she wrote, saying, "But Flora was mumbling to herself, as if seeing into a cloudy aquarium."

"She doesn't know what she's watching, but we do. And so we are seeing it through her eyes, understanding it, though she doesn't."

"That's nice. Details, please."

Every detail was in his description except the sight of the two people on the floor, the man hovering, holding the woman's ankles as he penetrated her, but in the way Steadman dictated it the whole room was suffused by the sexual act, the lamplight, the wallpaper, the flowers, the reflections from the wineglasses, the half-heard murmurs vibrating in furniture, the walls glimpsed incompletely from outside, so much of it a play of warm lopsided light on the ceiling and finally filling the imagination of the young girl in the street.

When he was done he told Ava he loved being alone with her, spinning his story.

"You're not making it up," she said. "You're remembering it."

He wondered at her certainty. He saw it all so clearly, peering within himself, his life so vivid in recollection it did not matter to him whether it was real or invented. He could see so distinctly into his early youth, memories of yearning and discovery, of the satisfying approximations of desire, when to his boy's lust, sex was everything, in the far-off country of the flesh.

"I want you to look at me like I am a piece of meat," Ava said, and laughed, and he could tell she meant it. "Salivate and then take me. I want to watch you eat me."

He was aware in his blindness that Ava closely observed him, remembering his reactions and using them to please him. Early on, his glance at the waitress's blond hair was one of her insights, inspiring her to wear the blond wig — a simple thing, but on her straight-haired and serious doctor's head it was a wild promise. In the first flush of his love affair with Charlotte she had done that — studied him in order to please him. When another woman flirted and he responded, Charlotte didn't scold but instead flirted with him and aroused him. It hadn't lasted. He had forgotten it until the memories were all returned to him in his blindness. And his blindness allowed Ava to explore his curiosity, giving her access to the hungry man within him who hardly had words for what he wanted but was obsessed by imagery.

Another summer day he chose to drive blind, walk blind, shop blind, get money blindly from an ATM machine, tap his cane near the ferry and take pleasure in the way he could part a crowd, cutting a swath through it like a prophet in a hurry. Men became anxious and helpless when they saw him; women lingered to watch, wishing to touch him. What was it about his blindness that roused women and made them protective, maternal, calm, sexual, all at once? Seeing him, it seemed they would do anything for him.

He tapped his way into a health food store on a side street in Vineyard Haven. He rummaged and by smell alone found a box of herbal tea bags and a jar of honey and a bag of garlic-flavored croutons and a package of sun-dried tomatoes, placing them in the basket that Ava carried. The shop's sections were defined and made logical by their delicious fragrances. But these too were memories. He had been there many times before. Years of being solitary had made him obsessive and turned him into a food crank. A preoccupation with health and the body was one of the consequences of isolation. Another was its opposite, disdaining health and order, damaging yourself. There was nothing in between. It was either self-denial or gluttonous indulgence; lonely people were either health nuts or chain smokers. He had told Ava that. He had told Ava everything. He repeated it that day as they left the place.

Ava said, "Now I know why you're a writer, because you're so sure of yourself even when you're wrong. Especially when you're wrong."

"And I know who waited on you," he said.

"You smell these women."

"That one for sure," he said, "in her white top, slightly torn sleeves, and her tumbled curly hair. She's hardly more than twenty. I liked her last year, when she was blond. She's dark-haired now."

He knew that Ava was staring at him as they walked through the parking lot to his car.

"Cutoff blue jeans and that halter top without a bra and those long legs." He slipped into the passenger seat, still talking, and handed Ava the keys. "What I liked most was that she was wearing that hillbilly getup with high heels. I loved hearing her walk back and forth, stretching to the upper shelves to get things for you."

"It's all true. What else do you remember?"

"The shoes are red. They have a teasing sound."

"What else?"

"She's Daisy Mae," Steadman said.

Back at the house, he needed to sit quietly to contain and enjoy the image — did not want to move or talk or eat. He was possessed by the thought of the busy girl in the ragged shorts and skimpy top, walking smartly back and forth — the breasts, the buttocks, the pretty hair and lips, the slender legs, the local girl playing at being a country girl, Daisy Mae, perhaps without knowing the innocent original, whose simple cartoon image had stirred him as a boy.

Steadman was so absorbed he did not bother to wonder where Ava had gone. He had had a good morning of dictation. The trip to Vineyard Haven had taken most of the afternoon.

Then, the sound of the shoes, the heels hammering, was unmistakable — the walking in the house, not toward him but back and forth, tantalizing him. He listened. They receded. They returned, rapping. He was on the porch, in the heat, and then she was with him, brushing past him, tidying the coffee table or, more likely, pretending she was doing so. Passing him again, she turned away and he reached out and touched her shorts, ran his hands over her, felt the softness and the rivets and the cutoff fringe and her warm thigh, and tugged her closer, slipped his hands up to her halter top, her shoulders, her curls. Her back was turned. He went on kissing her, touching her, her clothes, her skin, her shoes.

"Say something."

But the voice came from the far end of the porch, Ava's voice: "She's not paid to talk."

The woman he held began to laugh and, laughing, she relaxed and turned to kiss him, though he was unprepared — startled that the woman embracing him, groping him, was not Ava; shocked that he had not known; touching her breasts with his dumb fingers. He released her, but she lingered to lick his face.

"You can go now, sweetie," Ava said. "I told you, he's blind."

And with that the girl let go and laughed shyly, and as they heard the car departing up the gravel driveway, Ava led Steadman into the house, saying, "Now you're all mine."

3

"CERTAIN ITEMS of women's clothing unfailingly raised his lust," Steadman said in his dictating voice, with a cadence that helped him remember the narrative line. "The soft hand of silk, the open weave of lace, the tug of elastic, the neat cut of pleats in a short skirt, the way that satin smoothly bulked over skin — and particular loose combinations, warmed by a warm body. Much more than a woman's nakedness, the clothes were powerful aphrodisiacs. They were veils of enticement."

"Nakedness," Ava said, still writing, and in the tone that he was using, to let him know where she was in the middle of a sentence.

"Because a naked woman was someone stripped bare," Steadman said when she glanced up. "And he had never seen a naked woman his own age, only older ones, or pictures of them, looking so much like meat he wasn't interested."

Writing fast, her thumb driving the ballpoint, Ava muttered, "These are abstractions."

"To his terror-struck mind," he said, "such women seemed unattainable and far-fetched. And he was so young, the gaping straightforwardness of nudity seemed artless and demanding — nerve without guile, all flesh and hair. And where were the naked girls? He looked for young ones but he never saw them."

"Talk a little about his reaction to their nakedness."

"A naked woman was raw pork," Steadman said, talking over her mutter. "The word he used for 'naked' when he was growing up was 'bollocky.' It didn't apply to girls — they didn't have bollocks, but boys did. 'Swimming bollocky.' He didn't have a word for 'naked girl' and in a sense could not imagine what a skinny girl with no clothes on would look like. But clothed ones were everywhere."

"Go on," Ava said, encouraging him.

He turned to her and said in a sharp voice, "Why did you do that to me yesterday with that young woman?"

"Just having fun," she said.

He had no reply, because the object of his own life these days was his pleasure in his book. He said, "It was strange. I didn't realize. Those clothes threw me."

"Clothes," she said. "That is today's topic."

He resumed his dictation, saying, "Different clothes, the subtlety of styles, each one resonating with a year, a season in his life. He loved reading women's bodies through their clothes."

"Fetishism?" Ava said. "Role-play?"

"Semiotics," he said.

"Oh, please."

"Don't write that word. Write: red lips, tight sweaters, tight blue jeans, bare feet in high heels. Capri pants were popular when he was fifteen. Tight shorts, shaping the ass and giving it a smirk. There was so much expressiveness he saw that aroused him — the face in the crotch, the manner in which a girl's ass seemed to respond with a wobble in hot pants, silver lamé, ignescence from buttock to buttock as she walked."

"Delete 'ignescence,' I'm begging you."

"Okay. 'Sparkling.' More of the body showed because it was clothed, and it all beckoned because it was highlighted." He paused, then said, "One girl he remembered."

Ava's murmur now was both laughter and affirmation, but Steadman was staring, solemn, his voice croaky, dry with desire.

"It was madness. He watched her and thought, Your lips are a cunt. Your cleavage is a cunt. Your neck. Your ass. Your eager hands are fuckable. He wanted to come on her fingers and watch her lick them. It was more than madness."

He was sitting forward, upright, blindly seeing every detail he described, speaking in a scorching whisper as he listened to her writing as fast as the tape recorder was turning. The pad was in her lap and her exertion was audible, not just the rustle of paper but a peculiar sighing of her chair legs that was somehow plaintive, even sad, a loosening and sometimes a creak, like the complaint of a tight knuckle joint. It could have been her body, but it was always her chair.

"He loved it all. He wanted more."

He had drunk a pint of the datura and at the same moment he was dazzled. He saw a woman's face and other, separate elements at the margin of his sight — shoes, painted fingernails, breasts lifted against the filled bodice of an evening gown, a glimpse of lace, a bra strap showing, a full skirt pressed against crushable buttocks, a black veil over staring eyes — images from old magazines, fragments of drawings, memories of women he had seen and never forgotten, the wonderful covers of old paperbacks — the titles, too, *The Revolt of Mamie Stover* and *The Wayward Bus, Nana* and *I, the Jury* — depicting reckless women half dressed and dressed up. They had been the icons of his education.

"'All dressed up' was the expression that excited him then, much more than 'stripped naked,'" Steadman said. "He loved the drama of the event — the preparation, the clothes, the costume. He was possessed by the word 'girlie,' the word 'panties,' the word 'bra.'"

He was looking past Ava at a young girl in a gown, framed in a doorway, backlit by a bright lamp inside a house on a warm night, her hair piled up, knowing she was beautiful, realizing she was desired.

"How far back are we going?"

"Way back," Steadman said, and resumed, "Sex was the past, deep inside him, smoldering. Desire was mostly a memory."

The best sex was a second chance at something he had longed for and had never outgrown — datura had helped him understand that. Sex for him was not a foray into the fast lane. It was the recognition and recapture of a moment of intense longing in the past — reliving it, using it, completing it. And the best of it was that even then the longing was not exhausted of its pleasure.

"He was so happy and horny as a boy," Steadman said. "It was beautiful, but he wanted more. He burned and burned, wanting it all again. He renounced God for it, he turned his back on salvation, and if there was a hell he was willing to risk it for the luxury of enjoying a woman's hungry embrace. What is the greatest pleasure in life?"

Ava was writing, wondering whether she was being asked to suggest the answer.

"Pure happiness is the fulfillment in middle age of a childhood fantasy. Freud at his finest. Having now what you wanted then. At last the blind man could revisit the past and use what he saw."

"And what did he see?"

"He saw everything, and he could have any of it, any conquest, any moment. His special sight gave him access to the past." Steadman raised his hand to signal that he was delivering an aside. "I want you to know how serious I am when I say that the past is incomplete, unfinished. Certain occasions."

Ava had stopped writing, stopped moving. "The helpful cliché

'You're never too old to have a happy childhood,'" she said, and then there was only her breathing, like the softest swing of air. "Name an occasion."

"Prom night," he said. He wasn't dictating. He was tense with eagerness. "The thrill of it."

"There's the whole world to choose from and you choose a prom queen."

"Not a queen. A skinny girl!"

"For most high school kids of your generation wasn't the prom a letdown?"

"Of course. That's why it never went away." He sat forward. He said, "It was a golden moment that ended in frustration. What a thrill it was for him to uncover a yearning he had in the past, a tremendous sexual longing, and pick it up and complete it."

She resumed writing fast, to catch up, and remained attentive, snatching at the pages of her pad and flipping them.

"He wanted now what had been denied to him. He desired only what had been thwarted. What had been withheld, he hungered for."

He heard Ava's chair responding to her body as she wrote, and the chair sounded as though she were riding it.

"He wanted Rosemarie Fredella in a blue low-cut prom dress — bare shoulders, bare neck, her breasts crushed together and her hair swept up beautifully as he had never seen it before. And white high-heeled shoes and a pearl necklace."

"Pearl choker."

"Yes. And dangling earrings. Pink lips, pink nails. Mascara. A new face. He had never seen her look this way before. She had gone to a lot of trouble to change from a pretty smiling girl into a seductive young woman. And now he understood — in his blindness, from his experience as a traveler — that this was like a tribal rite of sex play, in which the choicest virgins in the village were dressed up in elaborate costumes, their whole being made more beautiful, for the sole purpose of exciting desire in potential lovers. A kind of betrothal, for their initiation."

The girl in the lovely dress, glowing with eagerness, his girl for the night, waiting alone for him at her doorway, looking fresh, looking willing, her smile and her whole posture saying, "I am ready. I am yours. Take me."

Ava's chair legs were murmuring, so he knew she was still writing. He said nothing more, even when she finished. He knew she was looking over the page, surmising what it was cuing her to do. An instruction was always implied in his narrative, implicit directions. She was glad. He needed her. Without her he was alone. With her his fantasy could live. There was no point to his blindness if his fantasy could not be activated. It had to be lived first and described afterward. The acting out of the fantasy contained the revelation.

He could trust her to be faithful to him, but he knew when he was being teased. She had tricked him yesterday, but playfully, proving that he was not as strong or as knowing as he thought. But he had liked the touch of the strange girl, and he had loved Ava's stratagem, how she had taken the girl's place, dressed as she was. He loved her for liking the game.

Now Ava said, "I need a little time."

"Then go now."

"Promise me you won't drive blind."

"It's wearing off. Don't worry."

She left the room, she left the house, he heard her car on the driveway gravel. He knew she would call and he hoped soon. She was serious, and always more alluring when the episode was formal, perhaps a result of her medical training — her instinct for order? Even though she sometimes rebelled against it, she found it awkward to be casual, took pride in preparation, and seldom explained what it was she was doing. Putting herself in charge — more medical doctor traits.

He found the right clothes for himself, the tuxedo he seldom wore, the black shoes, the stiff shirt. He set them out, the tux over a chair, buffed the shoes, and found himself pacing.

Without being conscious of it at first — for almost two hours had passed and he had not received Ava's call — he was impatient. Then he felt sure he was being kept waiting deliberately. *The doctor is busy.* There was absolutely nothing he could do except wait: could not read or write, or distract himself, or stray far from the telephone.

Such an old tormenting feeling, the impatience he had felt as a boy, wanting so badly to act on his own and hating the feeling that he needed permission, that he had to be summoned. Those were among the sharpest pains of his youth, impatience and delay, and they had created such yearning in him: his passion to vanish that he called travel.

All this was recreated in his mind without his having planned it. And how could she have known how much it had mattered to him, that delay itself made his desire greater and brought it to a pitch of lust? Almost five hours had passed.

His faltering blindness had turned to twilight, matching the actual twilight at the window, for he had been pacing in the house sightlessly, without switching any lights on.

When the phone rang, his blindness had moderated to the point that on the second ring he actually saw the telephone by the window in the last light of the waning day, almost eight o'clock this August night.

"It's me."

"Who?"

"Rosemarie, your prom date," she said, and gave him her address.

He dressed quickly and considered a swig of the datura while he did so. But though he rued the fact that his blindness — his lightness — was completely gone, and he squinted at the confusing harshness of the lamps, it meant that he could keep his promise not to drive blind. He brought some of the mixture with him in a hip flask that had once held his whiskey.

The address she gave him was a house number he did not know, on a side road off Franklin Street — probably a friend's place — but when he found it he could see it was perfect: a frame house with an open porch, a light burning on the porch, a lantern on a post beside the brick-paved front path.

As he approached the house, the front door opened and she stepped out in a blue prom gown, her hair upswept, white high-heeled shoes, white gloves. She wore lipstick and blue eye shadow, and he marveled at her resourcefulness. There was more detail in her appearance than he had suggested in his dictation: everything that he had remembered, and more, from the half-buried memory of his boyish desire.

"You look great."

"Thank you," she said in a small voice, seeming more uncertain than shy.

In the car, she said, "Are we going dancing?"

He said nothing. He hadn't thought of that. He only wanted to be alone and to hold her.

"I know a place," he said.

They went by the unpaved back roads to the beach at the harbor entrance to Tashmoo, where they parked, hidden amid the high rose bushes, facing the Sound. Satisfied that they were alone, Steadman took out his hip flask and drank two large swallows. He then sat quietly, feeling the drug course in his blood and rise into the bulb of his head and warm his brain.

"This does amazing things to your pulse," Ava said, her fingers on his wrist.

But he was smiling, he was blind, he got out of the car and went to her side and slipped off her shoes. Then, hearing music from a house in the woods they could not see, they danced slowly on the sand. He held her close, felt her frilly dress, the silks beneath it, all the layers against him, her body too, her sinuous dancing in his hands. He could hardly bear it.

He touched her, let his fingers slip to her buttocks and clutched them. Ava murmured but said nothing. He felt for her breasts in the crispness of all that cloth. She seemed to pull away, a tug of modesty, yet she allowed it.

They kissed. She kissed his ear, his neck, and he thought how holding her and kissing was a form of dancing.

"Not here."

They went back to the car, which was fragrant with her perfume, something sensual in its stuffy heat, all the windows closed. He helped her into the back seat and kissed her again, sucked on her lips, groped at the bodice of her dress and found her breasts and put his face between them and kissed and nuzzled her cleavage.

"Long ago the answer was always 'Please, stop.'"

Ava said, "Please, don't stop."

She sighed as he slipped his hand beneath her dress, all those layers, snagging his fingers on her petticoats, and found her panties. He extended his fingers to touch the lace trim and slid them under the tight elastic to the slick hair and soft lips, and as he slipped a thick finger into her, she moved her legs together and clasped his hand between her thighs and moaned and rode him.

Parting her legs again for him, she reached down and clawed at the crotch of her panties where they were binding his hand, and with her other hand she grasped the bodice of her dress and eased it down, bar-ing her breasts. Then she clutched the back of his head and guided his mouth to a nipple.

Her breath against his ear was hot as she licked him, panting, squirming against his hand, saying, "Suck me, bite my nipple, finger-fuck me harder," and she reached again and took his hand like something inanimate and pumped it against herself, frantically using it.

He submitted to her grip on his hand. He loved feeling the hot silk of her sex lips, which pulsed in a rosy glow beneath the lacy shadows of her clothes, the ripeness rising and mingling with the aroma of flowers, so that he could not distinguish her perfume from the hum of her sex, her satiny skin from the smoothness of her lingerie. The heavy odors saturated his eyes and excited his hunger and made him dumb with desire.

"Lots of times," she said slowly, "I touch myself like this, dreaming of you," and lifted herself slightly from the seat cushion to free his hand and give him more room.

Touching her vulva was like fumbling with dripping peach slices, covering his fingers in warm syrup, and her flesh was warm under her stiff petticoats. Her soft breasts propped in the brocade of her dress were like fruit, too, pressed against his face as he sucked the tender stem.

"We've got all night, baby," she crooned to him as she held him to her breast. "And when you're through with me, I'm going to take this" — she found the bulge in his pants and traced it with her fingers and squeezed.

She let go with a gasp, twisting away from him and snatching at her dress, just as a pair of headlights slashed the air. Above them the blazing blue gelatinous light atop a police cruiser flashed like a spaceship that had just settled to Earth.

Behind an overbright flashlight with a querying beam came a steady wide-awake voice.

"There's no parking on the dune, folks."

The flashlight swept across Ava's face — the smudged lipstick, the wisps of dangling hair — and briefly Steadman's. They were disheveled but dressed, and both of them so formal. In a tidying motion the beam lighted the empty front seat.

"You the owner of this vehicle, sir?"

Keeping his head down, hiding his hands, Steadman said yes, the car was his.

"Good. Now I want you to get out of the vehicle very slowly and show me your license and registration."

"What for?" Ava said.

"Please do as I say."

Steadman did not object. He flicked his wallet and found his license in a plastic sleeve, but as he swung the car door open and stepped out, he stumbled, and in a defensive reflex the cop jumped backward in what seemed a practiced move, clasping the handle of his pistol and directing his flashlight at Steadman's face and gaping white eyes.

"He's blind, Officer."

As Steadman's dead eyes accused him, the cop seemed unsure now, and he was startled into ignoring the license. He turned his flashlight from Steadman's face to Ava's. "You okay, ma'am?"

"This is a special occasion, Officer." In the interval of the policeman's confusion, she had adjusted her dress and smoothed her hair, though she looked more than ever like a prom date, rumpled, demure.

"You look kind of familiar. I've seen you."

"The hospital."

"Right. Emergency. You're the doctor." With each statement he became more polite. "And you're the writer. I've heard about you."

Steadman simply stared, looking ghoulish.

The policeman switched off his flashlight, another mark of respect, and said, "Sorry, folks, I thought you were summer people."

After he had gone, Ava said, "That was perfect. Now let's go home."

"No," Steadman said, touching her as he spoke, and with his touch finding a fragrance.

Sliding one hand beneath the hem of her gown, embracing her and delving into her bodice, fingering her cupped breast, he knew what she wanted from her sighs of encouragement. And when he found her warm damp panties he parted them, and clasped the wetness of her folds, stroked those lips, all the while kissing her face and murmuring into her mouth.

"Oh, yes," she said, reaching down to guide his fingers, steadying them and chafing herself with them once again. Then through her teeth she spoke into his mouth, insisting, "Fuck me, fuck me, fuck me," and seemed to thrash inside her dress as she gripped his hand, and the rustling of the cloth aroused him as much as her voice.

A scratching on the metal of the car, the stiff leaves and thorns of a

249

rosebush nudged by the night breeze, was strangely rhythmic — maybe the car was rocking against it? The sound was like a cat's claws. Then it was gone, lost in Ava's choking, as she came with a great grunt and gasp, as though, thrusting the orgasm from her body, she were giving birth to it.

They lay there breathless for a while. The claw-scratch returned on the car door. Steadman lifted himself to the window to make sure it was no more than a rose bush. The mass of blossoms was blue in the fluorescence of moonlight.

Ava, too, was luminous. She lay as if ravished, and blue-white like a fresh corpse in her soft dress, her hair tangled, her lipstick smeared around her mouth, her dress yanked down, one breast lifted from the bra cup and its own weight giving it an odd sideways twist of lovely plumpness.

She woke as he watched her, back from the dead, tucking her breast into her bra, lifting her gown to cover it, pushing down her skirt, leaning into the front seat to switch on the overhead light, and then studying her face, touching her hair, smiling, remembering.

"I look fucked."

Still smiling and peering intently into the mirror of her compact, she wiped the smears of lipstick from her face, dabbed at her eyes, combed her hair. And just as Steadman thought she had finished, she took out a pouch of cosmetics and applied mascara and thickened her eyelashes — slowly, paying no attention to Steadman, who watched with fascination as she prettied her face. She rouged her cheeks, reddened her lips again using a brush and lip gloss, made herself a new face, a mask of desire.

Only when she was done, having put herself back together and now looking again as she had in the doorway, did she turn away from the mirror and snap her compact shut, lingering in the light a bit before switching it off. She faced him. The dusty moonlight deepened the texture of her makeup and softened the planes of her face, and what had seemed an innocently questioning smile in the small mirror was now lust lit by moonbeams.

She leaned toward Steadman and her lowering arm crushed her gown as she reached down and slid her hand along his thigh. She touched his cock and kissed him, thrusting her tongue into his mouth and moving her fingers, playing with him through the cloth of his trousers. She unzipped him and slipped her hand inside, her warm hand clutching him, as though gripping a knife handle, until it thickened. Then she pumped it, driving it downward against his groin, again and again, thrusting hard, as if she had a dagger she was using against him. And still she embraced him, held tight to him, kissing his lips and his face as she held him, not stopping, not even hesitating. She had risen, and she hovered over him so urgently hers was a posture of assault, possessing him and pounding his cock with a murdering motion.

The sound of his pleasure came slanting from deep within his lungs and seemed like an echo of a softer sighing in her throat. Her breasts were in his hands, his thumbs grazing her nipples. Her touch was surer and so finely judged that she seemed to feel in the throb of his cock the spasm of his juice rising — knew even before he did that he was about to come. Then he knew, his body began to convulse, and as he cried "No" — because she had let go — she pushed him backward onto the seat and pressed her face down, lapping his cock into her mouth, curling her tongue around it, and the suddenness of it, the snaking of her tongue, the pressure of her lips, the hot grip of her mouth, triggered his orgasm, which was not juice at all but a demon eel thrashing in his loins and swimming swiftly up his cock, one whole creature of live slime fighting the stiffness as it rose and bulged at the tip and darted into her mouth.

Holding him with one hand, she devoured it and was still swallowing as he went limp and slipped out of her mouth. When she looked up at him with her smeared face and smudged eyes, she was still greedily gulping, licking droplets from her gleaming lips.

The car was warm and sour with the mingled odors of perfume and sweat and the fish glue of his semen. Ava was silent. The world was old. The moon looked brittle and barnacled, and down below in the Sound a breadbox of a ferry chugged through the greasy waves. He knew his blindness had worn off.

4

In the sallow morning light of glaucous summer seafog he could not tell whether he was blind or sighted. His uncertainty made him impatient to resume his book. He had woken alone, clearheaded, fixated on the notion that writing and sex were disappearing acts. Wrung out, too, as though, smaller and simpler, he had lost one of his limbs in an ecstatic ritual of eroticism.

Sex was a form of departure, a passionate sacrifice of farewell, and even his writing these days had the unanswerable finality of a suicide note. Take that! he thought with grim pleasure. He wanted to write everything down so there would be nothing more to say and no more to remember, to burn out his self so he could vanish.

Opening the drawer of his filing cabinet, he smiled at the large glass jar that held the dark tea of the datura. He wagged it slowly, stopping at intervals to examine how well the residue had dissolved, and this mechanical motion helped him look ahead to the morning of work.

He needed to think aloud in the form of dictation, because he was troubled by a paradox he did not fully understand. The act of sex, so well planned as an end in itself, seemed to suggest a sequel, by giving you courage, by helping to uncover a related desire, something else, a particular image — last night the glimpse of a pretty garter of lace on the moonlit skin of her thigh, her gown hiked up in a hurry. This enhancement was an invitation: certain clothes seemed to beckon. And he, who had imagined that sex with Rosemarie Fredella on that prom night had been his earliest sexual ambition, the origin of his desire, saw something deeper. This flimsy scrap of lace stirred him again like a fetish object, and he wondered what it meant and where it led.

Two other details also unexpectedly aroused him. He believed he had thought of everything, but no. The interruption of the policeman — the surprise, the drama, the suspenseful moonglow after he had gone — was one. And then, without having been told anything, the way that Ava had further tantalized him by pausing, switching on the overhead light in the car, and turning away with the coy hauteur of a high school coquette. Forcing him to watch and wait, she had put on makeup. He had sat back sighing, loving the chance to see her face change. He was transfixed by her vivid mask, the sharp symmetry of lips and cheeks picked out of the humid shadows of greens and reds in the highlights of her eyes. As though she were saying to his reflection in the mirror, knowing what she could stir in his guts, *I am making my face look fuckable.*

That was going into the book today, as soon as Ava appeared and he could levitate himself with a dose of his drug and begin dictation. His book would be the last word, something for people who had lived a lot — not a beginner's book, not even a book for those who praised *Trespassing,* not for children or schools, not to be studied but to be lived. The book's subjects were blindness and lust, offering no moral, nothing except the peculiar reality of one man's transgressions, the way back, as a sort of atonement for having been silent for so long.

How he hated the books people praised and recommended to him. Blindness had shown him what a sham they were. Blindness had shown him the folly of such praise. Blindness allowed him to hear the nonsense that people uttered. Blindness had rid him of his faith and all his sentimentality and had led him here, to contemplate his sexual history. And blindness had given him the strength to reenact it, for his book. There could be no other books.

"What would be the point of learning Braille?" he had said to a well-meaning woman. "What on earth would I want to read?"

He remembered everything he had ever read. There was too much. A great deal of it he wished to forget. He raised the jar of muddy liquid and, seeing a ring of residue darkening the bottom, the grainy dregs of datura, gave it another shake.

"Look who's wide awake," Ava said, entering the room looking aloof and casually efficient in a T-shirt and shorts. She was barefoot, carrying a mug of coffee in one hand, her doctor's bag in the other. Her face was scrubbed, a slight redness where his stubble had chafed her cheek and a small swollen serration on her upper lip where he might have bitten her — he liked to think of the bruise as showing his teeth marks.

In other respects Ava seemed a completely different person from the one of the night before, his prom date, a perfect memory of a longing accomplished — fulfillment. Had she seemed the same woman, he would have found it hard to dictate his book to her. Even so, he felt awkward, not sure of how to greet her.

"Got a letter for you," she said. She handed him a thick business-sized envelope.

Addressed to him through his publisher, it had been forwarded to his post office box. Steadman looked at the return address and saw *Manfred Steiger* scribbled in pen above the bold printed name of a German company. Using all his strength, Steadman tore the envelope in half and tossed it into the wastebasket as Ava looked on. She was smiling, but her smile was a question.

"No letter that long can possibly be interesting," he said.

"Maybe it's not a letter. Maybe it's a manuscript."

"Even worse," he said, and then, "What's that for?"

Ava had put her mug down and taken her stethoscope out of the bag.

"I'm wondering what that stuff is doing to you," she said. "Have you drunk your dose today?"

"Not yet."

He lifted his shirt and let her listen with her stethoscope. Then she cinched his arm with the black cuff and pumped the bulb and read his blood pressure, studying the gauge.

"How does it look?"

"A little above normal, but fine. Now have a drink. Keep that thing on your arm."

"Give me a minute," he said, and as Ava sipped her coffee he unscrewed the lid of the jar and poured half the mixture into a tumbler. Holding the tumbler in two hands, in self-conscious veneration, like a priest at an altar, he lifted it and drank the liquid slowly in a number of reverent swallows. And then he smiled and stumbled a bit as he went to the sofa, already cloudy-eyed, and when he sat a new day took shape around him — new colors and sounds, subtler ones, more birds, sharper odors, his mind fully engaged. Ava smelled of soap and talc, and her shampoo had given her hair a fruity aroma, and there was a hint, a tang, of freshly cut grass — green clippings on her shoes that were darkened by dew drops and a smack of mud.

"You've been out?" he said dreamily.

"Not far. A walk around the garden."

She was kneeling, pumping the bulb, inflating the cuff. And then in stages, letting out the air, she read his blood pressure again.

"It's a miracle drug. Your blood pressure is way down. Better than normal — a young man's heart." She took out a small pencil-shaped flashlight. "Look at me," she said, and shone the light into his eyes, peering in.

"See anything?"

"Nothing."

"Neither do I," she said. "Your pupils stay dilated."

Instead of the glimmer of the light, or any object, he saw her seriousness, and he smiled, feeling superior for being something of a riddle. Much as he was reassured by Ava's concern, admiring her medical skill, her deftness in using her instruments and examining him, he liked her puzzlement much more, a doctor saying *I don't know*. He enjoyed her confusion. On this one subject, at any rate, the effects of the datura, she was ignorant. So it was all still his secret.

She had put her instruments away and seated herself, had found her clipboard and pad, and was already clicking her ballpoint.

"Last night," he said. "That was everything I wanted."

Even so, praising her extravagantly, he was doubtful. He wanted her to deny what he said or to offer an insight. Maybe she, too, suspected an incompleteness.

"And you put your heart into it," he said.

"I'm younger than you, but I went to high school, too," she said. "I had a prom date."

"Who with?"

"That would be Jeff Ziebert." She smiled, saying the irrelevant name.

"And you went parking with him afterward?"

"Hey, this is your book, not mine."

"So while I was hot for Rosie," he persisted, "you were fantasizing about him."

She said, "I was struck by something you said about desire being located in the past. I tried to see if that would work with me. I looked deep into my own."

"And found Jeff."

She smoothed the pad on her clipboard with the flat of her hand in a cleansing motion, as if wishing to brush away the question.

Steadman considered this phantom rival and concluded that he didn't mind. He was liberated by not figuring in Ava's fantasy. It was better that she used him as he used her. He wanted her to feel free to fantasize as she liked, to fulfill what mattered most to her. Otherwise it was all self-deception.

"Better that we should deceive each other than deceive ourselves," he said.

With this reflection he began dictating the episode — the prom date, groping her in the car, the sudden policeman, the fluffy dress and the straps and stitches of all her underwear, the makeup, the final flourish. Ava helped him when he hesitated, and she gave him the right words for the cosmetics.

But he said, "I don't want too much detail. No brand names. None of those ridiculous lipstick shades."

And when he got to the point of describing his orgasm, saying "Not juice at all but a demon eel thrashing in his loins and swimming swiftly up his cock, one whole creature of live slime," she frowned and interrupted.

"Do you want to know how it felt to me?"

"Go on."

"That I was sucking the life out of you and that you were inert while I drank you. That I was in charge, draining you of your strength and swallowing it, to be strong myself."

Her exactness and her poise made him thoughtful. He was reminded of how much he needed her, and that she was half that life of desire he was reliving, and so half his book had to be hers.

"I'm sorry if I shocked you," she said. She changed her posture, recrossed her legs, and said, to encourage him to continue, "So time passed."

"No, wait." The experience last night had uncovered an earlier memory. That was the paradox. "There was something else."

"Another woman?"

"Another me. A younger me."

He was staring blindly at the window, beyond it, at the lifting seafog and slender dripping oaks and grizzled needles of the pitch pines, into the past, remembering.

"I grew up in the age before everyone had an electric clothes dryer," he said. "You probably had one."

Ava was listening.

"Let me see," he said. "This matters. Everywhere I looked I saw clotheslines — women's underwear on clotheslines, lifting with the breeze and fluttering beautifully, as beautiful to me as the nakedest woman. Those secret clothes were women to me, and the way the wind filled them made me gape."

He was gaping frankly now and lost in his gaze, consumed by his vision of silken whiteness, like the whiteness of a body. And Ava was writing swiftly as he dictated; she had no memory of her own to match his vision and was somewhat surprised by how remote this seemed from his description of yesterday's desire, the prom date, kissing and fondling in the back seat, an adolescent episode relived.

"I see clotheslines, and secrets on them — panties and slips and bras. Why so many? Did women need more underwear then? There seemed to have been more of it, or was it more elaborate — women perhaps making up for their outward modesty by covertly wearing seductive underwear."

"Sometimes it peeked out," Ava said.

"Yes."

Underwear was never totally hidden; that was the excitement and the tease. The ghost of a bra seen through a gauzy blouse, the neat curve of panty line under tight slacks, the ambiguous straps and ribbons, the imprint of lace showing through a skirt — always pretty — the notion of the beauty, the idea of tiny pink bows hidden beneath a woman's clothes.

"And so it seemed that underwear was a distinct and evocative form of nakedness. A woman in a slip or panties was the object of desire that a naked woman is now." Steadman pressed his temples with his fingertips. "But only the past matters to me. Underwear was an invitation, and a greater temptation than nakedness. I can see it clearly."

As though peering from overhead, past rooftops and telephone poles, he saw himself as a hurrying boy cutting through back yards to get to Carol Lumley's house. The boy passed clotheslines and ducked behind them, recognizing the women's underwear from the Sears catalogue and the Sunday newspapers. The Cronins' daughter was a nurse, but even a nurse's white uniform seemed like a version of underwear, and so did a man's bathing suit.

A great fluttering whiteness on this warm day in early summer. The wind lifting the underwear also lifted the forsythia and the lilacs, the irises and the two-tone leaves of the poplars that went on spinning, the sun-struck laundry, bluish white in the deep green.

Hurrying under the clotheslines, he felt the flimsy silken things fluttering against his face, the warmth of them, their fragile beauty. He was fascinated by the variety, the shapes and sizes, some of them pink or fringed in lace, their softly rubbed seams, the stitches on bras, and the way some pieces were perfectly matched — the pairs of them in silk or satin pegged up together, the revelation of the back yards of his childhood.

Needing courage, though he had nothing else to do — school had ended for the summer — he had waited until late afternoon. Carol had said, "If you want to come over and sit on my porch I'll probably be around. My parents might have to go out."

The casual way she had said this was a greater inducement than if she had made a formal invitation. They were tentative exploratory words, but each one suggested a promise. The danger was that the more specific you were, the greater the blame, and the worse the sin. Vagueness was the tone of innocence, and though he was attracted to Carol Lumley he had no idea what lay beyond this attraction. He wanted to kiss her, he wanted to touch her, he wanted her to let him and for her to like it. He was fourteen years old.

He moved, hunched and watchful, like an intruder, from back yard to back yard — the Cronins', the Halls', the Fasullos', the Flahertys' — on this hot bright breezy day, what his mother called a good drying day. In one yard Mrs. Fasullo was clothespinning her voluminous panties, and in another Mrs. Finn was harvesting her slips, and elsewhere the underwear flapped like flags or swelled with the wind, as if with the curves of a woman's body.

Ducking through the last back yard, he came to the Lumleys', and what stopped him was not Carol's underwear — though he saw lots of it on the line amid the whole family's underwear, from her mother's bloomers and her father's boxers down to the tiniest bras, the smallest panties, the half-slips, and the slips — what a small body she had. He caught sight of her blue nightgown, the kind he knew as a baby doll, and he paused and looked closely.

Trimmed with lace and pink bows, wooden clothespins holding its straps, the lovely thing hung and swayed as though Carol had just slipped out of it. He touched it and held it to his face, the blue satin warmed by the summer afternoon. And beside it, just out of reach, the matching blue panties. White satin ribbons were threaded at the shoulders, and the wide strip of lace at the hem was picked out with bows. It seemed to him both a gown and underwear, but it was designed for bed, and what mattered most to him was that it was meant to be admired by someone else.

"What the heck are you supposed to be doing?"

He was too startled to speak, and even when he saw Carol laughing at the window he was not calmed. He looked away. He felt he had revealed himself. Had she seen him clutch the baby doll and press it to his face? If so, he counted on the fact that what he had done was so absurd she would not understand it.

Anyway, she was gone from the window when he looked again, and a moment later, answering the front door, all she said was "What did you bring me?"

"Nothing."

"And I bet you want some lemonade and all kinds of stuff."

He shrugged and smiled and Carol made a disapproving face, what he thought of as a woman's expression. She wore a pink blouse and white shorts, and though she was fourteen, as he was, she seemed much younger. She was thin and slight, with small breasts and fragile wrists and fingers, a body so slender it was like a young boy's, a compact bum and skinny legs. But she had blue eyes, full lips, light curly hair — an angel's face.

"You might as well sit over there," she said, pointing to the porch swing, and she vanished from the doorway. She was gone some minutes, but he knew why when she returned with the glasses of lemonade and redder lips.

"You've got lipstick on."

"Big deal," she said, and pressed her lips together as if to make her lip color emphatic.

They sat apart, at either end of the porch swing. They held their glasses, and the only sound was the clink of the ice when they raised them to sip the lemonade.

"So, guess what, my parents just went out."

He was gladdened by her saying that, and sipped again from his glass, and looked off the porch to the house opposite — the Martellos' — to scrutinize the sky above its roof. He wanted dusk to fall, he wanted shadows, he wanted to be insubstantial himself, smaller and less obvious in the dark, his face in shadow, his eyes hidden.

"Did you tell them I was coming over?"

"I forgot to."

He laughed a little and saw that she noticed and got fierce.

"But I'm going to tell them," she said, "that you came over looking for trouble."

Horrified by the truth of what she said, he accidentally chinked the glass against his front teeth.

"Where did you tell your parents you were going?"

"Up the park. Softball game."

The park was not far, two streets over, behind a tall fence, the game in progress and audible — shouts, cheers, the sometime slap of bat and ball meeting in a solid hit. Their revelations were like complicity, like an admission they were doing something wrong, and knew it, and were glad of it. But because he could hear the sounds of the softball game it seemed to make sitting on Carol's porch with her less of a lie.

"What if they find out where you really are?"

"I don't care," he said. "I would have snuck out anyway."

She seemed to like that. She sat back, shoving herself against the cushion, and said, "So why were you trying to steal my stuff off the clothesline?"

He shifted on the swing and said, "I wasn't even looking at it."

Her blue eyes narrowed on him. He could not tell what she was thinking, for the lower part of her face was in shadow. As long as there were shadows he did not care what she was thinking. And anyway, he liked her giggly teasing voice and her pretense of scolding, even her threats — they seemed to show that she liked him and wanted him to stay.

"I bet you want more lemonade."

"I don't care," he said, although he did. But he was choking with desire and confusion and did not know what else to say.

She went for the lemonade and took longer than before, and when she returned he immediately smelled the perfume, stronger in the smoky dark of dusk on the porch. He loved the fragrance; he had never smelled such flowers; the odor pricked his eyes.

He thanked her for the lemonade. She tossed her curly hair. They rocked on the porch swing.

Finally she said, "My father says you're smart."

He turned to her. At the far end of the swing she was now mostly in shadow, except for her bright white shorts, so small on her body.

"I think you're a sneak," she said.

"No sah."

"Yes sah. So why are you sneaking over here to sit on my front porch and drink lemonade?" she said. She had hitched forward and was kicking the porch floor, propelling the swing back and forth with each kick and accusation. "You know my parents are out."

He felt guiltily that because this was so, he was a conspirator. His silence made her sharper.

"Or else you wouldn't be here," she said. She kicked again, a skid-squeak of her rubber sole. "And you were sneaking around the clothesline."

This was also true, and so accurate in its blame he said, "No I wasn't. What do I care about all that old washing? I was just taking a shortcut."

Instead of replying, she leaned so that he could see her smiling. She kicked the floor again, hard, and sent the porch swing backward, and he felt all her insistence in the movement.

"Please don't tell them."

"I'm going to," she said, and it sounded like *gunnah*. "I'm going to blab everything."

Now he wanted to go, but he could not rise from the moving swing, and when he finally got a grip on the arm of it and tried to hoist himself, she was talking again in that same teasing tone.

"I bet you want to come right into my house."

"No," he said, his voice breaking, and turned the small word into a squawk. He just wanted to leave. The day had gone dark, though he hadn't noticed it until now.

"Then why did you come all the way over here?" And seeing that he was flustered and at a loss for a reply, she laughed softly.

The lights had gone on in the park, illuminating the treetops, and he still heard the sounds of the softball game, the cries of the spectators, the shouts of the players — easy to tell apart. He was thinking of all that passion and noise, just a game being played, so innocent, so blameless, an honest ball game under the lights. And he knew that he was doing something wrong, enacting a secret in the shadows he could never explain or justify.

"So why didn't you bring me anything?"

He was silent. Another ball was smacked, another cheer: the players were harmless and happy and he was wicked.

"Because I got something for you. Want to see it?" She did not wait for a reply. "Stay here."

She went inside and closed the doors — the screen door, the solid inner door, and he heard the thunk of the bolt. He remained sitting, wondering whether anyone could see him. He felt conspicuous and impatient and sensed he should go home. After a few minutes he rang the doorbell to tell Carol he was leaving. The bell was loud, but even so, there was no answer, not even footsteps. He waited, feeling trapped by the silence. Like a gasp, an expelled breath, a light inside went off.

And then came the metallic swallowing of the door bolt and a movement of the inner door. He could not see past the screen — only the outline of the doorframe, the darkness within. He plucked open the screen door and saw nothing but the dim hallway.

"Go in there," she spoke from behind the door. He could see only her bare arm pointing to the living room. "Wait a little while. Then you have to find me."

As soon as his back was turned she hurried away. He did as he was told, continued into the living room, his heart pounding, excited by the suspense. The living room was shadowy, lit by the street. He sat, and fumbled, then stood and listened, tremulous, his hands damp.

Her muffled voice came from somewhere upstairs in the house. "I'm ready."

He went to the stairway and listened, and hearing nothing more, he climbed the stairs, looked into one room and then another, all in darkness, but he could make out the shapes of chairs, the lumps of beds, the glint of mirrors.

He entered a room at the front of the house, and though there was more light here from the street lamps, he did not see Carol at first because she was motionless, standing upright, almost posing. But he could see what she was wearing: short blue baby-doll pajamas and a pair of fluffy slippers. Her hair was fixed in two high bobbing brush-like ponytails, her shoulders were bare, her skin so pale as to be almost ghostly. The diaphanous blue cloth shimmered in the scanty, slanted light.

"Do you like it?" she said. "I dressed up just for you. I bet you don't even care."

She twirled before him and set the baby doll in motion, and then approached him and took his hand and brought him close to her, so close he could feel her but hardly see her, as if she were embarrassed to be stared at. And liking the darkness he clutched her, the silken cloth in his fingers, the warmth of her body, the odd warm saltiness of her damp flesh in the room that was like the promise of sex, the burnt perfume on her skin. She began to kiss him in a way that was new to him, sucking on his lips.

She moved from his mouth and said, "You better not tell anybody."

Then, before he could say anything, she kissed him again, her kisses like promises. And as he returned her kisses, answering back, he opened his eyes and saw the room beyond her more clearly — the chair, the small bed, the neat row of costumed dolls on the dresser. He led her a few steps to the bed and pushed a cloth doll out of the way and sat down, hugging her, still kissing her, tasting the saltiness of her moist neck, the lemonade in her saliva.

"Lie down."

"No," she said, in a tone of caution that was almost fear.

But she did not stop kissing him, and a moment later, when he took her free hand and pressed it against his lap, she let him guide her fingers. Then all the initiative was hers, as she touched him, rubbed him with her small hand and finally unzipped him and took hold of him, pumping, her whole hand enclosing him. The thought came to him that she knew a great deal and was unafraid.

She certainly knew more than he did — he could tell that from her grip, her confident fingers wrapped around his stiffened cock. And her other hand, too. Her boldness startled him, for he had hardly touched her body. He knew with a kind of dread that he was trespassing. He had entered a new country that was strange and dark and sinful and pleasurable, full of shadows and delights, and he was here for good, was possessed, was changed, would never return. Being here with Carol, kissing the lemony taste of her lips, her skinny hands bewitching him, was not a choice — there was no alternative. He loved it and knew he was damned.

She sighed when he touched her, slipping his hand onto her thigh, and fondled the lace of her baby doll, which was like part of her nakedness. She sighed again, and he knew her sigh meant yes. She parted her legs and allowed his hand to rise. Groping there, fumbling in the dark, was for him like uncovering a secret being, another person, a hidden woman, her scalp and cheeks, her lips, her mouth — everything but eyes — and when his fingers traced and hesitated at the tiny mouth of this damp-faced creature, she opened her legs wider.

"Put it inside," she said, as she kissed him. He slipped one fingertip in, and she said, "More."

Even unseen he could feel the lip-like folds glisten as his finger dipped into the slick pocket mouth of flesh. Sliding closer to him, crushing her nightgown against him, she kissed him harder, put her tongue into his mouth, showing him how, until he did the same to her.

She was leading him, teaching him. He used his tongue as he stroked her with his hand, in the same motion as she was stroking him. She was rocking, helping his hand, and in this fierce syncopation of desire he could feel her small damp body squirming beneath the satin, like a captive animal, a mewing cat trapped and twisted in silk. The lights from the street made the cloth glow. The bedroom, not so dark now, was fragrant with her perfume and her dolls.

He was looking at one of her Barbie dolls sitting flat on the dresser, its long legs straight out and slightly parted to keep it upright, when, pumping him and taking light skimming breaths, Carol gripped him, seeming to sense his whole body go rigid, as though concentrating. Then a sweet wound within him swelled and burst in a single stroke, and when he convulsed and clutched himself he also clutched her sticky searching hands.

"I can feel it," she said, and became girlish and curious and almost jubilant.

He groaned, for he had emptied quickly and now there was a void where all that heat and muscle had been.

"Let me see it," she said.

"No." He was bent over, slashed in half, reduced to a crouching guilty boy.

"It's on my fingers, it's all over my nightie," she said. "Look what you did."

He was sorrowful, ashamed, exhausted, almost feverish, and he watched with drowsy surprise as she dabbed her fingers, smelled them, put the tip of her tongue on them, and wagged her tongue at him. Then, seeing that he was shocked, she became assertive and shocked him further by snatching his hand and choosing his wettest finger and sucking it. She lay back and trapped him with her laugh.

With a slight catch in her throat from being overeager, Carol Lumley whispered, "Touch me some more."

Touch me some more, Ava was saying, in a mass of blue silk and ribbons and lace. *More.*

5

THE TWANGING MUSIC he heard as he approached on the whitish dust of the summer path made the solitary cabin more solitary, yet gave it life. It was a small, rough-wood bungalow with a song coming out of the side porch. Had Tom's mother left the radio on and gone out? It seemed impossible that she could be inside listening to something so loud, stammering and delirious music that knifed the steamy air like hot metal. Listening to it he seemed to see the sunlight glittering on sharp silver, and he walked faster, toward the melody. The music also seemed to give the cabin a face — eye-like windows, porch nose, door mouth.

"We're going out with Kenny," Tom had said at the lake, holding his sister Nita's hand.

Kenny was a fisherman, Kenny had a boat, Kenny was Tom Bronster's older friend. Tom talked about him all the time. "Kenny's got a gun. He's going to let me shoot it." Today, Tom's tone suggested that Slade was not welcome, or at least that he would be in the way. Kenny's boat was a small skiff with an outboard motor.

Nita was vexed: she wanted to stay with Slade, and yet Tom was responsible for her. That morning on the beach she had said to Slade, "I could be your girlfriend." She was ten, he was thirteen. Slade was glad to see her go.

"Never mind, I'll stick around here," Slade said, knowing he was lying.

As soon as Kenny's boat sped across the lake, tipping up and plowing white water aside, Slade turned and walked through the pines and up the dusty path by the margin of the meadow where a cow sometimes followed them along the fence. Nearer the cabin — as soon as he saw it — he heard the music, and now he was glad he was alone. Tom was his friend, but when Tom was with him, Slade was distracted. Slade was dreamy, he preferred to be alone with his reveries, he found more pleasure in them than in noisy games. Tom was a talkative, active boy with an exhausting shrieky voice.

Agreeing to spend this week at the lake with Tom and his family meant that he, the visiting friend, was obliged to accompany Tom every waking minute. So he was happy on the path; he liked having a break from the burden of this raucous boy who was always chasing his dog or challenging Slade to bike races or boasting about Kenny.

Through the side window of the cabin Slade saw a flash of white, Tom's mother in a bra, her thick hair plaited into one braid and fixed by a ribbon. He thought even then how no white was whiter than a woman's white underwear. She was playing a steel guitar, a table-like instrument resembling an ironing board with strings, plucking it and moving a wooden spindle at one end to create a quavering sound, a sweet hungering he knew to be Hawaiian music. Yearning melodies troubled the fretwork of the amplifier, a black boxy suitcase with a hole on one side.

Tom's mother, who was always dressed up at night, looked naked to Slade now. He was fascinated by each thing she wore: a bra that made her breasts into two white cones on a harness, loose shorts — her navel showing in her pale flat stomach — and wedge-heeled shoes with fake cherries attached to the straps, painted toenails, her thick braid sliding across her spine as, looking tall, she concentrated hard on her pressed-down fingers, making music.

Had she not been playing the instrument she would have seen Slade at once. Carelessly dressed, her braid swinging, she seemed playful, younger, like a very big girl. Steadman stayed at the window, looking at her bare legs and her white shapely breasts. She was half faced away from him, but she looked so lovely he found himself staring. He was dizzy with meaningless heat and numb fingers. He loved looking, but as minutes passed she became less and less Tom's mother and more and more like someone whom he knew a little and had never seen like this.

Imagining himself touching her eased his mind. She had sallow skin and green eyes. Mentally he placed his hands over the cups of her breasts and stroked them slowly. The thought so possessed him that he stepped away, ducked beneath the cabin window, and went back to the lake to wait for Tom and Nita to return from the fishing trip. Still, even sitting on the grassy bank with his feet propped on the exposed roots of a tree, hidden by bushes, he felt guilty and excited.

"You missed it!" Tom called out from the skiff when he saw Slade on the embankment. Tom held up a dripping foot-long fish.

That night, Tom's mother wore a pink pleated dress with short sleeves and white sandals. Her long hair was unbraided, combed out, hiding her neck. Each night she dressed differently. He loved her clothes, their color and variety, and he saw in her joy in dressing up how attractive she was. But it pleased him to know that he had seen her that afternoon in her bra and shorts. She was kind to Slade. She watched him eat and complimented him on his manners.

"And what a good appetite." She said to Tom, "I wish you'd eat like Slade."

"You're a good cook," Slade said, and saw the effect of his praise — the way she smiled, the way she leaned over and asked him if he wanted more. He averted his eyes from her neckline, but he got a glimpse of the bra.

Nita whispered to her and then clapped her hand over her mouth.

"And you've got a secret admirer," Tom's mother said.

In the bunk beds that night, almost pained by the thought of the woman and needing to talk about her, Slade whispered in the darkness from the top bunk, "Tom. You awake?"

"Yeah."

"Your mother's nice."

"Bull."

"No. She really is."

Slade wanted to have a conversation about Tom's mother, find out more about her, or at least just talk to console himself.

"She's horrible. She's a wicked nag. Always making me babysit Nita."

Tom wouldn't say any more. Soon he was asleep, and Slade saw how Tom was selfish and immature, no fun to talk to, a disappointment who was a burden as a friend.

The routine was the same every day. Up at seven, and after breakfast, the lake. Hot dogs and milk at the cabin for lunch, then bike riding or back to the lake in the afternoon. Supper at six, the meal Slade looked forward to, because Tom's mother would be dressed up. They played in the meadow until the mosquitoes started biting. Then to bed. The house smelled of its pine floors and newly sawn timber, and at night there was always a radio playing, Tom's mother downstairs alone, leafing through a magazine, *Collier's* or the *Saturday Evening Post*.

The next afternoon, Slade left Tom at the beach.

"I have to go to the bathroom."

He returned to the cabin, delighted when he heard the familiar music. He crept toward it, his head down, and he took up his place at the window to watch the woman in her white bra and shorts, to listen to her playing. He had been there only a minute or less when Nita stepped from behind the side porch. She had obviously followed him from the lake.

Fearful of revealing his secret interest, feeling discovered, Slade started to walk away.

Nita said in a whisper, "You're spying on my mom."

"No I'm not."

"Don't believe you." She squinted at him and smiled and in a wheedling voice said, "Want to see my special house?"

"Sure," he said, to humor her and avoid any more questions, and as he agreed it occurred to him that Nita looked just like a monkey.

Nita bent over and slipped under the porch, duck-walking into the crawl space. Slade followed her, hearing the mother's music, like bright light blazing through the cracks in the floorboards. The crawl space was cool and smelled of cat shit and sour dust; the shadows were thick with cobwebs. At its edge was a banner of sunlight, for the cabin was on blocks, no basement, only the crawl space and the splintery wooden underpart. Slade felt disoriented by stepping under the house and hearing the music from the room above, and by the insistent beckoning girl among the shadows and the smells. He was dizzy and distinctly felt that he was doing something wrong.

"This is my kitchen. I could fix you a meal. This is my living room." She had a hoarse husky voice. "Bedroom's over there."

The places she named were just sun-striped portions of dust and cat shit, littered with stones and blown leaves, an overturned bucket serving as a stool.

"And this is my bathroom," she said.

Slade was half kneeling because he was so much taller than she was and there was so little headroom.

"You can use it if you want," she said.

"Use it like how?"

"Like what do you think, silly."

She slid her panties to her knees and squatted, defying him with her mother's green eyes, seeming to hold her breath while he watched and listened. He stared at her, the little bare-assed monkey with the wicked look squatting in the dust, but all he heard was her mother's music slashing through the floor from the cabin just over their heads.

Even crouching, Slade could see nothing more of Nita than her bulgy small-girl knees, for she was compact and squatting. But when she stood up and straightened, with the same defiant look, leaving her panties at her ankles, he got a glimpse of sunshine through her legs, but little else, and it seemed a mystery. What was she hiding? When he went closer he saw the subtle, slightly parted mouth of what seemed a secret incomplete face, a simple frowning mask at her crotch. Only then did she tug up her panties, as though as an afterthought.

"Your turn now," she said, and hiked the panties up tightly.

He found he could not speak at first. He had a reply but couldn't utter it while transfixed by the way the slit-like frown under her belly showed through the panties. At last he said, "You didn't do anything."

"At least I tried." She was irritable. "Go ahead, fraidy cat, no one's looking."

The demanding sharpness in her tone aroused him and worried him at the same time. He wanted to linger, he wanted more of her. To be alone in the shadows of a summer cabin with a willing wicked girl was like a dream. But her body was skinny and incomplete, she was too small, she was reckless. The danger of her recklessness excited him but made him afraid, and in the seconds of trembling there he felt only panic. What if someone saw or heard them? He bent over and tried to rush out of the crawl space, but not bending over far enough, he

269

cracked his head against a low board under the cabin floor, and then was on his hands and knees in the sunshine, his head ringing.

His sensation of having been deafened by the knock on the head was heightened by something else that was wrong: the music had stopped. In the instant he realized this, still groggy, he saw a pair of sandals approaching. They were trimmed with fake cherries. He struggled to his feet and came face to face with Tom's mother, who was bent over — she was taller than he was.

"What's going on here?" she said, and the mother's demand had an echo of the daughter's scolding voice.

"Nothing," Slade said, but he glanced behind him and saw Nita climbing out from under the porch.

"Aren't you supposed to be at the beach?"

But Tom's mother was not speaking to him; she was addressing the little girl, who sulked and walked away. When Slade started after her, Tom's mother said, "Not you. You're staying right here where I can see you."

Slade went hot with blame, and looked away from the woman's face, and dropped his gaze to her shoes, the wedge-heeled sandals. The fake cherries on the straps were chipped, but her toes were lovely with pink polish.

"What would your mother say if she knew you were misbehaving?"

"I don't know," Slade said miserably. He could not keep the tone of guilty pleading out of his voice. "I wasn't doing anything."

"Under the house with Nita," she said. "I think you were being fresh."

Slade was terrified. He knew he had no control over what Tom's mother was saying. He could not contradict her, and he hated the little monkey girl for tempting him.

"Come in here," Tom's mother said, and she stood aside. "Do you hear me?"

"Yes, Mrs. Bronster."

Only then did Slade notice that Tom's mother was dressed as she had been the day before, in a white bra and loose shorts, the same blue ribbon on her braid, her winking navel in the sallow skin of her bare midriff. The steel guitar was set up where she had left it, the amplifier like a battered suitcase, the sheet music on a metal stand.

"I guess I'll have to keep an eye on you," she said. "I don't think I can trust you."

"You can trust me," he said in his pleading voice. "I didn't do anything."

In her thick-heeled sandals she loomed over him, and she turned on him and said sharply, "Your knees are filthy. Look at your hands. You need a good shower. Get over here."

She beckoned him to the back of the cabin where, on a slatted platform, there was a shower stall — a plastic curtain, an overhead pipe and nozzle. She turned on the shower and the water spattered and splashed on the boards.

"Go ahead."

Slade wanted to please her yet he hesitated, his hands on his shorts.

"I suppose you think I've never seen a naked man."

When she said "man," Slade did not think of himself; he thought of Tom's father, who was never there.

"Now make it snappy."

He turned away and slipped off his T-shirt and dropped his shorts. He entered the pouring shower, hiding in the torrent, his back to the streaming shower curtain.

But he could tell from the way the water splashed that Tom's mother was watching, crowding the shower stall entrance. Then she stepped away and the water fell straighter. Slade soaped himself, still trying to please her, and after he had rinsed off he saw her at the bathroom door, holding a towel.

"Here," she said, and dangled it, but when he walked toward her, naked, she held on to the towel, gripping its corner as he dried off.

"You're certainly not putting those dirty clothes back on," she said, and kicked his shorts away as he reached for them. She gave him a small limp handful of soft silk.

"Put those on."

He was uncertain, almost afraid.

"Do as I say."

He drew them on, black lace panties, consoled that his nakedness was covered yet feeling foolish. But the woman's seriousness helped him. She was matter-of-fact; she could have teased him but didn't.

"I want to trust you," she said.

Slade did not know what to say, but he thought, Test me, try me, I will do anything to earn your trust. The panties he wore were so flimsy he imagined that she could see through them, but when he looked down he saw he was covered.

"They're mine. They're silk," she said. "Sometimes you have to improvise. Make do with what you have."

He could not tell if she was smiling, but her voice was kinder than before.

"You'll find that, as you get older," she said. "What are you looking at?"

She touched her own shorts at a place where the side zipper had worked open, the gaping slot showing a blister of pink panties.

"Want to zip me?"

Eager to please her, he used two hands, one to pinch the zipper together, the other to lift the fastener into place, closing the gap, and as he worked on it, Tom's mother touched his fingers, patting them, and then smoothed the seam when he finished.

"You're good at that."

He said nothing.

"Now unzip me."

He was aware of being barefoot in damp panties, his head still wet from the shower, this woman in her sandals much taller than he was. But he obeyed, working the zipper open, and when it was down the woman plucked at a button and the shorts opened onto swelling pinkness. She tugged at them a little and they dropped to her ankles and she stepped out of them.

Feeling like a geek, he was looking away from the woman, toward the front door of the cabin, the blinding afternoon sunlight pouring through the squares of glass, when she stepped behind him. From the touch of the fabric on his shoulder it seemed as though she were draping him with a scarf.

"I think you need this."

She lifted the soft cloth to his head and wrapped it, blindfolding him. And just as she knotted it, he sensed a slight effort of her hands and arms, and got a whiff of her body and with that, contradicting it, the odor of her perfume on the silken softness against his face.

"Can you see anything?"

He shook his head, hardly daring to breathe. Yet as soon as he was blindfolded she was gentler, even submissive.

"Nothing."

"Don't be frightened," she said.

She must have noticed that his voice was thick with fear, because it was then that she touched him, holding him like a baby, and led him slowly across the smooth floorboards of the cabin to her bedroom. His feet shuffled, hardly leaving the floor, as he moved blindly, guided by her. He knew when they entered her bedroom from the sweetness in the air, the softness of the pillows. Then he was fearful, alone on the bed, but she had left him only to shut the door, and a moment later she was holding him again.

"Baby, baby, baby," she said, her hands on him. "Isn't that better?"

He lay slightly crouched in apprehension, not knowing what to say.

"I'm so lonely, baby." She sighed and sounded small.

He had entered the cabin knowing nothing, but he was learning, liking the strangeness of it, and now he knew that "baby" meant something different, someone strong, a man. Her mouth was against his ear, heating it, moistening it with her breath.

"You can be my boyfriend," she said. "Know what boyfriends do?"

He had no idea. He couldn't see, he couldn't speak. He thought, I am blind.

"I'm going to show you," she said, and when she touched him where he was tender, he drew back. "No, no. Let me, let me, let me."

Her hand was on him, but the heat that burned him was like a thickness of raw flesh after the skin has been peeled away, the warmth of blood and some throbbing, too. When he reached down to protect himself his hands found her head and became tangled in the hair of her loosened braid as she pushed her hot face against him, her tongue snaking, not devouring, not swallowing, but an audible ecstasy of the most rapturous tasting.

"Oh," she said in a small voice when it was over.

She murmured again sweetly but sounded disappointed, though she continued to nuzzle him. She held him tightly for a long while, then sighed and removed his blindfold.

"What did you see?"

"Nothing," he said.

"Good. Now get some of Tom's clothes and run along," she said. "This can be our secret."

He stared at her. Though she was damp-faced, with tangled hair and a redness on her cheeks, looking chafed, she was still in her white bra and pink panties, and she lay like someone who had just woken from an afternoon nap. She smiled at him.

"The first time I saw you I thought: This kid loves secrets. I'm going to give him one to keep, all to himself. And if he's good at keeping it, I'm going to give him some more secrets."

Ava put her pen down and leaned back and stretched. She said, "Didn't Tom ever find out?"

"He wasn't interested. Anyway, he had an older friend. That man Kenny, with the boat."

"But his mother was taking a risk."

"His mother, I see now, was a beautiful sensual woman, starved for attention. Long before that day she dressed up for us. She put on fancy dresses at mealtimes in that plain summer cabin. Even now I don't know the names for those clothes."

Ava said, "Your adolescence coincided with the age when women dressed carefully, the last gasp of extravagant fashion. White gloves. Pillbox hats. Veils. Girdles. Garter belts. Angora sweaters. Dresses with pleats. Women took pains to look . . ."

"Lovely?"

"I was going to say edible."

"Maybe that's why nakedness doesn't interest me."

"Maybe you're a woman's dream. We're so insecure about our bodies."

"I was so flattered that Tom's mother wanted me."

Ava was staring at him, and now she looked flustered and responsible, like Tom's mother.

"What else did she want?"

Instead of answering that question, Slade said, "A life isn't only about what you accomplished. It's also about what you desired. What you dreamed. What was in your head. All those secrets."

"Why are you smiling?"

"Because I realize that now" — all this time he had been sipping from a wineglass brimming with the muddy liquid of his dissolved drug — "I want to remember it all."

Ava said, "There was more?"

"Much more."

6

THE INTRIGUE between himself and Tom's mother, Mrs. Bronster (he was too shy to speak her first name, which was Lily), was so inconvenient, so filled with secrecy, uncertainty and misunderstanding, so many agonies of waiting, fears of interruptions and being found out, such a misery of insecurities and whispers and obstructions, of hardly any privacy, Tom quacking, "Where have you been?" and Nita nagging, and just the feeble pretense that he was a houseguest and she was his whining friend's kindly mother — so much nuisance and dissatisfaction, such confusion and thwarted pleasure — that he knew it could not possibly be love. He was thirteen years old. Only now, reliving it with Ava for his narrative, seeing it through the blaze of his drug, did Slade understand that all this pain and joy was the absolute proof that it *was* love.

Slade blinded himself to remember, blinded himself to write, blinded himself for desire; he was transfixed by the drug's blindness most of the time. The days at the lakeshore cabin had haunted and informed his life as a lover.

"Because everything I need to know is in my own head," he was saying on one of his dictating days after that, sitting to stare at Ava with blind eyes.

"She wanted me every day," Slade said. "And I wanted her just as much. I loved the routine that became a delicious ritual. I longed for her to blindfold me. It excited me to hear her heels on the floorboards of the cabin coming toward me after she finished locking the doors."

Then she would be next to him, and he could hear her sighing, smell her perfume, feel her body brush against him, the rub of the older looser skin of her arm or her belly.

"Don't move," she would say. "Keep your arms to your sides."

He stood like a small soldier, obedient and blindfolded in the middle of the wooden floor, its rough-cut timbers still so new they held the tang of the saw blade. Even blinded he knew that Tom's mother was standing in her shorts and bra, and could see her long legs rising into her loose shorts. Damp wisps of hair framed her face, which was bright with the blush from the day's heat. With gentle attentive hands she undressed him, helped him to put on the panties, reminding him that they were her best ones, expensive ones, and how lucky he was, as she brushed her fingers across the loose silk.

His mouth was gummed shut in panic and pleasure, for there were just the two of them in the house, and he knew that he was part of something illicit — his very desire was a proof of it. In the pistol imagery he associated with desire, he sensed the hammer was cocked on his libido in those hot afternoons with Tom's mother.

"I have to change," she said. "I have to get ready. You can help me. It'll keep you out of trouble, won't it?"

He could tell from her voice that she was bending over. He heard her shoes drop, and then the plop of her shorts, and the tearing sound of her panties skidding down her long legs, and the soft lisp and release of her bra; how her voice changed and strained as she reached behind her to unhook it.

"I need a shower," she said, and he heard her bare feet on the planks as she walked past him to the shower stall. He listened to the water coursing over her body. She was back in the room moments later, drying herself with a towel, gasping a little from the exertion, and he could hear the towel chafing her skin.

"Help me," she said, and put the damp towel into his hands.

His head rang as he pressed the towel on her smoothness, feeling her curves give, a new sensation to him, soft flesh. And all the odors — her perfumed soap, the sawn planks, the fragrance of the bedroom, the humid afternoon air still holding the lunchtime aromas of hot dogs and mustard — mingled with the distant yelling of children.

"Do you like doing that to me?"

Unable to think of a reply, he concentrated within the darkness of his blindfold and dabbed gently with the towel, loving the heat of her skin.

"Because you're so good at it you must have done it before."

"No," Slade whispered, wiping blindly at the woman's body.

"You're a fast learner," she said. "Can you see me?"

Slade made a solemn sound of denial in his nose that was more negative than the word "no."

"And don't peek. Peeking's against the rules."

Her voice was receding slightly. She had moved away from him and he stood still, holding the damp towel and listening hard. From the sounds, the same on every occasion, he took her to be kneeling and bending, sliding drawers, clattering coat hangers, and he gathered that she was looking in the dresser and in the closet, choosing clothes.

"Come here."

He went gladly, to please her, to please himself, but he stumbled, twisting the towel, as though for balance.

"Careful," Tom's mother said. "Over here."

The same game every time, one he loved. She was moving, there was laughter in her voice, and he could hear the throb of her desire in that laugh.

"You can't find me."

She spoke in such a teasing way that he laughed, too, and was aroused. He relaxed and in this mood of pleasure seemed to see Tom's mother as a big warm upright glow, giving off heat from across the room. He went forward with his arms extended, following the wisps of her fragrance, the creak of a floorboard, discovering that every perfume had its own heat.

"You're no good at hide and seek."

"Yes sah," he said, as though responding to a playmate, though a bit short of breath from shyness. "I'm wicked good."

"Then find me," she said.

"Why should I?" he said, so that he could hear her voice again.

She said, "If you find me, you can dress me."

He loved this game with his whole body. The blindfold over his eyes was silken, soft, fragrant, the odor of this woman's skin. He loved the darkness on his face, the soft weightlessness of her panties stroking his cock — that, and the summer afternoon of sunshine and pillowy heat in the small cabin bedroom, the hot tang of the wood planks, the whiffs of nakedness and perfume, the teasing girlish voice. It was all warm on his skin, and the blood in his head seemed to gag him with its heat.

He smiled, realizing that the blindfold helped him know so much: he could see, hear, and smell the whole enclosed room. In a silence that was rich with odors he turned his head and reached with his fingers. She had freed him and made him blameless by blindfolding him.

He touched warm smooth silk and moved his hands to the edge and raked his fingers across the stitched ribbon of elastic that lay tight against her flesh. He let his finger pads graze the length of the narrow band of lace that fringed it, caressing its netting, the fretted texture of its line, the lip of elastic, the scoop of loose silk. He felt there and found her hip, where her panties fitted her closely. She sighed and canted her body and thrust herself into his fingers, offering him a whole handful of soft silk, her warm body beneath it.

"French knickers," she said softly, keeping the words in her mouth and making them gummy as she savored them.

Her panties were warmer, more slippery than her skin, and when he touched her with his other hand he understood the little miracle that each part of her body was a different temperature. Had he not been wearing a blindfold, he would not have known that. And another revelation of his darkness was that she was breathing harder than was audible — he could feel the pulses of blood and air in the smallest muscles beneath her skin.

"I guess you found me," she said.

Encouraged by the smile in her voice, he traced with his fingers again and followed the strap binding her bra to the little clasp, played with it, and then found her breasts. He cupped them as he had imagined when he had first seen them and lifted slightly, feeling their weight in the thickness of stitches and ribbing, until his thumbs discovered them plumper where they swelled above the cups.

His face was so close to her bare stomach, her breathing was a repeated sweetness of soft pressure on his cheek, and when she spoke the words purred in her body.

"Want to help me get dressed now?"

Slade nodded, his nose nudging her skin.

"First we have to get some stockings on."

Just her mention of knickers and stockings filled him with a desire to taste her clothes, to have them in his mouth, but the thought was so extravagant he was too shy to tell her. He could not imagine overpowering her, and though he was aroused he had no idea of penetrating her but only of holding her. He wanted to nuzzle her, to smell her body through her clothes, to nibble her and nip them with his teeth — so near to him now, so delicious in her underwear, she seemed edible. He licked the edge of her panties with his tongue and then sucked on the silk.

One word from her and he would have stopped. But there was nothing, only her shallow breathing, her tightened muscles, the encouragement of her sighs, her fingers in his hair. He knelt like an acolyte before a decadent priestess, blindly, his mouth against her.

She pressed the stockings to his cheek and eased his face away.

"This is a garter belt," she said. She encircled her waist with it and hooked it. "Now you're going to snap my stockings on."

There was a catch in her throat as she bent over, and then came the faintest burr of silk on her leg as she drew up one stocking and then the other. She showed him, holding his hands, how to fasten the stockings to the clips. He loved fumbling at her thighs and failing, his knuckles against the textures and temperatures, as though creating a lover out of skin, elastic, and silk.

"Tighter," she said. "Yes, that's nice."

Still his face was against her, still he knelt, half naked himself in her panties, in a posture of adoration. He was excited that she was so much taller than he was, and that even when he stood, as he did when he finished clipping her stockings, his face was level with her breasts.

"What shall we wear?"

She led him to the other side of the room and opened a closet door. He groped a little until she took his hand and let his fingers roam through the dresses.

"Chiffon," she said. "And that's watered silk. Taffeta. Feel them — aren't they delicious? You choose better if you're blindfolded."

His inquiring fingers moved through the closet. He hesitated and began stroking slowly one hanging garment.

"This one," he said.

"That's a pleated skirt," she said, sounding doubtful. "But okay, if you like it I'll wear it for you."

Rattling the hanger off the rod, she shook the skirt as she removed it and then spun the hanger out of its waistband. She lifted the skirt over her head, tangling herself in it, then worked it down and shimmied into it.

"Now zip me."

He used two hands to squeeze the zipper seam together, to lift the slider and inch it upward, sensing the skirt fitting closely, letting his fingers glide through the deep pleats.

"That's nice. You did that so well you can help me pick out a blouse."

Already he was touching the clothes, tugging at sleeves, guessing which ones were blouses. A fold of sliding cloth fell across his hands, so cool and smooth it felt like liquid in his fingers. He raised it to his face and inhaled, saying, "This."

"I love this blouse," she said, and lifted it. From the way she spoke, straining a little, he could tell she was slipping the blouse on. "But it has very small buttons."

He touched them. They were small and fixed tightly to the blouse. They were cool, too.

"Seed pearls." She turned away and knelt down now and let him lean over her. "Button me up."

His blindfold was no hindrance; it made the game luxurious. He aligned the edge of the open blouse against the groove of her spine and worked from her neck down, fitting button to buttonhole. The seed pearls were tiny but his fingers were deft — more than deft, they were knowing, taking their time with each patient insertion. This sensual challenge enthralled him, all of it, for he had loved cupping her breasts in his much smaller hands, and he had adored the suffocation of his face against her panties. But buttoning the silk blouse, tugging each pearl and fixing it into a hole, this was the most pleasurable duty of all, for the tumbling of her hair over his fingers, the fragrance of her nape, the warmth of her shoulders at his palms, the way the buttons matched the pretty bones that ran down her back.

"You're a doll," she said. "You know that?"

He was smiling. And after that he chose her shoes, picking them for their slender heels, and when she stepped into them she was even taller, a warm giantess, her voice altered by her height. Still he stood close to her pleats and silks.

"Want to take your blindfold off?"

He shook his head. He could not say why he wanted it on — perhaps to prolong the intensity of her odors, to feel the fabrics more keenly, or to be blameless, for he felt no shame in the delirious in-between dream state where darkness was so revealing.

"Isn't this fun?"

Fun was not his word; for him it was unimaginable rapture. Having all this time to touch her, to attend to her, serving her. Yet he couldn't describe it, and he could only thank her by being ever more willing. He wanted to tell her through his obedience: I will do anything you ask.

"Have a seat, honey," she said gently, and helped him in the right direction.

But it was not a chair. It was much softer than a seat cushion, and springier. It was the edge of the bed, he guessed, but before he could be sure, her arms were around him, the soft white giantess enclosing him, her body against him. He was wooden, blind, inert, yet joyous from the crush of her clothes, the blouse he had chosen, the pleated skirt, the straps and softness of her lingerie, and her skin so damp where his fingers clung.

"Baby," she was saying, "baby."

He allowed himself to be stifled in all the textures of her embrace.

"Hold me, baby."

He did so, limply at first, testing her, then fiercely.

Her hungry mouth and soft lips were on his face. He had never imagined being been kissed like this — urgently licked, her flower-scented saliva on his lips and tongue, the heat from her nostrils on his cheek as she breathed and kissed him again. Her loose blouse slipped against her curves. He could feel her flesh beneath the cloth, her tight bra and the stiff cups of her enclosed breasts. He knew every stitch of her now, the skirt, the stockings, the panties, the garter clips he had fastened, the fringe of lace he had explored with his fingers.

She took his hand and eased it between her thighs, guiding it to the heat beneath all those tangled pleats, the pleasing roughness of lace, the straps and clasps. Everything he touched counted as her body, all the clothes, the silky hair, and, at its deepest, delighting him even as his wrist ached from the angle of his reaching under her, he knew he had found her secret self. This part of her body was not dark at all but highly colored, blood red and gleaming, a squashy pocket of lace and flesh, with something warm and damp alive inside it, like the secret of life.

She began to cry, at least it seemed as though she were sobbing, as she pressed her body against his face, rumpling his blindfold, so that he felt the silk and stitching against his lips. He remembered — not in words but as a yearning — how he had wanted to chew on her beautiful clothes, almost frightening himself with his memory of how he had wanted to eat her.

"Let me, let me," she said.

He did not know what she meant until he sensed the panties go loose on him, and she worked them free of his legs with her long arms.

Then he was naked, blindfolded, climbing on her as she toppled backward onto the bed. She pulled him nearer, balancing him and finally opening her legs for him, and as she snatched at her tumbling clothes to receive him, he marveled at how they fitted, his body on hers.

He was not raw anymore. Her cool fingers had enclosed him, and there was the cooler sensation of her silks as she stroked him and used him to push more deeply inside, to the hottest part of her body. She tightened on him until he could not stand it and could only whimper, as if among all the lips, silks, and flesh he were penetrating a flower, scattering rose petals. And after it ceased, the last petal falling, and he shivered and gasped and went cold, she was howling into his mouth for more.

He slept a little and woke drooling on her breast. His blindfold was off but the room was in darkness. He couldn't see, he had no idea where he was, he didn't know his own name. The woman's body was an island where he had washed ashore, cast up and saved by a furious wave.

He remained perfectly still, trying to remember, afraid to speak.

She said, "Playing isn't wrong."

The kindness in her voice gladdened him.

She said, "We can do this every day."

He wanted to say yes, but did not dare to say anything, fearful of how his voice would sound, for she had turned him inside out, and now he was at his nakedest.

"This is our secret," she said. "You can dress me. You're not going to tell anyone, are you?"

"No," he said, obeying her, hearing a note of urgency in her voice, needing him to say no.

"Will you let me make you happy?" she asked.

He said yes with his body, and she asked him again.

"Yes, Mrs. Bronster."

Then she let go of him. She pleaded with him, seeming to beg him with the heavy flesh of her own struggling body: "If you tell anyone, I'll harm you."

He turned away, reaching for his blindfold, but after the room went quiet there was no need for the blindfold. She was gone.

At dinner she was still wearing the clothes he had chosen. He loved sitting at the table with quacking Tom and cranky Nita, talking about everything except that. The clothes meant everything — that he possessed her, that she possessed him: that was their secret. She had made him her blind and willing lover. She had made him a man.

"First love," he said in a whisper to Ava, and she slipped off his silken blindfold.

Everything he had seen in his mind's eye, everything the datura made possible, that he had remembered and relived of his hidden life, of his sexual history, all that and more he had dictated to Ava. There was so much of it, for the larger part of his life he had lived in secret. He was gratified by the symmetry of it, its reality, its oddness, and he reflected that the rarest thing in books or movies, in which decapitation and rape and outrage were commonplace, was the simple joyous act of two lovers fucking.

In his interior narrative he had taken a longer and more difficult journey than the one he had described in *Trespassing*. There was frailty and failure, too, embarrassments and risk. Yet he never felt more powerful than he had on those nights and days, blindly revisiting his past. That power vitalized his belief in the chronicle of second chances that he had relived with Ava as every passion he had ever known.

Long ago, as a solitary boy, he had not understood the meaning of his desires. Now, enacted in the blinding light of the drug, they were coherent. The fulfilled yearning of youth was the only passion that mattered. He told himself that what he imagined was also real. What he had wanted and never gotten had made him who he was; what had lain buried in his memory was dragged out of the darkness and given life. And nothing was more sexual than the forbidden glimpses of his past, nothing truer than his fantasies. He called it fiction because every written thing was fiction.

So his work was done. The past made sense. At last he had his novel, *The Book of Revelation*, and he could face the world again.

FOUR

Book Tour

1

HE WAS EUPHORIC at having finished his book, relieved of a burden he had carried like an uncomplaining drudge for so long it had cut and wounded him, enfeebling his body. All that suspense, the thing not done and tentative, the fragment of a promise kept in a stack of notes and tapes, had made him feel incomplete. His shattered sense of having been injured, of needing to heal, was nothing glorious — not the secret agony that was said to be the source of art. The dull pain had made him feel like a lower animal in the slow process of regenerating a limb from a broken stump. Now his work done, he was active again, whole and happy.

Except for some tidying up — the last transcripts and edits — Steadman had his book. This reward for all the years of silence, something at last his own, was a sexual confession in the form of a novel. He was at first so lightheaded he did not miss the datura tea he had drunk every working day in order to find the thread of his narrative. He was jubilant, with the exquisite thrill of his past revealed and understood.

Throughout the year of writing he had never needed to tell his editor he was at work. The whispers had reached New York early on. This man was Ron Axelrod. As a new young editor he had inherited Steadman when Steadman's first editor had died. But for years that editor, and Axelrod too, had seen no new writing from Steadman and had merely shuffled contracts and processed the new tie-in editions of *Trespassing*.

Steadman phoned Axelrod and gave him the news. He said a disk with the first part of the manuscript was in the mail. He said, "I'm back in business."

"I don't know whether you're aware of it," Axelrod said after he had read the early chapters, "but there's a touch of mysticism in your book."

"Just tell me it's on the spring list."

"There's probably enough lead time. If you deliver the whole thing soon, we can try."

It did not seem that anything better could happen to improve his mood. And then another call came. Ava was at work; she had gone back to the hospital the day after the dictation had been finished and the last tapes sent for transcription. Lazing in bed on a Saturday morning, propped on pillows and relaxed, watching television, at first too drowsy to change the channel from *Teletubbies,* Steadman groped for the remote switch and pinched it and a new program flashed onto the screen. It was a stark cartoon in lurid colors, a wicked-faced man in a beaky green eyeshade tapping his stick under a stormy sky along a cobblestone road. Above his bony head was a swinging sign on a large old house, *The Admiral Benbow Inn.* He wore a black cape and hood that made him seem like a swaggering and wicked jackdaw.

"Will any kind friend inform a poor blind man who has lost the precious sight of his eyes in the gracious defense of his native country, England — and God bless King George — where or in what part of the country he may now be?"

A young cartoon boy whom Steadman knew to be Jim Hawkins, but drawn with a pale face that was meek and girlish, stepped from the shadows holding a flickering orange-windowed lantern.

"You are at the Admiral Benbow."

The blind hooded man whirled around and snatched at Jim's hand and twisted the boy's skinny arm behind his back.

"Now, boy, take me to the Captain."

"Sir, upon my word, I dare not."

"Take me in straight or I'll break your arm."

Steadman watched Blind Pew bully and terrify the boy. Then, as Blind Pew entered the inn, Steadman's phone rang.

"This is the White House, president's office. We'd like to speak to Mr. Slade Steadman."

His thumb on the remote switch, he muted the TV. As soon as Blind Pew delivered the Black Spot there was mayhem — old grizzled sea dogs ransacking the rooms and tipping over sea chests.

"Speaking."

Blind Pew was outside, groping again, and lost. Steadman watched in triumph, feeling contempt for the malevolent and stumbling blind man, who without any warning had been deserted by the others.

"The president wonders if you are free to attend a dinner at the White House on November tenth, for the visit of the chancellor of Germany."

As in silence Blind Pew struggled on the empty, shadowy road, calling out for help, the woman on the phone explained that this was a call only to see whether he could attend the White House dinner. If the answer was yes, an invitation would be sent.

"Delighted to accept. Does this invitation extend to my partner, Dr. Ava Katsina?"

"Of course."

Steadman spelled Ava's name, and the White House secretary went over the details ("This will be black tie"), and Blind Pew fell into a ditch. He climbed crabwise out of it and, once again on the road, was trampled to death by five galloping horses.

Ava was pleased by the news. She moved lightly, happily, restless with pleasure, still wearing her green hospital scrubs. "This is great," and looked at Steadman sideways, smiling uncertainly, because it seemed there was more and he was not divulging it. And when she saw the froglike expression on his face, heavy-lidded, his eyes half shut, his lips pressed together, she said, "Okay, what is it?"

He didn't say, he squinted and looked froggier, he paced a little. The thought *This is perfect* showed on his face.

Ava followed, staying with him, and then he turned and said, "They asked me about my" — he raised his arms and clawed a pair of quotation marks in the air with his hooked fingers — "special needs."

A slackening look of disturbance clouded Ava's face.

"And you told them — ?"

Steadman laughed, much too loudly, a honk of confidence.

With pleading eyes Ava held him. She said, "When you try to be enigmatic you can be such a bully."

"I can see in the dark," he said.

She screamed, howled in protest, which thinned to a cry of agony and betrayal.

"You can't do this."

He was in no doubt that he could, yet he knew from that moment he would never convince her of it.

"It's a lie."

In what was almost a whisper, but a heated one, Ava said, "I have just come from the hospital. We have real sick people there. 'Special needs,' all of that. We have sick children. We have people confused and upset because they've just been told they have macular degeneration, for which there is no cure. What an insult, what an outrage, for you to pretend to be blind."

"Not pretend," he said.

She shouted and left the room saying "No!" But he knew there would be more over dinner, and there was. She said that she had felt guilty about returning to work at the hospital so soon after his finishing the book, leaving him so abruptly. But now she was glad, she said. She wished she had gone sooner.

When he didn't reply she said, "I can't stand your smug face."

In the days after that he felt so idle and liberated he used the datura again and found the alteration powerfully hallucinogenic. Even his voice underwent a change, became declaratory, with a stammering vibrato. Datura was a friend. Blind, he was able to reconstitute his world and find his true place in it.

"Back from the dead," he said.

The whole day ahead was his, without any obligation on his part to cast his mind back and revisit his past; nothing to accomplish. He had written his book.

That day Axelrod called again with the news that *The Book of Revelation* was on the spring list.

"But you'll have to help me with the catalogue copy."

"Give me a hint."

"Tell me what it's about."

"The physical side of the act of creation."

"Yes?"

"The origin of art."

"Be a little more specific."

"Look, it's about itself."

He said it was more a book about transgression and trespassing than *Trespassing* had been; it was all interior travel. He did not say that datura was the means, its name like an elegant, darting vehicle that had taken him the whole distance, there and back.

In the days that followed, Ava sulked, stung by his insistence on going to the White House dinner blind, showing up impaired in public as the president's guest, someone who would be photographed and written about. When he talked Ava stepped away to give him room, for he seemed to crowd her, to look past her, as though he were haranguing a multitude of people, the wider world, speaking more expansively, like a man starring in his own movie. He appeared to be aware that a public process was at work on the Vineyard, a marveling at him for his prescience, the murmuring witnesses to his renewed fame, the triumphant second act of his life, more dramatic, more visible and original, than the first.

He imagined his face on his book jacket: eyes opaque with the drug and yet shocking, with a wounded corrosive stare on which nothing was lost, for this new book was like the oldest book in the world, a confession that was prophecy and revelation.

He had dreamed of writing such a book. He had yearned to create it but had been baffled and tentative, not knowing how to begin. The book he had envisioned was calculated to eliminate the possibility of any biography of him, to make the notion of a biographer a joke. A parasite, a hanger-on, an outsider, an intruder, a stammering explainer with his nose against a smeared windowpane, staring into thick curtains — who needed such a person? For someone who wrote the truth exhaustively, setting everything down without any inhibition, making the ultimate confession, a biography was superfluous. Why would anyone bother? There would be nothing to write, nothing new, nothing of value. So with the book he called his novel, he had taken over the work of all the prospective biographers.

"I've put them out of business," he said loudly, as though to the world.

Axelrod said, "We can get it into the catalogue now. If you deliver the manuscript on a disk before the end of the month, we can publish in the spring. Shall we say it's travel?"

"It's travel, it's autobiography, it's everything. Most of all it's fiction."

"Hell of a title."

As for the paragraph for the catalogue the editor asked for, Steadman said, "How much better *not* to have one." And when the editor seemed doubtful, Steadman said, "Just the title."

There was general approval for the two-thousand-year-old title, *The Book of Revelation*.

In a damp and breezy October of slapped-down waves in the harbor and discoloring and withering leaves up-island, the Vineyard had almost emptied of visitors and was returned again to its year-rounders. After his months of steady work it seemed odd to Steadman to be here with so little to do except process his manuscript. In the course of almost a year of dictation — they had returned from Ecuador the previous November — a woman with a secretarial service in Edgartown had transcribed the tapes he had made with Ava. The woman had said she was unshockable. "As the mother of three boys and a girl, with a husband in the Coast Guard, I've seen just about everything." At first she sent the pages using a courier service. Then, perhaps to save money, she delivered the printed pages in person. She had kept pace with the dictation, the tapes and notes, and not long after Steadman finished, she handed him the remainder of the first draft of the novel, with the tight-lipped smile of someone tested to the limit, as though holding back her disapproval.

The book was complete, needing only line corrections and slight revision. Having the whole book before him was a pleasure. But he worked without the drug. How plain the printed words seemed compared to the stipple of brilliant pixels in his drug visions.

He dabbed at errors, rubbing highlights into words and phrases, deleting preciousness ("frenzied and oculate waves" became "wild eye-spotted swells"; he crossed out the words "numinous," "ineffable," and "chiastic"). Now that his days were relieved only by his trifling with the manuscript, he found himself disoriented. He was glad to be free of the anxiety of the guilty lopsided life of a writer with an unfinished book, but he missed the day-filling routine of dictation, the drama of his sexual nights, the anticipation of taking the drug each morning. The music had stopped, the racket in his head was gone, the house was whole but predictable, colorless, no longer hallucinatory. One day was like another, the empty hours of silent mornings and much too long afternoons and dreamless nights that had no objective, not even the promise of Ava. She was always tired: her work, her life, was elsewhere. He was reminded of his life before Ecuador, when he'd had nothing to do, nothing to write; when he had felt cynical and impotent. He was not impotent now, yet he felt his desire slackening, the old disobedience that was like a deafness of the flesh.

He found he could not read easily; habituated to glowing shapes and colors, his eyes were unaccustomed to the severity of small print. The letters jumped and rearranged themselves as he blinked, making him feel dyslexic. So he put on earphones and listened to audiotapes. The glimpse of Blind Pew on the television that morning had stirred his interest. In his present mood of impatience he had a boxed set of tapes, Stevenson classics, sent to him in a taxi from Vineyard Haven. He shut out the world by clamping Stevenson to his ears. Some passages he marveled at, but the best of them saddened him with their exactitude and made him feel lonely. He had often felt this when he was affected by the truth in fiction.

He missed his datura, he missed its pleasures, he missed its benign guidance, the way it had helped him in new directions; he missed the way it had led him upward to a vantage point where he saw himself so clearly he could concentrate on his wholeness, like a man in front of a mirror sketching his self-portrait. He missed the complexities of color, the way one color appeared as separated layers, like leaves of innocent light given meaning when they were arrayed together. The drug had given him access, and now he was just a man on the outside.

The drug had allowed him to range widely in time and space, to peel experience from his body and mind, and now without it he was smaller and shallower, with an obscure sense of loss, like someone so stunned by the death of a loved one, he suffered all the more from the trauma because — so deranged by the loss — he could not recall the loved one's name or face. Under the spell of the drug, the future that had once been full of suggestion and promise was now unreadable. The past was distant and inaccessible. He was a small figure on the parapet of the present, feeling very little except the obvious and violent compulsion to jump.

He was sighted now, returned to the gray daylight and misleading surfaces of the visible world.

With nothing to keep her at home, and as if atoning for all the time she had taken off, Ava worked long hours, odd hours, spending arduous days at the hospital. She was like a missionary doctor on a remote Third World island, where everyone expected favors, every patient was hopeless and desperate, every case an emergency, and failure was common. Ava knew all the Vineyard families. "I have to do it. If I didn't, who would?" The sort of thing Steadman had seen in places like New Guinea and Haiti. Sometimes Ava worked twenty-four hours without sleep; she was often on call all night.

Cursing the pager, dreading the phone, the three A.M. emergencies, the midnight births, Steadman was reminded of the early days of their love affair. He had forgotten that she had a life of her own.

"This is normal," she said when he complained. "Look, we were writing all day and fucking all night."

"What's wrong with that?"

"It's nice, but let's say it's less usual," she said. "I'm a doctor. I think the difficulties of doctoring made me a reckless lover. But now I'm back to work. Get used to it."

She stopped using makeup. Her choice of clothes, even when she was not at the hospital, seemed clinical, even dowdy. Usually she wore green scrubs around the house.

"You got what you wanted," she said. "Your book."

"It wasn't only that."

"Okay. You got your reputation back. Your manhood."

But he resisted simplifying it. He said, "Are you going to make it all my trip and deny that there was some pleasure in it for you?"

"It was like a year of insanity. Yes, I found it exciting, but I am so glad it's over."

He stared at her, and seeing she was unmoved, he said, "Don't you see what's beginning?"

"I can do without excitements. We have enough of those at the hospital." She saw that he was still staring defiantly at her. "People die there. They give birth. They come in with bone splinters sticking out of their flesh. You should see a motorcycle victim sometime. These people are scared, they're in pain. Some of them do nothing but cry. And we have a psychiatric unit, too, you know. They need me more than you do."

He turned his back on her. He said, "It's like you've forgotten everything we did those days."

"When I start to miss it I'll read your book."

He wondered if he would ever feel as lost again as he had before he met her, but he told himself no, he had his book, he had no fear of solitude. Blindness was the ultimate in solitude, yet blindness had made him bold and filled him with courage.

"Listen to this," he said one day, on her return from work. He read from a sheet of paper, a rare example of his handwriting. "After I drank, the most racking pangs succeeded: a grinding in the bones, deadly nausea, and a horror of the spirit that cannot be exceeded at the hour of birth or death. Then these agonies began swiftly to subside, and I came to myself as if out of a great sickness. There was something strange in my sensations, something indescribably new and, from its very novelty, incredibly sweet. I felt younger, lighter, happier in body; within I was conscious of a heady recklessness, a current of disordered sensual images running like a millrace in my fancy, a solution to the bonds of obligation, an unknown but not an innocent freedom of the soul —"

"How can you write that arrogant shit?" she said, interrupting him, and when he began to laugh at her, she hissed at him.

"I didn't write it," he said slyly. "A doctor wrote that."

"Some quack," she said.

"Dr. Jekyll," he said. "He would have agreed with you!"

Without telling Ava — he wanted her to feel neglectful — he admitted to himself that his life was still full. He would have objected more loudly to being left on his own except that around the time Ava had returned to the hospital he began again to be in demand. He started to receive messages from intermediaries — Axelrod, the publisher's publicity department, helpful friends — telling him there were people who wanted to meet him. He got calls nearly every day — people tipped off that he was writing again, that the author of *Trespassing* had a new book.

One of the requests came from the television show *60 Minutes*. Would Steadman agree to an interview? He guessed how this had come about: Mike and Mary Wallace had been at Wolfbein's most recent party. The hook would be: famous recluse, stricken blind, produces a new book in his enforced darkness. The title of the segment would be something like "Edge of Night."

Axelrod had relayed the message. "They want to follow you around at home on the Vineyard and do an in-depth interview."

Other messages, nearly all from TV shows and photographers, implored him to return their calls to discuss what they might do together. There was no ambiguity in the requests: he was to be seen close up by a camera, to be observed at work and at home — they put it in a kindly way. He was at first flattered but easily saw the renewed interest as intrusive journalism, the voyeuristic wish to film him walking into walls, stumbling, and perhaps falling on his face in picturesque Vineyard settings. Steadman knew that they wanted to see his sideways gait, his faltering gestures, his groping fingers, his big blank face and swiveling head. Great TV, they were thinking — and what a surprise they would get when they saw that he walked headlong with a strut and a slashing cane, with well-aimed gestures and an animated gaze.

"Out of the question," he told Axelrod.

Someone from the *New York Times* called to schedule "At Home with Slade Steadman," and again he suspected an eagerness to see him bumping his head and knocking things to the floor, crumbs on his shirt, mismatched socks. *People* magazine suggested something similar, but insisted on an exclusive. The *Boston Globe* reminded him that he was a native son, but it was the travel editor who called. Would Steadman consider an interview on the sailing ship *Shenandoah*? Freelance photographers asked for sittings and portraits. There was no letup. And when the book was announced in the publisher's catalogue the number of requests multiplied. Bookstores urged him to visit, universities asked him to speak, and would he please be the keynote speaker at a seminar on travel writing "for seniors with disabilities"?

In almost every inquiry there was an allusion to his blindness: offers of assistance, a limo, a ticket, an escort, "anything we can do to make this as painless as possible for you." "We have many visually impaired students in our institution," one letter said. "I did Borges," one photographer claimed, adding, "I'd show you the contact sheets, but I guess you'll have to take my word for it." Subtler suggestions patronized him: "Lots of people ought to have the chance to share your story." And one of the universities, offering a large fee and promising a good audience, wrote, "We have a full range of handicapped access."

"They think I'm a cripple," he told Axelrod.

But seeing an advantage in creating buzz — his editor's expression — Axelrod advocated early publicity for the book. The *New York Times Magazine* had put in a request.

"They're not promising you the cover — they never do that — but there's an excellent possibility of it. Think of the sales."

The thought *No one knows me* — his sense of being a wraith, a phantom, an anonymous presence — had always driven his writing and made him content. But now Steadman laughed, because his book was done and his life and work, once so hidden, so widely speculated on, would soon belong to the world. There would be nothing else to tell.

"I'm differently abled," he told Axelrod. "If only they knew how differently abled I am."

All that was known of him was his blindness and his new book. He liked that, because the truth of his blindness — its gifts — was so startling. To the imploring journalists and askers after his appearance, he was a casualty, an object lesson, a freak, a moral parable, tabloid fodder; not a writer but a survivor. They wanted to hear about his pain. And he smiled because there was no pain, only joy — a bigger story but an unexpected one, and perhaps of more limited appeal, for people wanted to share his suffering.

So the word was out that he had a book. He suspected he would be marketed as a miracle, a survivor who had managed to tell his tale, batting the air with one hand and whirling his white cane with the other. He was eyeless and enigmatic, but also valiant and pathetic, a licensed bore, someone who made you shut up and listen so that he could be sententious, always managing to succeed against the odds.

All lies. He had never been more clear-sighted than when, drugged, he had blinded himself and entered the mind and heart of the small hopeful thirteen-year-old he had once been. Nothing was more important than finding that child and rewarding him. In that simple wish the book was born.

"I am not a cripple," he wanted to say to the prospective interviewers and TV people. "Blindness has been an asset. I could never have completed this book without it."

He said this to Ava, told her how he had valued the trip to Ecuador, learning the uses of datura. Blindness had changed him, living with her had changed him, the book had meant everything.

She was smiling as he spoke. She controlled her voice, holding her emotion in her mouth, and said, "So much for you. But what do you think all this did to me?"

Steadman scowled at her. Because she so seldom talked about herself, this question seemed irrelevant.

"I don't want to make you feel guilty," she said, "but can you imagine what your behavior did to my head?"

He still scowled and looked deaf. He was niggled by the word "behavior."

"I have a past, too," she said.

"That's for you to deal with," he said in a tone of *Who wants to know?*

He had become grim and uninterested. He wanted to turn away from her, for all this time, in her arms, lusting for her, he had seen her as every woman he had ever loved, and she had seen him as — who? — someone else, certainly.

"Your story," she said, "is not to be confused with mine."

Of course, another narrative had been unspooling in her mind, utterly different from his own, one he could not share.

"Be a doctor," he said. "Help me. Heal me. Don't tell me about your medical history."

Still, he was puzzled by the parallel life she must have led while collaborating on his book. Sexuality was so private, so fantasy driven, so dependent on the past. He knew what role she played for him in his blissful reveries of childhood, but what part did he play in her simultaneous recollections and rehearsals? Better not ask.

"What does it all lead to?" she said. "People will wonder."

"Happiness," he said. "Anyone reading my book will see that all they need to know is in their own head. That's my message. 'You are the source of all wisdom. Of all pleasure.'"

So he told himself he was content. He took no notice of the invitations and requests, for he kept thinking of that morning of the phone call forewarning him — a "save the date" call for November. The invitation from the White House was sent by mail, the state dinner for the German chancellor. And a handwritten note on an enclosed card: *The president is looking forward to seeing you.*

One night in the first week of November, Steadman was at the chessboard, waiting for Ava to come home from the hospital. She hated eating late, regarded it as unhealthy; she had stopped drinking alcohol, since she might be summoned to the emergency room; she was always too weary these days for sex. Even chess was a labor for her, a single game might take days, but at least they were able to converse over the board.

He sat lightly, studying the chess pieces in a posture of patience and concentration. He was like a diner about to finish a meal, some scraps still on his plate, a man who was rested and alert and not very hungry, perhaps saving some of his food for his friend, who was about to turn up.

Ava entered without speaking, and it was only when she sat down that she spoke. "Your move."

"Let's play rapid transit," he said. "I want to finish this tonight."

As she made her move, she said, "You're going drugged?" resuming the conversation that had ended the previous day when they had stood up from the chessboard.

"I'm at my best when I'm blind." He took his turn without hesitating.

"It's the White House. Everyone will see you. They'll know."

"Your move."

After her move he swiftly took her rook, swooping with his knight.

"I want everyone to know."

She let out a howl of agony, a surrendering cry of despair, not recognizable words but a dark lament that filled Steadman with horror for its sound of suffering. It was as though a knife had been plunged into her body, but she was not a victim, she was a witness, being given a long, hideous look at certain death — his death. He was fading as she looked helplessly on, and her howl at what he said was how she would feel at the sight of him dying. He saw that for her, with his certainty about being blind, he *had* died in her eyes.

Just afterward her voice changed to a gasp as she spoke with a scorched throat. "How can you?"

"I have to."

"It's a lie. It's a mask," she said, her voice catching.

"Blind Slade wrote that book," he said. "To go any other way would be deceitful."

"What if they found out the truth?"

"That *is* the truth. Please move."

She moved, she was bent backward, as though wishing for words. She said, "To pretend to be afflicted."

"I'm not afflicted," he said, and struck again with his knight. "That's the first thing people have to know."

"It is such bullshit," she said.

"Your move."

She poked at a bishop, and in the next move lost him, and began to cry, the same lament but softer, more sorrowful, rubbing her eyes. With wet fingers she moved a pawn.

"I help sick people," she said. "And you pretend to be sick. It makes a mockery of everything I do."

"I became blind. I lost my sight. You know that."

"People with brain tumors lose their sight. Diabetics lose their sight. People with detached retinas. Burn victims. Infected corneas. Serious head trauma. You should be ashamed."

"I never said I was a victim. I never whined."

"You're worse. You boasted."

He folded his hands and waited for her to move.

But she said, mimicking his voice, "I can write in the dark!"

"I *can* write in the dark. I am blinder than Borges when he wrote his essay 'On Blindness.' I wrote my book in the dark." He had not looked up at her. He added, "If you don't want to play, just say so."

Ava stared at the board for a long while, then made a move, another fatal one. As Steadman plucked at her chess piece, Ava said, "I'm not going to help you. I won't be part of it. Go to the White House blind if you like. What a mockery!"

He said, "It's the truth. It's who I am. Me at my best."

Then he moved. She glanced down to see the trap. He said, "Checkmate," and only then did he raise his eyes to her.

She recognized the bloodshot and glassy stare of his blindness as he sat triumphant over the chessboard. She put her hands in her lap and looked old and prim and distant.

He knew she would not howl again. No one could do that twice, with such a cry of horror. But she didn't have to. He still heard it within himself. The sorrowing sound had deranged something in him — no longer a sound, but a pain lodged deep inside him, something torn, an ache that had displaced all his desire.

2

EVEN WITH THE invitation propped on the mantelpiece and the decision to go settled, Steadman kept receiving phone calls and faxes to verify additional details: his and Ava's Social Security numbers, ages, birthplaces, home address, and — though Steadman had been explicit about his not needing help — a "Special Needs" form to be filled out and faxed back. Another form in the invitation package indicated that because rooms were unavailable, they were not being invited to stay the night in the White House. Attached to this was a list of hotels that offered special rates to White House dinner guests, with parking instructions, and "handicapped accessible" was mentioned here, too.

"'Special needs' describes me perfectly."

"Why do you insist on doing this?"

He had to think a moment before he realized she didn't mean the decision to accept the invitation but rather his insistence on attending the dinner blind. But he said nothing. His mind was made up.

Black tie had also been stressed — everything that was stated was stressed — and it was repeated that the chancellor of Germany was the guest of honor. Nothing was left to chance.

The morning of their departure, Steadman called Wolfbein to tell him the news and to ask for advice. Wolfbein was a friend of the president and a frequent overnighter at the White House.

"You putz," he said, and he bantered, pretending to be hurt because he had not been invited. Then he urged Steadman always to remember to call him "Mr. President," and not to bring a camera, and to observe protocol. "It's ground zero. It's the center of the world." Wolfbein then became concerned. "How are you feeling?"

"Great. I can see through walls and around corners."

When he put the phone down he was aware that Ava was behind him, leaning away, in a posture of disapproval.

She was silent on the way to Boston, silent on the plane to Washington, and it was only when they arrived at Reagan Airport that she spoke.

"I see the Jordans."

Vernon and Ann Jordan approached and said hello. They had just arrived from New York, en route to the same dinner party.

"How're you doing?" Vernon demanded in his hearty direct manner, fixing Steadman with a smile.

"X-ray vision," Steadman said, tapping his dark glasses.

That pleased Vernon, who laughed loudly, his muscular body radiating light and health and humor. He was a man who smiled easily and whose casual manner masked a shrewd intelligence and fastidious discretion. Yet he was genuinely friendly, and near him Steadman felt that he was in the presence of a man of power, a smiling sorcerer who remembered everything he saw or heard.

"You know my wife," Vernon said, and turning to Ann, said playfully, with a little bow, "Hello, wife."

"I know you from the hospital," Ann said to Ava. "We are all so thankful to you for your wonderful work."

"Can we offer you good people a lift?" Vernon asked.

They accepted the ride with gratitude, feeling rescued, for they had traveled in silence and had arrived in Washington bewildered. And now, having been swept into the limo, they were treated to Vernon's running commentary about the landmarks they were passing — the Pentagon, the Jefferson Memorial. He narrated tactfully, describing their beauty, using his enthusiasm for detail as a way of hiding the fact that he was doing this for a blind man.

"And here we are at the Willard. We'll see you folks later."

The formalities at check-in were brief and efficient, questions asked and ignored by Steadman, who brushed at his watch face with his fingertips and said, "We have to get a move on."

He had taken a dose of the drug in the morning. He took another one in the hotel room after he changed into his tuxedo. Ava sat apart from him in the cab to the White House; she was remote, she disapproved, she was sorry she had come. A shadow of unease lay across her features, while Steadman's were bathed in light.

After they were dropped at the side entrance, following the instructions on the map, they showed their IDs and were escorted ("This is the East Room") to where there was a receiving line and drinks being served. Steadman was aware of a glazed and shimmering room filled with excited strangers.

"I'm right beside you," Ava said.

"I know," Steadman said. And then, "Do you believe this?"

The smells of fresh flowers and floor wax and new paint gave the place a hum of something venerable, the glory of an old hotel restored to luxury. All this with the contrasting odors of perfume and aftershave lotion and polished leather. But more conspicuous than anything was the insinuation of decay beneath the sweaty faces and the glitter, the corruption and the untruth, like the decrepitude that stank under the White House timbers — Steadman could smell it all.

The discomfort, the awkwardness, was palpable, too — bumped shoulders, loud greetings, the hyperalertness of strangers. But though no one seemed at home there — the whole gleaming structure was like a stage set — they were all energized by simply being in the place. With an intensity that was like a fever of madness, the guests seemed to

Steadman like heavy animals in unnatural postures, tottering on their hind legs. They were clumsy, they were eager, they chattered and bantered in a way that made them seem skittish and tickled. Their attention was brief but vibrant, glittering for an instant and then flashing elsewhere, as they roved — the men especially — swinging their arms, shouldering forward, glancing sideways. Steadman was reminded first of ungainly athletes and then of greedy goodhearted apes.

Approaching the receiving line, Steadman was cued to the keen attention — gestures more obvious than murmurs — of people making way for him. They stood aside and let him pass, no one touching him, until the large warm arm of the president rested on his shoulder. With a firm fond hug, the president held on.

"So glad you could make it. And you, too, Doctor," the president said, gripping Ava's elbows. Then he turned and said, "This man is truly one of my favorite writers. And I can tell you, he's a hero. Slade Steadman, this is His Excellency . . ."

But Steadman was grasped again, and the chancellor said, in a slight accent that made him seem kindly and precise, "Yes, in Germany as well. So good to meet you."

He heard the soft bubble-burst of camera flashes and felt his face warmed as his picture was taken. He knew the others were smiling, he could tell by a tightness in their voices, but he did not smile. He tried to look serene and untroubled, indifferent to the cameras, for he knew these pictures would travel.

"You've probably been to Germany." The voice was unmistakably Vernon Jordan's. And Steadman was hugged and Vernon said, "How you doing now?"

He took the muscular hugs and the bantering to be reactions to his blindness. The making way, too — silence, pity, confusion, bewilderment, and head signals and hand gestures. He smiled at eliciting these reactions, and none were kinder than the president's.

"Beautiful paintings," Ava was saying as they left the receiving line.

No sooner had a waiter put a drink in Steadman's hand than the president caught up with him and steered him to the other guests and introduced him. He insisted on including Steadman in every conversation — "the author of *Trespassing*" — and he held on to him with a gentle guiding hand. The president was being a big brother, a defender, an explainer, a benefactor, taking personal charge of him.

Twice, Steadman overheard people saying variations of "I wish my mother were alive, so I could call her and tell her where I am. She would be so proud."

He heard voices with a clarity that kept the words in his memory, and the guests had the urgency of people trying to remember everything that was happening. They spoke in a mannered and self-conscious way, as though rehearsing what they would later report to their friends.

But with the words, the particular accents, he recognized the chief components of people — their lips, their ears and noses, their nervous hands and shuffling feet, the physicality of the guests standing in the room, the fleshy strangulatory handshakes, the way they kept patting him on the back, the fragrant iridescence of the women — was it their mascara? — the heavy faces of the men, the way they used their jaws in speaking, always aware they were conspicuous. The bulk and heft of their bumping elbows, the suggestion of sinew and fat, their long greedy arms, their impatient feet in heavy shoes. He was continually reminded of the density of their flesh, and aware of them as restless contending animals.

Although they made room for him when he moved, when he stood to talk they always seemed to be crowding him, backing him up, standing a bit too close, speaking a bit too loud, as if he were not blind but slow-witted.

Among themselves, in their odd unhesitating talk and movement, he saw the guests as wishing to be in agreement, all on the same side, all rooting for the same team, all delighted to be there in the White House. They were all in step, a great hairy hovering party, full-throated in solidarity and especially emphatic in their marveling bark-like laughter.

Steadman knew that the pretense of unanimity was a polite deception, and he felt only pity and condescension for these people. He was glad — proud, beaming, blind. But the roar of approval concerned him as much as the sweet perfume that masked the stink, for he could see it was the purest theater, the posturing and the falsehood, the insincerity, the fakery, the lies. The guests were nervous and unsure and grateful; if the president had asked, they would have agreed to anything. Ape-like, he kept thinking, and they had the moral blindness of primates too.

"We're being summoned," Ava said. "But I'm not sitting next to you."

They went into the next room for dinner, Ava steering him, and then he was shown to his seat. He knew he was being watched as he was served a glass of wine and as the first course was put before him.

"Consommé," he said, inhaling.

"That's a ten," the woman next to him said.

"No," he said, feeling that she was patronizing him. "A ten for me is when it's sashimi and I correctly guess maguro by the aroma alone."

"Liz Barton," the woman said. He could tell she was small and sure of herself, very young, with a confident gargly voice. "I know who you are. My father was such a fan."

He swallowed his rebuke and said, "What do you do, Liz?"

"I'm in the attorney general's office. Overseeing adjuncts to the Americans with Disabilities Act."

"So I guess I'm not your first blind dinner partner," Steadman said.

"Not at all. I had the privilege of escorting Stevie Wonder when President Mandela visited."

"I can see him now, grinning all over his face, wagging his head and shaking his beaded locks in gratitude," Steadman said, turning to the person on his right and gesturing to Liz Barton. "This young woman insists on flattering me."

By then the second course was being served. Steadman made small talk, realizing with disgust that this was required of him and already wishing to leave. He had shown up, he had presented himself to the president and the guests as the blind author, his picture had been taken. But he couldn't leave, not yet, for the dinner was formal: there were toasts, affirmations of friendship between the United States and Germany, the repeated mention of a trade fair in Hannover.

"I am so sorry my wife is not here to join us. As first lady, she is on an official visit to Africa with our daughter and sends you all her good wishes." Before the president sat down, he added, "I want to say a special word of thanks to my good friend and a great American writer, Slade Steadman."

Snatching at his cane, Steadman rose and leaned on it and smiled, showing the room his dark glasses and his grim smile, and sensing the explosive puffs of air and flashes of light as cameras fired at him.

Coffee was served and the president offered to show the guests more of the White House: the Truman Balcony overlooking the South Lawn, the Green Room where Jefferson had dined, the smaller family dining room, and some artifacts, including a Gutenberg Bible, which had been brought from the Library of Congress in the German chancellor's honor.

The crowd thinned, the women who had sat on either side of him had left, and Steadman was alone. As he wondered where Ava had gone, he felt a familiar hand massaging his shoulder and heard the president's voice.

"Slade, I'm so glad to have you here with us. I do hope you'll come back," he said, and then, obviously to Ava, "Hi, there. When am I going to see you on the Vineyard, girl?"

"I hope it's at the Wolfbeins', Mr. President, rather than the hospital, where I usually spend my time," Ava said.

"That's so great, being a doctor there. I could have used you when I twisted my knee." But when the president spoke, Steadman could tell his mind was racing, always elsewhere, on something else.

"I know your name," the man said, another German accent.

They talked of *Trespassing*, all the familiar remarks — the boldness of it, the danger, the originality, how it had inspired a TV show and a clothing line. Steadman mentioned his new book and hoped that, before long, *Trespassing* would be forgotten and his *Book of Revelation* would be the topic of discussion.

But something else bothered him, for the president's hand was still on his shoulder, and Steadman felt as he had back in the summer, that the president was a wounded man. A note of hurt and insincerity, of forced gaiety in his voice, a turbulence in his manner that appeared to be the opposite — such great poise that his equanimity could only be a pretense, the poise of someone with a secret, the grace and glibness of a man in pain, who wanted no one to know it, who hated most of all to be pitied, who never wanted his weakness, nor any of the many secrets humming in his heart, to be known.

All this time, the president and the German dinner guest were speaking — about writing, about cultural exchange, about the American Institute in Berlin. Steadman found himself saying, "Yes, of course, I would love to visit when my new book comes out."

"You will be welcome," the man said, and turned away to be introduced to someone else.

The president said to Steadman, "I hope you'll join us tomorrow in the Rose Garden for the joint press conference. There'll be a lot of journalists there who'd love to see you."

He gave Steadman's shoulder one last massage, the big brother grip of encouragement, and he moved away, into the throng of beaming guests who had lingered nearby, wishing to be noticed. Ava remained beside Steadman, her flank against his leg, and he knew by just this glancing touch that she was unhappy, inert, sullen.

"What's wrong?"

"I feel so humiliated. How could you do this?"

He said, "Why do you want to have a private argument in such a public place?"

"I can't help it. I feel awful. I should have stayed home. I hate being part of this charade."

"I am blind," he whispered.

"You're not. It's such a lie. And here you are soliciting all that pity. Is it that you need an audience?"

"It's not a choice. It's who I am."

Ava was silenced but not convinced, even as they stepped outside to await their ride. He had to remind himself that he was facing the world from the North Portico of the White House. Ava was glum; she brought her dismay and her shame back to their room at the Willard, where she lay bluish and disapproving at the far edge of the big bed. They lay apart, miserable, another unhappy couple, one angry, the other ashamed. And lying there, he could not help but think of the president in his bedroom, equally disturbed by his own fictions, his own secrets.

In the morning, Steadman drank datura with his breakfast, then said, "I'm going to the joint press conference."

Mortified, but claiming she had to pack, Ava said she would stay behind.

Steadman took a taxi to the White House. He showed his pass, and as he was escorted to the Rose Garden a man fell in step next to him.

"I'm from the *Post*. I'd love to do a piece about you."

"Maybe some other time."

He heard the murmur of the press corps some distance off. His escort said, "We've got a seat for you down front."

The chair was at the end of the front row. He took his seat just as the president and the German chancellor emerged from the White House.

Seeing him, the president approached and put his arm around him and said, "Great to see you here, Slade."

Steadman heard the sound of cameras, the hubbub surrounding his being singled out. He sensed this watching as a pressure on his physical being, and knew, as he had the night before, that he was being observed, the object of curiosity, with his white cane and dark glasses and Panama hat. That was his image now, no longer affectations but part of his public identity.

He was considering this — I am a new man — when a stranger knelt next to him. But perhaps not a stranger. There was something familiar in the way the man crouched, the odors of his skin and stale hair. Steadman recognized people from a particular memory of what they ate, as though the residue of their diet seeped through their skin. This man represented familiar food, and the unseasonal warmth of this November day offered an exhalation of his sour shirt.

"I know you," the man said, and his accent gave the rest away.

"Manfred."

"And I know your secret."

Steadman spoke again and then he was noticed, for he was addressing empty space. Manfred had crept away. Steadman reached out with a grasping, inquiring hand and said, "Wait."

"Did you lose something?" an urgent voice behind him said.

"No, I'm fine."

But he had to admit — and it was a revelation — that though he felt anything but impaired, he had a blind spot, and Manfred had vanished there, dissolving into that crack. Concentrating hard, Steadman was deaf to the press conference: until that moment he had forgotten the existence of Manfred.

In the taxi on the way to the airport, Ava said, "Did I miss anything?"

He said no. He did not mention Manfred — how to explain? Ava had never liked the man, and from his tone — Steadman kept replaying *And I know your secret* — Steadman could not discern the man's motive, if indeed he had a deeper one than simply teasing him.

Steadman felt low and limited. The existence of a blind spot bothered him, like a previously undiagnosed ailment. And he had expected more from his visit to the White House. It was theater, with a large cast, on a vast stage, but his role was undemanding: just show up and be polite.

Yet for him, singled out for being blind, it meant everything, a kind of dramatic debut. In his mind the president kept saying, *I want to say a special word of thanks to my good friend and a great American writer, Slade Steadman* — and as he rose, leaning on his cane, his dark glasses flashing, the loud applause that declared, as it continued with a sustained humility and praise, *We see you. We approve. You are brave.*

Yet he was discontented — not undermined but made insecure by a wisp of shadow, a doubter, as though at the periphery of all this praise he had sensed a spider descending on a long thin thread of its own gray spittle, preparing to spin a web.

3

HE HAD GONE to Washington to step out of his seclusion and to present himself to the world as a blind man. The president himself had vouched for him. Yet his keenest memory of the White House visit, the detail that he went on suffering, was not the president's praise but rather the needling accusation breathed into his ear by Manfred. *And I know your secret.* The statement grew more sinister in implication as the weeks passed. The heavily accented voice made the words clumsier, more hurtful, like a cut from someone using a crude knife, requiring the idiot force of a vicious thrust because the thing was so blunt. And those few words were all Steadman had. He wanted more. He needed to deal with the man.

He had no help at home anymore. As if out of spite, Ava opted for odd hours at the hospital. That was the trouble with doctors: at their most selfish they could claim to be unselfish. I have to do this! My patients need me! I have someone in labor! Get out of my way! Dr. Ava Katsina, anyway.

"I'm going," she'd say, and without another word would leave the house, trailing the settling dust of self-satisfied finality, as in the days before Ecuador when they had made the decision to split up. And here they were, facing another winter on the island.

"I need you as much as ever," he said.

"Who will be my pouting chatelaine?" she mocked. "Listen, there are really sick people at the hospital, who need me much more."

Her bossy doctor's voice was her most clinical and severe, always an order, like *Take your medicine. No backtalk.* Where was the compliant, agreeable sensualist of the past year who had aided him in his book? Here she was in baggy green scrubs, back at work, hoisting a sightless squalling baby that was dripping with womb slime.

With her help he could easily have corrected his book, she reading the galley proofs while he lay drugged and insightful, suggesting improvements or deletions. But he was alone and undrugged, reduced to the menial condition of sober sighted scrutinizer, certain that he was missing something as he read, mumbling, his fretful finger poking at the lines.

And yet in the task of publishing — all the minutiae of preparation, the discussions with Axelrod, weeks of it, choosing the jacket, planning the book tour — none of it distracted him from what had been hissed at him in the Rose Garden, Manfred Steiger reappearing from nowhere like an ugly-faced gnome in a folktale, accusing him of treachery, as if preparing to exact his price.

This memory nagged at Steadman. Over the year he had worked on his book, he had not thought once of Manfred, nor even remembered the man's association with the drug. He recalled the letter he had received; he was glad he had torn it up. Then, reentering the world, he had been confronted by Manfred, as though the man had been lying in wait all that time: the only other person in the world who had shared that secret experience of datura in the Ecuadorian rain forest. What did he want?

Exasperated, needing relief at the end of the day, Steadman drank a measure of the drug, blinding himself so he could stare white-eyed at Ava when she got home, scowl at her and say, "You're mad at me. You've had an awful day. You've operating on someone. Eight hours of invasive surgery! Massive trauma to the brain! Insult to the cerebral cortex!"

"You're thinking of yourself and that stuff," she said — he was still holding the cup he had emptied of the datura. "I was suturing a scalp wound."

"I can smell the blood."

"No blood on me."

"Buzzing molecules of blood."

He grumbled and accused her this way because he did not know how to tell her about Manfred. He guessed that she would say, "Your friend. Your fault."

Manfred had made no secret of being a writer. He had told Steadman he was a journalist. But so what? Steadman assumed he was based in the United States, maybe in Washington, but more likely in New York City. Steadman wanted to talk to him, find out his intentions. *And I know your secret.* Why had he put it that way? Sometimes it sounded coy, at other times a threat. Steadman was not afraid; he was insulted at being blindsided by the whisper. He imagined his phone call, or even better his confronting Manfred again, saying, as he had wanted to say in the Rose Garden, "Obviously it's not a secret!"

He had called the White House press office and announced who he was. The woman at the other end did not recognize his name. At an earlier time he would have said, "*Trespassing*? That book, that TV show, that movie? I'm the person responsible."

But he said, "I was a guest at the White House dinner a month ago."

"Do you know how many dinners we have?" was her putdown.

Who hired these people? But he knew: grovelers and climbers who dealt with rich meddling businessmen demanding personal repayment for their campaign contributions.

"The dinner for the chancellor of Germany," Steadman said. "I doubt you were invited."

He had silenced her, though he heard what sounded like steam coming out of her ears.

"I need the address of a reporter who was at the press conference."

"We can't disclose personal information."

"Just the name of his newspaper. German."

"Have you tried the Internet?"

"I'm blind. I am Steadman, the blind writer."

"I'm sorry."

"No you're not."

"I wish I could help."

"No you don't."

No wonder some blind people could be so bitter, so angry, so selfish, for they were always encountering oafs who said things like that, who sounded secretly pleased that they were able to be obstructive or worse, encumbering the blind with their smug pity.

She was a flunky — a blind man deserved better. His indignation was a pretense but his annoyance with the woman was real. He had no second thoughts about his decision to go public as a blind man. That woman was an exception, because most of the time he was amused by the attention lavished on him for his supposed disability. Yet he *was* blind. His greatest satisfaction was that he was hardly handicapped at all, that he was superior in every important way to the incompetents and gropers and busybodies who claimed they wanted to help him.

Manfred's contact number was all he needed. But as time passed even that seemed less urgent.

He began to go out alone, to Vineyard Haven to shop, to Oak Bluffs to have a drink at the Dockside bar where he had brought Ava on that first date, to restaurants in Edgartown. After so long in seclusion he loved being in public, enjoying the attention. A blind person was watched everywhere, like a fragile vase wobbling on a narrow shelf — what if it topples, what if it shatters? People hovered and held their hands out as though to break Steadman's fall. To alarm them the more he walked faster when he knew he was being observed by someone very nervous, and he took long strides, defiant ones, swiping with his cane, like a man whipping at long grass.

Women were especially solicitous: he loved their whispers, their soft sidelong glances, their fumbling concern, their warm, well-intentioned hands. Up to a point he accepted their help, just to smell them. They were redolent with longing, saturated with emotion, moist with desire, tremulous with thwarted motherhood; they touched because they needed to be touched themselves. He allowed himself to be stroked. He went no further, though he could have possessed them completely.

Ava was taken care of, preoccupied at the hospital, but she was still in his life. When she arrived home and he asked her how her day had gone, she refused to describe it except in futile terms, as a series of pious ordeals: "We lost someone today," or "A woman was medevaced to Boston." There were fewer patients than in the summer, but the ailments were more serious. She made a point of ignoring the Christmas holiday, and worked on Christmas Day and New Year's Eve, too, with her doctor's martyred cry, "They need me."

Everyone on the island said she was an angel, but Steadman knew that by taking on such responsibility at the hospital she had a free pass everywhere else — didn't have to shop, or cook, or clean, or give presents, or socialize, and so Steadman felt abandoned. He couldn't complain about being ditched by a doctor. No one would listen, for whose work was more important? From their commanding position on the moral high ground, doctors always had the last word.

Odd to think that she had been his reckless and sensual lover. But Steadman guessed that she looked back on their time together doing the book as frivolous. He wanted her to say this, so that he could reply, *You are mistaken. It was revelation. What revelation is there in illness? The pathetic truth that people are frail and they sicken and die. Only the vitality of sex reveals the human essence.*

But she was angry. He played the conversation in his head. He went for walks. He pondered what he had written of sexuality and risk, and one day the news came out — horribly, awkwardly, first as a rumor, then as a disputed denial — that the president had had a flirtation, perhaps an affair, with one of the young female interns at the White House.

The speculation was preposterous. The simplest version sounded bad enough. Steadman remembered how he had guessed at the poor man's confusion months before.

I want to say one thing to the American people. I want you to listen to me. I'm going to say this again. I did not have sexual relations with that woman, Miss Lewinsky. I never told anybody to lie, not a single time. Never. These allegations are false. I never had sex with that woman.

The president spoke, beating the air with his finger. Seeing the pink and sleepless face, the humiliated and guilty mask of an adulterer, Steadman said, "Poor guy."

But Ava was contemptuous. "How could he be such a fool?"

"He was smitten," Steadman said.

Ava's expression said, I don't get it.

The revelation of the president's waywardness overwhelmed everything else. It was all the talk on the Vineyard, and on the news-hungry earth. That the president of the United States had gotten blowjobs in the Oval Office from a chubby Jewish girl in her early twenties was world news.

Steadman watched closely as the messy story unfolded. He guessed that if Manfred was a foreign correspondent, he must be covering it for his newspaper. Steadman was provoked to do something he had avoided up to now. He typed "Manfred Steiger" into his computer and got seventeen hits: stories in the *Frankfurter Allgemeine Zeitung*, all with a Washington dateline. But he did not attempt to get in touch with Manfred.

People who disliked the president before now hated him and were gleeful. His supporters faced the dilemma of explaining his behavior, or even justifying it. Most people's marital embarrassments were minor compared to the president's from late January onward.

What was he thinking? It was the only topic of conversation these days, the president's face fixed in an expression of defiance and shame, looking like a fool.

Steadman was certain that his *Book of Revelation* would have greater resonance in a world bewildered by the fact that the most powerful man in the world had risked his whole reputation, his job, his marriage, the respect of his friends, in order to meet a pushy, privileged, fattish, and unappealing young woman and encourage her to fellate him while he sat glassy-eyed with lust in his White House office.

It wasn't strange at all, really, though you could hardly blame the president for denying it. It was at the heart of Steadman's book, for safe inside the White House, having his cock sucked, the president was briefly a happy boy.

With all the lies and evasions and half-truths he had told, the president was miserable, and yet he clung to power. He repeated that he would not give up, would not resign, would go on no matter how loud the mockery and the declarations of hatred. The hatred was not new, but the pity was something terrible. Steadman could tell that the president was chastened and weakened by the pity and that he found it hard to bear.

Seeing the man so embattled, Steadman took his side, but he knew in advance that the president's disgrace offered other ways for Ava and him to pick on each other.

"He stepped on his dick, I grant you. He's behaved like a fool. But what has he done wrong?"

"I'd be out on my ear if I did that," Ava said. "If I were caught fucking an orderly in my office I would be fired, no questions asked."

"No one is hurt by it. And he'll have to endure the worst possible punishment — the whole world laughing at him and feeling superior. That's a nightmare."

"My father was in the Navy," Ava said. But she spoke in a tone of resignation, not outrage. "If he had done that he would have been shitcanned or demoted and posted to Diego Garcia. The president is the commander in chief of the armed forces."

"So what? That's honorary."

"He's pretending to be innocent, like you're pretending to be blind."

"I am blind."

"What is it, an addiction? You can't deal with stress? You can't face the world? So you retreat. But instead of pot or speed, your drug is the Ecuadorian blindfold. The ultimate escape."

"It's the opposite," he said. The datura was insight, an asset, not evasion at all, not an escape from the world but immersion in it, the deepest possible confrontation with reality. "And if that's not so, then how is it, after so much failure, did I succeed in writing my book?"

"That's simple. I helped you."

He couldn't dispute this. He had repeatedly told her that he would have been lost without her.

"And now you have it both ways. People pity you and yet you're stronger than they are."

He had no answer. He knew it to be true.

"It's over between us," she said. "I'm busy at the hospital. I should get a place of my own again." As though thinking aloud, she went on softly, "All you've done is disrupt my life."

"Don't go," he said. With an effort of will, swallowing hard, he said, "Please."

"You don't deserve me."

She was so strong now, with a fierceness in her fatigue and bright feverish eyes that came from working long hours at the hospital. And she was so formidable scrubbed of all her makeup, pale and intimidating.

"What do you want?"

He said in a small imploring voice, "I want you to accept that I am dependent on this drug for now." He looked at his hands with mild surprise, as if he had just realized they belonged to someone else. "The basket is broken to bits. Someday soon I will run out of the juice. I won't have the option of being blind. In the meantime . . ."

"In the meantime I am not going to help you."

"Okay," he said, lifting his empty hands and holding them as though to propitiate her. He wanted to say more but did not have the words to describe the fulfilled dream it had been for him: their living there, just the two of them; inhabiting the house, his fantasies, his book.

"I'm not going on your book tour," she said.

"I can live with that." And saying so, he decided that it was better if she didn't come along in that mood, dragging her grudge with her, a nagging presence, casting a gloomy shadow, as she had on the trip to Washington.

As though still negotiating, he said, "I'm almost out of the drug. Maybe a month or six weeks more."

"Go ahead, then," she said, "make an idiot of yourself, like him."

The president was on TV, always shown before a crowd of delighted people. As he strode past a rope line, he leaned forward and hugged a grinning girl in a black beret — the fool embracing his fellatrix.

Ava shook her head, and he could tell from her upright posture, her hand, the twitch of her hair — not making eye contact, reflective, not looking for an answer or expecting to be contradicted — that she was in her clinical mode, delivering a medical opinion.

"God only knows what that stuff is doing to your nerves. But I can guess. Stressing the neurons. Toasting the ganglia. Burning out the synapses."

With a slow, dull smile he said, "It's easier for me to talk to you after I've taken a dose." He looked her full in the face; his eyes were glaucous and fish-like. "Because I can see what is really in your heart."

She seemed puzzled, not by that assertion, he knew, but by her realization that she had been home for more than an hour and had only just noticed that he was drugged, saturated, blinded. She had been able to be passive and playful as his sex partner, but in her doctor's scrubs she hated surprises and especially hated being told things she didn't know.

She quickly recovered and said sharply, "So you insist on wearing a mask."

"So what?"

"That makes you two different people. Yourself and your mask."

"That's my problem. Or maybe my special gift."

"Your problem," she said. "The fear that you will be unmasked. The fear of all mask wearers."

4

THE WIDER WORLD that Steadman entered as a solitary blind man was deranged, inside out, constantly expanding with obvious conspirators, subtle freaks, and the mouth-breathing ectoplasm of strangers. Using her lunch break, Ava helped him at the check-in counter at the Vineyard airport. He clawed the air, as though trying to seize it and understand.

"Just one person traveling?"

The nibbling mouse-faced clerk, with chewed and bitten fingers, shiny boots, a sweaty bag at his feet, was the first of many people who seemed to Steadman grotesque approximations — worse, weirder than when he had been with Ava in D.C., perhaps the more phantasmal because he was alone.

Sensing his unease, Ava said, "You'll be fine."

"I'm being met by an escort in each city."

"Great," Ava said, without any interest, her frowning face like bruised fruit. "Gotta go. I'm operating at two. Appendectomy."

She was gone the next moment, the woman whose beauty he had adored, who had inspired his wildest sexual fantasies, scuttling away in scrubs and tennis shoes, a medic on the move — so long, Doc.

Steadman boarded the Boston flight and at once felt tossed into the funnel of his tour, toppling toward the black light, past the peripheral voices, just chatter. Most of what he heard was pointless — "They have their big meal at lunchtime" — but now and then the public emotion concentrated in the departure lounge was inexpressibly sad: "I watched him die," and "Please don't do this to me," and "I don't care if I ever see him again," and "Ricky, did you remember to take your medication?"

He traveled as though in a foreign land where he was fluent in the language, a high-tech world of absurdities, inhabited largely by scowly sniffing furry-faced humanoids and now and then a bewitching woman trailing her odor of desire. Some people emitted a faint glow, others a ranker smell or a telling whisper. Nothing was as he had once known it. He was trespassing again. At Logan Airport he called Axelrod.

"Good news," his editor reported. "We've almost sold out the first printing. We're going back to press. Everyone wants to interview you. How's it going?"

He couldn't say. The dream-like distortions thronging the departure gates were not hindrances, more like revelations. A huge-headed fish-faced boy whining for candy, his teeth much too big for his mouth. Tramping bulky men burdened with satchels stuffed with fakery. Yammering old women, like a chorus of withered simpering baboons. The man next to him farting in fear and impatience. Scaly hands on him and unhelpful halitotic breath. All the world he saw anew; he was charged with his drug.

"I love you." That was a desperate clumsy man with sweat in his fists.

"I love you, too." Innocent, afraid, trapped, gabbling, speaking just to fill the dead air, and plainly insincere.

He found it so easy to tell when people were lying. He was the center of attention with his dark glasses, his cane, his hat, his handsome shoulder bag. He winced at the people gaping at him.

"Look, Steve, the guy's blind. Go ahead, help him."

"Get away from me." He swept them aside with a swipe of his cane and kept them off, taking long strides as people scattered, making way for him.

Down a chilly ramp, an effeminate man at his side said, "Just a little bit farther, soldier, and let's watch our step," the man's stinking fragrance like festering lilies and his hands pawing at Steadman's sleeve.

On the long flight to Seattle he was pampered by a monstrous male nanny who said, "Want me to feed you?" Steadman swore at him and sat and suffered the stagnant air. He then put on his earphones and listened to a Philip Glass tape, which lulled him to sleep. He could sense the other passengers' anxiety when he woke and groped forward to the toilet. The trip was an experience of jet howl, a racket of interruption and the passengers' squalid fear.

"Are you being met here?"

He hated the babysitter's tone. Already he was disgusted with bystanders' insincere solicitude. It all made him defiant, assertive in his singularity.

A hand on his arm as he reached the bottom of the escalator.

"Hi. I'm Pam Fowler, your escort."

She was a slow skinny woman who had forgotten where she'd parked her car. They roamed the lot for ten minutes until she found it.

"Just saw your *Post-Intelligencer* review," she said as she buckled herself in. "It wasn't very favorable. I had to look up the word 'meretricious.' Did I say that right?"

She drove badly, muttering the whole time in a nasal way, blaming herself for her ineptness.

"But it's flying out of the stores. Elliott Bay reordered. They're expecting you tonight."

He was due to read at the Elliott Bay store, though "read" was not the word. He would talk instead, something about blindness.

"Have you seen your schedule?"

"What is your name?"

"Pam."

"I am blind, Pam. I have not seen the schedule."

It was a low blow, but he was still smarting from "It wasn't very favorable."

"I'm really sorry. I know that," she said. "It's just that you don't seem blind."

Turning to look at him, she took her eyes off the road. He could feel the car edging into the rumble strip, the washboard battering of the tires, the car's echo from the nearby guardrail.

"Watch out!"

She braked, she apologized, she was now more nervous and her driving deteriorated. As if to placate him, she attempted small talk.

"Rainier's out. Too bad you can't see it."

"But I can," he said.

The hotel was large, with rank carpets and dust in the air. He was shown to his room by an awkward grunting bellman, and then he lay on his bed and dozed in the buzzing room until he was summoned to the event at Elliott Bay.

Stepping inside the bookstore, he knew from the stifling interior — the air sucked thin — that the place was packed. The day was damp. Only overdressed people on rainy days smelled worse than used books. People stepped away from him as always, seeing his glasses and cane, giving him room, as though he were fragile, as though fearing to touch him and topple him. One frightened pair of hands fumbled with his arm, trying to guide him.

"Just point me in the right direction."

Already he hated being touched by strangers.

"I'm not going to read to you," he said, taking his place at the raised table. "Instead, I'll say a little about my condition. How unexpectedly I became blind. How what I thought would be a nightmare turned out to have its advantages. My book is not about blindness, but blindness helped me to imagine it and to write it."

He searched the faces of the watching audience, and because he did not hesitate or look down at any notes, he seemed to alarm them when, with a kind of fierceness, he said, "'I have a way of always keeping my eyes shut, in order the more to concentrate the snugness of being in bed. Because no man can ever feel his own identity aright except his eyes be closed; as if, darkness were indeed the proper element of our essences.' That is Ishmael, in *Moby Dick*."

His speaking with his blind and staring head erect created an even greater silence and apprehension. He recited Sassoon:

> *Does it matter? — losing your sight? . . .*
> *There's such splendid work for the blind;*
> *And people will always be kind,*
> *As you sit on the terrace remembering*
> *And turning your face to the light.*

The audience's concentration was intense and seemed almost to crackle with attention. That calmed him and helped him pause and remember what he had planned. Rather than draw conclusions from the Melville, he plunged on. He disparaged *King Lear* for what he said was its crude depiction of blindness. "'Looking on darkness which the blind do see' is also wrong. Shakespeare is mistaken." With the exception of the prophet Ahijah, the blind seer, the Bible is even more misleading on the subject of blindness — just a litany of ignorant threats and half-truths and false metaphors and the usual stumblers, Isaac, Samson, Eli, Zedekiah, Tobit, and the frantic and guilt-ridden taxman Saul. There was scriptural authority, he said, for making the case that God is blind.

"Darkness is the one thing I do not see," he said. "Borges is right. The blind do not see black. The world is not dark to me. At its most indistinct it has a green glow, like the phosphorescence that is common in the densest rain forest. You see it on the narrow forking path, in the decay under the high canopy, exactly like an area in the Oriente province of Ecuador, where in fact I lost one form of sight and gained another."

He quoted Milton and another poem by Sassoon. He had made mental notes. He was aware that he would be giving the same talk in all the cities on his tour, improving it, using the parts that worked, dropping the quotations that made the audiences restless.

Tonight, finishing with some lines from Borges's essay "On Blindness," his thanking the audience was drowned out by loud hospitable applause that seemed to say: You are brave, you are brilliant, you are heroic.

He sat and made the semblance of a signature in the books opened to the title page. His picture was taken, he was stroked, people whispered their thanks to him; everyone said something.

"Should I read your book? I'm not too sure I'll like it."

"My father loved your first book. He was such a bastard. He hit on my best friend and then he left my mom and the last we heard he was somewhere in Alaska."

And one woman said in an urgent whisper, "I could take you home."

But he was driven to the hotel by Pam Fowler, and he lay in his room thinking, I like this.

The next morning she drove him to the airport for the flight to Portland. He was coddled again on the plane, but this time he did not protest. This was better than being at home. He did not feel nagged; he was well looked after, like a fragile adored child. When he got off the plane he called Ava. "I'm fine." She seemed surprised that he was calling. She did not want to know more. She said she was busy at the hospital.

In Portland the woman escort, Julie, took him directly to a radio station. The interviewer announced himself as blind. For the first time on this trip Steadman was conscious of a pitiless scrutiny, not curiosity or fear but a piercing intelligence, like a beam of light turned on him.

"My wife read your book to me," the blind interviewer said as he expertly worked the controls of the recorder. "I want to tell you that you write as only a blind man can — that's a compliment. Reality for us is hallucinatory. Sighted people don't know that. It's a different grammar, a different vocabulary, a different world. It's inside the world that sighted people see, but it's hidden from them."

After that, the interview went well. The blind man asked about the book — he was to be the only interviewer to address the book. Everyone else asked Steadman about his blindness. They sat face to face, blank stare to blank stare, talking amiably. And when the interview was over Steadman felt he had passed a crucial test.

In the evening he gave his pep talk about blindness at Powell's Books, another large turnout, the close attention of eager and sympathetic readers, the sour smell of unsold books on shelves, the pleasant aroma of his own new book, like the tang of warm muffins, the new paper, the freshly cut pages, the clean slippery dust jacket, and now and then an old musty copy of *Trespassing* thrust before him for his signature.

"Hey, did you know you got kind of a crappy review in *Time* magazine?"

"Thanks for signing my book, but the only thing is, I can't read your handwriting."

He had learned a new way of signing his name, with a flourish, deliberately making it elegant, defying the people who stared at him hungrily as though he were defenseless and edible.

Again he was asked by a woman, "Can I see you to your hotel?" She had been standing behind his table, sighing. This time he accepted. He dismissed his escort, Julie, but when he got into the strange woman's car he realized that she was heavy: she rocked the car as she slid onto her seat. How had he missed that before? Perhaps she had been standing behind him the whole time. She had a sweet small-girl voice. The car was littered with candy wrappers and cat hairs.

"*Trespassing* changed my life," she said in the bar of the Heathman Hotel. She had insisted on buying him a drink.

Now he could see everything, not just her bulk and her lank hair but the suture seams in her skull.

"I could show you to your room. I'm not making suggestions. I'm just saying I don't have to be anywhere in particular."

But she *was* making suggestions. She was sad-faced and forlorn. Her dewlaps shook as she sucked on a straw, nursing her daiquiri. What she did not know was that other people in the bar were staring, some in chairs and looking like figures in an altarpiece depicting fallen souls and damnation.

"I feel I owe you something. I believe in giving back."

Steadman saw again that for some women blindness was not simple allure but acted as a powerful aphrodisiac. He became sad, telling her gently that he had an early flight, and he refused her assistance to the elevator, leaving her to pay the bill. Upstairs, he fiddled with his radio, deciding not to call Ava.

He flew on, feeling lighter, to San Francisco, and was met again and driven up the freeway to the city in the clear air that was spanked with waterborne sunlight from the bay. After he checked into his hotel the escort, an elderly man, said, "There's time for drop-ins. Couple of chains near here."

He said, "Okay," and at the first bookstore, "I can handle this alone."

In the short distance from the car to the entrance of the store he startled a flock of crumb-pecking pigeons and they flew up, a fluttering of winged rats, shitting and spattering onlookers as they ascended into the chafing wind.

He moved with hesitation to the information desk, pursuing the brisk tap of computer keys.

"I'm here to sign my book."

"And you are?"

"Slade Steadman."

"Is anyone expecting you?"

"I don't know." He tapped his cane, as though to indicate time passing.

"The manager's on break."

Now with all his senses wide open he was able to discern the features of the speaker, a young man wearing a filthy knitted cap, with pale hands, arrogant as only a very dim person could be, too obtuse to understand his own arrogance, quietly sniveling, at the vortex of a hundred thousand books.

"What was the name of the book again?"

"The Book of Revelation."

A woman waiting at the desk near Steadman piped up. "You ain't going to find that here."

She was black and big, in a soft loose dress, with hair knotted like rug nap, her heavy-fleshed arms the color of undercooked ham and nipples like figs on her slack breasts.

"That there would be in devotional," she said.

"I wish I could be more helpful," the young man said.

Steadman yelped, something like a cry of pain, attracting attention, and then slashed with his stick and cleared his way to the street.

That gave him a story to tell interviewers. There were two that day, and each time he boasted of his blindness. The journalists were kind, yet he knew that they would mention the crumbs on his shirt front, his wild hair, and if his socks didn't match they would say so.

That night, in Corte Madera, half an hour north of San Francisco, he talked about his blindness at Book Passage. He elaborated on Borges and Melville and quoted from Shakespeare. He felt so intensely observed he thought that few people actually listened to him. A woman in the front row seemed to smile in fear, her teeth bared, holding her fist to her mouth in anxiety and seeming to bite it like a large dripping fruit. Most of the people were fretful, embarrassed, as though watching an amateur acrobat without a net inching his way across a high wire.

They gathered afterward for his signature, murmuring at him: women with backpacks, men with handbags, their pockets crammed with paper, one boy like an Inca slinger, his cap with drooping earflaps.

"My cousin is blind and he, like, learned to play bass guitar and is really good at it now."

"You should sign yourself up for one of them dogs. One of them Labs."

"I can't afford your book, but would you mind signing this picture of you I cut out of the paper?"

And as he left a flamboyant blonde offered him a lift and laughed beautifully when he declined.

Back in San Francisco, the streets were thronged with sprawling beggars demanding money. Steadman stared brazenly at them, poking with his stick and marveling how, at his refusal, one man farted an explosion of black swallows and green gas.

The next morning, on the way to the airport, the elderly male escort said, "I've been kind of wondering. You fully insured?"

Steadman flew to Denver and was met by a young woman who demanded to carry his bag. She drove efficiently, chatted to him without mentioning his blindness, then said, "Can't you tell I'm a hottie?" Another talk, more interviews, good news of his book sales, a glimpse of a young couple kissing in the parking structure of the Tattered Cover bookstore, where a worshipful crowd applauded him and bought copies of his book for him to sign.

"Can you say something like, 'To an amazing woman, from someone who knows'?"

"When does this come out in paperback?"

That night, a room-service dinner in his hotel room, and then an early-morning flight to Chicago.

The escort waiting at O'Hare was a powerful man named Bill, who held his bag with one hand and steered Steadman through the airport with the other. In the car he said, "You had a message," and dialed the publicist and passed the phone to Steadman.

"I've added another interview in New York," she said. "A German paper, but the interview will appear in English on the Internet. He says he knows you. Manfred something. Big fan."

All through the Chicago appointments Steadman was aware of being watched by a yellow-eyed owl perched in a round window, like a porthole cut into the sky. *Manfred something. Big fan.*

"You knew Bruce Chatwin, right? He's a fantastic writer, probably my all-time favorite."

"The guy that played you in the TV series doesn't look like you at all. Plus, he's got that phony accent."

"I don't know Braille," he said in the hotel elevator. "Will someone press seventeen for me?"

The elevator mirror reflected different faces from the one staring in.

No one had mentioned his book. Three newspaper interviews, one taped for radio, a photo shoot on Michigan Avenue — all centered on his blindness. He slept badly, thinking of Manfred. In the morning Bill sped him to O'Hare, saying only "This is the right direction at this hour of the morning. I'll have to get into that mess going back to the city."

At the departure gate Steadman was seated next to a porcine nun in a black habit like a witch's gown, and she was tugging at her ragged earlobes as she prayed.

Fingers touched his hand, not the nun's but those of a harassed tearful man, who spoke in a fretful voice, "You can preboard."

Steadman was crowded by the waiting passengers. "Back!" he said, and raking with his cane, pushed past men with roll-on bags and youths with greasy knapsacks and bipolar children on Prozac and a man with garbage on his breath.

The same yellow-eyed owl peered down at him from a porthole over Manhattan.

By this time he had become accustomed to the telling silence and the sign language — rapid overt gestures of people who did not realize he was aware of what they were doing. He was used to the grunts, the nudges, the puzzlement, the boisterous greetings, the condescending heartiness that was one of the worst expressions of pity. Pity was on most people's minds when they saw him. But he suffered it, because he did not want to reveal himself through his anger. And the pity was that of semiliterates and oafs.

Equally stupid, well-meaning people, like the taxi driver who took him to his first interview, tried to offer him hope.

"Maybe get one of them eye transplants."

"I like myself as I am."

"But what if you could find an organ donor?"

"Hit that jogger and we'll have one."

"You saw that woman?"

"No. You saw her and swerved."

Yet New York City seemed perfect for a blind person: the logic of the streets, the indifferent passersby, the unexpected politeness of people. At the bookstore signings there were the usual questions.

"Do you plan to see Ved Mehta while you're here in the city? I would have thought he'd be really supportive."

"Did you know visually challenged people are allowed to touch some of the sculptures at MOMA? Go for it!"

New Yorkers announced themselves beforehand, as though shouting ahead from a great distance. In New York, Steadman knew what people wanted long before they asked, knew what questions they were preparing to pose, knew when they were staring at him, when they turned away and pretended to be interested. New York was used to strangeness, for only true oddity was news, and so for his four days in the city he had a starring role, as the well-known and perceptive traveler who was now the blind novelist.

On his second morning, he was taken to the *Today* show.

"Mr. Steadman, you're kind of a legend in the book world, and the TV world, too, with the inspiration for that long-running TV series," the wheedling woman interviewer said. "There's so much to talk about. I want to ask you about your latest book this morning."

This morneen was the way she said it. She was puppet-faced and tiny and held a clipboard, tossing her scraped-aside hair as she spoke. She leaned forward and her voice became a quack.

"But first, what a tragedy it must be to have lost your cherished gift of sight."

Steadman welcomed the vulgarity of her gloating manner. Because she was not asking a question but rather making a mawkish pronouncement, he could respond with a dignified rejoinder, putting her in her place. It was always a mistake to answer a question. No one remembered questions anyway; much better to say what was on your mind.

"Losing my sight was a blessing," he said. "I would never have known how much I was missing. I may see less but I understand more."

"Yet isn't it incredibly painful to know what you've lost?"

Her persistence annoyed him, and he could barely control himself in his reply. "I have tried to make my blindness an asset. I believe my book is the better for it."

"Talk to me a little bit about the downside," she said.

"What you are doing to me now is the downside," he said, his voice sharpening. "You are asking the question that way because you think that you're superior, that you are whole and I am somehow incomplete." He smiled at her and knew from the light on his face that the camera captured his angry smile. "I assure you that this is not the case. You are mistaken and misled, and I, Tiresias, old man with wrinkled dugs, perceived the scene and foretold the rest."

At the mention of "wrinkled dugs" the woman became flustered and broke off the interview as soon as he finished his sentence. She thanked him for showing up and apologized for not getting to his book. Steadman had the impression that he had terrified her and she was relieved to see him go, eager to move on to the next item, which was an update on the president's disgrace.

Back at the hotel, there was a message from Ava. He called her on her cell phone. She said she had just seen him on the show.

"You were good. You looked so confident. You don't need me."

With a few hours free he experimented with the city. He strolled down the sidewalk, going south from his hotel on Madison Avenue. It was not easy. Pedestrians bore down on him, moving fast, tramping hard, sometimes pushing him aside, mumbling to themselves, some of them singing off-key, under their breath, with a kind of panic. But at least they didn't stare.

Taping a segment of *Charlie Rose,* he became aware that he could say anything that came into his head, because Rose, though portentous, was unprepared.

"Slade Steadman," the man began in his ponderous way, lowering his head, "you have written the best-known travel book of our time. For many years you were a virtual recluse, rarely venturing out of your house..."

This descriptive prologue continued, and when Rose showed no sign of finishing, Steadman interrupted him, confusing him, and described his book, explaining why he had chosen the confessional mode for his novel of a man's sexuality.

The face he saw later that night in his hotel room, that filled his television screen, a great animated head, the wild hair, the dark glasses, the confident sneer and frowning delivery, had him peering closely. He was glad he was alone, glad that the drug had worn off so he could watch himself. He paid hardly any attention to what he was saying, but he could not take his eyes off his face, which was distorted and heavy, masked by the glasses. He imagined a stranger seeing the face of this blind man and being cowed by fear and awe.

In contrast with Steadman's rumpled jacket and black turtleneck sweater, Charlie Rose was nattily dressed in pinstripes. He looked presentable but rather pained, even overwhelmed by the fierce presence of Slade Steadman.

He spoke at the Barnes & Noble in Union Square, and afterward, a woman looking for a signature said, "What do you miss most?" Before he could reply, she was gone. He appeared on a panel at the 92nd Street Y. He was interviewed at the National Public Radio station downtown, in a studio hookup with Terry Gross on *Fresh Air.* He was photographed on a bench in a part of Central Park that was near his hotel.

All the odors, all the transparent talk. He could tell the instant he was introduced what these people thought of him, of his book, of his blindness. He always knew what they wanted. He had a powerful sense, the whole time, of being watched from a distance, followed, hovered over, almost breathed upon, as though shadowed by a stalker.

"I'm glad you can't see me," the photographer, a young woman, said. "I am such a mess."

So rattled by his presence they wanted to say something, yet not knowing what to say, people often said the wrong thing. But still so new to it, and rattled by his anonymous watcher, Steadman was unforgiving.

"I can see you. You're not a mess. But you're angry, you're agitated. I think you're in serious debt."

She became still, staring at him, saying nothing. Finally she said, "Shall we get this over with?"

Perhaps as a response to his mixed reviews, interviewers went out of their way to compliment his book. But one man, setting up his tape recorder at the outset of an interview, laughed awkwardly and said, "I wish I could tell you I liked your book."

"I wish I could tell you I'm agreeing to this interview," Steadman said, and rose from the settee in the hotel lobby where they had just ordered coffee. He left, brandishing his cane like a rapier.

He was blind, he was blameless, he could say anything, he could write anything. He was forgiven his shocking book because he was so obviously maimed. One review said it: "The outrage and candor of his book is appropriate to the author's condition."

The reviews that were read to him did not surprise him. He knew his book was graphic — so personal, so revealing, so near the bone, it did not seem like a novel at all. But he said, "You know, everything is fiction," and because he was blind, he was not contradicted. Blindness was his license: blindness made him right.

"Never mind the reviews," Axelrod said, which meant the reviews that hadn't been read to him were perhaps worse than he guessed. "The sales are great. Your tour has been a huge success."

Still, he was distracted, waiting for the inevitable.

5

THE CONFIDENT VOICE on the phone said, with odd singsong stresses, "I think we have an appointment at this hour, yah?"

"No" was in his mind. Listening hard, Steadman heard the words as *sink* and *heff* and *zis*.

"I have it so in my agenda," the voice went on.

"Where are you?"

"In the lobby area. Just here."

Chust here. Steadman felt besieged and frail and weary.

"I come upstairs, yah?" The foreign cadences of the voice made it seem even more gauche and importuning.

"No, no," Steadman said, regretting that he might be revealing his weakness in overreacting. "Go away," he wanted to say. But he said, "Be right down."

Throughout the tour, whenever his concentration flagged or he lay sleepless in a hotel room, he had remembered Manfred — how the man had recognized him in Washington and said "I know your secret," how he had obviously pursued him. The prospect of meeting Manfred nettled him because he suspected it would be a confrontation; but it did not greatly disturb him. Manfred was like a distant relation in need of a favor. Manfred smelled a salable story. Steadman knew that smell; he also knew how to deal with it, not by fleeing but by facing him, staring him down with his blind eyes.

Beyond all this nuisance was the melancholy fact that Manfred was real, flesh and blood, a tedious tricky man emerging from a shared episode in an actual past. That seemed incredible. In Steadman's mind the trip to Ecuador had been like a fictional journey to a place of enchantment, full of dangers and unexpected discoveries, all the sorts of risks that an adventurer would have to overcome in order to find a magic formula. This potion, these twigs of rare datura, would deliver him from his feeling of futility and turn him into an engine of creation, would make him virile again, give him the book he longed to write, would inspire him and make his brain blaze like the prophet Ahijah's.

Steadman savored the Ecuador experience as a remembered dream. He likened it to a mythical spell in the wilderness. Over the past year he had embellished it, deleting the oil drilling and the degenerate town of Lago Agrio and the grease-soaked roads and noisy boats on the muddy river. He had replaced these memories with the looming presence of the shamans and the *vegetalistas* and the *ayahuasqueros*. The trip had the color and light of a classic quest, the teasing revelation of unexpected magic, the strange and appropriate justice of transformation. Although he pleased himself with the inventions, the highlights, and the deletions, the transformation was something he had earned and deserved. He had come back a different man.

Those other travelers, those gringos? He had deleted them, too. Who would want to remember those voices, the complaints, the facetiousness? One squawk he had not forgotten. The bitch with the book, who had waved it at him and said, "It's by this legendary has-been."

And he had deleted Manfred as well. He did not want to remember that the drug was Manfred's idea, Manfred's tempting suggestion; that he had paid Manfred for it. He wanted to go on believing that he had ventured on that solitary journey as a dream hunter, questing with Ava, with whom he had fallen in love all over again. He hated to recall that it was a drug tour, that a grubby German had patronized him, that he was being revisited; that there were consequences.

Manfred was waiting for him in the hotel bar, the place sour-smelling and somnolent in the midafternoon heat, stuffy, dusty, mostly empty, with dense stale air that stank as though it had been chewed and spat out.

"So?" Manfred was standing, but obliquely, and Steadman sensed someone else beside him.

"Who's with you?" Steadman said, walking past Manfred and the companion, someone he detected as a warm bulky presence.

"My photographer, Arnulf."

"Tell him to go. No pictures."

No words were exchanged. Manfred shrugged, the photographer pleaded a little, gesturing, screwing up his face, then shook his head and planted his feet more firmly.

Hearing the lisp and suck of a shutter, Steadman slashed at the camera and made contact. "Ach!" A yelp. Then, from the way the cane recoiled he knew he had made a direct hit and had also carved a stripe in the photographer's wrist. The man stepped away and stowed his camera in a bag and zipped it, while Steadman stood over him.

"You almost break my camera," the man muttered in a sullen way.

"I'll break your fucking head," Steadman said. "Get out of here and stop trying to take advantage of a blind man."

Only when the photographer had gone did Steadman slide into a booth. Manfred sat across from him. He was wearing a thick noisy coat — leather, with flapping lapels, too heavy for this warm bar. Steadman could sense the dampness of the man's skin, his sweaty face and glistening hair, his open mouth, breathing hard as he affected to be jolly.

"Never mind Arnulf. He is a fanatic for the pictures."

But slashing at the man had eased Steadman's anxiety and reassured him that he was never more alert than when he was on the drug: no one could deceive him when he was blind.

"It was so fantastic to see you in Washington," Manfred said. "I tell my friends, 'I know this man!' In Ecuador, I think, 'I will never see this man again.' But here you are, crazy man. Fantastic."

"Manfred, what do you want?"

"Cup of coffee. Little talk."

"Skip the coffee."

The leather sleeves of Manfred's jacket rubbed the table, the leather elbows skidded: the coat was still an animal to Steadman, its skin peeled from living flesh.

"You sound not so friendly."

"I didn't like what you said in Washington."

With a laugh-snort that wasn't mirth, Manfred said, "I forget what I said to you."

"You said, 'I know your secret.'"

"Everyone has secrets. Even Mr. President." He began to laugh again, but as though becoming conscious of Steadman's silence, he added, "Good memory you have."

"I don't forget insults."

"Yah! And me — I don't forget."

Steadman had reached across the table, his knuckles forward, and brushed what he suspected was a tape recorder.

"Nice machine."

Manfred covered the small tape recorder with his hands, as if to conceal it. But still Steadman heard it working, the obscure tick of its timer that was hardly audible, more like a change in temperature, like a pointed flashing light, a flickering flame of altering numerals that repeated as a low pulse.

"Digital. Swiss. *Teuer.*"

"That's a brand?"

"No. *Teuer* — costive."

Steadman seized the thing with his reaching hand, then quickly turned aside and dropped it to the floor. He crushed it with his shoe, feeling it go silent and die in pieces under his heel.

"No." Manfred wailed, stooping.

"That's for not asking permission."

"You make me in a bad situation."

Hearing the noise, a waiter had approached. He said, "Everything okay over here? Can I get you anything to drink?"

Coffee for Manfred, a glass of water for Steadman, and when the waiter had gone Manfred leaned across the table, put his face close to Steadman's, and said in a punished voice, "I have no other recorder."

"That's what I was counting on."

Manfred was still snorting. "You insult me in Ecuador. You say how my father is a Nazi. You call me a thief. And those people . . ."

Steadman was smiling at *fazzer* and *Nay-zee* and *seef*, and said, "I described what I knew to be true."

". . . and those people," Manfred repeated, "they tell Nestor to telephone the police. They make big trouble for me. The police they write a report. They threaten me. They insist for a heavy bribe, which I must pay."

"I think you made out fine."

"You tried to hurt me with the lies, despite I help you."

All that seemed so long ago, in the dream forest, in the rising tide of color and light, like fresh blood eddying in his head, the splash of it sounding in his ears, the detailed loop and retrieval of memory. It was his first experience of the drug's logic, the way his blindness had sorted and returned so much to him, the ordered images that helped him fit irregular fragments and overheard phrases and stray glimpses into whole smooth narratives, so seamless as to be absolute truths. The facts were so clear he had wanted to speak them aloud for their simplicity. Uttered, they sounded like accusations. He had marveled at the effects of the drug, its limpid truths, the purest consolations of blindness. Everything made sense with the datura; he was hopeful for more.

"My boss in America, he found out from the gringos. Those people on the trip were important business guys! I lose my job. No salary for almost a year. I write a little on my drug book. Now I am just doing a few stories for the Frankfurt paper. Did you lose your job?"

The mention of the job made Steadman smile: Manfred's outrage seemed almost comical. The news that he had been fired had no effect on Steadman, who regarded jobs as burdens that were eventually lost as you moved on, the better for having been rejected. In Steadman's experience the boss was always the worker's inferior.

Into Steadman's silence Manfred said, "Fuck you."

The two men were quietly brooding when the waiter returned with his tray, the clatter of coffee cup and saucer, the clink of tumbler and water jug. Steadman was aware of the waiter's abruptness, his resenting them for their paltry order that was like an intrusion. He fussed, yammering to himself, and then left.

"I hardly knew what I was saying," Steadman said, recalling the scene in the hotel room in Quito. "I was just repeating what was in my head."

Manfred was examining the smashed tape recorder, pushing buttons that didn't work, weighing it like a stone, frowning at its useless weight.

"Now you make the more trouble for me."

"It was the truth."

The way Manfred breathed through the gaps in his teeth showed Steadman how the man had seized on the word, as though holding it and shaking it in his jaws.

"The truth, yah," he said, his saliva sounding like juice in his mouth. "I think the same thing when I see you at the White House."

In his disgusted impatience he lapsed into Teutonic consonants and became confused, saying *sink* and *thame sing*, sounding furious and vindictive and simple-minded in the accented present tense.

"I see you with the dark eyeglasses and the shtick. I see the president viz his arm around you, all the press corps so impressed. This is the truth? I don't think so."

Subtlety had not been a quality that Steadman associated with Manfred: he was bullheaded and self-absorbed in Ecuador, always reaching for another helping, searching for an advantage, querying, looking for more — his journalist's traits, of which presumption was the most apparent. But his confident aggression was something new to Steadman, and it threw him, for he had become used to the gentle coddling of strangers confronted by blindness, feeling helpless, wishing only to propitiate him with their insistent "What can I do for you?" as they eased him forward and tried to make him comfortable.

Manfred was in his face, bristling, shaking his finger as though Steadman were not blind at all. And so Steadman exaggerated his calmness, so as not to rouse Manfred further.

"You pronounce that my father made a suicide." He was shaking, stiffening, as he bore down on Steadman. "This is something painful for me. So you say, 'Is the truth — too bad.'"

"I don't know how I knew, but I knew." And Steadman thought, Like I know now that you've just eaten, you are sour with the smell of meat and mustard and beer.

"Maybe I say something when I am taking the *yajé*. Or maybe asleep. Maybe you hear me. Okay." He hammered the air with his head as he went on. "Is a secret for me. But you repeat it to the others. This I cannot stand."

Steadman wanted to say, It was spoken somehow, it must have been true, and so what? Manfred seemed to go limp with loathing, and there was a sneer in his breathing, a kind of clammy heat that bothered Steadman more than the butting head.

"One thing I find curious."

He said *sing*, he said *koorios*. His voice was shrill. There was no arguing with Manfred, who had become much angrier. But when he spoke again he seemed to be smiling, as if he had just thought of something, addressing Steadman in the halting tone a person uses to tease someone with a contradiction.

"I know some few blind people," he said. "One thing about them. They always dress a certain special way. With special clothes. Beret. Cravat. Waistcoat. Colorful stockings, maybe yellow shoes, or boots. And why?"

"Tell me."

"So you look at the clothes and not at the blindness."

It seemed to Steadman a shrewd observation, the way in which a blind man may affect to be a dandy, using the style of his clothes to divert strangers' attention from his tormented eyes.

"But not you," Manfred said, needling him. "You want so much for people to look at your blindness. You need them to see you. You like their attention. Your clothes are nothing."

The truth of this stopped Steadman cold. And it was worse hearing this insight in a bad accent, as though the man were cutting him with a rusty knife.

"What the fuck do you want?" Steadman said.

"I'm sorry?" Manfred said. "You are speaking to me?"

"I've just published a book. I've laid my heart bare. I've told the truth about myself — I've told everything. And you're accusing me of being a hypocrite?"

"You ask me what I want," Manfred said.

Steadman nodded slowly, knowing that Manfred was seeing his reflection in his dark glasses.

As Manfred leaned closer, the leather jacket tightened on his arms and across his back, like a belt being cinched and strained. Steadman could smell the worn and chafed leather, the damp corduroys, the long hair. Being frugal, leering at Steadman's clothes and eyeing him sideways, insinuating himself into Steadman's life — all that was a certain smell, too. And Steadman saw how similar he himself was, for all of Manfred's traits marked him out as someone on the periphery, an ardent fantasist, a solitary eavesdropper, a lonely man, a writer.

Manfred said, "I want to know how it is happened that you are being blind."

"An accident. A disease."

"Which one, accident or disease?"

"Both. The disease was an accident. I lost my corneas." He could tell that Manfred was still leaning, trying to see through the lenses for scars. "They got infected after I was hospitalized. The transplant surgery didn't work. It was rejected. I have scar tissue. It sometimes happens."

"When was this?"

"After Ecuador."

Manfred's smile of triumph was like a crease that ran the length of his body.

"I like your explanations. 'Disease.' 'Hospital.' 'Transplant surgery.' You know why I like them? Because of the words. 'Corneas.' 'Rejected.' 'Scar tissue.' I like them — they are *scheiss*. You tell me that you like the truth, so I ask you a question and what do you do? You lie to me."

Steadman could not bear the man's certainty, for he searched hard and saw that there was not a shred of doubt in Manfred's mind.

"Like your president. He has done nothing wrong. He is blind too."

Manfred had turned as he spoke, and Steadman realized that a TV set was on in the lounge and the president's image obviously on it with a fragment of voice-over: "*Sources in the White House confirm that the president assured them there was never any relationship . . .*"

"You can ask my doctor." Saying this, Steadman had a twisted picture in his mind of Ava howling.

Manfred said, "Your girlfriend doctor who says bad things about me also."

His clumsiness made the accusation more hurtful somehow, and so

Steadman merely faced him without emotion, hoping to confound him.

"I want for you to say the truth," Manfred said.

"I'm not lying to you."

"One word you are not saying."

Steadman resolved not to let the man rile him, and he stared back, implacable in his dark glasses.

"It is the drug. Say that to me. 'It is the drug.'"

"That was the beginning. The disease came afterward."

"I don't think so." He wasn't finished, but as he spoke, he turned and swallowed whatever he was going to say next. He looked in the direction of an approaching sound, not footsteps but the swish and flap of loose clothes.

"Mr. Steadman?"

A woman. He summed her up in just the saying of his name. She was slight, rather thin, with fragrant hair and a perfumed neck and a click of small finger joints and something in her throat — a stickiness, a tension that told him she was anxious and sexual.

"They said you were in here. I didn't mean to interrupt, but would you please sign my book?"

Steadman was keenly aware of Manfred's hostility, which was also a smell rising from his angry stiffened body.

"Be glad to."

"Thanks so much," she said, and held his wrist and placed the book in his hand. She kept a hand on his shoulder as he wrote his name with the usual flourish.

"Maybe I'll see you later," she said. "This is so kind of you." And in an even voice to Manfred: "Sorry, mister."

At that moment, as she retreated, Steadman felt a heaviness in his eyes, and then in a flicker of faint light he got an actual glimpse of the woman walking away — yes, she was small, in a fluttery pantsuit, but plumper than he had taken her to be. She glanced back with regret and longing, as though leaving with reluctance.

And Manfred, too, was apparent, but he was not the man Steadman had summed up in his blindness. He was a plainer and sadder approximation, not foreign at all but like a distant relative. Steadman realized how differently he had seen the man when he had stared blindly, and he wondered which one was the truth.

The whole experience of this glimpse lasted a few seconds, like a bad bulb flickering on and then failing, for no sooner had he seen Manfred, his features raked by a skeletal light, than he was eclipsed, as the drug took hold again and gripped him, possessing him, in the trance of its own blinding light.

"What were you saying?"

But in those seconds Manfred had stowed his broken tape recorder and gone.

6

THE MEMORY OF Manfred's accusation gnawed at him. He headed into the remainder of his book tour feeling like a fugitive, his muscles slack with indecision. Because of his blindness he was treated like a celebrity, yet his low spirits killed his enjoyment, and the hearty welcomes he got — people always talking a bit too loudly, a bit too energetically, calling attention to themselves, as though he were not blind but deaf and dimwitted — made him listless and passive. He felt insulted when they yanked on his sleeve, vulnerable when they touched his body.

"I was so happy working on my book, so happy on the Vineyard," he said to Ava from another hotel room. "Maybe I should have stayed home."

"Maybe you should have stopped taking the drug."

"There's hardly any left."

She sighed. She said, "How can you face these people?"

"That's part of the punishment," he said. "The anticlimax, the violation of being in the world, being observed as a freak."

"You asked for it." Without any sympathy she seemed to gloat.

"The thing is, here I am, publishing this personal novel that is not even an inch from the truth."

"It's a bestseller. What are you complaining about?"

"No one wants to talk about the book."

"Then come home."

"A few more days and I will."

But the next time he called and spoke of returning home she said, "Why bother? I don't want to see you in this mood."

Ava was chilly, distant, back at work, busy: he had come to expect no consolation from her. She didn't understand his need to continue as a blind man.

He told her that he had to go on taking the drug as long as some remained. When it was gone he would find a way of living without it.

"That's what addicts always say. Sorry, I'm being paged." And she hung up.

To Manfred it was his secret. Yet it had never occurred to Steadman that he had a secret. His blindness was something he had discovered as a cure for his silence, which was also his impotence, his frustrated attempts to write a novel. The accident of the drug he had exploited with effort, finding a reward in it when he might have found pain or obstruction or greater impotence. The drug was his virility, yet because of Manfred he found himself reacting defensively, behaving like a sneak, with a secret he went on swallowing, and always on guard against a leading question.

A day and a night in Washington, D.C., followed New York. Steadman took the train and was met at Union Station by the escort, "Everyone calls me Jerry," an obliquely attentive man who used his deferential butler-like manner to be bossy, evasively insisting that it might be a good idea for Steadman to sign books in Rockville, Maryland. When that was done, they visited a radio station in Chevy Chase, seeming to surprise the interviewer.

"Your life must be so different now," the interviewer said.

They never used the words "blind" or "blindness." Were the words so shocking? Yet it was all that anyone wanted to talk about.

Ask me about my book, he thought. Steadman's reputation as a difficult, at times forbidding interviewee prevented him from attacking the tone of the question. Everyone patronized, no one inquired. Yet he tried to be helpful; he wanted to seem strong. Stifling his rage, he deflected even the crassest questions. And all he could think of was Manfred, who doubted him, showing up like a vindictive gnome in a folktale to undo the hero's magic. *I know your secret.*

By the time they got to the bookstore event at Politics and Prose, Steadman was hoarse with fatigue. Feeling frail, he spoke about his blindness, his overcoming almost twenty years of silence with this novel, to revisit the sexual life of his alter ego in *The Book of Revelation*. "I am a traveler, yet I discovered that the antipodes are within us, in the far continents of the mind," he said, paraphrasing Aldous Huxley in *The Doors of Perception*. He chanted some lines from Thoreau:

> *I hearing get, who had but ears,*
> *And sight, who had but eyes before.*

He commanded the attention of the crowd by describing the inner journey of his novel, so different from the stunt that *Trespassing* now seemed. And then he signed a hundred copies of his book.

Afterward, breaking the silence in the car, Jerry said, "They ask really great questions."

Regarding this as a dig, Steadman said nothing for a while, and then, "What do people in D.C. make of the president's problems?"

"What do they 'make' of them? They make jokes," Jerry said. "Notice how he's playing the victim? First he denies everything, and then he gets other people to attack the press. He brought it all on himself and he's blaming people for being interested. Hel-lo! Mr. Winkie is hanging out and you wonder why everyone's staring."

The man seemed triumphant and even drove his car that way, his head crooked in defiance.

"Power here is a zero-sum game," he said, because Steadman had not replied. "A lot of people are glad to see the president diminished by all his pretense. More power for them."

"How does his private life figure as pretense?"

"He lied," Jerry said. "He pretended to be someone he's not. People won't forget that." His lips were twisted in irony, and it seemed as though he were tasting it deeply, because he giggled a little and said, "I mean, Lordy, have you *seen* her?"

Steadman felt a surge of glee. He said, "How could I?"

It seemed so unreasonable for Steadman to say it — the woman's face was everywhere — the man took his eyes off the road and turned to look at him.

"I'm blind, pal."

"I keep forgetting," the man said, fussing rather than apologizing. "You are so damned on the ball."

The president was undergoing the sort of scrutiny Steadman dreaded being turned upon him for his blindness. Manfred's questions seemed like intimations of this intrusion. Under pressure, the president had begun to appear tricky and defensive, his denials hollow. It was obvious that he had dispatched his aides to attack his accusers. They had spoken of a campaign to discredit the president — it was all a right-wing conspiracy. Yet the president seemed guilty and hunted and sleepless, more and more like a man under a strong light of scrutiny, looking pale and insubstantial.

As the days and weeks passed, Steadman had watched closely the man who had appeared to him, when they first met, not a paragon of suavity and power, but a sheepish and needy boy, craving listeners, wishing to be a big brother, nursing old grievances, and hiding his secret life.

A ringing startled Steadman from his reverie. Jerry handed him a cell phone. "For you."

Axelrod again: "I just spoke with the manager of Politics and Prose. She was really pleased with the turnout. I hear the interviews went well, too."

"All they want to talk about is my blindness."

"The book's selling. We are going back for another printing."

"I'm being treated like a cripple."

"They don't like to think they're advertising your book."

"And some of them treat me like a freak."

"Slade, don't you see they're looking for a headline?"

Steadman hung up. He was tired, and Jerry wore him out just sitting there attitudinizing, doubting him, jeering at the president. The president had become the butt of all jokes and now wore a shamed cringing look, like someone brutally mocked and still trying to maintain his dignity.

"I feel for him," Steadman said.

"The smart money says he'll resign."

"Why should he?"

"For disgracing the office of president. For being a chubby-chaser. Listen, toots, I was in the service. If a senior officer was caught doing that, he'd have to resign."

Steadman said, "Would you like someone checking up on what you do in your spare time?" and felt he had struck a nerve.

Then they were rolling up the driveway of the Ritz-Carlton. Jerry stopped the car and got out quickly to dash to the passenger side and help Steadman. But Steadman had already gotten out, provoked by the man's fussy certainty. Wishing to be away from him, he swept with his cane, found the curb, and moved on.

"Can I help you?" A strange voice in his face.

"Yes, get out of my way."

As soon as Steadman entered the hotel lobby he felt lonely, his feet unsteady, as though the floor were aslant, for loneliness was also a sorry flutter in his inner ear, a loss of balance.

He went to the bar and eased his way through the drinkers, who cleared a path for him. Feeling for a stool ("Right here," someone said), he found one that had just been vacated, the cushion still warm. The acute perception of temperature had also become part of his blindness.

"What'll it be?"

He ordered a glass of wine. It was put into his hand. He was careful to sip without spilling: people were watching.

A warm body next to him kept him wondering at its softness. He knew women by their obscure sounds, of chafing silks, tightening undergarments, the clatter of bangles as they slipped to a narrow wrist. This woman's body spoke, and her breath, that fragrance. She stayed at his elbow, and she too was drinking wine — he knew by her sips and sighs.

He was thinking: Then don't come home. I don't want to see you in this mood.

"What's your name?"

"Dewy Fourier."

"That's an interesting name."

"It's French. Can I order you another cocktail?"

He was trying not to smile. "No thanks. One is my limit. But you can help me find the elevator."

"I'd love to."

She guided his elbow, crowding him, jostling him, because he knew the way out of the bar. At the elevator, she pressed the button before he could and was saying, "Where to?" as he tapped his way in beside her.

"Mind pressing fourteen?" The doors sucked shut, and when they were alone he said, "You only pressed one button."

"I'm going where you're going."

They ascended in silence. He inhaled a vaguely familiar aroma, a thick odor of fresh blossoms, like syrup in the air. When the elevator stopped at the fourteenth floor the woman got out with him, still touching his arm. Her fingers told him everything: she was nervous, eager, young, excited. Her leather bag was not large, but it was heavy and dense.

"I know the way."

She released him as he tapped toward the door of his room. She remained, walking slightly behind him.

He tucked his plastic key card into the slot of the door lock, but when it buzzed he did not push the door open. The woman was a warm breathing shape of perfumed flesh next to him. He heard the binding of her shoe strap. Her long naked body was apparent to him as a bright shadow, submissive beneath her insubstantial dress.

"Yes?"

"I was wondering if there was anything I could do for you."

"I'm thinking," he said.

She hesitated. She leaned toward him as though to kiss him. They stood at his door in an empty corridor, on a thick carpet, the distant sound of a food cart rattling out of a service elevator.

"I'm very oral."

Now he hesitated. She was faced away from him, not out of shyness but making sure that no one would interrupt, the edginess of a fox near meat.

"Good. Then you can read to me." He pushed his heavy door open.

He sensed her whole body reacting with relief as she passed him, still radiating warmth, and went inside. He followed her and kicked the door shut.

He put down his cane, took off his jacket, and threw it on the sofa. He found a bottle of mineral water and poured himself a drink. He jerked the drapes, closing them. Then he excused himself, went to the bathroom, brushed his teeth, and returned to the sitting room of the suite, where the woman was standing in the center, stiff with puzzlement, clutching her hands. She had placed her heavy handbag beside the sofa.

"Dewy?"

"I'm here."

"I know. What do you think of my suite?"

"I can't see anything."

343

Only then did he realize that he had not turned on the lights. He laughed and switched on a lamp next to the sofa. He sat and stuck his legs out.

"It's beautifully appointed. Very comfortable-looking. Exquisite taste."

The words made him frown, but as he pitied her he was aware that she had stepped to the door and hooked the safety chain. And she had glanced into the bedroom as she passed it.

He went to her. He caught her arm and held her hand and touched her face. She was not tall, and though she radiated heat she was fleshy, even plump. He could tell by passing his fingers over her face that she was pretty, and when he touched her she did not resist. She relaxed and took half a step nearer and smiled. So far, in the strange distortions of this book tour the only women who had offered themselves to him had been heavy and slow and unsubtle, incurious about his mode of living. But this one, Dewy, was bright and attractive and — he wondered why — very curious. From the moment he had switched on the lamp she had not stopped looking around.

"I can see in the dark."

"Incredible."

"I know you from somewhere."

She put her hand over her mouth to stifle her reaction.

"I signed a book for you."

"If you say so."

"I'm trying to think where it was. New York, maybe? What are you doing here? You're a writer, aren't you?"

"I do a little writing."

"You're following me. You were waiting for me in the bar."

The answer yes was a perceptible twitch in her body.

"What is it you want to know?"

Her silences told him everything, and she was still looking around the room, as if searching for clues.

"Nothing," she said.

He laughed, because he had made her so self-conscious and defensive. He said, "You said you'd read to me. What did you have in mind?"

"Something from your book."

"It's a little late."

She felt for him, her fingertips stroking his thigh. "I've got all night."

He was smiling at her, and she did not seem to be aware that he knew that as she was stroking him she was nodding at the corners of the room, pausing to examine the items on the tabletops, the clothes showing in his open suitcase, glancing back at his face to peer at his eyes.

"Something from my book." That had surprised him. Even though he was suspicious of her, he was flattered by the suggestion. He moved away from her and, sitting on the sofa, felt for a copy that he had left on a side table.

She sat beside him and said, "Mind if I get comfortable?"

She slipped her shoes off and drew her legs up beneath her and still, from where she sat, she was searching the room.

"I like the scene where you're in the car, making out," she said. "And your date goes down on you."

"Not me. The main character."

"He doesn't have a name — how am I supposed to know?" she said, and took the book from him and flipped pages. "Anyway, the back seat of the car. A hot night. It was a turn-on. Here it is."

She began to read. "'*I look fucked.*'

"*Still smiling and peering intently into the mirror of her compact, she wiped the smears of lipstick from her face, dabbed at her eyes, combed her hair. And just as he thought she had finished, she took out a pouch of cosmetics and applied mascara and thickened her eyelashes — slowly, paying no attention to him, who watched with fascination as she prettied her face. She rouged her cheeks, reddened her lips again using a brush and lip gloss, made herself a new face, a mask of desire.*

"I love that," she said. "It goes on.

"*She faced him. The dusty moonlight deepened the texture of her makeup and softened the planes of her face, and what had seemed an innocently questioning smile in the small mirror was now lust lit by moonbeams.*

"*She leaned toward him and her lowering arm crushed her gown as she reached down and slid her hand along his thigh.*"

As Dewy read, her voice thickened and purred, and she let one hand drop onto Steadman's leg. Though her fingers crawled across his thigh he was hardly conscious of it. He was listening closely, not aroused by anything she read but instead questioning the punctuation and certain words. "Lust lit by moonbeams" seemed purplish and pointless. She was racing ahead, reading with emphasis.

"The sound of his pleasure came slanting from deep within his lungs and seemed like an echo of a softer sighing in her throat. Her breasts were in his hands, his thumbs grazing her nipples. Her touch was surer and so finely judged that she seemed to feel in the throb of his cock the spasm of his juice rising — knew even before he did that he was about to come. Then he knew, his body began to convulse, and as he cried 'No' — because she had let go — she pushed him backward onto the seat and pressed her face down, lapping his cock into her mouth, curling her tongue around it, and the suddenness of it, the snaking of her tongue, the pressure of her lips, the hot grip of her mouth, triggered his orgasm, which was not juice at all but a demon eel thrashing in his loins and swimming swiftly up his cock, one whole creature of live slime fighting the stiffness as it rose and bulged at the tip and darted into her mouth.

"Holding him with one hand, she devoured it and was still swallowing as he went limp and slipped out of her mouth. When she looked up at him with her smeared face and smudged eyes, she was still greedily gulping, licking droplets from her gleaming lips."

She put the book down and moved her hand between his legs, and then he kissed her. Moments before he had sensed warmth, a glow of pleasure, but there was none on her lips. She was made of clay, going through the motions — he could taste her indifference, another low temperature. Her hands and arms were cold, her grip was perfunctory, as if coaxing a stubborn lever. She was placid, really; there was no thirst in her body.

But she said, "That feels nice."

He smiled at her lie. He could easily discern her calculation, a different sort of scrutiny, like the squinting gaze of a bobble-headed passenger sitting across from him on a train, sizing him up. As a blind man he had become used to that stranger's gaze — people staring at him in public. But in his own room it alerted him. She sniffed as she searched, and still her hand was closing on him.

Then she stood and slipped out of her dress, and when she sat again and was naked he sensed that he knew her absolutely. He reached behind her and turned off the lamp.

"Why did you come here?"

She let go of him. Her whole body contracted as though denying the implication behind his question.

"I have a feeling someone sent you here."

Her reaction, which was not audible, not visible, not an odor, nothing except a suggestion of furious molecules, her stiffening and becoming a fraction smaller, told him it was true.

"You're trying to find out if I'm really blind."

Again the whir of molecules, a swallow of air, her knees together, her surprise. He sensed all this in the darkness as a liquefaction slipping slowly past him.

"There's no story," he said. "Put your clothes on. You don't belong here."

She said, protesting, "You wrote this sexy book and I want to give you head and you throw me out of your hotel room? Tell me that's not a story."

But she had started to dress, trying to be calm, like someone woken and startled by the smell of smoke, preparing to flee a dangerous room.

"It was in New York," he said. "In the hotel. You asked me to sign your book when I was with Manfred."

"No."

"He sent you here to check on me."

"No."

"Tell Manfred to stay away from me."

She was fumbling with her dress, hopping a little as she pulled it on and straightened it. "Please put the light on."

"If you tell me the truth."

"Manfred said you were a kind of mind reader. I didn't believe him. But I believe him now."

Steadman switched on the light and said, "You have a yeast infection."

The woman began to cry, and her crying hindered her movements as she finished dressing, her sobbing slowing her and making her clumsy. When she was done and had put on her shoes, she stumbled slightly as she left, yanking the door, catching and straining the safety chain, and crying in frustration as she unfastened it and went out.

Steadman sat, a film of guilt like scum on his face. Needing to complain, he rubbed his eyes and dialed Ava. Just as quickly he hung up, realizing as he tapped the keypad how late it must be. He had not checked his watch — he unconsciously assumed that his watch face would be visible. It usually was at this hour. Touch was like sight: he stroked the hands of his watch — almost midnight. He cursed Manfred. And he imagined the phone call he had just aborted, Ava saying, *You pushed your luck — what did you expect?*

What happened next was odder than anything that had happened on that odd day. He was groping toward the bedroom when he remembered that he had not taken the drug since rising that morning in New York to catch the early train to Washington. He had been blind for more than eighteen hours — unprecedented, unexplainable. And the moment this disturbing thought occurred to him, he bumped into the bedroom wall.

7

HE WAS SHAKEN out of the soup of an obscure dream of interrogation by the ringing phone — a man's overbright voice saying "Hi" and nothing else, one of those needling people who do not identify themselves, but instead make you guess, as though to unsettle you or test your friendship. Who at this hour was so alert for this sort of teasing? But Steadman was certain — still limp with sleep, even as his unpleasant dream faded — it was Jerry, the escort from yesterday, saying in a more tentative way, "Are you there?"

"Right here."

"What train do you want to catch?" He seemed chastened by Steadman's abruptness. "I can meet you anytime."

"Don't bother. I'll take a cab to the station." And Steadman hung up before Jerry could reply. He was still annoyed by "They ask really great questions," implying that — blind, standing in front of the bookstore crowd, speaking without notes for a full hour — Steadman had made no impression. All that Jerry could commend was the brilliance of the audience. But it was a strategy, his belittling, like not giving his name on the phone.

Steadman's indignation was twofold. I am a writer, he thought, and I am blind. Bastard!

He had to put the phone down to concentrate. It was bad enough to be woken by an idiot call, but, much worse, he was not sure at that moment whether he was blind or sighted. In his confusion his mind was scoured of all thought. He sat up in bed stupefied. Feeling vulnerable, his memory impaired, he felt an animal compulsion to flee the hotel and the city.

He needed to leave, to return to New York; needed people to observe him in order that he could function. He felt lost when he was alone and blind, but the physicality of other people, their glances and gestures, the way they breathed and swallowed, all their human responses, their smells, their skin, their very nerves, helped guide him on his way.

He needed friends, Ava especially, a woman whose intelligence would match his, whose eager flesh was like a torch to bring the foreground into focus and make the wider world visible. That was nothing new; he had always wanted a woman near, someone to challenge him, to comfort him, a sexual friend, a listener, the ideal companion Ava had been throughout the writing of his book. The paradox was that while he had loved her for her independence, he had also wanted to possess her, so they could be sexual, wise and foolish together. He loved her for being so reckless and so bright, for often being the aggressor, for lighting his way, for her risks and her dares. Even now, though she seemed out of sympathy, she was necessary to him.

Alone, he saw the future as a grainy monochrome of days, indistinct and worrisome. He wanted color and perspective, the stabilizing echoes of human voices. He needed to be witnessed. This he realized anew as he moved through his hotel room, gathering his clothes and filling his bag. The young woman's perfume clung to the sofa where she had sat and read to him from his book.

He finished shaving and was about to take a measure of the drug when, mixing it in a glass of water, he faltered and batted the air and put the glass down untasted. He was already blind. He felt for the mirror, fingertips on the glass, saw nothing, felt nothing, except the hot lights framing the mirror on his face. I'm losing it, he thought.

Often he had gone to bed blind, but when had he ever woken blind? The effects of the drug had always worn off while he slept. Now his heavy eyes made him clumsier as he stuffed his suitcase. And at last he went back to the bathroom and drank the drug hurriedly, splashing his chin. And he stood, unsteady, as if he had swallowed a syrup of light.

The warmth spread from his stomach and whipped through his blood until the nerves throbbed behind his eyes and crackled, a phosphorescence that was electric.

Downstairs, in a suit like a school uniform saturated with the woolly smell of cigarette smoke, the bellman approached on big flapping feet to take his bag. The man was black and broad-shouldered, and the bag was insubstantial in his hand as he swung it into the taxi, holding the door open.

"You going to be all right?"

The man pitied him with a helpless, burdening concern, easing him into the taxi as Steadman studied him, summing him up as someone poor and unappreciated, living on his own but with children somewhere, who were kept away from him. Having to be at work at five A.M., he was already weary. His uniform was fairly new but his shoes were worn, the leather crushed, with thin soles. The man coughed, covering his wide scraped-looking face and his bruised lips. His lungs were spongy and rotten.

The taxi driver said, "How'd it happen?"

Strangers swept in, querying, seizing on his blindness like predators spotting a weakness.

"Long story."

"You think you got problems? Check out the president. That man is breathing hard."

"What's the latest?"

"Talking 'bout 'peachment."

The president's woes, the scandal, the repeated denials and counterattacks, were on the radio in Steadman's earphones all the way to New York. As he listened, he saw the president's pink sheepish face and blue uncertain eyes, the bags of sleeplessness under them, as naked as a man's features could be, as blank and pathetic and symmetrical as a target. He looked fragile and insulted and ashamed. He was everywhere on TV screens with the sound turned down, mouthing words and looking like a cornered man trying to persuade a gunman not to shoot. A man could not look more powerless, more hunted, more like prey, more bullied.

Steadman removed his headphones, and as though recognizing a decisive gesture, the woman sitting next to him on the train inclined her head and spoke in a gentle voice. "Going home?"

"No."

"Not a New Yorker?"

"Just visiting."

"I could show you around," she said with conviction.

He wanted to surrender to her, to hold her; there was such a purr of protection in her voice.

"Where might you be staying?" she said.

She seemed as she spoke to invite him onto her lap, and in his mood of self-pity he was prepared to call her bluff and crawl beneath her arms, to lie there squashed under her breasts and allow himself to be suckled.

Instead of replying to her, he lifted his head and stared in her direction and watched her dissolve, become a pale flesh tone and an odor of crushed flowers. And just as quickly she bulked up again into the fattened reality of a broad-faced woman with a sack-like body and thick thighs, a rumpled dress, and puffy sorrowful eyes behind old-fashioned purple-rimmed glasses.

I am not blind, he thought. Could she tell?

Fading, narrowing, as though liquefying, she became a small anxious girl again. She was inquisitive and sexual, and he was aroused once more. But who was that woman he had just seen?

"My uncle was blind," she said. "He had a kind of carapace. That's not a good thing. I reached out to him. But he wouldn't come out of his shell."

The imagery he found sad and exact, and concentrating hard and leaning toward her, he realized she had gone. They had arrived at Penn Station. She had given up on him and left without saying goodbye.

He thought again, I'm losing it.

New York, its sallow shadowy light, the blatting of its cascading car horns, its rushing people, lay at the top of the escalator. He rose on the steps, his bag at his feet, into the steep indifferent city, the dirty bricks, the flat-faced buildings, the surly windows, the fleeing pedestrians, the toxic air. Someone nearby, a young stupid man, was swearing loudly in a foreign accent, vile disgusting words, spreading hostility like foul-smelling fumes. No one reacted.

In the taxi on the way to his hotel, Steadman reduced the city to its separate components, the scorched oil stink of exhaust, the noise of engines, the dense and unforgiving flow of traffic, the unintelligible voices as of an asylum turned inside out — all that and the radiance of its limitless sky. The city was never dark, never silent.

But his hotel was quiet enough. He was welcomed back by the staff as though cherished, the pet blind man, like the beloved cripple on whom all friendliness was bestowed by sentimental strangers. They exaggerated their attention because it seemed they could not imagine how, unless they made a fuss over him, he would possibly remember them.

Instead of calling Ava, he called Axelrod.

"You still have Boston and Philly," he said. "And there's that party tonight."

The party was news to him. He asked for details.

"It's in a private room at Waldo's Grill. I'll meet you at the hotel at six. We've invited media."

Dreading it, he drugged himself, and the event was every bit as awful as he had feared, a hot overcrowded room above an overcrowded restaurant. The downstairs howl of diners reached the private room on the second floor and filled it with stinging sound. Steadman was introduced to the guests, who snatched at his free hand. He knew them from their hands and their voices.

One said, "I loved your book. They say you have a sixth sense. Tell me something."

The man's hand was clammy, unwashed, scummy with the city, impatient, insincere.

"I wouldn't want to presume," Steadman said.

"Go ahead."

"You're agitated. You have a lot on your mind that is all trivia. You are looking for a quote from me. You didn't read my book."

The man let go, shook Steadman's hand free, and said, "That's like an all-purpose answer, right?"

"Take my hand," a woman said, bumping other people aside.

In a sudden glimpse that was soaked with dirty light, Steadman's sight returned just as she clutched his hand. He saw the room — the guests drinking and taking food from trays, the cluster of people around him waiting to speak, all of them looking hungry and eager. He was confused by the faces, the reaching, the jostling. He was embarrassed and defensive, as though he were gazing through a one-way mirror. They had no idea he was looking at them. He couldn't help it, and worse, he hated seeing them. These flashes of sight were like awful glimpses into his own past, like his mind coming alive to offer the vividness of shame and remorse he thought he had forgotten, visions like bad memories.

The woman seized his fingers. He saw her clearly, he saw everything. The flood of faces brimmed in the room, putting it in shadow. He was overwhelmed by the sight of it, and then his blindness took hold again, a glittering curtain descending over his eyes.

"Are you all right?"

Had he betrayed his brief ability to see? It was terrible the way the drug had become so unreliable. He drank it these days and saw the sorry unresolved reality of daylight. Then he skipped a dose and without any warning he was blinded, as though there remained in his body an undissolved sediment of the drug, a residue that was stirred by his blood flow, taking away his sight.

But his blindness now was not the blindness that had revealed the innermost world that was also his past; it was an obstacle, a kind of ignorance, a puzzlement. These days — tonight, for example, in the stuffy room of guests and spectators — he felt weak and defenseless, a blunderer, trying not to wave his arms at the walls.

"Cindy Adams. The *Post*. I was hoping you'd tell my fortune."

How could he tell her that he was no longer capable of the party trick of prescience? He turned away, and an insistent man at his elbow said, "Can we talk somewhere quiet?"

People still touched him all the time, and they talked too loudly, poking or pawing him on each word. The man persisted. Steadman sensed that he was being tugged into a corner, away from the bump and shriek of party guests.

Where it was quieter, Steadman could tell that the man beside him was calm and inquisitive, confidently moving him against a wall as Steadman prodded the floor with his stick, almost losing his balance as the man nudged him.

"I've got a few questions."

"Yes?"

"I really did read your book, but I want to talk to you about your blindness. Like, do you feel it gives you an edge?"

Though the tone was neutral, the question seemed hostile, especially now, jammed against the wall, beset by strangers in the stuffy room. He had been thrust into the party and was expected to perform. He had not had a drink, his eyesight had flickered, dark to light and back again, from one world to the other, the simpler world of sight to the tortured one of this new version of his blindness that was unfamiliar and overwhelming. Not just beset by strangers. He felt he was among enemies: the sour air in the room, the mutters, told him this, but he knew no more.

Reaching as though to restore his balance, he was reminded of the toppling figure of Blind Pew in the cartoon, arms spread in a gesture of appeal: *Help me!*

"No edge at all," he said. "It's a struggle." He sensed skepticism in the way the man exhaled. "Please excuse me."

"Some guy has a Web site claiming that you've been taking a drug."

The word "drug," uttered for the first time by a stranger, filled Steadman with such dread he was too numb to show alarm.

"Maybe a performance-enhancing drug. Like I say, maybe to get an edge."

Steadman said, "Do you think that anyone would choose to be blind?"

"Right. That's what I was wondering."

Steadman had never felt blinder or less in control. He had swallowed a dose of the drug in the hotel room just before setting off for the party, and here he was, baffled, seeing nothing except when, in an occasional burst of ugly light, he had gotten a glimpse of the room and winced.

"I find that an insulting suggestion," Steadman said, and felt for the wall.

"I'm sorry you think so," the man said. "Hey, I was just asking."

"Excuse me" — he recognized Axelrod's voice. "I was wondering where you were."

"This man was accusing me of faking."

"I didn't say you were faking. I was just trying to verify the rumors that you're on some kind of drug."

"Back off, asshole!" Axelrod said, shrieking at the man. "How dare you say that! This man has lost his eyesight. He has just published a great book. And you're a guest here. How about showing a little respect?"

As Axelrod cowed the man with his fury, Steadman thought, Why didn't I say that? Why wasn't I that angry?

"I am so sorry," Axelrod said. "You look tired. Maybe you should go. People will understand."

Steadman left the party, and later in his hotel room he was so rattled he could not think straight. He reasoned that Manfred had put the word out, to expose him. And it was likely, as he had suspected, that the woman in Washington had come to his room to check up on him, to look for the drug, to see if he was really blind, to relay the information to Manfred.

He would go on denying it — there was no proof. But there was a greater problem, and it horrified him. He seemed to have no control over his blindness now. The drug was at times irrelevant. That night he lay in a sweat, waiting for the usual glimmer of light, the dull glow that told him the drug was weakening in him. But there was nothing, only the throb of New York, the city howl vibrating in his guts. He wondered if, after all the months of taking the drug, he had saturated himself with it, that his flesh was drenched.

He slept. He woke. He could not tell whether it was day or night, and he was terrified.

8

So he remained in New York, and each morning in his hotel room he opened his eyes hoping that he was waking from the nightmare, that something had changed, that he was able to see. He would have been grateful for the merest glimmer of light. Each morning he was desolated. There was nothing but the city's roar, like the endless slosh of muddy toppling surf, and though he could not understand it, there was something in that noise that always mocked him. He went to the window and was deafened by the traffic strangling the dust-thickened air. New York was an ocean and he was trapped at the bottom of it, suffocating at this black depth, dense with sound, struggling against the suck of the tide. He had lost even the memory of light, and sorrowing, he thought, I am in hell.

He had stayed in the city for its protection, for the way it seemed to accommodate every human type. Still, he suffered — why was it not luminous? — and he was too timid to leave. He canceled the rest of his tour: Philadelphia, Boston, the C-SPAN segment, the photo shoot for the *Time* interview.

"It's not a problem," Axelrod said. "The book is doing great."

But the city was not benign. He was a cripple here. He had slipped into a diabolical darkness that he had once denied ever existed. He was reminded every second of his ailment; he was seriously disabled, among strangers. Nothing was worse than to go to sleep miserable, trying to hope, and to get up the next morning just as miserable, and hopeless.

A call came, a voice said, "Mr. Steadman?" and when he said yes, "This is Trespassing. Please hold for Mr. Gurvitch."

The next voice he heard was a gruff and displeased one.

"Shel Gurvitch, Trespassing Promotions." And after a deep and pitying breath, "Slade, I don't think we've met. I won't waste your time. I just want to say that we were not told anything in advance about your publicity tour and, wait a minute" — Steadman had begun to object — "we couldn't be sorrier about your accident. But we are seriously questioning what sort of a message your headlining is sending to the branding emphasis of our licensing base."

"I have no idea what you mean."

"Give you an example. The Limited Edition package."

"Of my book?"

"No. The Trespassing Limited Edition that we proposed for the redesign of the new Jeep. We've just been turned down. We think it's related to your accident."

"What accident?"

"Your thing. Your eyesight. Your infirmity."

Steadman put down the phone. He took no more calls. He hardly went out. And who was that always following him? He only needed to pause at a curb for someone to offer him money, believing he was panhandling. One person, passing him, pressed a bill into his hand. He was so startled he held it as he walked along, and moments later he was bumped — a whiff of acrid sweat — and the money was snatched from him.

Some awful logic was chopping him small as his book was being elevated. Yes, he had his book. His quest had been a success. Now he knew the price.

To control his fear and gain confidence, he folded the remainder of his crumbled drug in paper and made a parcel of it. He left his hotel, the Carlyle, took small slow steps one block up Madison, turned east, and tapped his way down 77th, across Park Avenue and onward, past Lenox Hill Hospital. He sensed a slackening of attention in passersby, which allowed him a shadowy intimation that he was being followed again — someone close behind him. He turned sharply, tottering in darkness.

"What do you want?"

Whoever it was shadowing him halted and took a breath.

"You think I don't see you?" Steadman said. He gestured with his stick. "I know you're there. You're not fooling me. Is it Manfred?"

There was no sound except the slapping tread of a pedestrian striding through the murk. Never mind the darkness, forget the worrying voices — he could not breathe. It was as though all the air had been sucked from the city. In that vacuum, Steadman heard his own hollow voice in his ears.

"I know it's you, Manfred. Or is it another of your whores dogging my heels?"

A woman's voice inquired, "You want a hand, mister?"

"No." He turned away from the voice.

"The outpatient entrance is right over here," a man said.

"There's nothing wrong with me!" Steadman shrieked.

He slashed with his cane, trying to emphasize the point, but he stumbled and someone said, "Careful with that stick, fella. Poke someone's eye out."

Clearing his way with the cane, he kept on to the end of the block, where there was an uprush of air at the subway entrance, a gust of urinous dust and warm human-scented air. He allowed himself to be helped across Lexington. He smelled fresh-baked bread, pizza, coffee. The helper said, "Spare any change?" Steadman gave the man all the coins in his pocket, and the man said, "This is chickenshit. I'm hungry and I just saved your sorry ass. Give me five bucks, fuckface." Steadman kept going. He tapped his way to Third, to Second, moving very slowly, fearing that another abuser might try to ambush him, yet needing someone at each avenue, and fearing even more the sound of cars. He had hated the way people had touched him before. Now he needed their hands, the pressure of their fingers, their reassuring voices.

"There's a footbridge somewhere near here," he said to a man next to him who offered help, when he heard the cars at FDR Drive. It was a raceway; he was terrified.

"Few blocks down." This gentle voice guided him, bucking him up as they walked. "Almost there, my friend. Few more steps."

He was at last at the edge of the island, above the enclosed trough of speeding cars.

"Just get me onto the bridge, thanks. I'll be okay."

"You're the boss."

"Get me to the handrail."

Already he was learning the cranky authority of the blind, hearing himself make demands and give orders and be obeyed by these invisible fingers, prodding and pinching his clothes.

But something was amiss: the man had hurried away. Steadman slapped his jacket and realized that the man had lifted his wallet.

Across the walkway he found the stairs, and at the bottom of them the rusty rail. He heard the wind slapping at the surface of the river and raising a chop. In the sluicing current, the lick of waves spilled past him and slopped at the embankment at his feet.

He took out the paper parcel and tore it open, scattering the crumbled twigs and stems of the drug. There was hardly any left, yet he wished this to be a ritual, an outward renunciation, ridding himself of it all. Some innate strictness told him that if he made an effort, as he had in the painful journey to this spot, and if the ritual was formal enough, he might get his wish: his sight back.

Then he would be abject. He would admit in public what he had done, how the vision and the recaptured memories in his book had been achieved. The journalist at the party had given him a truthful expression for it: I needed an edge. Until then, he would remain the man he claimed to be, Blind Slade. The wind was tearing at his jacket as he bowed and mumbled an apology, wanting to weep for his error. He had once worried about running out of the drug.

"You drop something?"

Steadman inclined his head to hear if this man's voice was familiar — one of those sneaks he suspected of following him. It was a horror to stand gaping and not to know when people were watching him.

"No," he said, and asked the voice for help in recrossing the footbridge and finding the street. When he managed this, the man steering him, bumping him along, he turned aside and thanked him. There was no reply. Though all noises rattled him, he found silence worse than any noise.

The man had stolen his watch. A craftsman on the Vineyard had made it for him. The watch face had no glass, only the sturdy hands, which Steadman traced with his fingertips to tell the time, and his continually touching it made the watch something precious, a talisman, and a friend.

"Bastard! I can see you!"

But his voice calling into the darkness sounded so tearful, so filled with woe, he stopped. He kept on walking. His footsteps were feeble and tentative; so was his cane. He pitied himself for his own anxious, searching sounds. He was terrified all the way back to the hotel, afraid that he would be flattened by a car, one of those honking taxis or a roaring unhesitating truck. He scowled each time he heard a horn, for every blare was warning him to back up. Having to be alert exhausted him, and he felt at any moment he might step into a hole.

What had gone wrong? He knew that Manfred was out to expose him, but any suggestion that he was faking his blindness could not be proven. He had never been blinder, his world never blacker. The quality of the darkness was complete, like a curtain of utter ignorance, a mangy blanket of evil, like the black drapes of a tyranny. This persistent night bore no relation to the peculiar illumination he had known before, brought on by the drug that had made him so happy. This was a stinking bag dragged over his head as though by a hangman, the doom-laden obstacle to perception. His hands and legs were useless too. He was frightened and felt childish. The intimation of death in this was made worse because he was trapped in New York, city of terrifying noises and hostile voices and ambiguous smells, where he was treated like a trespasser.

He paused to rest near Madison Avenue, and someone with a dog — the creature snuffled at his shoes — said, "Hey." But thinking he was being assaulted, he thrust with one hand and struck the person, and only then, as he smacked a hand holding a rag-like piece of paper, did he understand that the person had been offering him money as a handout.

"Fuck you! You broke my nail. You should get cancer!"

Cowering back in his room, he flinched when the phone rang: Axelrod.

"We are being flooded with requests for interviews."

"No more interviews. I want to go home."

"You don't sound too perky."

"Lost my coordinates." Steadman became breathless with fear. "Can you get me a ticket to the Vineyard today?"

"Easter weekend," Axelrod said. But the desperation in Steadman's voice had alarmed him. "I'll do what I can."

He called back to say that all flights were full. The only free seat was two days off.

Despair, the memory of that dreadful walk, and the thefts made him feel so helpless he wanted to weep. He was intimidated, he was a child, and he sorrowed for himself, for his book had been so bold.

Out of the hoarse pathos of this solitary regret, like a dull murmuring aria of lamentation, he was reproached by his forgetfulness, the emptiness of his memory. His seclusion in the present had turned him into a sunken-eyed traveler who had strayed from his path and was lost on the bank of a jungle river. He could see it all, his wraith-like shape on one of those scoops of sand on a long reach between the overhanging foliage — some skimming birds, the muddy eddy bubbling like chocolate milk, the shadow of a chalky wide-winged ray shooting just beneath the surface. High up, a dark hawk floated in the hot gray sky.

This recollection, seeing himself as a castaway, was not a vision of horror but rather one of profound sadness, a memory of himself at his most innocent. There was an insistent voice, too, Manfred's, urging him to get up, tempting him with the drug in the nearby village; the man loomed over him, his hands working.

I know a little about this one . . . It is great. It change your head, it give you experiences. Only the question of money, but you have money.

All other memories were closed to him, but this one he saw was him at his happiest, driven by hope, on the verge of his discovery of the drug. Manfred had revealed himself as a friend.

The drug tour, the quest, the surprises in Ecuador, which he had seen as a leap in the dark, had given him strength. Now he saw himself as the hawk might have seen the castaway on the crescent of wet sand on the riverbank, a raptor's meditation. And this memory gave him more by offering him glimpses of the aftermath, the illuminations of blindness, the sight of him dictating his book, the months of seclusion, like years of enchantment in a remote castle, in which he had lived the narrative. Manfred had been right in his promise: he had been uplifted, he had achieved his book, he had never been happier.

And now he had sunk to this: the airless overfurnished cell of a hotel bedroom, the sense of being captive. He knew now he should never have come, but he had made his worst mistake in continuing the drug, to call attention to himself. Even the offering of his book had been a hasty decision. He had allowed himself to be hurried into the anticlimax of publication, the inevitable disappointment, the misunderstandings, his dubious performances on the tour, in bookstores and lecture halls — it had all been like a secret revealed, the disclosure of a weakness, a loss of power. He had once vowed never to go on the road. Why hadn't he been satisfied with the writing of his book? He was in agony thinking of the purity of that task, and he reproached himself — he had Ava's words — for his pride and his posturing.

Manfred was hovering, casting a shadow, looking for a story. But Steadman knew there was no vast plot, no conspiracy. No one had laid a trap for him. It was his own fault that he was being punished for pretending to be blind, his poisonous pride. And now, without drugs, without trying to deceive — in fact, against his will and to his shame; perhaps his body was saturated with the dirty drug — he was blinder than it was possible to imagine, as all the idle speculators had described. His blindness was the blindness of every cliché. He was in darkness like a wilderness of wool, his head wrapped, mummified, bent down and suffering the black misery of a frightened panting creature who expects at any moment to be pounced on.

Lost in the seamless darkness of his despair, he was accused of faking. The news was out. People were talking. Even in his blindness and seclusion he was not spared. Somehow — was it self-punishing? he wondered — he was still able to tell when people he knew well were lying to him. He heard hesitations, as though they were trying to minimize the rumors, but the hesitations only made them seem worse.

"I've heard a few things," Axelrod told him when Steadman asked, hoping to be reassured that there was nothing. "Pay no attention to them. They're cheap shots."

"Like what."

"Cheesy items on Page Six in the *Post*. 'Sightings.' No one takes any notice of them."

But Steadman knew that everyone read that column, and Axelrod's saying "items" alarmed him.

"Probably on the Internet, too," Steadman said, angling for a denial.

"Who looks at that crap?"

So it was true: accused of faking on a Web site, or more than one. He said, "Why don't we put out a statement — like a press release?"

"You mean a formal denial?"

"Why not?"

Axelrod hesitated so long, Steadman was demoralized before his editor finally replied.

"Overkill. It'll provoke questions. It could sink your book." Axelrod sounded as if he were trying to convince himself as well as Steadman. "Besides, why dignify this slander with a rebuttal? Take the high road."

"Take the high road" was worrying, too, for it meant a campaign had been mounted, and it always implied that, in the attempt to undermine him, some damage had already been done.

"The important thing is, how are you doing?"

"I've been better."

"The writer Eric Hoffer — *The True Believer*? — he went blind as a child," Axelrod said. "At the age of fifteen he suddenly got his sight back. Turned him into a reader."

"I hate heartwarming stories," Steadman said. "I went for a walk. I was mugged twice — lost my wallet and my watch. Couple of people swore at me."

"That's really horrible."

"Someone else gave me money."

"At least the sales are great," Axelrod said. He clearly wanted to change the subject.

Steadman took no pleasure in the news of his book's success. He saw his stumbling in the dark as punishment for it. Only now was he able to understand that he had not been blind before. He had been drugged. The condition that he had known was the opposite of this. He had to learn how to cope with his blindness, for instead of feeling liberated he was limited, he was diminished, and the pain was hard for him to bear.

Still he was accused of faking. He could not read the newspapers, nor would anyone read them to him. But he knew. One measure of the gossip was the number of requests for interviews, and they were incessant. Some were needling, others were meant to scrutinize or embarrass him. They used the seriousness of the gossip as the pretext for his breaking his silence.

"You'll only lose by hiding from the press," one woman told him. She said she was a journalist from a wire service; Steadman's statement would reach millions of readers.

"I have no statement."

"Give me a few minutes. Let me come over. It could help your credibility."

The very suggestion that his credibility needed help saddened him.

Saying no to everyone and screening his calls, he was condemned for being uncooperative. His insistence on seclusion was like proof of his guilt.

In his favor, the presidential scandal was being played out. People were obsessed with the unconvincing explanations for the president's behavior — talk of secret meetings and phone sex with the young woman, extravagant talk of trysts, the repetition of the expression "oral sex." And the accusations of another woman as well, who said the president had once exposed himself to her in a hotel room. She claimed that she could accurately describe the president's penis. This took up so much space in the papers that attention on Steadman was diminished, though several importuning journalists said, "You're behaving just like the president." The president, too, was saying nothing.

There had been a time when he had imagined that the president might become his protector, that his power might be useful to Steadman in some way — an asset, perhaps, that the president read him and recommended him and had invited him to the White House. That was no help now. The favor the president had done him was to become involved in such a steamy scandal of his own that the newspapers were crowded with stories of his duplicity, eclipsing the rumors about Steadman. Steadman imagined the rumors to be repeating that, far from being blind, he was a reckless fantasist who had experimented with a psychotropic drug that produced spells of blindness and a glow of hypersensitivity.

The basis for his imagining such details was that he knew the supposition to have been true. It was no longer. He was sightless, he was weak, and being in New York was like being in enemy territory. Even at the height of his fame as the author of *Trespassing* he had not been in greater demand. And it was all an agony to him.

He had given explicit instructions to the hotel that he was not to be bothered or phoned; no one was allowed to enter his room. And so the knock on his door early on the morning he was to leave for the Vineyard was unexpected. As always, he woke and felt like clawing his eyes when he realized that nothing had changed. He groped to the door and opened it, seeing nothing.

"No visitors," he said.

"It's me" — Ava. She thrust herself into the room and shut the door as he grasped at the air, flailing.

"I'm taking you home."

But he was struggling, saying, "Who's with you? There's someone else. Who is it?" Finally he allowed her to hold him, and when the door was kicked shut he began to cry.

FIVE

The Blind Man's Wife

1

From the moment he stepped off the clanking plates of the ferry ramp he was fearful. He stubbed his toe on the rim of the ramp's steel lip and stumbled ashore, flapping his arms for balance, feeling foolish as he toppled forward. Fog had delayed the flight to Boston, so they missed their connection; Ava drove a rental car to Woods Hole, where they caught the *Uncatena*. And when he was on the island, tasting abandonment, he thought, with a castaway's woe, What am I doing here?

There was something else on his mind, but it was unformed, a wordless worry, like a lowering cloud with a human smell. He was unable to work it out and frame it as a whole thought, because the Boston shuttle had so disoriented him. The fussing of flight attendants, the offers of a wheelchair, the unhelpful hands plucking at him, the puzzled fingers twitching on his arm, people jerking his sleeves, patting him in idiot attempts at consolation; the mutters of "Hang in there" and "Go for it, big guy" and "Right this way, sir" — the gauntlet of well-wishers every blind person ran into each day.

And on the ferry, he had stood at the forward rail, near the blunt bow — for the air, and to get away from Ava and her noisy pager and clamoring cell phone. A man and woman crept up behind him — newcomers, eager visitors — to coo at the seascape.

"Lookit, lookit, lookit."

"Whole buncha whitecaps," the man said. "And that sailboat, see, she's heeling over."

"Seagulls," the woman said.

"Following that fishing boat," the man said, "for the scraps. And the baby gulls dive-bombing for fish."

"Will you look at that," the woman said. "Ever see anything so gorgeous?"

They were talking to him, Steadman realized, and in the moment of addressing him and drawing level, they saw his dark glasses and his slender cane, and their mistake.

"Awful sorry," the man said in a voice he suddenly hushed, sucking it into his cheeks, abashed at seeing Steadman was blind. They made faces at each other, as people did in the presence of a blind person, and they whispered and stepped aside, chewing on their self-reproach.

"They're terns," Steadman said, "not baby gulls."

He remained facing forward, the southwest wind tearing at his ears.

Another voice, Indian or Pakistani, said, but not to him, "Is the Winyard," and soon the ferry was sounding its horn for the arrival in Vineyard Haven.

He was unsteady, he walked like a drunk, he was a stranger here, he did not belong to the place, he was intruding on someone else's island, trespassing again. The smells here were not just foreign, they were hostile; he did not understand any of the voices; he was shoved and jarred by the bumps in the road, battering the tires, and felt insecure being driven by Ava — faintly nauseated, anticipating more bumps, more curses.

Stiff and breathless with panic, he did not recognize the odor of the sea in the wind, which was like a flapping blanket, ragged with the smell of garbage, and the low-tide hum of dead fish and decayed kelp and the whiff of diesel oil. The sharpness of the sounds and stinks made him timid in the same way as, at the ferry landing, the sudden laughter of the crew had put him on edge. He imagined that they were laughing at his unsteadiness, and they got away with it because he was so cowed, so feeble-looking.

What was worse, the other wordless fear — and its cloudy ambiguity made it awful — was his sense of a third person with them. He had an intimation of another body in the rental car from Boston; someone with them in the passenger lounge of the ferry; the same person in the taxi and again in Ava's car from the Vineyard airport, where Ava had parked it, always sitting in the back seat ("You sit in front, Slade, with your long legs"), staring at the nape of his neck. They had not been alone. There had always been this third person with them who did not speak yet, who gave off a vaporous aura, a small breathing body humming with warmth.

He sat in the car, his damp hands holding the knobs of his knees, sensing this stranger behind him, a smirking eavesdropper — who?

"Aren't you glad to be back?"

Unusually for her, Ava drove badly, even worse when she was talking, too fast and then too slow, stamping on the gas pedal, cursing the car ahead, pitching Steadman forward when she braked.

He was mute with worry, retching each time he tried to swallow. He spat out the window and thought, Where am I?

"You're not wearing your seat belt."

She pulled off the road, spilling him sideways as the car rocked on the ridge of the shoulder. She fastened him in with reprimanding fingers, as though buckling a child into a baby seat, and then resumed the drive.

She was in charge; she made him feel lost and helpless. She too seemed like someone else, bigger than ever. The way she touched him had seemed rough and abrupt, and all the way from New York she had stayed on her cell phone, setting up appointments for her patients and picking up messages. She seemed less like a lover than a caregiver — one of her hospital words. Nevertheless he had no idea what he would have done without her. Yes, he knew, he would have died in New York, where a blind man was a victim of every stranger's indifference or fussy attention or reckless cruelty.

The lopsided fear of impotence that he recognized in himself from long ago heightened his notion of not belonging. He was frightened but he was passive, unresponsive, in a place that was so foreign he felt like a trespasser. That was another old feeling, but this time like a eunuch in a harem. The Vineyard was just a name; everything else was withheld from him.

He wanted to speak to Ava but did not know how to begin. Two thoughts tormented him — that he was in a strange place, that he had been abducted. The rest of his fragmented feelings he could not express. Had he been hit on the head and dragged away? He concentrated to listen to the harsh breathing of the person behind him, and realized the breathing was his own.

Ava said, "I've been talking to some lab people. I'll need a sample of your drug. I want to have it tested for toxicity. I don't know why I didn't do it before."

A crumbled plug of datura splinters was in a jar in his desk, hidden like an addict's stash. He had kept it just in case he might crave it. But he did not crave it; he was disgusted by the very thought of stewing it and drinking the brew.

He struggled to speak. He finally said with self-reproach, "I poisoned myself."

"You're alive. Your book is a hit. Be happy."

"I'm mutilated."

He was miserable, and when he got to the house he felt like a hostage and hated its harsh smells and thought, Who lives in this place?

Ava was on call. She was paged as soon as she entered the house. She tapped at her phone as she led Steadman to his study and eased him into his leather armchair.

"I have to go to the hospital — an emergency. I'll be back as soon as I can."

She put earphones into his hand and set a CD player in his lap, and she left. He did not switch it on. He sat with his head cocked, hearing someone sneaking around, two rooms away.

"I know you're here. You can't fool me."

Without conviction his voice sounded timid. The feeble echo returned his words to him.

"Who are you?"

Of course, by his blurting this out, whoever it was became very quiet.

"What do you want?"

The person had stiffened in a corner and was flattened against the wall.

"I may be blind, but I'm not stupid!"

He hated his weak screechy voice, and sitting there he reflected, sifting his thoughts, searching for reasons to hope. His discovery in his luminous phase, and the gusto of making his book, was that his sexual history was his own and not in any textbook, or any novel, or memoir. Similarities did not matter. All his travel and trespassing had prepared him for this revelation, which was a true epiphany, an actual encounter, something like being visited by an angel of desire, who had wakened in him the urge to be bold.

You carried on blindly in your life, never daring to believe that one day you would be granted the gift of sight. It was like travel to a strange land where you knew the language and loved the culture — strange and secret to everyone else but the only place on earth you could call your own. All his intelligence, his eloquence, his savagery, his pleasures, every fantasy that existed inside him, everything he wished to see manifested, all his desires realized — that was sex for him. He had lived in a state of apprehension; he had relived it with happiness and understanding, making it new, turning it into a book. Everything he had done in his life had been a preparation for this discovery, a rehearsal for that pleasure.

Now he was dumb and sightless and impotent once more, plunged into darkness, in a place where he didn't belong, not knowing (and still he heard the mewing of someone else in the house) whether he was alone. There was no safety here. His only home was inside his head. The blinding was like a castration.

He dozed in his chair and a door slam woke him. Either he had slept soundly or else Ava had not been long — whatever, he was hardly aware of having been left. He was not reassured; he felt ever more like a captive.

He wondered if by some diabolical ploy she had taken him to a different house, one that would trap him by being strange, for nothing in this house seemed familiar. But why would she do that?

Ava's confidence made her seem all the more important. She made announcements, loud declarations, as though to a roomful of listeners. "This is absolutely the best time of the year," and "I love driving on the island now," and "You see lots of migratory birds around."

Late spring, the trees in leaf, the branches bristling, each opening bud a gilded green, new growth like small healthy claws: that was how Steadman recalled it, yet he stared into empty air, trying to imagine the dusted buds swelling into blossoms, the lawns thick from the rain. As though describing a distant planet, Ava told him that the island was chilly and damp, but lovely with flowers — the magnolias were a mass of creamy pink petals with no leaves, the lilacs had never smelled sweeter, robins hopped in the driveway, looking confused in the chill. The roads were empty. Some roadsides were scattered with the last of the daffodils, going brown.

She must have looked at him then and seen that he was simply gaping, unmoved by her attempt to cheer him up with the description of the Vineyard spring.

He said, "I think there is someone in this house."

"Why do you say that?"

He marveled at this. "You didn't say no!"

"Because it seems such a paranoid thing to say."

"I knew there was no point in my mentioning it. I knew you'd deny it."

She did not reply. It maddened him when she fell silent.

"Who is it?"

After a long pause she said, "You're being unreasonable."

"Why don't you say 'There's no one here'?"

"Okay. There's no one here."

He tried to discern where she was standing. He turned to face her, to bear down on her. He said, "I don't believe you."

Her unexpectedly calm voice came from a different part of the room, behind him. "That's your problem. I think you're tired."

"Tired!" he shouted, sitting forward on his big chair and rocking as he spoke, like someone grieving. "I'm not tired, I'm half out of my mind. I can't see, I can't walk, I'm half deaf. I've turned into a lump. You have no idea. At the beginning of my book tour I was bursting with health, I could see everything, I had my drug — I hardly needed an escort. I was hallucinating in a surreal world of interviewers and bookstores." Saddened by the memory of it, he became breathless, but began again, his voice breaking. "And one day, without doing a thing, I lost it. I noticed the drug wasn't working in the same way. I got flashes of eyesight without drinking anything. Then my vision just clicked off and stayed off. And it wasn't like anything I had known. Some of my senses went with it. It was like I was being stifled. I felt small, I was in the dark. It's how I feel now. Don't you understand? I am terrified."

Ava knelt before him and took his hand. He could tell she was wearing her scrubs — a whiff of the hospital disinfectant still on them, and her hands so clean.

"I'm going to help you."

Her saying that, suggesting that he needed help and that she was turning him into her feeble patient, made him more miserable. He was reminded of how helpless he was without her. To be her patient was to be her captive; a sickroom was a cage. But he was too unhappy to say anything more.

Blind, illiterate, dumb, forgetful, stupid, sick — he felt less than a lump. The fact that she was in good health, and busy doctoring, only made him feel worse.

"After we get the lab results of the drug tests we'll know what our options are," she said. "I've got a lot of confidence in the people who'll do the analysis."

That did not console him, because he had not told her his deepest anxiety, that the darkness covering him now was like a funeral shroud. He was cold to her touch, he was mute unresponsive flesh, he was without a spark of desire, he was dead.

"Don't worry," she said, and touched him again.

Her uttering that empty expression filled him with despair. He shivered and drew back a little, covering himself, nudging her hand aside in an awkward gesture, almost prissy in its rejection.

Even his bed was unfamiliar, even Ava's body beside him, even her breathing. He had thought it was horrible to be blind and stumbling in New York, robbed and misled and abused, a jostled victim in the city. How could anything be worse? And he was mocked by everything he had done and said in the pompous elation of his drug vision. But it was so much worse to feel lost at home, for being a stranger here meant there was nowhere else to go.

Being outside the house was sometimes like being submerged, but more often he likened it to living under the great dark dome of a gigantic insect. An enormous spider had lifted itself and was poised upright on its long legs — that was the sky, the world, the darkness; and he was underneath the thing, in its prickling shadow.

Over the following few days, haltingly, sometimes tearful, he told Ava this. At first she seemed sympathetic. But when he complained more loudly at the injustice of it, she went quiet. Her silence was like an accusation that he easily imagined in her mind: *So whose fault is that?*

He had needed a key to unlock his memories, to gain access to the past. Manfred had found the datura. Sometimes he saw the German standing in the smoky village, beckoning him, not the Manfred he knew but a cleaner, devilish Manfred with a fiery light behind him and the ayahuasca vines twined in the trees around him, the vines that were smooth and coiled like the biggest snakes.

He had gotten the drug, he had finished his book, and the book had succeeded; he was famously blind. There were doubters and whisperers, but they had not seriously damaged him, and yet . . .

"I'm a prisoner," he said. "I'm completely dependent on you. I can't do anything without you."

He knew she was listening, sensed she was smiling — not in triumph but mildly amused at his choice of words, the melodrama. He was sure of it when she spoke next.

"Now you know what it was like for me."

2

HE FOUNDERED IN DARKNESS, choking and blowing and sculling with his hands like a drowning infant. He had lost the subtle syntax of his vision, his face was flooded, and he who had mocked the word "darkness" was drinking it, and hacking as it fouled his throat like muddy water and stung his nose like soot; he was submerged in it as it streamed past his eyes. He was upended, just like the nosy child who had wandered off and tumbled into a brimming barrel. He had not drugged himself, so he was fully awake in his unhappiness. He had listened to Manfred, but he had not volunteered for this.

The world he knew in this phase of his blindness was not passive. It was busy and hostile, and his own house rose against him, smacked his head, clawed his hands, twisted his legs, rapped his shins, tripped him, toppled him over. He had to be cautious; he had to creep. He sat for long hours fearing to move too much; he hardly walked. He had fallen and hurt his wrist and banged his elbow. Ava told him he was lucky it wasn't anything more serious. The darkness was hot, and summer was now upon the island.

Work was out of the question, and he feared the gaze of strangers. He felt wronged and old-womanish, unable to read or write. The radio was no relief; it blared the president's misery and satirized it. Steadman could not listen to the rumors and innuendos without being ashamed of the president's reluctant schoolboy confession, the ghastly details of it, a sneaky joyless muddle of cocksucking and cheap gifts and cold pizza. One rumor had the president on the phone, a wet cigar in his hand, the fat girl on her knees, her chubby fingers steadying his cock in her mouth. Another rumor concerned the existence of a semen-smeared dress.

The gleeful howls of the whole country against the president for his unconvincing denial and his paltry pleasure unnerved Steadman. People seemed not just glad that he had been exposed but giddy with relief that they themselves had not been caught. This summer everyone felt innocent and indignant. And the sanctimony of the reaction had its echo in the criticism of Steadman. Some people had listened to Manfred; some were howling in their own way against Steadman, believing that his drug-induced blindness was a ruse. But while the Internet buzzed with it, the press was single-minded in pursuing the president, overshadowing Manfred's whisper campaign with shouts of accusation and demands for the president to resign or risk impeachment.

"I have no intention of resigning," the president said. That emboldened Steadman. The president was facing and debating his critics, defying them, insisting that he was entitled to a private life, even if that meant enticing the fat girl to his office and groping her and making her kneel and ejaculating on her cheap dress.

Compared to this, Steadman's scandal was a trifle; nothing was pettier than a literary fuss. And who cared? *The Book of Revelation* was still selling well. There was no drama, only unanswered questions, and even these had died down. Yet Steadman was stone blind and crippled by it, beset by fugitive noises in the house that no longer seemed his own. He did not wear his stereo headphones anymore, because they interfered with his monitoring the movements of the intruder he suspected. The sounds of this stranger were incessant.

"Who's that?"

The faint scrape of guilty feet, perhaps the thin soles and light tread of a woman's shoes, then silence.

"Who's there?"

The click of a door shutting, the pad of retreating footsteps.

"I can hear you!"

But his shout created silence, and then he knew that the stranger had fled and that he was alone.

On the evenings when she wasn't at the hospital, Ava comforted him. She nursed him, sat and drank wine with him. She made the simple meals he requested, French fries and fish sandwiches and raw chopped vegetables. He ate with his hands, could not manage a spoon or fork; he often bobbled his glass and spilled his wine. His clumsiness at meals frustrated him. His stumbling enraged him. He was depressed by his inability to work.

He wanted to write a short story, something related to his condition. He imagined what it might be, not the details of the story but how it might look — like a folktale, that sort of compact narrative, full of shocks and reverses, of a blind man lost on an island, ironic with horror. He wanted to publish it to dramatize his pain, to show the world how he was suffering and to prove he was still writing. But the effort was more than he could bear, and except for the physical ache of his sadness, his head was empty.

Now and then he talked on the phone. Axelrod was a regular caller, giving him updates about sales, and the news was so good he felt fraudulent. He was embarrassed by the gusto in his book, shamed by all his hubristic boasts, for the truth was somber, a sad man in a dark house. He was not the character in that book; he was a damaged man, suffering a self-inflicted wound. Some people were still whispering about him: he knew he deserved it.

Ava seemed tender, yet he was convinced that she stayed with him unwillingly, just treating him and failing at it. She was dissatisfied, and who could blame her?

He told her this. He found a way of saying that he was unworthy of her.

Her reply was unexpected. She said, "You're the one who taught me that sex is selfish."

What sex? But he didn't ask. They had been home for more than a month now, and he had no desire; he had not touched her. Some days he was so absorbed by darkness he hardly recognized her.

He said, "I don't deserve you."

"Maybe it's nothing to do with you. Maybe I'm here for my own reasons."

This was a different Ava, the doctor not the lover, the pulse-taker, the clinician in all things. She seemed genuinely concerned with his condition: his blood pressure, his headaches, his tremulous hands, the effects of the drug on his nerves.

She was breezier, seemingly happier, more content now that she was spending so much time at the hospital. It was clear to Steadman that the amanuensis, the facilitator of transcription, and the checker of manuscripts were not roles that Ava had had any liking for. And that suggested to him that the sexual roles he had assigned her she had acted out with some reluctance. How was he to have known? She had been frenzied, so convincing a sex partner he had known her only as his lover.

He was chair-bound now most of the time; they had not made love. Yet she did not comment, didn't reproach him, didn't even allude to it. All those steamy druggy months of dressing up, trawling in his memory, and now nothing.

She said, "I'm expecting the results from the lab any day now."

Bucking him up with science and changing the subject, she put no pressure on him.

The results came as a computer printout, perforated pages that she rattled and unfolded. He imagined it as something like a DNA report, with inky furrows and squiggles, a smudged hand-drawn document with the look of a musical score.

He prodded her several times with questions before she said, "It's inconclusive."

"But what does it say?"

"There's some heavy-duty alkaloids in that residue. They're trying to sort out how they combine with enzymes. How they affect the synapses. They also think that there have been Latin American studies on people who've regularly taken it. Maybe case histories of those Indians."

"What does that mean?"

"According to this analysis, datura contains a group of alkaloids called beta-carbolines. The psychotropic trigger is a substance called harmine."

The very word seemed dangerous and hurtful.

"Its overuse can lead to insanity or, it says here, blindness." She was speaking reasonably, interpreting the document, folding it and turning pages. "But there's a note saying that the lab is still trying to separate these elements of the drug. If we know the cause, we might find the cure."

Steadman said, "You're right. This is my own fault."

"I never said that."

"But you thought it."

"No. I was on that trip too, remember. I admired you for taking a risk."

"And look where it got me."

He was sitting upright, rigid, like a man in a straight-backed chair about to be electrocuted.

377

"There's something called atropine in this drug. I know what that is from med school. We use it to dilate the pupil. Maybe it's combined with another chemical that affects the whole of the eye and the optic nerve."

He had risked that poison for an ambitious idea. And now he contemplated the book's success as he sat alone, lost in his house, a parody of the man the papers had praised on his tour: "a visionary writer more dazzling as a blind man than most people are who are blessed with eyesight." He had secretly believed himself to be a prophet, the tiger of a new religion. He had boasted of x-ray vision and declared, "Blindness is a gift." All that showboating, flourishing his cane like a huckster in a carnival. And it had begun with Manfred, downriver in the Oriente. He had drunk this toxic cocktail of murky jungle chemicals; he had been granted his wish, and now was in the dark.

He stumbled constantly, shuffled like an old geezer, not daring to lift his feet; he knocked things over, he fell. In his own house, the world he knew best, he was like a phantom. When Ava was at the hospital he sat fiddling with the radio, listening to the news of the president's deceptions. He was appalled at how people hated the man, the things they said, the jokes they told, the merciless mockery. He imagined them turned against himself. He longed for Ava to return. He urged her to work at night so he could share her waking hours. He felt needy and superfluous and humiliated.

He drank more and, drunk one evening when Ava got home, he confided in her. Embarrassed, yet determined to bare his soul, he told her of his insecurity, his timidities, his dreads; he reproached himself, he was abject, he said he was being punished for taking the drug.

"I knew what I was doing. It's just a cop-out to blame Manfred. I'm in a hell of my own making."

Ava listened. She seemed very calm, but it could have been fatigue — she was so weary after work. She said, "I'm in the business of healing people. I want you to trust me."

Shamed by his dependence on her, he saw that she welcomed it; she seemed to be strengthened by his pitiful surrender. He knew he was not imagining this, for she took him on her lap and cradled his head. The effect of his dependence roused something that was both maternal and sexual in her. As though gratified by his expression of helplessness, she held him with tender hands and stroked his hair; she had not touched him that way for a long time.

"You're going to be fine."

She could have been talking about his impotence as well as his blindness. He was mortified by her pity.

She was wearing her scrubs, which were stiff and slightly rough to the touch. No lingerie, no perfume, no silks. He wondered, as though he were a patient supine in a hospital bed, whether she was comforted somehow by dressing in this clinical way and caressing him.

"Just relax. Clear your mind. Don't even think about sex."

He had not been — far from it. If only she knew. He had been imagining with horror the remainder of his life in darkness, the shadow of neglect, the obscurity of seeing nothing but the prison cell of blindness, which was both a tiny suffocating space and the emptiness of the entire unavailable world.

She was touching his face softly with her fingers, tracing his features. She lifted the shirt of her scrubs and supported her breast with her hand, grazing his lips with her nipple, saying, "Take me into your mouth. Bite me a little, suck me."

Her taking the initiative now, as he was suffering — her attempt to interest him in sex — left him feeling awkward and faintly repelled and ever more the captive. He had no hunger, and dread had killed his desire.

One of her hands was behind him, steadying his head; her other hand, feeding her breast to him, pressed her nipple against his mouth. Lying against her, he heard her sigh, her whole body rippling with satisfaction.

She was warm and sexual, yet he was heavy, tense, unresponsive, and he was on the point of asking her, "What do you want me to do? Tell me, I want to please you," as she had once asked him.

She seemed to understand, and in her crooning way she said, "You've got to stop thinking about your anxieties. Just let yourself float free. Can you do that, baby? It's like finding the confidence and relaxation to be buoyant in a deep sea. Remember the first time you lay back in the ocean and let yourself float?"

But he lay as though afraid of drowning, his body locked and thick with misery.

"I want you to imagine being in water. Just let go, relax, and let it happen."

She went on gently encouraging him, as if he felt apart, like a spectator at the edge of sex; and powerless, he sank in her arms and prepared himself to be weightless.

"Sex can be a way of seeing. You know that."

He was hardly listening. His mouth was on her, he was comforted by her, and he was so absorbed, lying against her bare stomach, he really did seem to become less heavy, almost buoyant, her arms glowing on him. With this levitating sense of pleasure seeping into him, he felt detached and stopped listening to her. And Ava went on talking in a low regular cadence, as though to someone else, as he lay sucking on her nipple, the softness of her breast squashed against his cheek.

"Is that nice?"

As she spoke another hand crept across his leg from below and followed the seam on the fly of his jeans, feeling for his cock through the dense layer of cloth, the busy fingers asking a general question. And a moment later he felt his jeans being unfastened and loosened and tugged down. How could this be? He felt Ava's two hands, one under his head, the other directing her breast. He was outstretched on the sofa, sleepy and slightly drunk, yet aware of the odd number, the insinuation of the third hand.

He made a move to pull away. Ava said, "Just let it happen," and the ghost-like hand groped further, the fingers manipulating him until it was no longer so strange. Then the searching of a licking tongue and the heat of an eager mouth.

Burying his face in Ava's breast, Steadman became fearful as the other mouth nuzzled him and enclosed his cock, at first gently, in a tasting way, and finally with gusto, sighing, the sighs sounding within his flesh and swelling. In a twinge of alarm, he let one hand trail down until he could feel the long hair of the woman below. She was wearing a studded leather dog collar that was tight on her neck. He felt further, into the warm declivity of her shoulder, and grazing his knuckles on her smooth cheek, he let his hand fall, and was greatly relieved when it found the fullness of her breast. She must have been kneeling next to the sofa, leaning across his legs, as though drinking at a fountain. Her breasts hung loose, slack and soft, and danced in his hand.

Unexpected light blazed in his mind. He surrendered to the caresses, and for the longest time on the sofa in the warm room he lay half smothered, half floating, while Ava consoled him. Or was she speaking to the other woman? There was a confidence in the way she spoke, almost as if she were gloating. It ceased to matter, for at last the separate strands of his desire became a knot, and the knot began to twist in his guts, and it slipped and tightened in his groin until it was an animal's cramp of tortured muscle. In an instant it was yanked hard and it liquefied, spilling warmth all over him. He cried out once, and then he was raw and innocent again.

He sank into sleep, and was unconscious, wrapped in a happy dream of release. He had regained his eyesight. Sex had freed him. He recalled how he had suspected that there had been another person in the house — the shadow, the presence, the odd sounds. In his dream he was in the White House, at a jostling press conference in which he was doing all the talking to a respectful crowd. But he was defiant, tearful, saying "See? I was right!"

3

Feeling for Ava with creeping spider-like fingers in the bed when he woke, not knowing whether it was day or night, he found her arm and grasped it. At once he was doubtful, remembering. "Is that you?" She kissed him and drew him to her. He kissed her shoulder in a grateful way. She was happy, he could tell, not by anything she said — all she did was murmur — but by the teasing sigh in her throat, a simple grace note of irony.

"Who was that woman?"

"What does it matter if you liked what she did?"

He wondered whether he had really enjoyed it, because it had been so unexpected and unasked for, too sudden to savor. He did not reply at first; he considered that Ava, with her customary doctor's thoroughness, had been preparing the encounter for weeks. He had to admit that he had finally been aroused, coaxed out of his impotence. But the truth was that he had felt lost in the act, slightly panicky and bewildered, too startled to be possessed. He had been foundering and flailing at the periphery of her pleasure. Her enjoyment had disturbed him.

"I loved it," he said.

From the way her body settled as she was pressed against him, he knew it was the answer she wanted. Still, he felt the need to apologize.

"Maybe it's because I'm feeling so anxious about my eyes. I can't believe I'm so feeble."

"You were blind before. You were blind for months. And you managed."

"It was nothing like this. That was a kind of insight — you know! This is a prison. It's punishment. And I'm not taking the drug"

"There's such a thing as discontinuation syndrome."

"I'm afraid to go very far." He was too humiliated to say that he feared to leave the house at all.

"You should try. You're stronger than you think."

"Find me an eye doctor," he said. "Please help me."

"I have one lined up. She's in Boston. She makes a monthly visit to the island. She'll see you and run some tests."

"What do I do in the meantime?"

"Write your story. You said you wanted to."

He had told her of the short story he had planned, something like a Borges tale, compressed and allusive, something he would publish to prove that he was able to work. But all he had was a vague notion of the form; he had no narrative, no characters, no names or incidents.

"Nothing," he said, summarizing what was in his mind.

"Can't we do this?" She felt for him, but playfully.

Sex was like an intrusion, a hovering threat that made him feel small. When she touched him he felt clumsy and ignorant, like a big goofy boy intimidated by the mysteries of life and death, darkness and light, thinking, What will I do when I grow up? He had lost the ability to take a walk, to drive down the road, to sail a boat, to swim. He was a cripple, blind and incapable in the most fundamental way. Listening to the radio humbled him by reminding him of how futile he was, twisting a knob, holding his pathetic earphones. Though he struggled, mumbling to himself, he could not read or write, and even his speech seemed to be impaired. Half the time he stammered, unsure of whether he had a listener. For sex, for any pleasure, he needed the insight he had known before: the liberation of light.

What convinced him of that was the third hand of the night before. At one point in the intensity of his arousal, during the cramped convulsive unknotting, the sudden slippage of his ejaculation, he had sensed a sliver of light pierce his eyes. But no sooner had it blazed within the crevice of its narrow entry than it was gone. It was another reminder of what he had lost. He could not think of sex without feeling sad.

"Anyway, I was right," he said, remembering the niggling thought. But it was a victory of sorts for him, something he badly needed. "There was someone in the house."

Instead of speaking, Ava kissed him, but in a thoughtful way, holding her lips against his as though replying. She was always so scrupulous. She might refrain from responding but she never lied to him. He wondered what lesson there had been in her life that prevented her from deceiving him. Perhaps her study of medicine: the exactitudes of science had kept her truthful.

"Maybe I'm not as blind as I thought I was."

"Gotta go," she said, and bounded out of bed. "I'll be late."

He lay in bed trying to recall details of the night before. He had resisted, he had felt enticed, but he had little memory of it. The third hand had been like a wicked imp emerging from the darkness.

Before Ava left for the hospital, she said, "Try to get out today. Call a taxi, go into town. It'll do you good."

But when she was gone he became self-conscious, believing the other woman might still be in the house. He listened hard for a telling sound. Walking, he held his arms out, feeling his way forward, prepared to defend himself. His greatest fear was that without warning a stranger would touch him.

"If you're here, say something."

From the way his voice rang in the room he guessed there was no one, that she had gone.

He moped all morning, and toward midafternoon he called the taxi service and asked to be dropped on Main Street. "You going to be all right?" the young driver said with the bossy insincerity all the rest of them showed. In Vineyard Haven Steadman could tell that the sidewalk was busy with shufflers, but he also heard the remarks of people making way for him, even heard his name whispered several times, and "the writer."

Moving slowly, tapping his cane, he did not fall, and he was encouraged to walk farther than he had planned. He made it past the deli, the gift shops, the Bunch of Grapes bookstore, the drugstore, and kept going, past the bank and the bagel shop. He was still going slowly but, more confident, more upright, now he guessed he was on West Chop Road — no people crowding him. A car with a rapping engine pulled beside him and a man's voice called out, "Slade Steadman."

Steadman stopped and, taking care, angled his body toward the street.

"Let me give you a lift."

The car door slammed. The man was close to him, nudging him.

"Do I know you?" Steadman asked.

"Don't think so, but I sure know you. Here, get in," and the man guided him into the car. Steadman was too tired and confused to resist. "You're not safe stumbling around like that," the man said.

"I wasn't stumbling." Steadman spoke so sharply the man was silent. "Who are you?"

"Whitey Cubbage?" the man said in a querying way. "I guess your friend didn't like that," as if he had already forgotten Steadman was blind.

"What friend?"

But the man didn't seem to hear. He drove on, narrating: "Lovely day . . . Damned cyclists . . . God, they're tearing down the Norton place" — and soon made a turn. The car engine strained, seeming to climb a steep driveway, and with the car on this incline he stopped and yanked the hand brake.

"Where are we?"

"I live here," the man said testily, as though rebuffing an ignorant question. "Come on in. Bet you could use a cup of coffee."

He helped Steadman out of the car, and was so abrupt and impatient, leading him so clumsily, that Steadman stumbled on the porch steps. Seeing Steadman on his knees, holding the handrail, the man apologized.

"Can't kill *you*," he said. "You're the writer."

"Yes."

"And you've got everyone dogging your heels."

Cubbage guided Steadman like an usher, cupping his elbow, steering him to a chair. The house smelled of unwashed clothes, and though he heard a clock marking time like a metronome, there was a great stillness, as of tightly shut windows. A trapped fly buzzed and bumped one windowpane. A faucet dripped, drops plopping into a brimming sink basin. Cats, too — Steadman smelled the litter box and heard the complaining purrs, some of them like swallowed bubbles. The whole world was shut out, and the stinks shut in.

"I know it's a mess."

"It's fine," Steadman said. "But I have to go."

"You haven't even heard my story yet."

The man's voice was wet-eyed and jowly, and the implacable ticks of the loud clock made his procrastination absurd.

"Got the plans of this house out of *Popular Mechanics*. Want to buy it? If you don't, my idiot son will get it. It'd cost you less than a million. You could write a great book here."

Steadman said, "Is that your story?"

"Of course not," Cubbage said. "Listen, you shouldn't pay a blind bit of notice to what people say. There's no connection between anything you've done and this damn president."

"Who said there was?"

"I don't know, it's going around," the man said carelessly. He seemed to be stirring his hand in a cardboard box of oddments, because he made a clattering, the scrape of loose paper and the clink of trifles. Then came four clear notes of a banjo. "This is a little thing called 'Sleepy Time Gal.'" He began strumming, but his plucking slowed and stopped as he began to sob miserably. "It's my wife," he said. He snuffled snot and tears. "Cancer took her. Forty-two years we were married. You can't replace someone like that."

"I'm very sorry," Steadman said.

"Do you know what true love is?"

In a voice like stone Steadman said, "No."

"Go ahead" — and he plucked the banjo again, a twangling note — "make me an offer on the house."

"I can't stay here any longer," Steadman said.

"What about my story?"

"I'm late for an appointment."

"Don't you realize I saved you back there, from those people?"

"What people?"

"The ones following you. Looked like they wanted to pester you. And that man?"

"What man?"

"Dogging your heels."

"Can you describe him? What did he look like?"

"How am I supposed to know what he looked like?" Cubbage was on his feet. "You're the writer — you describe him."

In a mood of resentment Cubbage fumbled and bullied Steadman down the stairs and into the car. Because of all the one-way streets, he took him by the back route down to the taxi stand at the ferry landing.

"That's the thanks I get," Cubbage said.

"I'll call you," Steadman said, to pacify him.

By the time he got home he could tell from the descent of cool air and the dropping of the wind that night had fallen. He also suspected from the way Ava spoke to him that she was not alone. Something dense, like a thickness of cloth, blotted the echo of Ava's voice in the room.

She said, "I was beginning to think you'd taken up residence somewhere else."

The choice of words, too — the sort of facetious and brittle formality a person used when someone else, someone who mattered, was listening.

Steadman was too rattled to banter with her, and he was acutely aware from the pulse of the stranger's breathing that this other person was watching closely.

"What about that doctor who was going to examine me?"

"All in good time." Another stagy and supercilious phrase, meant to be overheard. "Now, how about a drink?"

It was all like theater, all the obvious talk, but he was lost here. He said, "Okay," and felt for his armchair. Sitting, drinking, he was weighted with a sense of captivity. Ava had put the glass of wine into his hand. She lingered beside him.

"I've been waiting for you."

Her growly affection was unambiguous: she wanted sex. Yet he had hardly recovered from the old man's weeping and bullying and the crazy interlude in his house, which was like an abduction. *Do you know what true love is?* and *Dogging your heels* — what was that all about? He was rueful: a blind man was everyone's victim.

"I had an insane afternoon," he said. "I did as you suggested. I went into town. I almost fell down about fifty times. I think I was being followed. Some crazy old bastard was after me."

"Come over here," Ava said. "You need to relax."

She helped him to his feet. She led him onto the carpet and had him crouch and lie down. She put a pillow under his head.

As he lay, letting her fumble with his belt buckle, she radiated warmth, hovering over him. He tried to imagine her propped on one arm, leaning to tug his jeans off. But apart from a vague picture of her warm presence, he got nowhere and was conscious only of his naked legs stretched out. Even when she touched him, using her fingers and then her mouth to arouse him, he felt unfocused and unprepared.

"I'm sorry."

He struggled to fantasize, yet his sense of being trapped, a reminder of the afternoon, crowded and distracted him. A hardening spark in his flesh gave him hope, but was more light than heat. He wanted to be overwhelmed, and he knew that was what Ava wanted. He lay on his back as though adrift, and she worked on him, squealing, her mouth filled with his flesh. When he was harder she mounted him. She rode him with furious impatience, and he was like a woman again, wincing beneath her thrusts.

"Now, yes, that's what I want," she said.

From the directness and practicality of her tone he knew she was not talking to him. A moment later he was nudged, something pressing his ear, and then his head was gripped and a mass of moist flesh settled against his face, warm soft skin at his ears, his nose and mouth brushed by the lips of a dripping vulva.

As Ava rode him, the other woman's body rose and fell against his face, as if in the saddle of a cantering horse. Each time she lifted herself, releasing his ears, he could hear her squeals — and the sighs of Ava's rapture, too, as she steadied the woman and kissed her. It was not the fierce kissing he had known, but a gentle chafing of soft lips and the pressure of fondling hands.

Her version of pleasure was so single-minded she made him feel more like her prisoner than her lover. Ava had taken charge again, but hers was not the tentative and maternal breastfeeding embrace of the night before. It was a piling on, aggressive and deliberate, an act in which he was a passive supine detail, something for the women to sit on and ride while they hugged and kissed. Lying there, he understood that he was an aspect of Ava's fantasy, but not the object of it, not the center of her attention. There was no rapture for him, no tenderness, and now, as he was pummeled, hardly any arousal.

The nameless person, the silent woman, was smearing his face, stifling him as he gasped for breath. He was pinned to the floor, the weight of the two bodies on him, his cock feeling twisted and raw from being ridden, his whole head burning from the hot clamp of the bare legs. They went on, like delirious children assaulting a giant. And he was rubbed and smacked, the heat of that wet rag of flesh like being slapped in the face with raw meat.

In the women's concentration on each other he was denied his orgasm, though they enjoyed a moment of frenzy together, yelping in triumph, sounding girlish. They didn't seem to notice him then, but when they were done, laughing softly, shivering into each other's arms, they gathered him up and helped him to bed.

"I hope we didn't hurt him," the woman said as they left the room.

There was so much he didn't know. He lay there feeling bruised. All this time and he hardly knew anything.

For the following few days Ava worked odd hours again. Steadman brooded on his humiliation. The next time she was on the day shift and they had dinner together at home, he tried to broach the subject. He did not know where to begin. Never mind the visiting woman; who had Ava become, and what did she want?

"Shouldn't we be talking about that" — he fished for the right word — "that encounter?"

"That was my encounter, not yours," she said, sure of herself. "So there's nothing to talk about. I just want you to know it's not retributive."

But he thought "retributive" was exactly what it was — retribution for the months and months of making his book, for the years of living his life, for his choosing the drug. And the retaliation was her way of showing him that she now knew what he had known all along, that sex was a different route, a different destination, for each person. Approaching that land of desire, one person saw a mountain and another a valley, a foreign landscape and culture, a confusion of language and costume. So that in any act of sex one person was at home feeling all the gusto and satisfaction of security, and the other was trespassing.

"I want to talk about it."

"You'll just interrogate me. I hate your writer's questions." As she spoke she got up and busied herself in the kitchen. "I'm happy. Therefore, there's nothing to discuss."

He didn't pursue her, but he was sorry. He had wanted to explain that fear had robbed him of his libido.

A few days later he slipped into bed and was embraced. He did not know at first that it was the other woman until she kissed him and sighed. Bodies could seem almost identical, but a voice, a murmur, a kiss, they were a person's uniqueness. And there was an odor — of breath, of skin and hair — that was singular, too.

He let himself be embraced and caressed, and he almost apologized for his futility when Ava slid into the bed behind him and snuggled up to him. Though she was against his back, everything about her was familiar. He was in the middle. He knew that he was somehow necessary to them, yet from their gropings that they were more interested in each other than in him. And so they lay tangled, but he knew that only he was in darkness.

The next morning, finding himself alone, he called Ava on her cell phone and left a message saying that they had to talk, and how about a drink somewhere? Ava returned the call later and said that she had reserved a table at the Dockside, overlooking the harbor in Oak Bluffs. She would pick him up after work. He took this as a good sign, something sentimental; it was the place he had brought her on their first date, where she had wept, realizing that he was the author of *Trespassing*.

"Your table is outside, as you requested," the waitress said. She led them to it and took their order, two glasses of Merlot.

When she was gone, Ava said, "I love to see the island people waiting to meet the ferry. The bossy posture. The way they stand on the pier with their arms folded, searching for their friends on the boat. They seem so confident. 'Here I am. I belong here. I'm going to take care of you.'"

She was not looking at him. Was she glancing down the pier where the *Island Queen* had just docked?

"What are you talking about?" Steadman said. She was speaking like a woman in a play, not listening, just making a superfluous pronouncement, pleased with herself, thinking she was giving information.

"Ah, here's our drinks," Ava said. This was also spoken like a line in a play.

Steadman sulked, thinking of his unwritten story, while the glasses of wine were set down. When he was sure the waitress had left, he said, "Can't you see I'm miserable?"

Ava said, "It's a beautiful evening. The harbor is full of sailboats. You've got a drink. We're together. Why don't we simply enjoy what we have?"

"What *is* this?" he said. She was haughty and enigmatic, and everything she said sounded stilted and fictional, as though she were not talking to him but merely reciting lines. "I don't want to hear about the boats. I can't see a thing."

"I'll be your eyes for a while."

"I can't read or write. I can barely think straight. Find me that specialist. Why don't you help me?"

He meant to challenge her, but she surprised him, saying with amused detachment and with an archness he had never heard her use before, "Maybe what we're doing with my friend will help you."

It was the sort of thing he might have said before: sex as a cure, sex as vision, sex as blinding light, sex as a miracle drug.

He said, "Maybe you're just using me."

"This is an opportunity. Don't ask me to explain it, but I know I won't have another chance like this again."

Women were usually spoken about by men — and by other women — as casualties of indecision, fretful, always on the hook, helpless, forever trifled with. But that had not been his experience at all. Men were the ditherers, the smilers, the feckless triflers. Men were fritterers, too: they took their time, because they had plenty of time. But women were remorseless timekeepers, ruthlessly so sometimes — certainly the women he had known in his life. They had given the impression of being passive and submissive, but they were not indifferent, far from it. They were watchful, perhaps silent, but obsessively alert, like raptors awaiting their chance.

And when the opportunity arose they knew it, and they pounced and gave it everything they had. He admired that, the way they singled out a choice and went for it.

"You like that other woman," he said.

"You can't imagine."

Ava was smiling, he was sure of it, but he could not say how he knew — something in her tone.

Ava was another raptor. She had found someone else, and it so happened the lover was a woman. He was in between and felt weirdly privileged and perverse. He had never seen this ferocity in Ava, and he took it to be love.

"How was that Merlot?" the waitress said when Ava asked for the check.

"Very nice," Ava said.

"Fine," Steadman said.

"And how about that frozen daiquiri?"

What frozen daiquiri? Steadman thought.

"It was fabulous." A woman's voice at the same table — how was that possible? But as soon as he asked himself the question, he knew the answer.

And that night was another night with the other woman.

4

SUMMER NIGHTS on the Vineyard, thick with humidity, saturated with the rush of the tide, its lift and splash, its ebb that left bubbling mudflats, and the warmed blossoms of *Rosa rugosa*, a dustiness of daylilies and the sweet decay of leaf piles and pinched acorns under the scrub oaks: he knew every detail and still felt that he was trespassing. The sociable people on the island for the season rushed from party to party. Even Ava was on the circuit, perhaps with her woman friend — how was he to know? His friends called — Wolfbein was persistent — but Steadman made excuses and stayed home. He had discovered that going out was dangerous.

The seamless dark turned him into a pedantic clown in a gloomy farce, intending to be serious as he stumbled and fell. He was so lost he began to question whether he had been blind before. He repeated to himself with disbelief that this was like nothing he had ever known.

Even those times years ago on the *Trespassing* trip when he had woken in a reeking room in the middle of the night, gasping and swallowing black air and the shit stink of a rural village, not the slightest idea where he was. Burma? Bangladesh? Assam? That simple confusion, which cleared up at daybreak, was better by far than this. What he knew now was trespassing with the direst consequences. No way out. He seemed to exist in a deep hole, with all the stifling cushions of night stacked upon him, making him very small.

How could he beg for pity? Yet he wanted sympathy. Ava had a bystander's slack attention. Would she listen to him? The curse of his involuntary blindness she seemed to regard as no more than another distraction, hardly amounting to an event, more like the continuation of his extended and episodic egotism as the famous recluse. He was another patient clamoring to be seen — at least that was how she made him feel. Her cold gaze held him in an unsubtle way as merely disabled, rather inconvenienced, somewhat bothered. And he felt he was dying.

His state of mind was the opposite of his old settled writing mood — the drug mood, which was bliss, and which he assumed by drinking datura. The mood that he put on, the mood that wore off. That was in the past, a game he had learned, and it no longer served him. He was now desperate. He had no control over this imprisoning shadow. He had not used the drug for months.

"I like the imagery," Ava said when he told her these things. "But it's like poetry, pretty but vague. It doesn't help in making a diagnosis."

Her pauses made him suspect that she might be taking notes about his condition. Something in her nose-breathing, air pauses like punctuation, suggested she was writing. She didn't deny it.

"I always update my case histories."

He tottered toward her on crooked unbelieving clown's feet, his arms extended. "I'm a case history?"

"Just an expression."

Still, it baffled him. And the confident way she said that, the way he was unsteady, groping for the arm of a chair that had been moved — and where was the sofa he had always used for dictation? — it all threw him. His disorientation robbed him of his sense of security and, worse, seemed to whisper that the house was not his anymore. The whole carefully built estate belonged to her and to her passions now.

"I don't mean to minimize the bother."

"Bother?" He tried to get his face close to hers, to show how strongly he objected to this belittling word.

"Slade, you've been this way for a year and a half."

Even she, the physician, avoided the word "blind."

"Not like this." In spite of himself he could not contain the scream in his voice, and that also made him feel small.

She didn't understand that the prescience he had experienced before as a mind reader, and the dark helplessness he felt now as an ignorant cripple, were two opposite modes of being. Maybe the drug had not really blinded him before but only given him a convincing illusion of blindness.

He knew that drinking even a drop of the drug had heightened his perceptions to the point where he was hyperreceptive to all physical stimuli. But there was an imaginative dimension, too. He was given so precise a memory that all experience was available to him — not just his ability to view the present: he was granted such an exalted reverie of insight that he saw both past and future illuminated in the diamond-bright datura darkness of his drug trance, which was a starry night of unlimited knowing in dripping stipples of color.

But now he had a bag over his head. He could not walk without stumbling, and his speech was affected, too. He spoke in a tentative and halting way, in a calling-out voice, never sure whether anyone was listening. Stammering and stumbling were similar uncertainties, and his loss of sex drive seemed to be related — blind and faltering in every way.

Wasn't it obvious to her that feeling powerless terrified him?

"Are you there? Say something."

"I'm listening."

"Who is that woman?"

Ava made a mirthful noise in her throat. She said, "Don't you like her?"

"I've got other things on my mind."

"But I don't."

He had suspected all along, but he was sure of it then: the woman was her opportunity. And what was he? "So you really are using me."

"I promise I will do everything I can to make you well," Ava said. "The specialist, the tests — I told you."

"I think you're playing some kind of game with me."

"Nothing that should surprise you."

"That woman —" he began to say.

Interrupting him, she said, "Don't tell me you're shocked." She was playful, slightly mocking and resentful. "I don't want to be your dolly. I *was* your dolly. And now are you saying you don't want to be my dolly?"

While she was speaking he screamed, a horrible incompetent honking, just to shut her up, and then he screamed again, "I can't see a fucking thing!"

He shattered the air in the room and shocked her into silence. He hadn't wanted to raise his voice and betray the extent of his fear. But now she knew. He sensed her coming near him. Before, he would have known what was in her mind; would have seen into her heart, would have been able to turn away and sweep out of the room. But all he knew now was a lurking shadow and her unsteady breathing. She clasped his hands in hers.

"I'll look after you," she said. "Please don't worry."

He wanted to weep with confusion.

"But don't deny me my pleasure," she said. "I've never denied you yours."

He didn't believe her. That was another effect of his darkness. Nothing was real; even voices were false. Ava's reassurance just depressed him. The more certain-sounding the promise, the less he was convinced. He was sure she was procrastinating, and selfishly, so she could go on involving him in her dalliance with her woman friend. And what he would have found pleasurable before was a torment to him now.

The woman did not show up after that conversation. Maybe his scream of "I can't see a fucking thing!" had given Ava pause. Or maybe the woman had been present and had heard it, and had fled.

The echo of that fearful scream went on booming in his mind. It finally resolved itself into an angry idea, like a tight whipping wire. He saw a wicked fable, not as a narrative but as a vivid picture.

He remembered *The Sleeping Herdsman,* a postage-stamp-sized Rembrandt etching he had once seen, showing a man with a beard dozing in a grove of trees and near him a smiling and impish young woman, his wife or lover, fondled by a young man while the older man snoozed and his cow gaped. But there was a wickeder version. Not a sleeping man but a blind man trapped by his lover, the man a naïve blunderer, the woman a calculating plotter.

The picture in his mind was a summing up of the whole drama. In the foreground, the blind man was sitting blank-faced in a garden, while nearby a gleeful woman with her legs apart was being mounted by a goggle-eyed youth — and the long-haired youth could have been a girl. The drama was straightforward and the image stayed in his memory, like the Rembrandt or a stark woodcut in a book of fables. This one would have been titled "The Blind Man's Wife."

She was the central figure, with her welcoming embrace; the blind man was helpless and fooled, the embodiment of inaction. It was impossible to tell from his ambiguous expression whether he knew what was happening, but even if he did, what could he do except rage at his blindness?

For that reason — the shame of it — Steadman did not rage. He persisted, though. He was so demoralized by seeing nothing, by writing nothing, by his dependence on Ava, that only this mocking picture of a betrayed man gave him hope.

Ava went on promising that the doctor would visit. And some days later the doctor came. Was it a few days? Was it a week or more? He didn't know. He was blind to the passage of time, too.

"I'm going to ask you to sit right here next to me."

It took him a moment to realize that the doctor was a woman. She was all business. This was not the lover — he understood that immediately from Ava's deference.

"Let me give you a hand," the doctor said when she saw him groping.

Her big hands wrapped his in their soft pads. An odor of strong soap and salty sweat told him that she was plain and heavy. She led him haltingly to a chair.

"Darling?" he called out.

"Dr. Katsina's in the other room."

Her familiarity with the layout of the house perplexed Steadman, and it made him feel like more of a stranger himself.

"Just relax for me."

She held his chin, and he could tell from the warmth on his eyes that she was shining a light into them, one then the other.

"Are you taking any medication?"

"No."

"No drugs?"

His mouth was woolly as he said, "No drugs."

"Any discomfort?"

He hesitated then, for the agony of his blindness was like a raw seeping wound in the torn-open meat of his body, which prevented him from being able to think about anything else.

"None."

She put a cuff on his arm, cinching it with Velcro, and took his blood pressure. She made notes; he heard the rattle of the paper, the click of her ballpoint. She was hovering near his face. He sensed her breath, felt her fingertips positioning his head; she was peering at him.

"What color is this?"

"I don't know."

"Can you see the light?"

"No."

She seemed to be taking measurements and noting them. She did not say anything more to Steadman, but after she left the room, he heard her speaking in an undertone to Ava.

"I've got a slot later this afternoon."

Such was Steadman's vagueness that he did not know the doctor had gone until Ava told him. And then he said he resented the fact that he had been left out of the discussion. Ava ignored this and said if he was willing, he could be examined further at the hospital. He agreed but halfheartedly: he had little willpower. His blindness had demoralized him, lowered his spirits. These days he woke in the morning and expected nothing except more darkness.

On the way to the hospital, nothing was familiar. Even his own car, the sound of the gravel in his driveway, the route to town with all its turns and stops, it was all strange. He stood, gangly and hapless, while Ava signed him in. Then, assisted by an orderly, with Ava holding his arm, he was taken to a room.

"Hello again."

The same doctor, greeting him. But she might have been anyone. Ava helped him to a cushioned chair, where he sat listening to the clicking and shuffling of metal instruments chiming on a metal tray.

"Rest your chin here," the doctor said, tipping his head forward.

He heard switches being thrown, the snapping of toggles, a slight diminution of heat on his face; lights out.

"Can you read the middle line?"

"No."

"How about the top line?"

He sighed and said, "I can't see anything."

"Please try."

"What do you mean, 'Please try'? I can't do this."

And then — was it the odor? was it her prodding voice? — he realized she was the doctor who had examined him at Mass. Eye and Ear in Boston.

"I know you," he said.

"I'm Dr. Budberg."

He shrank, settling into the chair in embarrassment, remembering the rest. He said, "I'm so sorry."

She was brisk, she ignored him. She said, "We'll need bloodwork. And a glaucoma test. I'm going to schedule an MRI and a CAT scan, too."

Fitting his face to the mask-like frame, she shot puffs of air into his eyes, one at a time, and scrutinized them with more light, which heated his eye sockets and warmed his head.

"Have you had any ear infections?"

"No."

But she wasn't through. Any trauma to the head? Severe headache? Migraine? Stress? Significant pain on one side of the body? Diabetes?

He made his replies with glum certainty, his mind on something else. He remembered how he had rattled off the lines of the eye chart from memory, every letter, defying Dr. Budberg to find him blind and confounding her diagnosis. But his pedantic memory was gone now. All he had were the instincts of a burrowing animal, a blunt mole-like awareness of heat and cold and bad air, of trailing fingers like rootlets raking his face, a confining darkness.

He had insulted this woman. He remembered it clearly because he had enjoyed it as a victory, and he had seen only when it was too late how sad she had been, heavy and gasping with grief, lumpish, bereaved. He wanted to apologize again, but she had left him and was at the door, confiding details to Ava.

"Pressure's normal. No apparent retinal detachment. No apparent nerve trauma. I'm getting responses. I'd like to see him again."

Ava was murmuring. Steadman heard "idiopathic" attached to some other, even less intelligible words. He called out in a trembly voice, "What does that mean?"

"You haven't damaged your eyes, so there's hope," Ava said.

A wheelchair was brought and, feeling useless, he was pushed to another room, where blood was drawn from his arm. He had no idea who did it; he was jabbed in silence. Someone said, "You'll be fine. You're going to surprise everyone." Drops were splashed into his eyes, and whatever they were seemed to scorch him. He imagined a distracted nurse using the wrong drops and blinding him, or someone wicked doing it deliberately. He was left alone after that. Ava was outside the room, conferring again, but with whom? He sat drooping, as though learning how to be stupid.

On the way home, Ava was so preoccupied with driving she said nothing at first. These days he imagined that when she was silent she was thinking of her lover, that nameless grateful-sounding woman. Past Vineyard Haven and the worst of the traffic, she spoke up.

"You're going to be all right."

That sounded like surrender. He said, "Really?"

"Dr. Budberg knows her stuff. And she's upbeat."

This was so unpromising he didn't reply.

"You've got plenty of options."

She was telling him it was hopeless: they couldn't help. All they could offer was lame, unconvincing encouragement, which was like the worst expression of despair.

In the days that followed, he wondered when the nameless woman would return as a sex partner. But there was no sign of her. Perhaps Ava was meeting her somewhere else, or perhaps she was so concerned about him that she was not meeting her at all. Given his condition the frivolity of a threesome was simply reckless. More worrying than anything, Steadman found Ava's diminished desire a sign of pessimism.

"They're still running tests on that drug you gave them," Ava said.

Did she believe she was helping him to be optimistic? Crumbs of hope only made him feel worse and woeful. And she spoke to him as though to a fretful child.

He said, "What are they not telling me?"

"The contributing factors."

"Such as?"

"Okay," Ava said. "Maybe it's an undetectable ear infection that spread and deadened your optic nerve. Or it could be a brain tumor compressing the synapses, a compression lesion of the optic nerve. Or a brain aneurysm, something we call an arteriovenous malformation, intertwined blood vessels that clot, creating an outpouring of one vessel. That compresses, or leaks, and affects the brain tissue that controls optical functions."

"So it's not the drug?"

"I've read some of the literature. It's pretty unscientific. Most of it is anecdotal, and all from small-town dopers. But the message seems to be that the alkaloids affect the visual center of the brain."

"Great news."

"You asked for it."

After that, his low spirits kept him in the house. The invitations continued coming for the summer parties, but he was too sad and ashamed to accept. He couldn't face the questions, and the prospect of all the good humor of party chatter saddened him further. He could not bear to be pitied, or worse, beset by partygoers who had come to regard him as a marvel. Steadman the blind man who could read minds and see through walls and trot up and down swinging his cane — the showoff, the bore in dark glasses who claimed to have acquired the gift of total recall, the White House dinner guest, the world traveler and writer who had announced to one interviewer, "A perfect memory is prophetic."

He was satirized by everything he had done and said under the influence of the drug. He saw nothing now, but he understood the hateful fact that the drug had truly blinded him.

Wolfbein called repeatedly and left messages. Steadman avoided picking up the phone. But one day when Ava was at work and Steadman suspected that she might be calling, he answered and heard Wolfbein at the other end.

"You're coming to our party, you schmuck," Wolfbein said in his friendly bullying way.

"No, Harry, please."

"How about a cup of coffee?"

"I'm pretty busy."

"Okay, if you won't come over to see me, I'll pay you a visit."

Half an hour later Wolfbein's heavy vehicle was rolling down the gravel driveway. Steadman heard the car door slam, the feet on the porch, the front door rattle open.

"So you don't want to see your old friends anymore?"

Steadman stood with his arms at his sides, not knowing where to look. It was true: he did not want to see anyone.

"I haven't been well."

"You look okay to me, fella."

"Harry, I'm blind," and his voice cracked on the word.

"Let's go for a ride."

The big man took him by the arm and guided him out of the house, across the porch, down the steps. Steadman moved like a child, resisting, scuffing his feet but inarticulate. Wolfbein helped him into the passenger seat and buckled the safety belt. Steadman's head lolled on his loose neck; what was there to see?

"You were blind a year ago," Wolfbein said, driving away. "I read the newspapers. I know what you've been through."

"The papers have been accusing me of faking."

"Don't pay any attention to that shit."

Steadman had mentioned the papers for effect, hardly expecting a response. But Wolfbein's reply confirmed his fears.

"Fuck all those people," Wolfbein said. "What do you care what they say?"

He cared deeply, and Wolfbein's defiance alarmed him and made the whole issue seem much worse. "All those people" were like a formidable army of naggers and detractors.

"Next month we're hosting the big guy again," Wolfbein said.

"The president?"

"Listen, Slade, he's hurting too."

"Too" meant he had seen the pieces in which Steadman and the president were compared in their deceptions and denials: two hollow men who had trifled with the public trust, a pair of liars.

Wishing to be contradicted by his sympathetic friend, Steadman said, "People think I'm like him. Hiding something. Lying. I know I'm being lumped with him."

"So what?"

"So what" was the same as yes.

"Where are we going?"

"Anywhere you want. Feel like an ice cream?"

"Go to town. Take West Chop Road," Steadman said. "I want to hear the ocean."

"You got it, buddy."

His hearty tone made Steadman feel more pathetic, like a loser in need of encouragement.

"As if my book is somehow invalid because I wasn't really injured."

"But you are injured, I can see it," Wolfbein said. "People who run you down are horrible. Hey, I heard the drug stories. Please!"

It was like a question in the form of a hint, inviting an explanation. There was too much to tell, and where to begin? *A few years ago I decided to go to the Oriente in Ecuador, downriver* . . .

Wolfbein was still talking. "Just because the president got a blowjob in the White House from a girl sneaking into his office, does that mean he can't get credit for the economy and for balancing the budget? He erased the deficit. We've got a surplus!"

But Steadman was thinking of the girl sneaking into the White House, another trespasser; and the president groping her, more trespassing.

They had come to a stop. Steadman heard the wind in tall trees and, in the distance, a sunken sound of cavernous water, the rush of the current, the slop and splash of windblown waves beneath the West Chop lighthouse. He could hear the snap of the flag on the pole.

"Just let this guy go by," Wolfbein said, and shouted, "Go ahead! I'm not in your way!" He panted in irritation and said, "Look at him."

Steadman heard the car accelerate and pass by them.

"Some people," Wolfbein said.

"Who was it?"

"A schmuck — I don't know. He's gone. Want to get out?"

"Help me."

Wolfbein unbuckled the safety belt and hoisted him out of the car. Steadman smelled the sea air on his face, and the flowers — daylilies here, heavy clouds of fragrant pollen. The wind thrashed at the leafy boughs of the tall oaks.

"It's a sunny day," Steadman said sadly.

"Beautiful day," Wolfbein said. He seemed at times to forget that Steadman was blind, or at least to think that Steadman was as alert and prescient as he had been the previous summer, the miracle man in dark glasses, amazing the guests. "Lovely. Kids on bikes. Lady walking her dog. Sailboats on the Sound. And here he comes again."

A car rolled slowly past, the tire treads pinching small stones and snapping them to the curb.

Wolfbein sighed. "Schmuck."

"Let's go down to the beach."

"You don't want to do that, buddy."

But he did. After all the resistance he had put up, now that he was here, he craved to be nearer the racing current, to tramp on the sand, to smell the tide wrack and hear the gulls and the riverine rush of the tide.

"All those fucking steps. Go down there and we'll never get out."

Steadman remembered that Wolfbein was heavy. The man hated walking, and there were three long flights down to the beach. He was impatient. But he was indulgent, too.

"I want to help you, buddy. You need a medical procedure. Don't worry. I know people."

Another extravagant apology, like Ava's and Dr. Budberg's and whoever had drawn his blood at the hospital. Everyone wanted to help; no one could do a thing. But they never admitted it, and that was the worst of it, the false hope, the hollow encouragement — bucking him up because they needed to be bucked up themselves. And meanwhile, as they were undermining him, they were getting on with their lives.

He went home, his head full of his story.

5

THE BLIND MAN was someone like himself, a traveler and writer and recluse. He lived near West Chop, in the lane on the bluff where the paved road ended and the steps to the beach began.

That was the character in his story. Steadman could see him clearly, as though beckoning, inviting him into the narrative. But he found he could not continue. On the brightest days in his drowsy up-island solitude, with the sun baking his face and his dense eyelids, his grief was a physical pain. In that golden heat the agony he felt was like a terminal disease. He wondered how to go on living. His awareness of sunshine made him desolate, gave him the detachment, the fatalism, of someone very ill.

The rain, the fog, the days of drizzle, he could bear: he stayed indoors and brooded in the appropriate gloom. There was a frown of unresolved crisis in his features that made a crease of blame in his face, and the sour stillness in his house suggested the blurred stink of a sickroom.

Outside he could smell the tang of the summer's heat curling the cedar shingles and drying the tussocks of tall grass. He was imprisoned then, pierced by odors alone. He lamented what he could not see: the box hedge, the dry stone wall, his field thick with daylilies, the pitch pines and the birches. He hated that they belonged to other people. He could hardly recall Ava's face or body. Whom did she belong to now? He had become a big clumsy ignoramus who ate with his hands and seldom ever shaved. From highly colored dreams in which he was nimble, he woke to darkness, hardly knowing how to get out of bed.

He was more reclusive than ever, avoiding everyone. He knew what they thought. The blind were not scribblers; they were celebrated in their evasions as storytellers and talkers. People patronized the blind, tried to propitiate them for their gloomy emanations, tiptoed around them, sat at their feet, feared them, asked them for stories, tried not to stare at the stains and crumbs on their shirt fronts, were jittery listeners, fearing what might come next.

Grieving, Steadman remembered the story he had angrily begun in his head about the blind man and his wife. The ugly drama it portrayed seemed an expression of his hurt. He was repentant, self-accusing. He needed to invent, to ease his mind. The story of the weak, credulous man and the opportunistic lover was like a fable of his failure.

With nothing else to do, Steadman felt that resolving the elements of the story would help him live. Yet even in his imagination the story scared him. He made it out of the materials of pure horror, hoping that when it was done he might know more about himself. His familiarity with the facts of it did not make it less brutal, but he suspected that the act of creation would make it easier to bear.

And so he resumed, concentrating on the blind man, who was someone like himself, a traveler and writer and recluse. His house was near West Chop, in the lane on the bluff where the paved road ended and the steps to the beach began.

Before he lost his sight, before he met the woman, the man believed that the active part of his life was over. He accepted that no great event would befall him, that he would grow smaller, his life narrower, less accidental, and he would die here in obscurity. He imagined one of those small rainy funerals in an up-island cemetery of old chewed-looking gravestones and pitted crosses.

In his self-imposed retirement, he seldom ventured out. When he did he kept to the same safe walk. He was not seeking anyone, not looking for anything, just passing the time. He was supremely content, steadied by his indifference.

There had been one scare, but that was on his former route. A wet-eyed elderly pedestrian named Cubbage ambushed him, saying "You're the writer," and feebly bullied him into his house. "Got the plans out of *Popular Mechanics*." Cubbage detained him. "Want to buy it? If you don't, my idiot son will get it. It'd cost you less than a million. You could write a great book here." The man seized a banjo off a tattered hassock. "This is a little thing called 'Sleepy Time Gal.'" He strummed a bit and began to cry miserably. "It's my wife," he said, his face streaming with tears. "Cancer took her. Thirty years we were married. You can't replace someone like that. Do you know what true love is?"

The man said he had no idea.

"Then make me an offer on the house."

Cubbage watched him flee. The man changed his route. He believed that he was happy because he had conquered desire and was floating, having achieved some sort of Buddhist ideal of nonattachment, as he sometimes joked.

On good days he walked in the woods behind the lighthouse, loving the smell of the trees and flowers, the pitch pines, the chokecherries, the scrub oaks, the leaf mold, the squirrel-bitten acorns, the sun warming the long grass, hot clumps of timothy, and cushions of moss like dense velvet that made him feel weightless.

He stuck to West Chop because in Vineyard Haven he saw women he had known years ago, swollen shapeless creatures like big bosomy men, and he realized that he had slept with them in his early days of fame, after the appearance of his celebrated book. He was chastened, for now they had come to look like him — solitary, unexercised, asexual, faintly mustached. He felt guilty and apologetic, for one that he took to be a former lover, a misshapen woman in a familiar knit, was in fact a man he had never seen before and the sort of person he knew he would keep bumping into afterward at the post office and the market.

Everything changed for him one end-of-summer day on the bluff of West Chop near the lighthouse when he saw a lovely woman standing alone. She faced him, looking fascinated, and then turned away and walked toward the tennis courts. He felt panic, a kind of hunger. He needed this woman. She was the one person who had been missing from his long life.

Understanding this, he was briefly happy, then he was ashamed and finally sorrowful, knowing for the first time the despair of love. He would waste away and die without her; with her he would live. He now knew that the reason he had taken the same walk every day was to meet this woman.

That night he lay in bed and could not call up her face. Her beauty was too subtle to remember with any accuracy. The next day he found her at the same spot and she hurried away — her sudden rush like a flushed quail, calling attention to her flight — down the road at the set of mailboxes reading *Loss, Titley, Ours, Levensohn, Lempe*. Which was she? In the days that followed he saw her twice more.

Self-conscious, he was reduced to being stealthy, glancing sideways to stare at her, to satisfy himself; but staring only made him hungrier. He was reminded of his distant past, of being small and poor, rather young, ignored by more powerful people while he toiled at his book and felt fameless. His book's bold title provoked his friends to patronize him, until the book was reckoned a masterpiece and was then the occasion of their envious jokes.

Now people said to him, "How are you, buddy?"

He said, "I'm miserable," but misery made him truthful. Speaking bluntly released his feelings of frustration. In the past he had often said the opposite of what he meant: "You seem perky," to distracted souls; "I'll try to remember that," to pedants.

Now he said, "People might call themselves perfectionists, but at the bottom of pedantry is an abiding laziness. Raise enough objections and you never have to accomplish anything."

The next time he saw the beautiful woman at West Chop he said hello.

"I was looking at that sailboat," she said.

The windjammer *Shenandoah*, out of Vineyard Haven.

"Isn't she beautiful?"

Emboldened by her directness, he said, "I hadn't noticed. I couldn't take my eyes off you. You are so lovely."

Her laughter told him he had made an impression. They talked inconsequentially about the ferry schedule. He said, "See you tomorrow."

That night he thought, And I hate my saggy face.

He had fallen in love with her, and he knew it was love because it was agony, the sort you died from. He felt famished when he saw her — her bright eyes, her full lips, her clear skin. He sought her out and felt humiliated by his longing for her.

To his delight, he began to run into her everywhere — at the drugstore on Main Street, the beach below the lighthouse, walking along the ferry landing, in the bagel café, and in the camera store where he was buying a pair of binoculars. Melanie Ours was her name.

He wooed her in the open air, doing most of the talking. Melanie was unaffected, soft-spoken, appreciative, and loving. One day she was clutching a small dog in the crook of her arm, nuzzling it and cuddling it in a way that suggested: I could treat you like this.

"It's not mine," she said. "It's a friend's."

Wondering what friend made him unhappy. But he saw Melanie Ours again and loved her more. He mentioned to her that he was older than she by twenty years. She said, "So?" He feared she might want children. She smiled and said, "I want you."

Nothing could have been simpler. They married, she moved in with him, he was joyful. They lived together in his house on the bluff behind West Chop.

He sometimes mentioned the places where they had bumped into each other.

She said, "I knew you'd be there," and explained that she had known his movements and had contrived deliberately to appear at these seemingly chance encounters. He laughed shyly, feeling desired. She said, "I found you fascinating." What more was there to know? Perhaps nothing, except that he learned that she was devoted to him, responsive and loving, forgiving as only a friend can be.

"I'm sorry, darling," he said, early on, in bed, feeling futile. She held him, kissed him, and he wanted to weep with gratitude.

Months of bliss. He sometimes became alarmed when she was out of his sight. Setting eyes on her, he blessed his luck. She was a light to him. "I thought I knew what happiness was." He was reminded that in the early, active part of his life he had been deluded.

This clarity of vision — his life now — was figurative and philosophical, but a paradox, for he found that in fact his eyesight was failing. He had trouble reading, even with glasses. He could not drive at night without being dazzled by the headlights of oncoming cars.

He had his eyes tested. He failed the exam. "It's to be expected at your age," the doctor said. "But new glasses won't help. You have cataracts."

He regarded this as good news, the promise that after his operation he would see better and be bathed in the glow of his lovely wife. But why was he asked to sign the waiver?

The doctor said, "There's less than a one percent chance of the procedure going wrong."

After the operation, still bleary-eyed and groping, he was given drops for his eyes. Melanie helped him apply the drops, and his eyes became scorched and infected. He lost his corneas, he got a transplant, and then more drops. The transplant failed. He howled.

As though rehearsing his defense in a malpractice suit, the doctor sternly reminded him of the odds: "Someone had to be in that one percent."

Because he had signed the waiver, he could not sue and was not compensated. He did not need money anyway. He wanted his eyesight back, even the feeblest sort, as on the days when he had said, "I can see your face, sort of dark, but not your features." He would have settled for that. He was the blind man now.

And, blind, he could not bear to be away from Melanie. Yet even when she was with him he was not consoled. He spoke to her, but she did not seem to hear him. Something wintry in her manner — why? He had never sensed it before, perhaps because her adoring eyes, her face, and her luminous skin had always overwhelmed him. Now he was aware of her as a different presence — her thumping clumsy footsteps, the sharp odor of her body, her harsh voice.

When she touched him her hands chilled him; her fingers felt reptilian. He was appalled even as she said, "Of course I love you."

He was now confined to his house. He was bewildered in it, in rooms like obstacles. He tripped over his own furniture. He could not go anywhere without her, yet more and more she was absent.

"I need to shop. Everything takes longer when you come along."

Shop for what? She had never shopped before. He began to ask her where she had been.

"Getting my nails done," or "Having my hair colored," or "At the dressmaker's."

But why? — since he could not see the nails, or the hair color, or her clothes.

"It's for me," she said.

He was confused by the mingled smells of her perfume, her nail polish, her shampoo, her new clothes. His blindness had wakened his other senses — he was hyperalert, sensitive to all stimuli. "I smell onions," or "Smoke — tobacco smoke — in your hair."

He smelled a man, he smelled sex, something humid and dog-like, and a roughness like razor burn on her chin. He was too sad to kill her. *Instead I'll kill myself.*

What kept him from it was that she was sadder, and tense, as if she had received some bad news.

"What's wrong?"

"Please, leave me alone."

"You're never home."

"I was sick! You don't care!"

After all that time, their first argument. She insisted that she loved him but was like someone else, someone cruel, a stranger. She returned with a new smell on her. These odors overwhelmed all other impressions and became like colors and shapes, some of them as layered and complex as unanswered questions.

Was he missing something because he was blind, or was he seeing her as she really was? There was that voice. Sometimes, speaking to him, she seemed a little formal and overinformative, as though she were also addressing someone else, as though she had a listener she was teasing with irrelevant detail and a sort of mocking pomposity.

"I certainly would not expect someone like you to understand the priorities of a woman whose primary goal is to find some sort of focus to give balance to her life."

"What's that noise?"

He was stifled by unfamiliar creaks in distant parts of the house.

"I didn't hear anything."

One evening at a party he felt awkward and lost in the host's house, so he stood to the side, out of the way of guests, waiting for Melanie to bring him a drink. Brushed by a stranger, he inhaled a familiar odor.

"You've been sleeping with my wife," he said without thinking.

He was surprised when a woman snorted and pinched his arm and said, "You're imagining things!"

Guilty people in farces often used that platitude, but farce was so near to tragedy. He saw that he was becoming shrewder; he had a clear vision of that woman's drunken face, purple, putty-like, with weepy reddened eyes.

He was nimbler in his own house. Melanie stumbled in the dark, banged doors, fuddled with simple things like the telephone and the bath plug, and faltered in corridors where now, to his astonishment, he was completely at home.

There was someone else lurking, he knew it clearly one night, in the big cluttered front room that looked out on the Sound. He had become accustomed to the dark. The other person was lost in it and made an uncertain canine shimmy, a backing up: someone making way for him.

"Who's there?"

"Who do you think?" And she laughed in a rehearsed way, as though she had an audience and was laughing on someone else's behalf.

"A man."

She jeered much too loudly, attempting a convincing denial, a bit of theater.

Using his fingertips, he traced his way through the room, surprised by how well he knew the route, and went upstairs, where he paused and heard the front door click shut. Then he heard his wife unsteadily on the stairs.

"It was a woman. That's why you laughed that way."

Memory helped, desperation helped, blindness did the rest. He could see with his teeth, his tongue, his lips, his face, his whole body. He knew later that the two must have been making love — an unmistakable vibrato, the specific sounds irregular, like a lapse from ordinary life. Not like sex between a man and a woman, a pattern of slaps he knew, a familiar rhythm, a top and bottom, an act writhingly echoic, but instead a tussle of equals, the percussive kisses, the whappity-whap of two women: a sudden sapphic sandwich with no filling.

From believing that he was always alone, he began to understand that he was never alone. Even when there was no conversation he was aware of another presence, a muffled physicality that filled a space in the room and blunted the sounds he made, something molecular and cloth-like. No darkness at all, only light that was loosely or tightly woven, always revealing a coarse or helpful light. What people called darkness, and feared, for him had a face and features: he now knew the whir of human atoms.

Smells, too, perfumes that pierced his eyes, duskier aromas in his nostrils, a further fleshier suggestion that he tasted on his tongue, the distinct earthiness of swallowed food. Another person — had to be a woman; a man would have been less circumspect.

He tried to follow these smells, to account for them.

"I don't smell anything."

If she believed that betraying him before his blind eyes was working, she was wrong.

"It was a man last week, but this week it's a woman."

She laughed again, the conspiratorial, informing laugh, and her laughter roused an unmistakable movement that jarred the room.

"Or two women" — guessing that was why she laughed.

Sometimes the sound of kissing was like a certain sort of secret eating, furtive snacking on dripping overripe fruit. At other times the lovemaking resembled two soft bodies plopping through heavy clouds, encountering turbulence, or was like the thrashing of a single person sleeping poorly. They were bold in daylight, but even bolder in the dark, believing that because they could not see, they could not be seen. The eroticism of their solitude was the opposite of the crackly randomness of ordinary life.

People held in the rapture of sexuality were trapped animals. He shamefully remembered, *I'm sorry, darling.*

"I know what you're doing."

To test her sympathy, he pleaded for help and found himself alone. It was a ruse: he knew his way around the house, but he could expect nothing from her. In daylight he understood much; at night he understood almost everything. He was not confused by shadows: he thought of night as a friend, blindness as a gift.

His dead eyes made his wife reckless. He was not fooled. He knew her better, knew that she had taken lovers, thieved his money. His blindness was her opportunity, but he was not deceived.

There was worse to come. At another party he sniffed at a vase of flowers and said, "That water smells like my eye medicine."

"You wouldn't want to put that in your eyes," the hostess said, and she explained that the chlorine in the water kept the flowers fresh longer by killing the bacteria.

Now he understood exactly who Melanie was and what she had done to him. She was the one who sounded lost and said in the dark, "Who's there?" The woman was simple, greedy, and obvious. She had blinded him. He knew her and pitied her; he knew himself with a fatal disappointment.

All the beauty he had once known was false; he conceded that the world was an illusion. His book was false, history was false, what you saw was false. His life was not a tragedy but a revelation of unanswerable facts. He now knew what it was like to be dead, to be a specter, to see everything without being seen. What did you do with this enlightenment? You became obnoxious, truthful, stubborn.

A man said, "I've been on a diet."

He replied, "You've got a long way to go."

The editor of a magazine introduced herself. He said, "Not at the top of my reading list, I'm afraid."

"That is hateful," he said to a boy in Oak Bluffs who was listening to rap music in a convertible.

Explanations were pointless; understanding was like torture. It did not help that he now saw clearly his wife's crime — not the dallying but her stratagem, her blinding him. How the woman who had plotted to marry him, whom he had loved, had substituted another solution for the one that had been prescribed to counter his eye infection. She had blinded him with the drops. He had lived through a mystery. He had solved a crime. Would anyone believe him? He interested a lawyer in the case, demanding secrecy, and rid himself of Melanie Ours.

The man Cubbage, who had accosted him and played the banjo and wept over his wife? The blind man met him again on the road and Cubbage was happy, pitying the man for his blindness, no longer bereaved. He had remarried, and was delighted that he had not sold his house. "We're sitting on a fortune here." The old misshapen women friends that the blind man had shrunk from before he now saw as contented souls, healthier than he was. "I am so sorry," they said.

He sometimes wished for his sight back, so he could be calm, generous, and deluded. He was not pathetic, he was powerful, another life was beginning, but a harder one — he had no faith. He read nothing. He did not believe the lies of written history, the daily news, or the consolation of friends. His own book he regarded as little more than a lunatic fiction. Every written word was fiction or a half-truth. The worst of the visible world was bearable only because of its deceits and the way its truth was always hidden. But as a blind man liberated by a selfish woman he saw everything, and so he suffered, not from blindness but from clear-sightedness. Love was a dirty drug with hideous side effects.

He had no answer: He could not leave the island and live in a place where people identified him as blind. He knew with sorrow that all that awaited him was a sort of undeserved fame that was no different from failure. The paradoxes of his recent past exhausted him.

How did this thing end?

As Steadman went on imagining the story, he felt he had rescued something from his situation, like someone who finds meaning in a personal tragedy. And as long as the story remained unfinished, he felt he was not lost.

6

ALTHOUGH HE HAD not written a word of it, although it was all still stewing in his head, he was buoyant, possessed by the fable, with the sense of wellbeing he always felt at having imagined something whole. His pride in the plain facts of it matched his faith in his extravagant invention.

But his happiness didn't last. The story made him secretive, for the woman in it was the villain and Ava had usually been kind, and even in her infidelity had been solicitous toward him. He was reproached by her kindness. And she went on indulging him, urging him to be upbeat, reminding him that she admired his work and that she would go on looking for a medical solution for him, more tests, another specialist.

He was grateful to her for her words; they were sincerely meant, but they were still only words. All praise these days sounded to him like the hollow pieties of a premature obituary. He was soon low again and unsure and as incomplete as his story. Maybe Melanie personified the blinding drug that had a feminine name — datura.

The simplest things reminded him of his helplessness. One day Ava said, "The mailman asked whether we have a red Corolla convertible. Apparently there's one that's often parked in our driveway."

"It's got to be a rental. Some tourist."

"That's just what I said."

"So who's the busybody, the mailman or the tourist?"

"You're yelling at me," she said, stating a fact.

Angry and hot-faced, he shouted again, "What do you expect me to do about it?"

"I just thought you'd like to know."

"Why are you telling me? Tell the cops!"

She never shouted at him; it was always doctor and patient. Faced with his howling, she said softly, "I'll deal with it. Now why don't you let me take you out to dinner?"

Food was meaningless to him, yet he did not say no, did not say that a restaurant for him was just a charade, that he could hardly use a fork without stabbing his lips, that people would stare.

He said, "Maybe."

"Or anything you want."

"Anything" sounded like a sexual invitation, so he said, "If you mean your friend," and didn't finish.

"It's up to you."

The very thought of the three of them again overwhelmed him with sadness: being sat on and fondled, all that seething. Sex was an expression of health and optimism, and he was a pessimistic wreck with an unreliable libido.

"I'd do anything to help you. I care about you."

He heard that as a note of farewell, different from caring *for* him. She wanted him healthy so she could leave him. They were back to where they had been in the weeks before Ecuador, the trip they had taken as a means of splitting up. They had no life together now, nothing to hold them together except his disability. They didn't talk about the future or of love.

They had never used the word "love." They avoided it as some people avoided red meat or refined sugar, and for the same reason, that abstaining from the word would make them healthier and stronger. They believed in love but hated the word, and loathed the moth-eaten expression *I love you,* which had been diminished and become so meaningless it had been reduced to a casual salutation. "I love you," people said at the end of a casual phone call. It had taken the place of "See you later" and "Have a nice day." It mattered less than his father's farewell at the end of a phone call: "Be good." His father had never used the word "love" either, yet he knew that the man had adored him.

Housebound among memories of his arrogance, Steadman said, "I think about only one thing. Getting back my eyesight."

"I'm working on it," Ava said. "And at least you have your book."

He didn't say what he felt — it was too melancholy. The book was pointless; it was incomplete. His life was not the sequence of his sexual history, it was everything that had led to its rediscovery, its periphery, all the circumstances, the landscape of his search, from the flight to Ecuador onward, how he had written it, the book tour, the president's duplicity, the delusion of the drug, his failure, even the subsequent revelation, Ava's dallying with her woman friend as he lay blindly supine. The sadness he was living through was the truest part, and yet it was not suggested in his book. His book was the narrative he knew now — this, the raggedness of reality, all of this.

But he said, "Right. I've got my book."

The Book of Revelation was over, though. Good or bad, it was not his anymore. What preoccupied him now was the story of the blind man's wife, the fable of his blindness.

Ava did not ask him how he spent his days. He knew she hated hearing that he did nothing but sit and brood. Asking him anything was like challenging him, and would have implicated her, made her feel partly responsible for his apparent indolence. He had no helpful reply. At least he had his short story. He clung to that with the tenuous hope of improving that fragment, looking to fiction for a solution to his dilemma, as he had once looked to travel for solace. Going away had always helped.

But if Ava had asked him what he was doing during the day, he would not have told her. What he was thinking was his business. The story was his secret, and anyway, the fictional lover was wicked. What would Ava make of that? Writing the story showed him how he wanted to blame

Ava for his own trespassing, because he resented her freedom and her health.

He took some comfort in being able to recognize the changes in the weather. Some days he sweltered, the Vineyard afternoons when the wind dropped and there was no air, the long summer days of humidity, bright sunshine at seven in the evening, and some nights could seem suffocating. But then the wind would rise, the air cooled, and within a short time, hours sometimes, he would fumble in drawers for his sweater. These simple perceptions seemed to him necessary victories.

Weather was missing from his story, so was the physical texture of the island. The narrative hovered between being a mystery and a fable. He wanted it to be both more concrete and allusive, more of Borges in it, some sparkle, some magic. Not a pandering moral — that was just shabby — but persuasiveness, a greater sense of place, so that a reader would at the end find it the more disturbing for being familiar and unexplainable.

Perhaps that was what was also lacking in *The Book of Revelation,* a sense of place. As erotica its problem was its preoccupation with foreplay and foreground: interiors. Apart from the long gothic shadows, the role-playing in the château — wild nights, wild nights — there was no visible island.

Yet if his novel was a failure, his story had saved him. His secret inventions had always sustained him. He was more inclined to laugh at anyone who questioned how he spent his time and to ask other people how they could bear living without writing. The fact that he had published very little of it did not matter. He had been engaged in some sort of writing every day of his adult life. He loved the title "The Blind Man's Wife." He liked the way the story was full of intrusions.

How do I spend my days? he could have replied to Ava. *I ponder my story.*

Fearing that he might hear his own name, he avoided listening to the news. The scandal of the president's affair, and his hiding and denying it, seemed to be the only topic, always speculating on the most vulgar details of the concealment. Every detail put Steadman on the defensive. He imagined being hounded in the same way, challenged and humiliated.

The president's lame denial had alarmed him, but months later, in the period when Steadman was pondering his short story, the president admitted his mistake. His apology was horrifying, and though Steadman did not hear it the first time, it was replayed again and again, for it was not an apology at all but a statement of wounded defiance.

Steadman got to know the phrases by heart: "Questions about my private life, questions no American citizen would ever want to answer . . . I did have a relationship . . . a critical lapse in judgment and a personal failure on my part . . . I misled people . . . a desire to protect myself from the embarrassment of my own conduct . . . It's nobody's business but ours . . . Even presidents have private lives. It is time to stop the pursuit of personal destruction and the prying into private lives . . ."

Steadman did not hear sex in the president's message; he heard his own voice speaking of drugs and blindness. The president was acting out Steadman's own humiliation.

He was on his own. The story was all that he had written since his book, and as with the book, he had not touched a pen. He wrote in his head. When it was complete he would speak it into a tape recorder and find someone, not Ava, to transcribe it.

Ava had slipped away and lost herself in the hospital. She still lived in the house. She left meals for him, helped him find his clothes. But he knew her heart wasn't in it. Her concern was professional now, a matter of ethics; he was a patient, a case, and her motto was "First do no harm." She had not been able to find a cure. He was waiting for a chance to say, "I need a referral."

In the meantime, "The Blind Man's Wife" was all he had. He would use it like a man whittling a stick — rewrite it, improve it, polish it. Until it was done he would not have to think of anything else. The story was his patience and his consolation. Ava would have said "your dolly."

In pitying him she had taught him that pity was useless. He needed to help himself.

Wolfbein called again, using the same tone of friendly bullying a nurse would use with a morose and bedridden patient.

"Something's come up. You're having lunch here today. The only question is, are you coming on your own or am I going over there to get you?"

"Harry, I'm useless."

"I'll be right over."

He arrived a half hour later, honking his horn, and after Steadman got into the car, he drove fast, hardly speaking.

"What's the hurry?"

"No hurry. Nice to see you," Wolfbein said.

But the man was preoccupied, his hectic driving proved it, and he gabbled at the traffic. Although sunk in the depths of his blindness, Steadman understood the simple trip from his house to Lambert's Cove to be a matter of reckless urgency.

"I told them to start without us," Wolfbein said. "It's all guys, by the way. The women have other plans."

Then Steadman knew that Wolfbein's picking him up and driving him to lunch had been unforeseen. Yet Wolfbein, seriously inconvenienced, had acted out of friendship. They arrived in a flurry, Wolfbein whispering to other people. Steadman was too bewildered to hear anything clearly. The house on the bluff that he had known so well seemed unfamiliar to him — strange elevations, sudden steps, echoes.

Wolfbein guided him through the living room to the sliding screen doors, then across the terrace to the wide lawn. Steadman had expected just the two of them for lunch on the terrace, Millie serving sandwiches. But this was something formal and unreadable. Steadman heard the chatter without making any sense of what was obviously a sizable and organized event.

"These guys will take care of you," Wolfbein said, and seated him at a table. "I'll be over there at the head table if you need me."

Head table? Steadman's own table companions were murmuring men, sounding British and inconsequential, talking about people they knew, none of whose names Steadman recognized. He felt for his glass and, finding a water tumbler, sipped from it, but cautiously, guessing he was being observed. His fingers tested the table, then encircled a fork handle. He pushed some food around his plate but did not dare to raise any to his mouth, for fear he would make a mess of it and embarrass himself. He sat, he knew, with a look of consternation on his face, trying to listen.

After a while a diffident voice beside him said, "Are you still working on that?"

Probably the waiter, but because Steadman was unsure, he said nothing. What if it was one of those other men at the table?

Dessert was served, the same diffident man saying in a querying voice, "Tiramisu?" Steadman worked a spoon into it, then nudged it aside. Coffee came. He risked a sip but slopped some of it on his chin.

Most of the talk seemed to be generated by the other table, or tables; Steadman couldn't tell how many people were present. The voices were earnest, insistent, sounding strident at times; Steadman did not recognize any of them. The odd thing was that the men at his table, who had been murmuring about mutual friends, had stopped talking altogether and seemed to be listening to the conversations at the far tables, carrying across the lawn.

"Good Lord, is that the time?" the man next to him said, a lazy genteel voice. "I must push off."

Some others said the same. Steadman had a sense that he was being acknowledged and thanked. One man said, "I'm so sorry we didn't get a chance to talk." Then a creaking of wooden folding chairs and all the voices shifting, becoming like whispers as the men moved off, up to the terrace, the lunch party ending, just like that.

Steadman sat, wondering if he was alone. He heard the wind chafing the trees, the chirp of birds, the trill of insects, a distant dog, a far-off ship's horn skimming across the water. He was happier left like this, and in the sudden solitude he wondered what had been the point in coming? What he had taken to be Wolfbein's impulsive lunch invitation had been something semiformal, a catered affair with rented tables and creaky chairs. He heard Wolfbein squawk from the terrace.

"Sorry, sorry," Wolfbein called out as he approached. "I thought someone had come to get you."

"I'm okay." Saying that, he sounded feeble.

"The thing is, there were lots of people I wanted you to meet, but they all had to leave in a hurry." Wolfbein had grasped Steadman's arm and was helping him up. "These are strange times, my friend."

"Who were all the other people?"

"You were sitting with Prince Andrew and Evelyn de Rothschild. I was with the president. Like I said, it was spur of the moment. He's on the island to escape the press. He's putting on a brave face, but believe me, you do not want his problems."

Then Steadman knew: he had seen nothing. Apart from the story he was trying to write, he hardly existed.

On a fragrant morning in late August, his wide bank of lilies sweetening the breeze, at an hour when he was certain that Ava was gone, he called Information and ordered a taxi from Vineyard Haven.

"I need to get to West Chop."

"Street and number?"

"Just the lighthouse."

Setting off, he was less than a child. He took so little with him — that was a measure of his futility. No pen or paper, no tape recorder, no camera, nothing but his cane. He had money but could not tell one bill from another; a one could be a fifty. He could easily have been cheated. Yet he was going out in search of factual detail to relieve the starkness of his story.

He would carry everything in his head, but for all his bravado he was unconfident. His head was clouded with fear. He had sat like a wraith at Wolfbein's, and here he was trying to be a writer again. He was making a narrative using the simplest tools, like a tribal storyteller squatting on his haunches before a fire.

He felt undermined by not having any idea of the route the taxi was taking, and he was too proud to ask the driver. The turns made him queasy. He guessed the stop-and-go traffic was Old County Road, but it could have been Main Street. His blindness made him carsick. This man was in a rush. He was reminded of Wolfbein's speeding and swerving. A long straight stretch of slight ups and downs he took to be West Chop Road.

When the taxi stopped the driver said, "You sure you're going to be all right?"

People said that because they didn't care and didn't want to be responsible for him. Everyone blamed him for being helpless.

"What are you suggesting?" he said, to confuse the man.

"You're the boss." He chose some bills from Steadman's hand and cranked the door open to let him out.

"Just point me in the right direction."

"Where would that be?"

"See some wooden steps leading down to the water?"

"Right over here, sir."

The man's hands were careless, only approximating the direction — he was in a hurry to get back into his taxi. But as he led him toward the stairs, Steadman could hear the sea slopping and splashing, like a vast tub filling, far below the lighthouse at the corner of the Chop.

The man's loose grip was like rejection and made Steadman stumble. He said, "I'm okay now. Thanks."

Without another word the man left him. Steadman told himself that he was glad for such lessons in indifference: he needed to be reminded that he was on his own.

The notion that this was literary work pleased him. He was walking in the setting of his story and would be grateful for any details — a smell, a sound, the texture of a leaf or a boulder. The age cracks in the weathered handrail that he felt now, the smooth split wood — that. He was looking for authenticity, for writing about a known place, he tended to take too much for granted.

"Hello."

His first stab of fear today — not the voice alone but the fact that he had not known he was being observed. He could not tell whether the person on the stairs was going up or down. It sounded like an old woman.

"Going down to the beach?"

No, it was a small boy.

"Yes, I am," Steadman said, trying to sound confident. And he heard the boy pass him, going up, the stair treads creaking, the boy climbing too fast.

"Take your time, Brett. You're going to trip!"

A man's voice beneath him on the steps. And then he addressed Steadman, talking a little too loudly. "Can I help you?"

"Can I help you?" was the typical Vineyarder's rebuff when confronted by strangers — trespassers, all of them — and was the local equivalent of "Go away."

Steadman ignored him, but the man persisted. "Visiting the island?"

"Never mind."

"Manage all right?"

"Doing fine," Steadman said, his anger rising. He had come here to be alone.

"Watch your step."

This was too much, "Watch *your* fucking step!" — and he swiped with his cane as though swatting a fly, slashing twice and catching something hard, a protrusion he thought was the handrail, until a moment later the man uttered a strangled cry.

Then the man called out, "Daddy's all right, Brett! Go back, son!" — warning the child who had preceded him up the stairs.

Steadman imagined the panting boy with red eyes and sweaty cheeks blushing with terror at seeing his father thrashed by a crazed blind man wheeling on the stairs. He had a glimpse of Blind Pew tottering on the road and snatching at Jim Hawkins, and he smiled at the confusion, father and son trying to reassure each other.

"Get the fuck out of my way!" Steadman said, and jabbed his stick at the man's murmuring.

"Are you nuts?" The man was still gasping, probably nursing a wound, a welt somewhere the width of Steadman's cane.

He slashed again, cutting the air with the sound of a whip and stepping to a lower tread on the stairs.

"Brett, be careful!" the man cried, his shriek turning womanish in panic. "Don't come down here!"

And as Steadman raised his stick to strike once more, he was bumped again but softly, and sensed that the man was pushing past him, shaking the wooden stairs with his stamping feet, climbing up toward the road, hauling himself with desperate pulls on the handrail.

The angry energy of the confrontation still shivered in his muscles. He was exhilarated by his sudden aggression. And when he collected himself and resumed his descent, picking his way down, he thought, I can use that. It was why he had come, to collect such asides for his story, to verify impressions. He wanted to prove to himself that he could find his own way.

He wondered whether there was anyone else on the beach. He had been down here only a few times. He knew it was a narrow pocket beach, bouldery, with patches of sand, at the foot of a high vertical bluff, north-facing, of crumbled stone and loose gravel. The secluded spot was approachable only by the long wooden stairway that was like an old-fashioned fire escape at the rear of a tall tenement.

The water crashed and collapsed, the continuous slosh of Vineyard Sound, small lumpy waves that nagged at the shore. Steadman listened for voices and almost tripped when he got to the bottom of the stairs and stepped onto a pillow shape of soft sand. Then he let go of the rail and tapped his cane, whacking rock, poking pebbles, making his way along the wall of the bluff.

"Hello?"

Hearing no reply, he turned to the right, where he knew the widest beach was, but even so, after a few steps he strayed into the water and wet his shoes and trouser cuffs. He stopped again to listen for voices and thought he heard the stairs creak, trodden by weight from high up at the cliff face. He concentrated hard: nothing.

Seeing a blind man, a stranger would say, as all the others had done, "Want a hand?" and would encumber him with insincere assistance. He hated being asked, hated being noticed, being visibly crippled, with a perpetual frown of consternation. He smiled remembering his fury: *Get the fuck out of my way!*

"Who is it?" he called out, because the wash of the sea at the shore obscured all other sounds,

He was alone. He had to be, or what was the point? He crawled onward like a dog, using his hands on a stretch of sand, and soon found himself bumping his way through waist-high boulders. They were set in a slope, like a revetment against the bluff. Touching them he was able to trace veins and cracks in the granite, and moving slowly he noticed with his slick fingers that many of them had bunches of kelp pinched between them, or swags of sea-rotted rope.

One slab of ramp-like rock was lying aslant the beach. It was so smooth, so warmed by the sun, he crept onto it and braced himself, and then he lay with his back against it. Its hardness and its heat penetrated his spine and soothed him.

In the rise and fall of the breaking chop just offshore he replayed his story of the blind man's wife, moving through its current — the narrative seemed to him like moving water — reminding himself of its progress. The reclusive, unsuspicious man of some accomplishment was content until the younger woman tempted him. As though drugged and bewitched he fell in love with her, became possessed, then disenchanted, and finally blinded. Only when he was blind did he see the truth. He had been greedy, he had succumbed to temptation, he had wanted too much.

He liked it for having the rough splintery elements of a folktale. Was this a short story or an episode in a larger narrative of temptation and possession? He posed this question in a dark room — as dark as where he lay now — where two temptresses were teasing each other and tormenting him. He drowsed as these swaggering and tumbled waves, topped with mermaid's hair, shouldered their way toward shore.

Then he was asleep, and the sound of the water washed away his story and imposed on his receptive mind a dream in which he lay canted on a raft like the black castaway in the Winslow Homer painting that showed sharks' fins in the water. He was that castaway, and the raft was sliding down the deep and rounded face of a swell as he struggled to stay on board, the wind twitching at one side of his face and his palms and fingers pressing the barnacled edges of the raft. He sensed he was sliding to his death.

Spatters of sea spray reached his eyes, and the tearing sound of the sea became louder until, startled, he awoke as a wave washed across his feet and lower legs. He stood and stumbled in water up to his knees. Instinctively he scrambled, but the wrong way, into the sea, then fell and foundered in the cold water and believed he was drowning. He was too alarmed to cry out. He lost his cane in his fall but felt for a handhold on a rock and gripped it, raising himself for air.

Listening for the shore and slapping the water around him, he found some boulders and braced himself more securely. When he got his breath he hauled himself to the larger boulders that he guessed were part of the sea wall at the base of the cliff. He was soaked, he was in darkness, the sea was loud, and he was trembling. But he was alive.

The water had risen while he had napped. He had forgotten the unforgiving tide. This was to have been a brief foray down the steep stairs below the jaw of West Chop, a search for color, a literary outing, something to give him confidence. Now he was in sodden clothes and heavy water-soaked shoes, and he was gripping a rock, slashing his fingers on the sharp crust of button-like barnacles and periwinkles. The important thing was to remain calm, but he knew he had to find the stairs and climb out of this place, for there was more of the tide to come. High tide took away the beach, washed over the rocks; high tide was a flood of deepening water, way over his head.

"Anyone here?" he called out. Then, reluctantly, in a timid, testing way, "Help!"

He hated his small tentative voice. But he knew he had to call out. He tried again, louder, like a hoarse boy trying to be brave. If anyone had been there and heard him, they would have come to his aid. No one replied.

He moved as quickly as he could across the boulders, but after a few steps he lost his footing and became frantic and fell. Toppling, he went stupid, and he thrashed, twisted his arm, grazed his ear, banged his head like someone at the mercy of a bully. The physical pain made him more fearful. Still he scrabbled forward, crabwise on the boulders. They were slippery now with wet thickened seaweed.

Where were the stairs? The markers he had mentally noted — the boulders, the pebbly patches, the cushions of sand — were underwater, sunken by the tide.

All that was left of the shrunken beach were the boulders massed at the foot of the cliff, a vertical eminence that was the island's wall. And he kept being assaulted. The brimming tide slammed his back with clouts of cold water.

Hanging on to the biggest boulder he could find, he felt for the steps, gasping all the while — frenzied breaths, gulps of air, salt water in his mouth. The sound of his own breathing was like the harsh wheeze of desperate fear, and it terrified him further. The splash of the water was loutish, indifferent, brutal — rising, falling; and though his head was teeming, the water was like a muscle without a mind, pushing him, pulling him. He would be separated, he would float free of the island, to be dragged down to choke to death in the sea.

As he lifted his face to the bluff, seeing only darkness, something plopped against his forehead. It just missed his right eye, and he knew when it fell farther, dropping to his shoulder, that it was a pebble. Had it been loosened from the cliff wall? He ducked, afraid there might be more, then looked up again, and again was staring into darkness.

Another pebble hit him, striking the top of his ear, hard enough to sting. And before he could react, another. He snatched at that last one and pressed it in his fingers. A pebble sucked smooth as a bead by the rolling water.

"Hey!" he called out.

And like a reply, something blunt and deliberate, another pebble struck his sore ear.

7

THE WELL-AIMED PEBBLES proved that someone was watching him and gave him hope of being saved. Yet there was no answer to his cries except more pebbles. *Pock!* He was popped on the shoulder with another one as this thought occurred to him. So it seemed like a game, a child's game, a wicked child's game of torment — and he was hit again, he called out again. What heartless bastard would torment a helpless blind man struggling in a swirling shore break?

Yet he had felt safer as soon as he guessed that the thrown pebbles were deliberate. He hugged the slippery boulder, his legs dragging in the push of the sea, the waves strengthening on the flooding tide. He called out again with thinning breath, his throat narrow with fear, and turned his hopeful face to the cliff. There came another targeted and bigger pebble. It stung one of his dead eyes and he thought, I'm lost.

The pebbles that had reassured him now threatened him, convincing him that whoever was watching him struggle wanted him to suffer.

"Who are you?"

A heavier hostile stone hit him on the head. Steadman clawed his hair and panicked at the thought of more of them, of being stoned to death.

"That hurt!" he called out in a child's pleading voice.

The force of that last stone told him that whoever was chucking the stones was not far away. But while the first one had struck him lightly, as if lobbed, this one punished him with a painful lump.

A demented person was doing this, someone enjoying the sight of his being shoved by the rising tide and bullied by the slap of waves.

"Why are you doing that?"

Another pebble struck him. Reacting to it, he twisted his head and got a mouthful of seawater from a reaching wave. He gagged, and as he spewed he was hit again. He was quick enough to drag it off his shoulder as it landed and fling it back. His throw was so awkward he thought he heard a mocking laugh, though the sound of mockery could also have been the sound of the rough water around him.

"Please help me," he called out.

A mass of small jeering pebbles smashed against his wet head.

"Can you hear me? I don't know how much longer I can hold on."

A single pebble struck his cheek like an insult.

"If it's you, I'm sorry I hit you," he called, remembering the man he had thrashed on the stairs. "Mister!" There was no response. He called again, "Ava?"

This time there was laughter, a low cough, the mirthless vindictive laugh of a man unused to laughing. It came again, a dry bark of unimpressed surprise.

In saying Ava's name Steadman knew he had given himself away.

"You think your girlfriend hates you like this?"

He heard *sink,* he heard *zis,* and he said, "Manfred."

The two pebbles that hit him after that were the equivalent of "Of course."

"Help me," Steadman said, glad again but scarcely audible, splashed by the rising slop of the surf as he spoke. He felt foolish, his whole head dripping as he tested the boulders beneath him. He attempted a firmer footing, bracing his heel.

"Stay in the place where you are."

The truculent voice was nearer and it, too, suggested the wavering sound of a man dodging waves and trying to keep his balance.

"How did you find me?"

"I never lost you."

"The car in the driveway?"

"I was ever following you."

Steadman remembered: the car that had been tailgating them when Wolfbein took him out, and the person that the old man Cubbage had mentioned.

"Ever since New York!"

"Why?"

"So to see."

Hearing him, having this conversation, Steadman was giddy. Manfred! Moments ago he had felt lost, and now he was sure he would live.

"What do you want? I'll give it to you. Just help me."

Manfred's low cough was a laugh of defiance that seemed to say "Never."

"What I want? Maybe I want to see you die."

"Manfred, please."

"You make me a jackass in Ecuador, on the river. And in Quito. After I helped you find that amazing datura, all those lies. And I lose my job and my credibility because of you. I try to talk to you and you smash my tape recorder. You try to punish me. So, maybe I punish you."

"I'm sorry. I don't know why."

"I know why. Because you felt strong."

"Maybe." And as he spoke the water bellied under him and lifted him and almost tore his fingers from the rock. "Give me a hand. Where are the stairs?"

"You are not strong now. I could let you die. I could just watch you."

"I'll give you whatever you want."

"You are nothing now." And *nossing* said it all.

"Please," he said with a piteous catch in his voice.

"But I am sorry — yah — you are really blind."

With a shriek that was so assertive it sounded like a boast, Steadman cried, "I can't see a thing!"

"That is so incredible, yah." Manfred was unmoved. "It spoils my story, my exposé, to get my job back. I want to unmask you."

"I have no mask. I'm blind. Manfred, I can't hang on."

Steadman wanted to say more when another wave hit him hard and thrust him against the embankment. Before he could recover the water plucked him and dragged him down, rolling him underwater. He surfaced with pleading hands.

"Take this."

A piece of cloth slapped Steadman's arm. He grabbed it, the sleeve of a wet sweatshirt.

"Just hold it. Don't touch me. I don't trust people in the water. You keep one side of the shirt, I keep the other side. Do as I say or I let go and you drown."

"Where are the stairs?"

"So incredible to see your desperateness. You are weak now."

"Manfred, if you don't help me I'll drown."

"A big scoop for me. Maybe I can find your body."

"You wouldn't do that. You're joking."

After a pause there came a growling chuckle. "Did you ever hear me make a joke?"

The wind had picked up, the sky went dark. Steadman felt the chill of the building clouds on his face. The cold salt spray soaked his head.

427

Now he realized that because Manfred was implacable he had no hope. Manfred seemed glad to see him trapped. Steadman thought he might weep, dissolving in his darkness at this noisy edge of the ocean, pressed against the West Chop cliff, dying so near home.

"What is it you want from me?"

"I want my job back."

"I can make that happen."

"And for my researches I want you to describe the drugs and the blindness. Some people it works on, others it has no effect. It is useless for me, just makes me sick. But for you it is effective."

"I'll tell you everything," he said with a kind of timid gratitude.

"And the skull. You talked about it. You must say you are a liar and a cheat."

"I promise. I swear to you, I'll let you tape-record it."

Another dry bark of laughter and "Sank you!" With a click like a thrown switch came a whir, and another click, and "*let you tape-record it.*"

"Please don't let go," Steadman said, because in concentrating on his tape recorder Manfred had loosened his grip on his end of the shirt.

"You were taking drugs for your book. And you lied. Not a poor unlucky man with an accident, but a liar and an arrogant."

"I admit it."

Steadman felt the sleeve of the sweatshirt go slack.

"Maybe I just let go and leave you here."

Steadman was chest-deep in swirling seawater, treading the submerged rocks. The loud tide slapped the cliffside. He was reaching with his free hand, snatching at the soaked shirt with the other, when he heard a commotion above him, a rackety agitated voice.

"That's him. That's the man!"

In a different, denying tone, Manfred said, "I do nossing."

"The one in the water, Officer. He tried to knock my son down the stairs. He assaulted me. Don't cry, Brett, it's going to be all right."

"What's going on here?" A different voice.

"It's okay, Officer," Manfred said. With that he pulled on the shirt and brought Steadman nearer. "I am helping my friend."

"Not that one — the other one!" said the angry man.

"This man is blind," Manfred said.

"He threatened me!"

"Hold on, sir."

"He hit me! That's assault with a weapon! A stick. A shod foot."

"Back off, sir. Give them room."

"Officer, I am an attorney!" the man screeched, but his voice was receding, as though he were being led up the stairs.

Feeling the wet sleeve tighten further, Steadman lowered his head. He steadied himself in the water with his free hand and gripped harder and let himself be tugged to the foot of the stairs.

"Easy," Manfred said, and helped Steadman up, placing his hand on the rail.

He was soaked, trembling with fatigue and panic as if tumbled in a black barrel of water, and still in darkness. He groped on the stairs, pulling himself onward, aware that Manfred was bumping along beside him. He sobbed and laughed and said, "Thank you!"

At the top of the stairs he fell to his knees and breathed deeply. Out of the wind, away from the water, he was hot, as though he had crawled up the cliff into a different day. In that moment his blindness didn't matter. Nothing mattered except that he was alive.

Then he heard from a little distance, "Aren't you going to do anything, Officer?"

"Step away, sir. This man is in shock."

Manfred said, "I take him home." He guided Steadman to his car and helped him in. As soon as he shut the door, he wrapped Steadman in a blanket and said, "I would not let you drown but I like to see you in trouble. That was nice."

Feeling tearful, Steadman did not reply.

"You thought I was your girlfriend throwing things at you. That is very funny."

Steadman wondered why he had called her name. Perhaps an effect of "The Blind Man's Wife," his belief that their love affair was over. He said, "I've been desperate. She found me a doctor — for my eyes. Nothing works." He fell silent. "I've had a hard time."

"Too much of cars on this island," Manfred said, braking. Then the familiar cough and bark — he was amused. "You went to a doctor! Ha!"

"A specialist."

"Even more funny."

"They've prescribed all sorts of medicine."

"There is only one medicine."

Driving, grunting at the traffic, Manfred spoke almost without thought, in the most literal way.

"You are unhappy. You are sick. You take medicine. But this is not the same. If someone gets sick because of a shaman, only a shaman can make it right. The way up is the way down. You don't know this? The medicine that makes you sick, the same medicine will cure you."

"You think so?"

"This I know."

"You could have told me in New York."

"No. I thought your blindness was false." He said, "I hear of it with datura but I never see it. Why you behave so bad?"

"It was different," Steadman said. "I was blind but I had a kind of inward vision. I had perception. I could move. I was happy."

"Yah?"

"Then I had no control. Everything went black."

"With how much of the drug?"

"No drug. I had saturated myself, maybe destroyed some nerves."

"Funny, I never hear about this before. But the shaman, he knows."

"That man on the river?"

"Yah. Don Pablo — my friend. A healing shaman they call him."

Manfred was making turns through the outskirts of Vineyard Haven, all the narrow one-way streets, cursing the other drivers as he spoke. Then he seemed to remember again.

"You went to a doctor!"

Steadman said, "Help me, Manfred. Take me there. I'll do anything you ask."

"You must pay. And I want my job back. I want my good name back. I am not a thief. My father was a good man. You must help me."

"Yes."

"And I want your story."

"My story is all I have."

"That's why I want it. Your story must belong to me. You must belong to me." He kept driving, straighter now on the up-island road. "Say yes and we will go."

Steadman stared into the darkness. He said, "You want directions to my house?"

Manfred said, "You think I don't know the way?"

430

SIX

The River of Light

There was so little he could tell of the journey. Dark — so dark it was not travel at all. He saw nothing, he heard hardly anything, he was numb with despair. It was a stunned and fatal fall through a tube of air-softened space, like an endless burial, a vertical night drop into a narrow and bottomless hole. He had surrendered himself to Manfred and the trip, as though to be sacrificed. He was prodded by Manfred's ignorant fingers, and Manfred's meddling voice misled him. He was soaked in darkness, he was hardly human, just a hostage, dying in stages.

The passing scene was indecipherable, the dark places meant nothing but delays — the wait in Boston, the change of planes in Miami, the long flight to Quito. They offered nothing to remember. The blindfold mask he had once worn was now his own face.

Before he left the Vineyard, Ava had said, "Are you okay?"

Doing her duty, Ava was more efficient, because she was out of love. But her nurse-like kindness and unselfish attention mattered more to him than her exhausting passion. Her awkwardness was like the clumsy shame of atonement. As an invalid, he understood.

Terrible for her, he thought: the healer who can't help, sensing that she had failed him. He knew very little now, but one thing was certain — standing there trying to console him, she was not alone. Her new lover was with her and she was happy.

She had repeated her question.

"No," he said. "Not okay at all."

A whisper leaked through his mind, saying *Find the heart of the flower.*

And with that he left with Manfred, a man he despised, to return to Ecuador to try to undo everything that had been done: to rid himself of the first journey, and the drug, and his story, seeking to be healed. The long slow trip unfolded in darkness. He forgot each thing as soon as it passed. Manfred never stopped saying "Money." He was a noisy eater and he ate constantly, chewing, swallowing, smacking his jaws.

After they arrived in Quito, Steadman could not say if the trip had taken a day or a week, or whether it was true they had arrived. Manfred's gabbling was no proof of it. Steadman was still falling, but through thinner air, and he thought, All cities are dreadful in the dark. The hotel room was a tomb in which he lay mummified, waiting for Manfred's knock.

Another plane, a narrower seat, a bumpy landing. Manfred said "Lago," and helped him down the stairs.

He was clasped by a big man, and then Nestor's voice: "Sorry."

"It's all my fault."

"That's good. You're humble. That will help." Then he spoke to Manfred. "*Hola, Alemán.*"

Another night in a hotel room, this one stifling, Manfred next door watching soccer on television.

The boat trip nauseated him, the fumes from the chugging engine, the tipping seat, the empty reassurances of "Not far."

"They believe the river is a snake," Manfred said.

Nestor said, "You don't believe it?"

The moment he said that, Steadman felt the boat muscled from beneath by the coils of a snake.

Not long after that, on one reach of the river, they were spun in the outer eddy of a whirlpool. When they stopped circling and the gurgle of the eddy ceased in a softer bubbling, the engine stopped, too. Steadman heard the chatter of villagers, the quacking tribal welcome, the sterner voice of Nestor negotiating, speaking Secoya. The incomprehensible language in the darkness completed Steadman's sense of being nowhere.

That night he lay on the platform, Manfred not far off, first eating in his loud snaffling way and then snoring. When he woke Manfred was talking to Nestor, making demands. He was uneasy here, just another visitor, an ineffectual consultant among specialists.

How many days passed? Steadman asked himself, but couldn't say for sure. He woke, he napped, he had nothing to do. He did not need to know anything except that he was where he wanted to be. Here his sickness had a name. Hope here was a smell of vegetation and decay, the nagging of birds, the ripsawing of insects, the giggling of children, and most of all the muddy surge of the river snaking past, sucking at the hollows of the soft embankment; hope in the dusty stink of pollen, hope in the foul wood smoke, hope in the human odors of the village, hope in Manfred, the man he hated.

Cross-legged on the platform, he smelled what he could not see: the smoke, the river, the rotting forest. He was calm; as long as the shaman was not here, he had not failed. He knew why he was here. He belonged here.

Manfred was impatient. Something in the way he ate, in the very way the man breathed beside him, conveyed to Steadman that he was feeling helpless and upset. He asked, "Where is the *curandero*?"

"The messenger has been sent. But Don Pablo is afraid, of course," Nestor said. "He might not come."

So it was Don Pablo who was to perform the healing.

"To make you well he must become ill. He was very sick once. That was how he became a *pajé*. A man can only have that power after he has been cured of a bad illness. It is the only way. The sick man becomes a healer. Maybe our friend here will be a healer."

Steadman heard in Manfred's mutter an objection to this, not specific words but a sound that meant "It will never happen."

Nestor said, "And you will have to drink poison."

Don Pablo arrived that night. It was as though he had descended through the boughs of the forest canopy, settling slowly into the village like a spider on its thread. He had not announced himself, yet he created an atmosphere, a silence, like dense space around him. Steadman was aware of his presence, and he smelled him, an odor of vines, a sweetness of tobacco smoke. Don Pablo asked no questions. He mumbled in Secoya and took Steadman's hands in his own and pressed them.

The Secoya words meant nothing, but at his touch, Steadman began to cry.

In a tone of approval, Don Pablo said, "*Listo*."

Manfred woke Steadman early the next day. He had become like a keeper, inattentive and meddling, yet suspicious of others.

"Don't take food," Manfred said. "Nothing to drink."

Without saying so, Steadman knew it was the day.

"He says you are dead."

Naked before this man, unable to object, Steadman understood this to be part of the process. He grew weaker in the heat as the hours passed, yet it was still light when he was led to the pavilion, Manfred on one side, Nestor on the other. From the way Manfred helped carry him, his grip on Steadman's arm, Steadman could tell that Manfred was proprietorial, the pressure of ownership in his grip.

Steadman's sightless eyes prickled with the sharpness of wood smoke. That his useless eyes could still smart with the sting of smoke he took as a hopeful sign.

"Daytime is better for a healing," Nestor said.

"Because there are demons in the dark," Manfred said.

"*More* demons in the dark," Nestor said. "There are demons all the time."

Led like a prisoner to be slaughtered, shuffling flat-footed without his shoes, Steadman lost his fear of death. Don Pablo was right: he was already dead. This was the meaning of his illness, gone with everything else. Infection had emptied him of vitality.

Nestor said to Manfred, "You can go. I will stay with him."

"I must stay," Manfred said. "This is my story now."

Steadman was lowered to a mat, and he lay listening to the preparation — rustlings, pourings, squeezings, the chuckle of liquid in clay jugs, the mutters of the Secoya, the children's whispers, their breathing. The afternoon sun heated his face. He heard murmuring, which could have been dismay or a prayer, and then the first of the chants.

"Don Pablo is drinking," Nestor said. "He has found his stool."

Steadman could hear Don Pablo scraping the stool nearer.

A cup was placed in Steadman's hands. He drank, he retched, he drank again. Altogether he took four cups. Then he lay on his back, lumps of earth or broken-off brush stumps poking against his spine. He was soaked with sweat, his cheeks flecked with vomit.

Groaning over him, Don Pablo hovered, puffing a cigar. He blew smoke in Steadman's eyes. He brushed them with a bundle of wilted leaves. All the while he continued groaning, a rhythmic chant low in his throat.

Feeling slight pressure on his eyes, Steadman lifted his arms and touched two smooth stones that Don Pablo had placed on his lids. His arms became very heavy as the drug took hold — the first stage he recognized from so many other times: the sound of rain drenching his mind; the trembling would be next, then the stars, the snakes, a milkiness in his vision, and finally his slipping free of his body and ascending to stare down at himself in trance-like concentration.

Don Pablo was anxious. He choked a little, he gagged and spat, and finally grew quiet. He placed his fist on one of Steadman's eyes, pressing the stone. Using his clenched fist as a pipe, he put his lips on it and began to suck air through it. Someone else, one of the acolytes or helpers, was singing like a novice monk in long organ notes of harmonious groans.

Sucking, spitting, Don Pablo began to work on Steadman's other eye. The drug had given Steadman a sense of being wadded in cotton. He was watching his mummification from the wooden rooftree of the pavilion, his stretched-out body like a smoked corpse, as though his soul had left it.

And it had. He was the soul observing the men tinkering with the shell of his being. Drunk with the drug and groaning in pain, the men led by Don Pablo were drooling over him.

Steadman sank deeper into a darkness suffused with green. He was underwater, enclosed by a snake, wrapped in its coils, being swept downstream. The pulsing of the snake's slippery entrails was like the suck and rush of a river.

With a stinging sense of being bitten, Steadman's whole body contorted, his muscles wrung like rags, his brain convulsed, until he was twisted small. With a mild sinking acceptance, he thought, I am dying. And his eyes were wet, not weeping but bleeding, wounded by the stones that had weighed on them. *I am dying, meester.*

He was turned inside out — another old feeling. This time the song was within him, the lowest notes in his belly, the chorus like colors in his eyes, not simple colors but the familiar mass of pixels. He was so small that when he fell he sped like a dropped pebble and kept falling fast, past the snakes and the moon men, until he came to rest in a tangle of filaments like a collapsed web.

There he stayed, vibrant, atomized, yet tranquil. Nothing else mattered. In a ritual of presentation, the shaman approached him with a brimming cup. He was shown his reflection in the liquid, and he took this to be the meaning of life. He did not recognize his face. He had an insect's head, bulbous eyes and mandibles like a pair of sickles. He did not know whether he had woken from a dream or had gone under again, reentering a dream.

The cup of mirroring liquid was offered amid swirling smoke. Words came; he was not sure whether he or someone else was speaking, or they might have been thoughts floated from his mind.

"What is it?"

"*Cura.*"

"The cure?"

"It is poison," the old man said in his dusty voice.

Steadman did not hesitate. A commanding instinct within him told him it was a cup brimming with death. And that he must drink it all, that he must die. He raised the cup to his lips to empty it.

His drinking of the bitter poison was a renunciation, a long kiss of farewell, and in this close embrace, the cup against his lips, he saw the passing of his life, the reminder of all his hopes, all the promises he had made, the miles he had traveled, the betrayals, the consolation of friends, the years of work and waiting — anger, fear, nights of desire, laughter, all his escapes and stratagems, meaningless memories of invention, all in that long swallow that ceased to be bitter, that grew sweeter and sadder as he gulped the last of it.

Then the cup was empty of poison. Night had fallen, burying him. He was so used to seeing nothing he merely stared with blank eyes when the torch became visible. He was staring into the hollow, at his fingers on the rim of the cup, holding the cracked thing nearer his face. With its ragged lurid flames and its unreliable promise of light, the torch was like the morning sun. He had surrendered. He was no one. His journey was over.

In the smoky pavilion he raised himself and looked into the bottom of the cup he had emptied. He saw active light among the droplets, something alive — a spider, glittering, lifting itself on its crooked legs, working its jaws. Steadman smiled as at the face of an old friend on waking from a bad dream.

read more ⓟ

PAUL THEROUX

If you enjoyed this book, there are several ways you can read more by the same author and make sure you get the inside track on all Penguin books.

Order any of the following titles direct:

0141011122 THE STRANGER AT THE PALAZZO D'ORO	£7.99

'A decadent, engrossing collection' *Mail on Sunday*

0140281118 DARK STAR SAFARI	£7.99

'A wonderful, powerful book, a loving letter to Africa' *Sunday Times*

014029936X HOTEL HONOLULU	£7.99

'A novel of enormous ingenuity and vitality' Sunday Telegraph

0140249796 THE OLD PATAGONIAN EXPRESS	£8.99

'One of the most entrancing travel books written in our time' *Financial Times*

0140245332 THE PILLARS OF HERCULES	£7.99

'A terrific book, full of fun' Jan Morris, *The Times*

014024980X THE GREAT RAILWAY BAZAAR	£8.99

'Funny, sardonic, wonderfully sensuous, consistently entertaining' *New York Times*

0140159762 THE HAPPY ISLES OF OCEANIA	£8.99

'Theroux's finest, most personal and heartfelt travel book' *Observer*

0140112952 RIDING THE IRON ROOSTER	£8.99

'Anyone wanting to know what China is really like should read this' *Mail on Sunday*

Simply call Penguin c/o Bookpost on **01624 677237** and have your credit/debit card ready. Alternatively e-mail your order to **bookshop@enterprise.net**. Postage and package is free in mainland UK. Overseas customers must add £2 per book. Prices and availability subject to change without notice.

Visit www.penguin.com and find out first about forthcoming titles, read exclusive material and author interviews, and enter exciting competitions. You can also browse through thousands of Penguin books and buy online.

IT'S NEVER BEEN EASIER TO READ MORE WITH PENGUIN

Frustrated by the quality of books available at Exeter station for his journey back to London one day in 1935, Allen Lane decided to do something about it. The Penguin paperback was born that day, and with it first-class writing became available to a mass audience for the very first time. This book is a direct descendant of those original Penguins and Lane's momentous vision. What will you read next?